The Free and Easy

ANNE HAVERTY

The Free and Easy

Chatto & Windus
LONDON

Published by Chatto & Windus 2006

4 6 8 10 9 7 5 3

Copyright © Anne Haverty 2006

First published in Great Britain in 2006 by
Chatto & Windus
Random House, 20 Vauxhall Bridge Road,
London SW1V 2SA

Random House Australia (Pty) Limited
20 Alfred Street, Milsons Point, Sydney,
New South Wales 2061, Australia

Random House New Zealand Limited
18 Poland Road, Glenfield,
Auckland 10, New Zealand

Random House (Pty) Limited
Isle of Houghton, Corner of Boundary Road & Carse O'Gowrie,
Houghton, 2198, South Africa

The Random House Group Limited Reg. No. 954009
www.randomhouse. co.uk

A CIP catalogue record for this book is available from the British Library

ISBN 9780701179748 (from Jan 07)
ISBN 0 7011 7974 0

Papers used by Random House are natural,
recyclable products made from wood grown in sustainable forests.
The manufacturing processes conform to the environmental
regulations of the country of origin

Typeset by SX Composing DTP, Rayleigh, Essex
Printed and bound in Great Britain by
Mackays of Chatham plc, Chatham, Kent

To Tony

I

To everybody, however complacent, the moment will come
when their oneness with humble and suffering humanity is
rudely revealed. This moment came to Pender Gast when his
always rugged good health suddenly failed. He found he was
unable to eat. Alcohol, always before a cure and a comfort, was
repugnant to him. Most ominously he experienced for three
days on end a terrible sensation at the pit of his stomach. With
stricken eyes he looked at Cerise. 'Call the medic,' he groaned.

It took Cerise some time to find Pender a medic, since in all
her tenure as his assistant he had never requested medical advice
or intervention of any kind. Doctors did not number among the
few things he believed in. And his personality could be
discouraging to someone who didn't know him. But, always
good in a crisis, she found one she believed would be mutually
acceptable. The doctor had a cheerful and reassuring manner, to
which the patient responded with a striking lack of grace.
However, he gave himself over eagerly to examination.

The doctor emerged from the encounter unscathed but
grave. 'I have my suspicions,' he told Cerise. 'We'll have to run
some tests.' In a hushed and tearful voice, Cerise at once
summoned Tom Blessman, Gast's grand-nephew and only
relation, to the bedside.

Tom was alarmed and moved by the sight of his more or less
speechless great-uncle. He had never seen the old man hapless
and pitiable before. 'You're going to be fine,' Tom assured him
in several different but equally unconvincing phrases. In reply

Gast made weak and poignant groans. The tests were quickly arranged.

Supported between Cerise and Tom, Gast tottered into the clinic, a broken man. Under his light alpaca coat he had the bowed back of an old-style Irish countryman, hooped over from a lifetime of working in the fields and weighed down by heavy winter country garb. In the waiting room he sat slumped in his chair, suddenly looking hardly taller than Cerise, and gazed around at the other patients, anxiety etched on his face. For the first time in his life, he knew himself to be not only as vulnerable and tragic as they, but infinitely more so, for Pender Gast never held views by halves. Over a couple of hours he endured the intrusive ministrations of medical technology, submitting to the barrage of ultrasounds, scans and X-rays with an uncharacteristic absence of complaint. Also uncharacteristically, he displayed no interest in the prettier of the personnel who operated the machines. Invulnerable to fate, they looked alien to him now; people from another world.

In the late afternoon he walked out of there a different man – his old self, really. Dropping his coat into Tom's keeping he strode ahead of his escorts, his large head raised to breathe in the air of the Manhattan spring, and ordered the driver to take them to Larry's, declaring that he would drink a last gin martini before he started on his medication. Gast hadn't been in Larry's for years. He didn't seem to care that it had changed. He did not speak of the diagnosis he had received, but it was obviously minor and perhaps embarrassing, comical even as misfiring bodily functions can be. In a mood of celebration that was rare in Pender's company, they stayed on in Larry's for three martinis.

Pender went home then, took the medication and stayed off the drink for a while, as he had been advised. In a matter of days he was right as rain again. Tom went back to his life downtown – 'that so-called life of his' as his great-uncle had been heard to call it – and Cerise to her desk. The moment of illumination had passed and left behind it no after-effects that any of them could see.

2

Not long after, however, Pender began to dream. This was significant because he had never been a man who dreamed, whether awake or asleep. Gast detested dreamers; he was devoted to what he called the hard facts of life.

Oh, he brooded, certainly he brooded. In fact you could say brooding was all he did these days. Looking down with unseeing eyes on the slow-moving waters of the East River, one hand gripping a glass of red wine of a superb vintage, the other spread with a slack but undoubted authority on the arm-rest of his plush and stately couch, he would brood on past events and on past wrongs done to him. Occasionally also he remembered wrongs – the few and small wrongs of course – he had done to others. It was then that he might emit one of those long, deep, groaning sighs such as splendid beasts are said to make when they're grievously wounded. This brooding tendency did not however normally find expression in dreams, or even nightmares. Gast always claimed to sleep the blank and innocent sleep of a baby.

Whether this departure from his former habits had anything to do with his recent health scare is open to question. What are dreams? What are they for? Can anybody say for sure, any more than we can say what life is for? A dream might mean anything or nothing. Or possibly everything. Maybe all you can say is that they must have their season. Or if you're unburdened by dreams all your life, as in Gast's case, could it be that you're obliged to have them in old age?

Whatever, the fact is that one night Gast had a dream. His dream was, like so many dreams, strange, melancholy and disturbing. And, like most dreams, it had no beginning or end. It was not however a nightmare-type dream since it didn't frighten him or wake him up with a start. Indeed his first impulse on waking was to get back there, into the dream. Naturally, having little or no prior experience of the general strangeness and middleness of dreams he was very struck by it.

It was an important dream, he informed Cerise. Telling it to her his air was more portentous than usual, as if to measure up to it. He had seen a vision of the old country. The people of the old country were calling out to him. Wan, gaunt, but in spite of that strangely beautiful, they were appealing to him, beseeching him.

Cerise nodded knowingly. 'Ah. Like they called out to that saint. Saint Patrick.'

'What?' demanded Gast. He was alarmed but flattered.

'I saw this programme on PBS. *The Story of Patrick, Patron Saint of Ireland*. He had a dream where the Irish people were calling out to him to come back.'

'Yeh? Back from where?'

Cerise shrugged. 'He'd left them, he'd gone back home to wherever he came from. They needed him I guess. Anyways in this dream he had they were begging him to return.'

'In my dream, there was no word whatsoever of returning.' Gast was insistent on this point.

'Hang on there a moment,' instructed Cerise. 'I want to get myself comfortable to hear this. Let me get my coffee.'

While he waited impatiently she settled herself on the couch opposite, crossed her short plump legs, and balanced her cup and saucer on a lap that was tautly wrapped in the new season's pink little boucle skirt. 'Okay,' she announced at last. 'Go on.'

He told her that he had found himself standing by a road or a paved track. 'A kind of a Roman-type,' he suggested.

Cerise nodded sagely and sipped her coffee.

It was a broad white road that stretched across a great plain and vanished into distant hills. A crowd of people were coming up the road, walking towards him. There was rain falling on them, a mild but steady rain. As regards Ireland, the rain was dead on. But the weird thing was they were nothing at all like the Irish that he believed he remembered from his infancy. They were clad in trailing and ragged garments that he was sure he had never seen anyone wearing in the old country.

'They seem to me like people you'd see in a movie,' suggested Cerise. 'About refugees. From a war, maybe?'

Gast ignored that. He himself, he continued, stood by the side of the long, undulating ribbon of road. The people approached, walking rapidly but in dignified file, three or four abreast, men, women and children, and passed him by. The men and women were remarkably tall, the children all young or at least very small. Hounds, little and large, padded alongside them, calm but watchful like good dogs guarding the tribe and its domestic beasts. But there were no domestic beasts to guard that he could see. Nothing edible on the hoof went with them, nor any baggage train of grain or fruit. Empty-handed, possessionless, wretched, they passed him by, noble of mien, not looking at him, but their expressions somehow beseeching. He got the impression that they were aware of his presence but were too dignified, too proud to speak of their need or the plight they found themselves in.

With a distracted hand, Gast smoothed down his sparse, well-oiled hair that was still streaked with black. 'The women were beautiful.' He looked at Cerise with a rapt but absent gaze. 'They were like madonnas.'

Cerise regarded him doubtfully. From what she knew of Ireland the scene he described did not strike her, apart from the rain factor, as being in any way Irish. It suggested to her more an Arab or an Asian country in some previous century. Medieval times. She thought of a documentary she had seen about the Crusades.

'How do you know it was the old country? Are you sure it was Ireland?' she asked.

'In the dream it was Ireland. I knew it was Ireland,' Gast said impatiently.

'That's how it is in dreams,' agreed Cerise. 'You just know. You are told by an interior voice.'

'There was no voice,' growled Gast.

'It wasn't audible,' Cerise informed him. 'You weren't conscious of it.'

'Whatever.' Gast lapsed into silence.

'What happened then?' she demanded.

'Nothing happened.'

Dismissing both the dream and Cerise, he gave himself some wine. He picked up the remote control from its place on the small table next to his couch, flicked on the TV and pretended to be deeply interested in a news show, one of those that he ordinarily dismissed as babble.

Stranger still than Gast having a dream in the first place was that a week or two later he had it again, and more or less precisely the same. All he would say was that it was no different from the last, still the same enfilade of noble misery passing him by with its mute appeal. And Cerise understood, though he refused to discuss the recurrence, that he had dreamed it for a third time when she found him one morning pale and dry-skinned from a disturbed night. His large fingers shook slightly when he pushed aside his morning coffee. Three times . . . she knew this was serious. Ten minutes later he called her in. He had his shearling rug pulled close around him and was already started on the wine.

'Get Tom over here,' he instructed.

'You want him right away?'

'Right away. Pronto.' He flicked to an animation channel.

3

Pender Gast had been borne away from his native land as a small boy and his fierce resolve never to set foot in it again or have anything to do with it had not diminished with time. Should Pender ever consent to analyse this resolve, which was not at all likely, a psychologist would probably explain it as an expression of an elemental fear. His memories of Ireland were few but awful. The most vivid and the most awful of these memories had to do with death.

A wake is in progress; one of those time-wasting, self-indulgent rituals that primitive folk go in for, as he sees it. This wake is not one of those rampageous Dionysian assemblies designed to rally the spark of life if it continues, or re-ignite it if it doesn't, or to persuade the not-quite-departed to return to the joys they are leaving behind. It's a sedate and gloomy gathering – a dead person displayed for a final viewing by the people she moved among in life. Hers was a short enough life; he knows now what it is to be old and that she was not old. She lies stretched out on a large matrimonial bed between starched white sheets.

Her pose strikes him as an outrage, a pretence at the normality of sleep, the pose of a woman confident in the certainty before she drifted off of the imminent arrival of her husband. But no husband comes, no floorboards creak beneath his steps, noises so familiar and companionable that she would not stir, to sit on the bed and unlace his boots, remove his various country garments and climb in beside her supine form. Only he, a boy three years old, comes.

With dragging feet he is brought, hand tightly gripped, to the bedside by some female, a forgotten relative whose status is obscure. She is probably an aunt. His small hobnailed boots creak with an eerie strangeness on the boards. Despite his reluctance he is pleased by the noise they make. Until now, he believes, he went around barefoot and these boots were bought especially for the occasion. He is presented to the corpse. Whether she is there for his inspection or he for hers he cannot tell. This bride – she seems to him in her white gown to be bridal – is terrible. In her smooth yellow mask, she's a ghost, an apparition, the incarnation of a witch. His story-book has pictures of witches, brides, goblins . . .

The room around him is vast, as all rooms are to a child. In its shadowy distances an audience is seated, among them his father with his head bowed, on serried circles of hard chairs. They are there, he is sure, to watch, to judge, to extract acts or promises from him. But he will give these people nothing, nothing . . . His gaze is level with the bed.

'Go on now pet, and give your poor grandmother a kiss,' commands the aunt. She pushes him forward. She means to be coaxing but her whisper has the aggressive nature of the goose that hisses and flaps its wings at him outside in the yard. He is enraged at the malevolence all about him, at the blatant attempt to pass off this travesty as his grandmother, to have dressed its yellow skull in his grandmother's soft greying hair. His grandmother is the only mother he has known.

'Go on, Pat.' The aunt's voice is more insistent.

'I won't.' To his own ears he speaks suddenly with the voice of a man, hoarse and firm. 'I won't.' Like a bucking colt he backs away from the bed.

The promptness with which the refusal is accepted surprises him. Unlike the goose that would come after him hissing and flapping, the aunt's firm grip on his shoulder slackens. On their straight-backed chairs the spectators seem to have forgotten him already. They break into one of those alien chants that since

8

then he cannot endure to hear, which evoke for him clouds of suffocating smoke, oppressive odours of a chapel, rain-sodden clothes, the hostilities and mud of the farmyard.

Head down he goes running from the room. His flight is unhindered. He has learned that a no can result in a win. The chant fades into silence and as he remembers it he keeps on running in a hectic but straight line, away from Ireland and away from death.

Next he is standing by the rail on the deck of a great ship. All ships are great to a child. Though no less vivid than the other, this memory is all too brief, evanescent as a scene glimpsed in a sun-bright spray-washed mirror. Down all the years he has often yearned to remember it better – in particular to remember more about the girl. He is already an American. He has escaped. As they swoop around the sparkling sky the sea-birds above are calling with the wild, exhilarating cry of escape.

The ship is cool and white. Above his head the polished wood of the rail glistens like an infinite coil of dark gold. Regularly he clenches his eyes, but always a second too late, against the rhythmic assault of the ocean spray. He tests his lips for the exciting taste of salt. He drinks hot chocolate from a thick white cup and it tastes of salt. The taste of salt is a pleasure to him still.

Along the wind-bleached boards of the sunlit deck a girl skips, whipping a blue and red-painted top. She's a big girl, much bigger than he is, she could be eight or nine. She's wearing a fur-trimmed hat and low-cut fur-trimmed boots. She enthrals him. She is the first, perhaps the only person he has truly loved. But she ignores him; she has no interest in him in the wide world. All too soon she vanishes, whipping her top into the dazzle of sea-spray and light, into the bright trajectory that leads the quick and truly living across the ocean, across the prairies and into the abstract infinite spaces of America's skies.

He would never go back. He was fierce about that. The ship is his true birthplace. He would never again have anything to do with those people, with she who drew him towards the jaws of death or those who watched.

When he was a young man and embarking on his business life – though of course he was never *not* in business; from the start he was one of those kids who trade in dodgy cellphones at the school gates (in his time the trade was in cigarettes) – news would arrive at intervals of their individual demises. His father's eyesight was so poor by this time that he didn't see the letters, and his heart so stricken that he didn't care to see them anyway. Pender glanced at them and then grimly put them away.

If he ever knew their names, he has forgotten them. In America, people with the strangest of names pass on everywhere, all the time, and the names recited in these letters were as unknown to him and as uninteresting. Briefly, he might wonder whether the letters were coded ... Implicit requests for the purchase price of a few neighbouring acres or the passage money west for a youth, or worse, funeral expenses – the kind of letter, the kind of request, that his few Irish acquaintances talked of receiving, and understood. This was no more than an idle thought, tinged with distrust and fear. He was convinced that in the old countries Americans were regarded as little more than sources of funds to be sentimentally disbursed. He sent nothing.

Very early on, he took firm avoiding action. He changed his name, adjusted it to be snappy, cleaner, more American, and himself harder to trace. He is unreachable by those chanting suppliant voices, those hands eagerly reaching out to grasp grimness and death, which could stretch far across the ocean and grab hold of you if you weren't careful. At one time Tom Blessman had been told that his great-uncle's given name was Patrick but he had forgotten it. Gast was unimaginable as the bearer of an ordinary name like Patrick. As for Paddy, Pat or any other derivative ... Impossible. His American name suited him, the uncompromising sound of it suits his emotional austereness, the hooded detachment with which he looks out on life. Mr

Tough, Mr Pender Gast – he grew into the name like a tall quick-growing tree. Then he stopped growing. He made sure of that, kept himself well-pruned, meagrely fed . . . Well, once a man finds his comfort zone does he have to keep on growing away from it, like a garden growing wild, allow its neat blooms so carefully cultivated to be choked by rampant stuff nobody planted or wanted? That was his philosophy and you couldn't say he hadn't thrived on it.

He would be the first to admit that love was not the least of the obstacles that stood in his way. But he had steered his way around it with some success. There was a brother of his, a great deal older, on whom his father, already discouraged, was depending to ease their path in their new life. But when they landed in New York they had found this fellow in a bad way. As soon as the younger boy was able at all, the living of all three was more or less down to him. It was a duty, but oddly not onerous. Somehow it came easy to him. By the time Pender went away to war in the Pacific, aged twenty, he had the title to three small dying-on-their-feet businesses that had a potential only he could see.

He had been attached to his brother, but it was a reluctant and censorious attachment. And when the brother died, just another Bowery bum, he loved the small daughter he had left the same. His niece was soft, she had a weak character. She was a disappointment to Gast. People generally were a disappointment to him. And true to form she made as he saw it a bad marriage to another softie, a man of German descent called Hank Blessman. In his opinion, their son Tom was no better.

But the past was catching up with him. This dream of his had him in its clutches and wasn't about to let him go. He was blown out of his well-tended patch by it. Tom had a sudden oddly moving image of him, a movie image. One of those spiky balls of tumbleweed sent skeetering along a forlorn dirt road somewhere in the Midwest, looking for a hole to roll into out of the wind . . . It wasn't like Gast, to seek to help anybody or anything . . .

4

When Cerise had led Tom into the presence of his great-uncle he had found a freshly uncorked bottle of vintage Pommard awaiting him on the couch-side table beside two tall gleaming glasses from the crystal cabinet. Normally Gast's drinking-vessel of choice was a tumbler, whatever the drink. The TV screen, which normally supplied him with a companionable and silent series of moving pictures, was dark. He was clearly in business mode.

'Tom, honey. Good to see you, baby. Good to see you.' He took up the bottle with a flourish. 'You'll join me in a glass.'

'Sure,' Tom said warily. He could see he was going to be asked a favour, his great-uncle always prefaced his requests of anyone, man or woman, with 'honey' or 'baby' when he wanted a favour. That he used them both now, and the prodigious look of the encrusted Pommard, suggested the favour he wanted was going to be big, something really out of line. And Cerise, Tom suspected, was in on the plot.

She had greeted him with her usual warmth and enquired with her usual sympathy and implicit encouragement about the progress of his novel. However she hadn't seemed to listen with her usual attentiveness when he was explaining the difficulties he was experiencing with the sub-plot, though she had straightened out a tangle for him before. He was only half through when she broke in to say he should go in to Pender. 'He's impatient to see you.' There had been no chit chat today, no little confidences about Pender's latest manifestation of eccentricity, or what her latest husband – Mike, wasn't it? – was up to, or her opinion of the latest show she'd seen.

And despite her implication that Pender had some urgent news to impart Tom was still mystified. So far he had listened with attention to his great-uncle's account of his dream. As dreams go, it was certainly impressive, possibly even archetypal. But if what he wanted was some kind of an explanation Tom was not the guy to give it. The many semesters he'd taken on sundry arcane subjects had not included the interpretation of dreams.

'You know, I believe there's a problem over there. They want something. They're in trouble. I think that's what they're trying to tell me.' Gast swallowed a mouthful of Pommard as if it were water. 'D'ya see? It's still the same, Tom.'

Tom found himself addressing his grand-uncle Pender as 'sir' which he'd hardly done since his childhood, when he'd lived in a constant state of wariness of his demands. 'I'm sorry sir, but I haven't the least idea what you're talking about. What's the same?'

His great-uncle leaned forward and looked fervently into Tom's eyes. 'I want you to go. Do a recce, Tom. Find out what I can do.'

'What do you mean, go? Where go?'

'To Ireland.' Gast enunciated the word with a deep and sighing resonance. 'I'm being haunted,' he groaned. 'That poor rock in the water. They're haunting me.'

'I guess you could say to be human is to be haunted,' said Tom flippantly. He was hoping to lighten the mood.

'They looked at me,' moaned Gast, as if he hadn't heard. 'They looked me in the eye. Next time who knows what they'll do?'

'What can they do? They're not real.' Tom attempted a laugh.

'They looked me in the eye,' repeated his great-uncle. 'What'll they do next? Take me with them?'

For a moment, before he gulped back the wine left in his glass, Tom saw the stricken look on Gast's face that he'd seen in the clinic. 'I can see you're scared,' he ventured.

Gast was immediately belligerent. 'Scared? Why should I be scared? I'm not scared.'

'I'm glad to hear it.'

There was a longish silence.

'We're not talking Timbuktu, honey,' Gast said at last.

'Maybe I'd rather go to Timbuktu, now you mention it. But I'm not going anywhere.'

'Ireland is your country too, you know. Your father would've liked you to visit,' said Gast cunningly, as if this was his trump card. 'In fact you should have gone before this. You should have gone a long time ago.'

'There's no way he'd expect me to go,' protested Tom. 'My father gave me a bad impression of Ireland. Very bad. He didn't want to know the place. And now we're on the subject, what about you? You gave me a worse impression. "I got the hell out and I'm never going back." That's what you used to say.'

'Well, I was right,' conceded Gast. 'Nothing over there, only misery. Misery and oppression.'

Through the tall glass sheets of the penthouse windows Tom looked down on the water of the East River far below. Once upon a time, sure, he'd considered a trip to Ireland. But it was at a time in his life when he was avoiding the thought of his mother and the thought of anything connected with her. He was avoiding many subjects at the time. And besides, his great-uncle had not been encouraging. Now he seemed to think he could order him over there on a whim.

'You've travelled. You like travelling.' Gast returned to the attack.

'What's that got to do with it?'

'Are you telling me you don't want to help these people?' demanded Gast.

14

'It's *your* dream, sir. Remember? They're your people, not mine. I didn't dream them.'

'So you'd let them drown?'

'Drown? How are they going to drown? They weren't even swimming. They were walking along the road for God's sake. There was no water you mentioned that I recall. Well, besides the rain. I guess somebody could drown in a pothole but it'd be pretty difficult.'

'You don't know the rain over there,' brooded Gast. But his gaze faltered. 'You went to Russia,' he tried then. He spoke with an involuntary note of distaste that expressed his contempt for travel and travellers, anyone with the odd and incomprehensible desire to leave America. At least for any reason other than for business or army service.

Tom was silent. 'What do you think they're in need of anyway over there?' he asked after a while in the uninterested tone of the merely polite. 'You know, I believe I saw a report – must have been in *Newsweek*? – about Ireland being a land of wealth and opportunity.'

Actually he'd only glanced at the report. He had picked up a copy of *Newsweek* or some journal like it when he was waiting at the barber's but was called up to a chair before he'd got very far. It wasn't the kind of report he'd have gone far with in any case.

Patiently his great-uncle sighed. 'Maybe. But starting from what base? A breadline base, that's what. You know nothing about it, Tom. It's not your world.'

'Okay. So tell me. What do they want?' Tom was sullen.

'How do I know? I told you, I can't figure it out. They're not telling me. That's why I want you to go. It's up to you to do a recce. All I'm asking is you find out what they need. Whatever is in my power to do, I'll do. Anything to get rid of this goddam dream.'

'Are you thinking something material? Or could it be some kind of spiritual thing? The way you describe them they sound kind of spiritual.'

'Spiritual? The place is coming down with spiritual. All these religious guys running around . . .' Gast sighed. 'The religion is what keeps them under, I guess. Fills them up with visions of the good life in the great hereafter and keeps them fatalistic. Stamps out their initiative. Do you know what they look towards? The day they can lie safe in the casket soaked in holy oils and saturated with holy water. They'd never think of getting up off their asses in the here and now.'

'Dad wasn't all that good for getting up off his ass. And he wasn't Irish.'

'Cool down, Tom. Your father was a fine man. I won't hear a word against him. Only thing is, unfortunately he had no ambition. He could have bought me out twice over, he had the brains. Twice the brains I had. But he never had the thought to do it. He was happy with his little two-bit property portfolio.'

'Nothing wrong with his little property portfolio, as far as I'm concerned.'

'It was okay, I guess,' said Gast generously. 'But it could have been a lot better, only he wanted a good time. There's another thing. He was like the Irish in that respect. They hanker after a good time over there. But they don't believe they have to work to earn that old good time. It's the education, you see. The education is no goddam good. Do they teach them the hard facts of life? Do they teach them the right attitude? Do they tell them that, okay, maybe you work the requisite eight hours in the day – but that doesn't entitle you to go to the bars or sit all night in front of some smartass on the TV who's earning more in a day than you bring home in a year? Not if there's another dollar to be made it doesn't.'

Tom felt he was now on familiar and comfortable ground. This was one among several of his great-uncle's old refrains. The youth, the Hispanics, the women, the men in the bars . . . All any of them wanted was a good time. But what they failed to see was they couldn't have a good time in any meaningful sense except they worked for it. He'd been hearing it since he was knee-high.

'I worked every hour I got,' Pender proclaimed. 'And hell, I'm still working.' He sounded tired now. 'I really need you to go, Tom. Why don't you sleep on it? But you know, whatever you say about your father, you should remember something. Your mother would've wanted it. It's the old country. These are her people, Tom.'

Gast lay back in his chair and closed his eyes. 'Look, sleep on it. Think it over and get back to me.'

5

In drawing his mother into the argument his great-uncle had touched perhaps the most sensitive of Tom's several sensitive spots. Tom had never known his mother and his knowledge about her was sparse. In his childhood a photograph used to hang in the dining room of his father's apartment that he had always accepted was his mother, though he did not remember being told who it was. The photograph was of a dark-haired laughing girl in a kaftan-style dress, her smile directed at someone invisible to her left. In those early years he had been given to understand by his father, his great-uncle or anyone else he'd asked that she had been obliged to go away somewhere mysterious and inaccessible on some mysterious and pressing business. He had been allowed to form the impression that it was not unreasonable to expect her imminent return. Later, when he was older, he was told that she had died. That in truth his mother was always dead, she had died when he was an infant.

'How did she die?' he had asked. The question was not consciously painful to him but afterwards he always remembered the day of the announcement as bleak and oddly dark, though it was a regular hot summer's day on Long Island where they were visiting his great-uncle.

'An accident,' his father told him. 'A car wreck.'

Around the time of the disclosure, as far as Tom could recall, the photograph was removed to the back corridor, the site of bathrooms, closets, utilities. It was replaced with a screen so that he and his father could be occupied by watching TV as they ate.

The mendacity about her only being absent was invented of course in his interests. Invented and insisted on particularly by his great-uncle, as his father costively told him, to protect him from the idea of death, from the realisation of its existence and its finality; to inculcate in him American optimism and a buoyant outlook.

Later again Tom discovered that she had died not in a car wreck but of a heart ailment.

'Why did you lie?' he demanded.

His father had mournfully spread his hands in the helpless manner that Tom thought of as European. 'Uncle Pender doesn't admit illness into the family. You know how he's in denial.'

But in the meantime, between the invention and the revelation, Tom had formed images and fantasies of his mother that he had never quite been able to give up. At the sight of a tea-room – 'Your mother,' his father had once remarked, 'was fond of drinking tea' – for instance, passing the Hedinbourg Salon du Thé off Fifth Avenue, he would imagine his mother in such a place in some foreign city. A glamorous dark-haired woman but vaguely tragic.

Somewhere on the Riviera she sat outside at a windswept table taking her tea alone. Her expression was unseeing and wistful because she was thinking of her absent son. Of course she was a busy woman, busy with thick slabs of esoteric documentation. Later, in the company of clean-cut men and briefcases she travelled demurely in open-top cars, her beauty appropriately but attractively faded. But her daily hour of solitude in the Salon du Thé was the time she kept aside for a secret purpose, to think of the son she held across all the years close in her heart . . .

Maybe his great-uncle was right, he sometimes thought. Maybe it was better to deny, to pretend. Then it was easy to keep a person you loved alive. But he had never imagined his mother taking her tea in Ireland. Would they even have *salons du thé* over there?

6

'You know anything about Ireland?' Tom casually enquired of Jacques Delaporte.

Though he seemed to be fairly settled now into the banking life at Leduc Lefevbre, Jacques, French-Swiss, was impressively well-travelled. He was renting one of the four apartments in Tom's modest downtown building, the last remaining property of his father's never substantial portfolio. His apartment was the best in the house. It had the water-bed, a good-sized kitchen with an excellent oven, a view of the square . . . Jacques always demanded the best and generally he seemed to get it. Tom often had a drink or dined in Bazaar with Jacques. This evening his question about Ireland was asked purely of course on his great-uncle's behalf. He clearly needed some up-to-date information.

Jacques eyed him over his French cocktail and gave his charmingly sardonic Gallic laugh. 'Ireland? You've never been? Typical American. You don't travel, you guys.'

'I've travelled. I go to the Caribbean. I've been to Europe.'

But Tom was defensive. His trip to Europe after graduation had not been successful nor particularly adventurous as far as he could recall. On an inter-rail ticket he'd flashed through the various cities, staying in a succession of the regulation two-star hotels and eating from cans – he had had unpleasant associations with sardines ever since – and tinfoil wraps in the company of two college buds and their enormous backpacks. After a week they'd given up on the hotels and used the train to overnight. Mythical cities fled by in the early hours as a series of lurid lights and bizarre smells. In Paris Tom baled out to hole up in a shamefully fancy hotel and spend his time drinking with compatriots like himself in the American-style bars around Montparnasse, an embarrassing attempt at aping the big boys of former days. His memories of that time were blurred. Later, with Katya, he'd travelled to Russia. Already by then they were in mourning – ostensibly about the revolution and its work of destruction – but actually maybe about their relationship . . . All in all, 'abroad' had forced Tom to conclude that anywhere else was little more than a botched simulacrum of the US. He preferred now to get his America at home.

'Well, you been to Stacey's Irish Bar?' Jacques was asking.

'A couple of times.'

'You got it. There's Ireland for you.'

Stacey's Bar? Tom gulped. The old country must be nearly as bad as Pender claimed. Stacey's was no fun. A place shrouded in ancient dust, the harsh lights of yesteryear lending the bartenders a ghoulish pallor like men who shunned the daylight, while whooping youths raised on a view of the world as a series of theme parks got stoked up on Stacey's special brew. Although to be fair Stacey's brew was pretty good.

'But isn't Stacey's archaic?' protested Tom.

'I guess,' agreed Jacques, though with a certain reluctance. He looked thoughtful. 'All the priests are in jail,' he remarked.

'In jail?'

'Les pedes.' Jacques gave a philosophic shrug.

'Surely not all?' demanded Tom.

'Not all,' Jacques conceded.

'But you're saying the religious thing is gone over there?'

'Comme les neiges . . . Well, let's say it's going.'

'So things are different over there,' mused Tom, his note of satisfaction mixed with an unexpected sensation of disappointment.

Jacques threw his hands in the air. 'They are living among the ruins.'

'Ruins?'

'The ruins of their culture. Civilisation. Of course, economy-wise . . . You are talking economy?' Jacques looked doubtful. He was aware of Tom's vagueness about matters such as economics.

'Oh, I am,' Tom assured him. 'Sure I am.'

'They're doing real good. They're prospering.' Jacques talked economic signifiers, elevated rates of GDP year on year, irresistible tax breaks, eager job markets, dizzy growth figures, hot investments, hot Irish investors. 'Awesome. They're really on the button over there,' he concluded.

'I'm not too surprised,' murmured Tom. 'But to hear it confirmed . . .'

'I think you'd like the girls.' With an appraising look Jacques was contemplating his agreeable reflection in the rose-tinted flamboyantly curlicued mirror. 'Nice eyes.'

Tom nodded in agreement, remembering the photograph in the back corridor.

Suddenly, disconcerted, Jacques said, 'Hey, you will be getting back with your wife, won't you?'

'Doesn't look that way, I'm afraid.' Tom's smile was brave but stiff.

'By the way, *on mange pas mal* over there,' Jacques offered after a pause, looking up from the menu. He spoke like a man weary of travel, who has found after all the arrivals and departures, the sights and the smells, the crazy colours and the eager conversations that the best thing to do abroad is to cut to the cuisine.

'They eat well?' queried Tom. 'That kind of surprises me.'

'The best butter in the world. Rich and yellow as a good béarnaise.' Briskly Jacques summoned the waiter and ordered him to bring a '*steak à la sauce béarnaise*', cooked rare. Bazaar did an excellent steak.

7

Tom made a trip uptown to give his great-uncle an account of this research. 'You don't have to worry about them,' he told him. 'They're doing fine.'

Gast refused to listen. He dismissed it as being of no relevance whatsoever. 'You think I haven't been seeing these so-called reports? A flash in the pan. It won't last.'

He was more pressing now. His hand trembled when he brought a glass to his lips. He had had the dream again, and more than once. The people traversing the plain were assuming individualised faces, faces he anxiously grasped at in the hope of recognition but that he also recoiled from. He feared to know them. It was so bad now he was getting to fear sleep itself.

'I can't drop everything on a whim,' protested Tom. 'I have a deadline.'

Gast adopted a wheedling tone. 'You know something? It'll be good for your writing. You're a fine writer, Tom. But my opinion is you could do with a change of scene. Rejuvenate the brain. Take a break. You're working too hard. Did this Frenchie – Delaporte was it you said? – did he tell you what they do over there? Okay, they breed scrawny cattle – but they sure breed big writers.'

Tom turned slightly pink. His great-uncle had hardly referred to his writing before and then only with a thinly disguised attitude of disrespect. Tom's novel, *Up Side Up*, published some eighteen months before, was lingering, as far as he could tell, unread somewhere around the apartment. Tom had also sent him a copy of *Fest*, the highbrow literary quarterly in which his novel was reviewed. Reading between the impressively obscure lines referring to 'the accessibilities of the occlusions' and 'a dizzying annotation of undermined ambivalences' it could be discerned by an alert and seasoned reader of *Fest* that the review was a rave.

But his great-uncle was not a man for reading between lines. He emailed Tom to say he had received the copy of *Salon* and that he would turn to it at some future undefined date when he was in the mood to concentrate; but that in any case the important thing was 'you're getting a bit of notice, my boy'. Neither *Up Side Up* nor *Fest* had been referred to again.

To Gast, writing was akin to an infection or a weakness, one of those misfortunes life threw at you, like a propensity for drugs or the wrong type of woman. He had made movie investments in his time and was sure he knew the species inside out. Writers were hacks, gamblers, drunks, always broke, always being divorced, always complaining . . .

'You really do want me to go,' Tom said heavily.

'Tom honey, let me tell you a thing. I never wanted anything more.'

Tom reminded himself that his great-uncle was given to hyperbole. But there was no one to match his tenacity once he had set his mind to something. He was stretched out now on his chair, apparently dozing. One eye he raised blearily to half-mast. 'Get moving,' he said. 'You don't want to waste good marching weather.'

On his way to Bazaar a couple of days later Tom was passing by Vogel's on Howard Street. He surprised himself by turning in there and ordering a pair of strong all-weather all-terrain walking boots to be made. One thing the Blessmans shared with Pender Gast was a liking for hand-tooled footwear.

'You going on a trek, Mr Blessman?' Mike, the assistant, enquired.

'Oh, I'm thinking maybe of a few days in the Catskills in the

Fall,' Tom told him. This was not wholly a lie. His old college bud, Georgie Hertz, always went hunting in the Catskills with his dogs in the Fall and often asked Tom to go along. He had never taken up the invitation but there was nothing to say he wouldn't the next time Georgie brought it up.

'Very nice, Mr Blessman. Well, should be ready in six weeks or so. That all right for you?'

'That's good. Should give me more than enough time to wear them in.'

The thought flew into his head: 'I can send for the boots.' Analysing this impulsive purchase the next morning Tom saw that it must indicate a subliminal response to Gast's reference to marching. He had succumbed to a mysterious and irrational wish to be appropriately shod for the long trek towards the horizon as he accompanied, or even led, the people along the dusty – or had Gast described it as muddy? – road to their unknown destination, even possibly to their destiny. But whatever his unconscious was up to, it didn't mean he was going to obey it.

8

'That bee in his bonnet just keeps on buzzing,' Cerise told him. 'All other business is postponed. He's got me calling up travel agents. An open ticket. He's insisting on business class,' she added hopefully. She was convinced that would sway him. Cerise adored travelling business class. 'If you want my opinion, Tom, you could do with a vacation. You've been through the wringer, breaking up with Katya . . . Breaking up is tough, believe me. I know.' She was on her fourth husband, after all. 'You must be still in shock. It's only natural.' She was getting to be nearly as persuasive as Gast. It was clear to her she would get no peace until she'd seen Tom safely onto the plane.

'It's not a vacation he has in mind.'

'Sure sounds like a vacation to me.'

'I can't just run out on everything,' Tom protested. 'I have a life, you know.'

Cerise gave one of her discreet coughs that implied doubt about a proposition. 'But of course. You're doing too much. It'd be quiet over there. No distractions. And your accommodation would be class. I've been looking at some hotels. I can get you the best.'

What could 'the best' mean when you were talking Ireland? In Tom's experience, limited though it was, what it usually meant in the small countries of the old world was great numbers of lugubrious bell-boys in antiquated tailcoats, the glare of 1950s chandeliers and five courses of bad food when all you wanted was one you could eat.

Indignantly Tom strode off to confront Pender. 'Cerise is moving far too fast here.'

'You know Cerise.' His great-uncle seemed neutral, even sympathetic. 'Although I bet,' he mused, 'your mother could have done with Cerise's organisational skills when she went.'

'My mother? Where did she go?'

'To Ireland.'

'My mother went to Ireland?' demanded Tom. 'When? Why did she go?'

'It's the old country. She got sentimental about it, I guess, like a lot of them do.' Pender made a dismissive gesture. 'She went on a vacation. Never said much about it after. Must've been when she was around the age you are now. It's a long time ago. I don't recall . . .'

Gast, of course, had never been in any doubt that Tom would go. His wants were neither many nor various. But whatever Pender Gast wanted he got.

'So where do you want him?' Cerise asked.

'Whaddya mean where do I want him?' barked Pender. 'In Ireland. I want him in Ireland.'

'Where in Ireland?'

'Drop him into Dublin. Put him in the capital, for God's sake. Get him a good hotel.' An unadmitted sense of guilt at sending Tom off on what could be a fool's errand made him indulgent. 'Get him the best.'

Happily, Cerise got on the net. She was proud of her instinct for these things. Wherever she was her impeccably attuned nose led her straight to the best restaurant, the best dress on the bargain rail, the best hotel. She would have loved to be given the go-ahead to construct a full itinerary for Tom, to present him with a sleek folder containing the details of a complex tour involving hire cars, guided inspections of ruins and monuments, and a brisk dining schedule.

'Forget that,' instructed Pender. 'He's going there to do detective work. Let him find his own way around.'

'I just want to nip into the annex for a few minutes,' Tom told Cerise on his next visit a few days later.

The annex, situated behind her office, was where Cerise kept all Pender's old files neatly boxed and shelved. He went straight to the faded buff-coloured box marked 'Blessman' and rifled through the meagre and sundry collection of documents it contained – the Blessman birth certificates, including his own, the school certificates, his father's death certificate, his will, a few photographs over-familiar from regular perusal in the distant past . . . He knew exactly what he was looking for. This was a photograph larger than the others, and dog-eared as if its present tidy and capacious resting-place was not a habitat it had been always accustomed to. Taking it out he examined it with a fresh keenness, paying particular attention to the yellowed back.

The photograph showed a couple on their wedding day, a plump-faced girl in a bouffant white dress and veil, and a slender young man in a natty but comically old-fashioned suit. The bride's hand, holding a knife, was poised over a tiered wedding cake. On the back a stamp read in faded blue 'Kennedy's Photographic Studios, Dublin'. Above it a girlish hand had written 'To Hilda. From Baby (Kinane!!)'. The 'Hilda' was Tom's mother. But all he could say about the 'Baby Kinane' was that the two exclamation marks she'd put were totally girlish, expressing – what? Surprise? Triumph? Hard to say what exactly. But they definitely implied a shared joke, intimacy, a confidence in being understood by Hilda.

Cerise appeared in the doorway and counted off on her fingers the arrangements she could complete in a trice once he gave her the word. 'Your accommodation, your tickets . . . Your cellphone with tri-band, for use in the remote areas of the world . . . Your signatory authorisation on his cards that's about to be set up. The bank account in Ireland is all ready to go, with your own authorisation, his co-signature required only on the really humungous payouts . . . And concerning that account, let me tell you Tom, you're getting a lot of money to play with. A lot.'

'How much?' asked Tom.

It was too awesome to say out loud. She leaned over and whispered a sum into his ear.

Tom whistled. 'Hell. What does he think I'm going to do over there? Go head to head with MacDonald's?'

'You'll find something,' said Cerise cheerfully. 'Something to make them happy, I guess?'

'Hey, that'll be easy, right?'

'Dead easy,' Cerise assured him.

They seemed to be moving seamlessly out of the conditional tense now and into the future.

9

The tall sashed window of his room in the Shelbourne Hotel framed a modest mountain range that rose up behind the low, rambling skyline of the city of Dublin. The mountains changed colour with an alarming speed as the light changed – blue and optimistic one minute, grey and menacing the next. This was disorientating but then jet-lag generally had a disorientating effect. The window was swathed in voluminous rose-patterned drapes that shadowed the room. An elfin Polish girl had come to unpack his bags and hang up his clothes. At what he hoped would prove to be an inviting angle Tom arranged his laptop on the mirrored table that would serve as his writing desk.

Emails from Cerise were coming perky and fast. She wanted to be told the whole deal. Was his flight good? Are the Irish needy? Isn't her choice of hotel cool? How he's doing?

The Shelbourne was grand, he told her, adopting the quaint adjective the Polish girl had used. 'Facade like a frosted cake, ornate, Boston-ivied. You'd like it.' And so indeed was the room service. Cerise believed in making full use of room service. Lest she imagine he was pining for Katya he mentioned the pretty steward on the plane who'd been particularly solicitous about his comfort.

'I haven't met any of the Irish yet,' he told her. 'A shoe-shine I spoke to turned out to be Hungarian and the cab driver was Latvian. We went through a few dodgy areas but nothing you wouldn't see in NY. The skyline is littered with construction cranes, looks like there's big money around. The Latvian wanted to know if I was here to build office blocks. Office blocks! Is Pender thinking of office blocks? I don't know what the hell he wants me to do over here . . .'

'Attaboy, Tom,' Cerise mailed back. 'He's happy as a sandboy now you're on the case. All you have to do is give it a whirl. Enjoy!'

Cerise was happy when the boss was happy. Maybe it was something, to make somebody at least happy. He had not made Katya happy. There were no emails from Katya, he hadn't got an email from her for a long time and then it was hostile.

He woke too early and went down and had a long 'full Irish' breakfast in a stately dining room. It was a good breakfast but it seemed pretty American to him. There were no Irish that he could discern among the waiting staff. All the same Pender's belief that the race was dying out for want of sustenance was hardly likely.

Back in his room he ordered up a telephone directory for the city. With a hand that very slightly trembled he placed it on the table and found the entries for Kinane. Immediately he was heartened. They weren't very many, the Kinanes. No Baby among them, however. But that would have been too much to hope for. Probably she would be hidden, invisible under her husband's listing, whatever his name was. He thought of the young man in the wedding suit in the photograph and tried to match him with a name: Andrew, Conor, Paul, Patrick, Alan . . . All of them or none could fit.

Beneath his window across the thoroughfare there was a public square. Behind the black railings surrounding it the trees were wearing their early summer frou frou and there were lawns bright with petunias and tulips. Today the sky hung creamy and plain over the city roofs. It was like a vast bowl of farmer's milk. The big acreage of sky gave Tom a feeling of exposure. It was like finding yourself on the top of some plateau in Colorado. Katya used to speak yearningly of Colorado. She wanted them to go there and live romantically in a frugal cabin, to be cleansed by its mountain springs and invigorating air. Crazy, he told her; she wouldn't last a week. He wouldn't, for sure. But maybe he'd been wrong. He was suddenly wistful for Colorado. He pictured Katya striding along a mountain-top, her face raised to the big sky as she took in draughts of cold, uncluttered air.

Freshly braced he picked up the telephone and dialled the first Kinane in the book; one A.T. Kinane. The number rang for a long time and he was about to hang up when a woman's quavering voice answered.

'I'm trying to find somebody by the name of Baby Kinane,' Tom said. 'Might you be her?' He knew from the aged quality of the voice that it was unlikely. But she could be a relative. There was a long silence.

'Who's calling?' the voice said then. That sounded positive, as if Baby could be near at hand . . . possibly in an adjacent room and easily summoned. Tom's pulse quickened.

'The name is Tom Blessman.' He emphasised the 'Blessman' so it came out portentous, significant. A name she would recognise.

'I don't think I know you,' the voice said plaintively.

'Of course you don't. But I thought you might know Baby—'

'I certainly do *not* know Baby. And I don't know you.' The voice was gaining strength. 'But I know your type. Ringing up women and harassing them and trying to ferret out information about them. But you're not going to get very far with me and you won't get far either with any more poor unfortunates, let me tell you, because I'll have them onto you. You just keep on talking now, young fellow and they'll be onto you in two shakes of—'

'I'm terribly sorry,' Tom gasped. Quickly he put down the phone. He found he was perspiring, as Cerise would say. The first Irish woman he'd spoken with, but what an exchange! She had accused him of harassment. Could cold-calling be construed as harassment? He was in a country of whose laws he knew nothing. They could be Kafkaesque for all he knew. But if a number was listed in a directory surely you were entitled to call it to make a legitimate enquiry, even if you didn't know the person?

It took him a while to calm down. Then, defiantly, he dialled the next number. Nothing else for it.

'Hello?' A man's voice, friendly. Country music in the background.

'I'm sorry to intrude,' Tom said. 'But I'm looking for a Baby Kinane. I wonder if you might happen to know her?'

'We have a Baby Kinane here right enough,' the man replied.

'You have? Can I speak to her?' This was incredible. To have tracked her down so soon . . . Tom's nervousness was replaced by a mounting excitement.

The man laughed. 'Sure you can. But she won't be able to speak to you I'm afraid. And she won't understand a word you say. In fact Baby's only interest in the telephone at the moment is in trying to chew it. She's bright but . . . well, a six monther. You know what they're like . . .'

Third time lucky Tom told himself as he faltered before dialling another number. This resulted in a relatively polite but brusque and negative exchange that left him tired and discouraged. However, tomorrow was another day. Stretching out on the rose-sateen bed he slept.

In the late afternoon he awoke groggy and peckish and went out. In the public gardens girls strolled across his path, oblivious, talking laughingly, fetchingly to their cellphones. On the grass couples were entwined in one another's arms. The arms were often pale and freckled. These probably belonged to the natives. An occasional whiff of dope mingled with flowery scents from the bright and tended parterres. At regular intervals one of the snouted lilac-coloured trams bossily clanged its bell and set off southward towards the mountains. Back on the shady street the usual city's traffic jostled around him, snarling and restive. He and Katya were like stalled engines, Tom mused; they had come to a stop, pulled up by some obstacle up ahead they could not see or some event behind in the line. Or just the old story? Incompatibility of temperaments, ambitions . . . Or had simply married in haste, impulsively, romantically . . . Lustfully, he thought with a rueful twinge. And mysteriously, imperceptibly the chemistry changing, until only the clash of temperaments was left.

Katya was convinced that the obstacle was the absence of Tom's mother, an unexamined trauma exacerbated by the appearances and disappearances of the women who slid in and out of his father's life.

'Your issue is that you fear the woman – and presently she is me – is going to leave you,' she asserted.

'The correct phrase is "at present",' he had corrected her. 'You could be right. Though maybe my fear is that I'm going to leave her. At present, you.'

Why had he said that? He didn't even know if it was true.

It had grieved her deeply. 'You make it sound like a decision, not to leave. If you loved me it wouldn't be a decision, it wouldn't be a choice.'

'I do love you,' he had said. But it sounded lame even to himself.

After that she had hovered uncertainly between retreat and attack. She was right, of course, and she knew it. She always did know everything. Her elliptical Russian eyes gazing at him with increasing outrage, silently enumerating his deficiencies. Once she said, exasperated by her own failure of judgement, 'What a cliché – I'm with a guy who can't commit.'

'I am committed,' he insisted. But no more convincingly.

'The truth is in the heart, not in the words.' How tragic, how accusing she could look.

Soon, gradually and methodically, she was removing from the apartment her files, her documentation, her driving licence, her passport, all the paraphernalia necessary to effect a rational and purposeful departure. One night he had come home after a difficult dinner with his agent to find her wardrobe doors swinging open and her favourite outfits gone, most of her collection of playful shoes; lots of other items he couldn't particularise.

'She's run out on you?' Pender had said in a tone of respect. 'I always liked that little dame,' he ruminated. 'But I always knew she'd be hard to keep a hold of. Too independent-minded. Too fond of a good time.' Her departure made Katya rise even higher in his estimation. In his eyes any woman worth her salt ran out, did the dirty, screwed her business partner, and her business partner's husband as she was at it. A real woman was as red in tooth and claw as her expertly lipsticked mouth.

'We had some good times,' Tom protested.

'Of course you did. Katya's a sweet kid. But not recently, right? You grew apart. It happens.'

'We ran out of steam, I guess. I don't know why.' Tom sighed.

'You gave her too much rope. A woman wants to own her man, that's all she ever wants. You own her, she owns you. Maybe you didn't let her own you.' His great-uncle sighed. 'But why should you?'

'I had no objection to letting her think she owned me.'

'You're no good at deception, my boy. You have to deceive 'em to keep 'em happy.'

To Pender Gast a successful relationship was a deadly but heady *pas de deux*, a performance where each played out his and her role of lover, deceiver, speculator, supporter and in which the guiding theme of individual survival was mutually agreed.

'You just sit tight, boy. Don't you let her know you give a damn. Go chasing after her and she'll keep on running.'

'Won't stop me worrying about her, how she's doing.'

Gast chuckled. He liked women to show the voracity of foxes, equipped with nothing but their wit and a Gucci holdall. 'Don't you worry. That little Katya is kicking up her legs out in California. She'll make out. You can be sure she's making out just fine as long as you're not hearing from her.' He said 'California' with the 'r' silent, like a hard-boiled character in an old-time movie. From his mouth it sounded like a good fit place, rich and tough with a good hard sun beating down on you and everybody making out.

'You'll be better off over there without her,' he told Tom. 'It's no place to take a smart girl like Katya. Did you ever see her walk down the sidewalk of a poor neighbourhood for her entertainment?'

'And for sure it's my favourite thing,' Tom had retorted. 'She'd be a drag at my heels.'

'You're going on a mission,' wheedled his great-uncle. 'This is a man's job, honey.'

Along streets Tom wandered, lined with old houses built of brick, wine-hued, orange. The houses could look pale and ethereal or solid and grim as the light took them. Old but trim, the brasswork burnished, the doors painted . . . The opposite of poor. At the outside tables of the bars, laughing groups of high-maintenance babes sat smoking and getting sozzled on expensive sundowners while the guys stood about in the pugilistic attitudes of high rollers, smoking, drinking black beers and doing swaggering high-volume talk. Any bar he looked into was lush with giant potted palm trees, stuffed leopards, tropical wood carvings. Or maybe there was only one such bar, only one leopard. In the exotic world of jet-lag still, brain cells zapped . . . Might have been zapped before I ever left Manhattan, in fact . . . Have to get some sleep.

IO

At breakfast he picked up a newspaper with the furtive and shameful hope of finding stories of famine and upheaval in the country districts. But the stories were the predictable ones of prospering places. There had been a murder the evening before in a neighbourhood described as 'a northside suburb', suspected of being drug-related . . . Some political scandal to do with kick-backs from the construction industry . . . The country's youth was said to be dangerously high on drink and drugs and sex . . . On the business pages there were articles about the remarkable rate of economic growth and whether it was sustainable. The pundits were taking the view that it was more than sustainable, 'in the medium term'. Tom was no economist but he could see they weren't hedging their bets.

With rather more keenness he read an interview with a native film director. The director's new movie was described as 'a wry and appealing comedy', a 'love triangle located in leafy suburbia'. 'The rain, the drunken father . . .' the director was reported as saying, 'all that sob stuff, the mangy dogs, all that shite, it's over. It's over historically, it's over cinematically. Don't get me wrong, it happened. No question. And the people who had to live through those times, they have all my sympathy. But I want to look at the real stuff, you know? I want to look at the present, the positive, something we can all relate to. Love, money, multiplicity of choices. We're global now, we're multi-cultural, let's celebrate. We're done with whingeing, right?'

Tom thought he'd email the interview to Cerise.

Demonstrate to Pender how things really stood in the nobly wretched isle of his dreams. He should know the difficulties his emissary was facing over here.

He took up a supplement that came with the newspaper and inspected the properties for sale. There was a good supply of great country houses, a plenitude of bijou townhouses, cute little country cottages . . . Maybe he should send that too to his great-uncle. There might be a property in it to light up the shrouded spaces of his memory, some little house at the foot of a hill might restore the knowledge of the place he came from all those years ago. Could that be what the dream was telling him? The unconscious desire to find the lost place where he began, a wish even to return? No, definitely. Pender never went back in any sense if he could help it.

He took a long bath and then with renewed determination turned again to the telephone book. The column of Kinanes seemed longer today. He submitted five more numbers to interrogation, returned with varying degrees of incomprehension, curiosity and irritation, before giving up. The fourth had rung out unanswered however, persuading him on no rational basis that this might be the one. He marked it for future investigation.

Room service came and went with refreshments, lunch, more refreshments. In the intervals he sat at the table bent over his novel. But he was finding it hard to concentrate. Manhattan, where it was set, seemed very remote. He had always known he wasn't one of those guys who walk into a strange hotel room, open up the file and set to work. It was why he wasn't a traveller, for God's sakes. Outside the water-laden sky was fitfully splashed by a lemon-coloured sun, watery but optimistic.

'Can't work over here. And no sign of the old man's people. What do you say I come home?' he mailed Cerise.

'Sure you can't work. You need to settle in, Tom. Give yourself a break.'

He looked at his watch. Not too long to dinner time. Certainly soon be pre-dinner-drink time . . .

From the bars along Dawson Street came a rising current of hilarity, a wave gaining momentum that within a couple of hours would rise to its evening crescendo. I am wandering on an island, among islanders, Tom thought. A reason maybe for their hilarity. The laughter of captives, fretful at confinement, but fearful too of ejection into a landlocked world . . . A Russian characteristic? A Russian tendency generally, you could say. The tea habit, drink habit, potato habit . . . But the Russian more reserved? 'The Russian is a serious person. We are sincere,' Katya had said, looking at him soulfully and with the expression of disappointment she had come to regard him with of late.

Off the melée of Grafton Street, at the outside tables of the hip bars where the smokers assembled, girls were clustered, glasses in hand, under the awnings. In a liquid mass they spilled onto the pavements, free-flowed around the corners of the lanes. The constant state of expectation this whimsical Irish sunlight engendered, again and again, and just as constantly disappointed . . . The girls' light and skimpy clothing displayed patchy gradations of tan. False tans, fragile, temporary . . . Could Pender provide tanning booths for the masses? Boost the morale, liven up those white and shriven faces he sees in the dream.

Tom sat at a rosily polished mahogany bar and drank a beer. Cavernous, opulent, the place was a fantasia of excess, a reliquary of looted civilisations. Lanterns and candelabras, a frolic of fronds and palms, demure statues in stone and marble, Etruscan type urns, Egyptian, tapestries, friezes from the ancients.

Shards of the past, shards of illusion . . . That was the phrase Katya had used in one of her philosophical pronouncements. 'Let me tell you what is life. A stony path littered with the shards of illusion.'

Stonily gazing at him as if he were at least partly responsible for all the disillusions in all the world. She must have read that somewhere. Or heard it sexily muttered by the moody protagonist in some gloomy European movie she watched all alone with a tub of ice-cream. Strawberry ice-cream, her favourite. Nowhere, Tom realised, had he ever been so alone. He took deep breaths, intensely solitary, but alarmingly, excitingly free.

In a small pedestrianised street where people hurried from one thoroughfare to another, there was the intimate old-world smell of drains. And across the familiar acrid note of exhaust fumes there came sometimes on a roaming breeze an enticing whiff of something fruity and toasted. The smell of dark beer cooking up in the brewery, according to his guide book. The humidity had dispersed. He made his way through the homing crowds as far as the river and turned west into a dazzling evening sun. The river water was flowing thick and dark between its steep walls, outpacing the patient lines of traffic inching their way onto the motorways, towards the lone stretches of estates housing the families, their hopes and desolations. He had seen them the other morning when the plane swooped low as it was coming in. It seemed a long time ago. Out there maybe the real-life versions of Pender's dream-pilgrims were waiting. But what did they want that he could give?

Taxis loped past in the lane reserved for them. All the poor guys stuck in their cars – if they rode in taxis wouldn't they be home a whole lot quicker? The sad fact was they wouldn't. A simple case of numbers. Most of the problems and troubles and annoyances in the world caused by everyone wanting the same thing, living their lives the same. Tom walked along in a mildly noxious fug. The river was giving off its retro stench. Further down the ebbing tide was draining its bed, revealing a dank and oozy silt, ages old, the effluvia and accretions of the generations. Gingerly he breathed it in as he gazed down at the objects mired in shrouds of mud like discovered artefacts from a recent and mundane civilisation. Twisted umbrellas, fallen traffic cones, a boot or two of an archetypal make . . . Like a rackety ark a bedstead tilted above the receding flood.

No bodies, no melodramas, no scavengers, only the mundane detritus of the not-destitute. Crossing a bridge over the river into the grimmer northern sky he passed into small, shady, domestic streets. From the dim sanctuaries of small rooms came the metallic fuzz of televisions and computers, breaking the almost silence. Parked cars were slumbering, snout to tail. Well, they seem to have enough cars, enough screens.

As he meandered along Tom imagined an ancestor living in a row of houses like this one, or that. The sounds they would have heard, the cries of children playing archaic games, a clip clop of horses on the cobbles . . . but the same brewery smell borne on the air, more pungent then. He was feeling kind of high. Were the whiffs from the brewery making everybody high? He imagined a different kind of mother, not the tea-drinking career woman but a girl made giddy and wild by floating beer-molecules.

The frenzied lilt of fiddle music issued from a pub. There were pubs at every corner, one or two not unlike Stacey's. He could do with another beer but decided to hold off. Wouldn't want to regress to the Paris days. Once or twice his great-uncle had made dark references to the perils of drink. 'Very easy to slide into over-consumption.' Yeah, tell me about it. A family weakness. But it was a reference quickly dropped. Pender didn't admit weaknesses into the family.

A broader street now, a thoroughfare, active and noisy. The warm dense smell of fast food, shadowy pavements broken by pallid pools of neon. From an alleyway a man's deep husky laugh echoed. A party of big-bellied men, a bevy of girls in tiny skirts.

'Hiya mister,' they sang out, coaxing but hostile . . . sure, you can have me, but you don't mess with me . . . Like a pearly beast, a tram loomed up between a pair of brightly painted apartment buildings and with the light thunder of urban rail moved off again. Ecclesiastical, the quaint clang of its bell.

In New York Tom did not frequent streets like this one. But he knew of them well enough, knew what they were like. The commerce, the low-life that any town worth its salt contains. He knew the routine. And as if on cue along came the dealers now, the guys sidling up to murmur, 'Are you looking? You in the market?'

Back home Tom was content to be no more than an occasionally browsing guest at the table when a line or whatever was put out.

'Thanks. But no, I'm just out for a stroll.'

'Nice night all right for a bit of a stroll.'

Irony hanging in the air, and a ruminating menace. The busy hum of unspoken hostilities being meditated?

As he moved on with a new briskness he caught sight of his reflection in a window. The natty Armani set of his linen jacket, the neat button-down, the haircut that suddenly struck him as preppy . . . A jaunty ingénue look all told. Ripe for the picking. Only lately Georgie Hertz was telling him about a college bud who was jumped on in some foreign city. 'What do you expect,' Georgie had remarked, 'going around in his preppy get-up the way he does.' Tom felt the stirrings of anxiety, slight but insistent. A girl stepped out into his path.

'Come on, Captain America. Are you interested? Or what?'

Tom paused, halted. He knew the type. Druggie but not terminal declined. Not yet. Mischievous still, perky. Freckles like they were sprinkled from a sugar-shaker. Cute little face. Hesitating, looking away and down to avoid her narrowed eyes he saw, planted insinuatingly close to his handmade loafers her small, pale, bony feet tied insecurely into slack gilted thongs. They were at least a size too big. A poignant metaphor, a metaphor for the great, sad and grim parade of life. Where, if he took her up on her offer, would she take him? Did she have a room nearby? Or just a shady patch by the wall in a parking lot?

Only once in his life had he paid a girl, a long time ago. As an experience it definitely didn't rate. Still, he wavered.

A breath, a low hiss, brushed his ear. 'If I were you I'd get out of here, man. They'd eat you alive.' With a start he looked up and saw a guy in a ponytail who'd passed him by, apparently oblivious of his presence, a small dog at his heels. He was walking on, his gait lithe and careless. But turning around to check the dog, he gave Tom a brief but meaning glance.

Hey, the guy looked streetwise. And he was flashing the warning lights. If this was New York, Tom saw in a moment, he'd be out of here. In fact he'd never have been anywhere like in. What was he thinking? Some kind of a rescue mission? He glanced again at the chlorotic girl with her winsome spatter of freckles. Maybe the thought had crossed his mind . . .

She inserted her hand into his. The bones were frail, insubstantial, but her grasp was firm. 'Come on,' she coaxed. 'Don't spoil me buzz, mister.'

In his head he heard his great-uncle's voice, exasperated, irate. 'Get out of there, and pronto. It's you wants rescuing, boy, if you think I'm going to prop up any dopeheads or sleazeballs or two-bit whores. Are you crazy? I see more than enough of them all around me. Okay, these guys have to live. But that's their game. Anyways, who's obliging anybody to get addicted? Nobody, that's who.'

A taxi was coming down the street, its sign thankfully lit. Tom pulled his hand from the girl's persistent grip, ran forward and wildly waved it down. 'The Shelbourne Hotel,' he instructed the driver. Lying back he closed his eyes with a sensation of escape. A close shave clearly, from some now never-to-be-known mishap. Let's get back to town. The lofty, clean, safe side of town. It was what he had come to see as his side.

II

In the Shelbourne the evening drinking was well underway. Thirstily Tom ordered a beer and sat with it on a sofa in the marbled and columned lobby. From this vantage he could watch the doors in their ceaseless revolution and the habitués they spilled out. Late workers from the offices, their pastel shirts crumpled from the wear and tear of the day, loudly laughing with a self-conscious assertiveness . . . Pampered people, rested, smooth-skinned, sauntering past. Practitioners of suspect trades, the kind who conduct their day's business in the gathering dusk of city bars, their freshly showered insouciance not quite masking a hungry and hunted look . . .

One of those chauffeured hugely expensive Augustas, of which he had seen quite a few already, pulled up at the hotel portico and a porter in his quaint uniform hurried out to assist its passenger from the back seat. With an impatient gesture the chic young woman shook him off and strode past into some inner sanctum. A pretty face, but not good-tempered.

Now a grizzled but winsome guy in a duster coat . . . Is he a resting actor? A pale, thin young woman, eating-disorder graduate-student type, wrapped in an unseasonal coat that hung limply to her ankles. Tom finished the beer and retired to his room. With renewed determination he took up his post again with the telephone. This time he would get through the whole damn Kinane listings, even if it took all night.

It didn't take that long. Maybe because he adopted the businesslike tone of a professional enquirer, the responses were equally brisk and to the point. But they were no more fruitful. He drew only blanks. Baby Kinane was not to be found at any of the numbers.

'She could be anywhere,' one helpful woman offered, engaging with the problem. 'She could be in Australia. She could even be . . .' She did not finish the sentence, but Tom knew what she meant. He could very well be chasing a ghost. There were a few listings where the call rang out unanswered that he marked for a redial. But he had an instinct that she wouldn't be found there, either. Somehow they wore an aspect that he would have described as cold. He decided he deserved a drink.

The smaller hotel bar was high-ceilinged but intimate, the mahogany fittings glossy and weighty, the light sombre. Traditional, tribal, the faintly bleak but ebullient air of a gentleman's club where men are let loose to do their man thing, to bellow, to boast, to drink too much. Tom had to push his way through hordes of them. The women, even the graduate-student type with her scrubbed face, clutching her big coat to her small chest, looked slightly louche or illicit. As if they had dropped caste and purpose at the door. Maybe that was the draw for the women. A version of slumming.

Tom thought he'd have a Guinness, the drink of choice it appeared, for the guys. A bartender fixed him in his sights, compliant.

'Evening, Rich. The usual?'

Rich! What was that about? Okay, familiarity might be the house style, could even be what the patron pays high tab for . . . but Rich? More than familiar, nothing less than presumptuous . . . And what did he mean by 'the usual'?

'I want to get a pint of—' Tom began coldly. But the bartender had already turned away and was pouring out a treble gin.

'Excuse me.' Tom's voice rose. 'I wanted to get—'

Behind him somebody chuckled. 'He's squinty-eyed.' A

man's voice whispered warmly into his ear. 'Takes a bit of practice to work him out. What are you having?'

A casual hand was raised. 'A pint here, Joe, when you're ready . . . The Rich – he wasn't talking to you; he was talking to Richard Quill. You know Rich? Longford man. My own part of the country. Big cattle man.' That chuckle again. 'Of course you wouldn't know what fires Rich might have his irons in.'

'I guess there's a fair number here could answer to Rich,' suggested Tom. He took a tentative sip from the drink Joe had placed in front of him.

'Yep. Though half of them would only be letting on.'

The speaker was a big fellow, maybe late thirties. A Midwesterner, Tom might have characterised him as, back home. Thick sandy hair, pink complexion. A full soft mobile mouth that made his expression amiable, but his grey eyes incongruously restless, watchful. He appraised the scene reflected in the ornate mirror behind the array of amber liquors and added, 'There's big money here all the same, I'll tell you. Enough to keep the tribunals going for a while yet.'

'Oh yes,' Tom said eagerly. 'The tribunals. They're, like, weeding out the corruption, right?'

The eyes seemed to darken. Soulfully they fixed Tom in their sights.

'You're American. East Coast?'

Tom nodded.

'In business?'

Tom nodded again, this time with a certain diffidence. 'I'm looking at investment possibilities.' He put out his hand. 'I'm Tom. Tom Blessman.'

The man's grip was meaty but less firm than you'd expect. 'Glad to meet you, Tom. I'm Denis. Denis Grogan. You're interested in investment potentials?' Denis considered his own question. 'We're on a roll. But you'd know all about that. Great stuff. But you could be getting in a bit late in the day. Right now I'd say everything could be overpriced. A decade ago now and it was a different story. Still, there's always something to be got if you keep your eyes open. You have a few bob?'

'I have a few bob,' agreed Tom.

'Joe,' Denis called out. 'Are you going to leave us standing all night here like a pair of camels? Give us another there.'

Joe threw a smile somewhere to the far left and bent with alacrity to the pumps.

'Can I ask you something?' Tom heard himself saying. 'You don't happen to know of somebody by the name of Baby Kinane, do you? I'm trying to locate her.'

Denis appeared to be racking his brains. 'Can't say I do,' he said finally. 'I know a Carey Kinane. Would he be any good to you?'

'No reason to believe he would.'

'You've looked in the telephone book?'

'I sure have.'

'She could be ex-directory,' Denis mused.

'Can I get listings for ex-directory?' inquired Tom.

'No way. That I know of, anyway. But of course there's always ways and means.'

'Like never say never?' said Tom wearily.

'Maybe.'

Tom saw a prospect of conspiracy ahead, weeks of embroilment and stealth involving payouts to a succession of operatives in the dark corners of bus stations and backstreet bars, all for a number that had become defunct a decade or two ago. Was that how they did things here?

'It's all mobiles now,' Denis was saying. 'What about the mobile listings?'

'Don't know,' Tom said without enthusiasm.

'Funny thing,' Denis mused, 'but I find myself forgetting about the residential listings. I turn to the business listings first off – natural enough I suppose. While Marguerite – that's the wife – Marguerite turns to—'

'The business listings?' interrupted Tom.

47

'Yep. They're in the back of the book.'

'You know, I believe I've been looking only in the residential,' Tom exclaimed.

'There you are now. You'd never know what you'd turn up in the business section. You a golfer, Tom?'

'No. Never got into golf.'

'We should do something about that. All the boys do golf.' Denis placed his glass on the counter. 'Well. Gotta move. I promised Marguerite I'd be home early. Have to keep the women happy, Tom.' He put out his hand. 'We'll meet again.'

'You bet,' said Tom heartily.

With the easy authority of a player Denis went striding away through the crowded salon. The grad student was eyeing Tom over the rim of her glass. She gave him a small but he thought rather sweet smile.

'Would you like a drink?' he asked.

Yes, she said, actually she would like a vodka cranberry.

He was favoured with a brisk nod from Joe, his astigmatised glance directed to a distant corner.

12

He awoke around noon, headachey, his eyes bleary. A tall blond Belorussian from room service brought up a large pot of strong coffee. Returning to bed to drink it Tom mused on the inevitable fall from his heady state in the early hours. Over-excitement. His memories were fuzzy to say the least.

Flushed faces, hilarity, wild talk . . . Even fuzzier, a person with a torch leading them along a narrow path, himself taking up the rearguard in the dawn light; though in this chimerical land of quasi midnight sun what seemed like dawn could have been the post-midnight glow. A cab's interior scented with something cloyingly sweet from a spray can. A girl next to him, her dress rustling on the leatherette, her head inclined towards his. And the delusion, sweet but dumb, that he was in some kind of a candy store, girls for the taking.

Lurching towards her, his hands reaching out. And her cool fingers prising him off. No sweat, no bother as they say in these parts. As far as he could recall, anyway. Who was she? His mind was a blank. A corn-fed quality. Definitely not the graduate anorexic girl. But the anorexic girl had been somewhere around. He – they? – had ended up in one of those bleached-wood bars. Could really knock it back, hard to keep up . . . But a guy has to stay in the game.

Must have left together. Travelling off to some place he never heard of – well, how could he have heard of it, even *compos mentis*? Some place out of town, some far-flung suburb of this low-sized straggle of a town. The cab had stopped. And in a decisive movement she wrapped herself around him and her tongue was in his mouth. Vividly he recalled the thrilling nip of sharp incisors.

And then she was gone and he was trying to tell the driver to go to the Shelbourne, but that was proving mystifyingly difficult. He remembered her scent, grassy and salty, saw a vivid image of a meadow by the side of the ocean, pale grasses nodding in the breeze ... Was that real or imagined? Steady up there. That damn romantic tendency, there it goes again. Has to be resolutely shunned as a reformed alcoholic turns aside from the nectar winking in a glass. Gets you into nothing but trouble.

Tom poured himself more coffee, raised himself gingerly to a less recumbent position on the sateen quilt and flicked the TV control. As moving pictures the swish savagery of twenty-first century life came into the room – and Ireland had it as much as anywhere else. They set his head throbbing all over again. Wincing, he let them go and roved through the fizzing radio channels. A man's voice came out loud and clear. It was a strangely soothing voice. 'What we need in Ireland now,' said the voice, 'may not be something a government or an agency or anyone else can supply for us. We may not have our hands outstretched as so many in the distant continents stretch out their hands to us in supplication. We may not be walking, Ed, in sad procession to far away aid centres. But we are conscious of a deep hunger all the same, a gnawing hunger.'

Tom sat bolt upright.

'Don't get me wrong now, Ed,' the voice continued. 'I'm not against progress. Not at all. I rejoice in progress. I like to see riches and plenty. I like to see my people sitting down as to a feast, with a groaning board spread out before them . . .'

The voice washed over Tom, mellifluous, inspiring. It was a brogue sweeter than any he had heard. It was a flavour, dark and thick and honeyed and matured in oaken vats. And as a bonus, it seemed to speak from deep inside the territory of his great-uncle's dream. Tom couldn't believe his luck.

Ed, the presenter, was attempting, annoyingly, to stem the flow.

'Now Ed' – there was the suggestion of an authoritative, even stern finger being raised – 'I know we are not all getting on as we would like. I know that very well. But material hunger is not what I am talking about now. What I am talking about is a hunger of another kind, a hunger equally real, equally consuming. It doesn't show up in the statistics. You won't find it described in government reports and you certainly won't be finding it in the reports of our myriad financial institutions . . .' The word 'myriad' was richly rolled, conveying a mild and chiding contempt.

'You're talking about the spiritual aspect?' asked Ed with a suggestion of boredom.

'Spiritual is not a word I use, Ed. We have heard it all too often in this country. And we have heard it from people who wanted to keep us in another kind of subjection. But make no mistake. The people are appealing for something, for a form of nourishment, for some form of sustenance they are not getting. They are crying out. Their hands may not be held out in mute appeal, their faces may not be gaunt from starvation, but they are in a state of want. What do they want? I do not claim to have the answer to their question, but if it is to be my task, my life's work I may say, to define what—'

At this point, to Tom's irritation, the voice was silenced.

'We've run out of time,' Ed broke in hurriedly. 'You'll come back to us some other time I hope, Mr Maconor?'

The dulcet voice was heard faintly to say, 'I'd be happy to do that.'

It was replaced by a brash advertisement for faux-German kitchens. 'All the expensive look of chrome and steel that you love . . .'

The guy had been rudely interrupted. And just when he was getting to the really important bit. Who was he? Sounded like Maconor, but hard to say for sure. Did he have a plan? It was all rather vague and aspirational. But God, he was good . . . Somehow he'd have to find him, arrange a meeting. Tom leaped out of bed, washed, dressed and ate some lunch. He was feeling a whole lot better.

Enthusiastically he opened the telephone book at the Mac listings. There was nobody in it by the name of Maconor. Must have got it wrong. But whatever his name was he was obviously well-known. He couldn't be all that hard to find.

With reluctance Tom turned once more to the Ks to pore over the Kinanes. The half-dozen he'd marked for further investigation drew blanks. Four were still not replying and the two who did were polite but negative. It was wearisome work, a needle in a haystack, a . . . But what was it that fellow Denis Grogan had said last night? The business listings . . . Unlikely. The Baby Kinane in the photograph didn't look like a businesswoman. The very name sounded unlikely for a businesswoman. All the same, he turned to the back and there, sure enough, were the business listings. And the minute he turned to the Ks a Kinane leaped out. Large black typeface, lots of white space around it. An optimistic listing. 'Kinane Kitchens. Design And Fit. Traditional And Modern. Wm. Kinane. Sandalwood Road, Ranelagh, Dublin 6.'

William. No reference to a Baby. Pointless obviously but . . . Wearily, he dialled. Little point either in leaving a stone unturned.

'Baby?' repeated a young woman's voice with a hint of incredulity. This was a response to which Tom was well-accustomed by now. It was followed by the usual silence as the question and appropriate answer were considered. Followed then by a laugh . . .

'My mother hasn't called herself that for yonks,' she said then. 'Hold on there. I'll get her.'

13

In good time the next afternoon Tom went downstairs and laid claim to a tasselled couch in the Shelbourne's Tea Lounge.

'I'm waiting for someone,' he told the waitress. He spoke with the air of confiding an intimacy. 'Afternoon tea for two, please.'

He was tremulous, both excited and anxious. It's not my mother I'm about to meet, he had to tell himself more than once. She's only my mother's friend. He could have done with a drink, but forbore. Had to keep his wits about him. Through the chunky revolving doors he could see the sleek Augusta of some regular, impassive and complacent as it waited. He took up a newspaper but, failing to make any sense of it, folded it again with an unwonted neatness.

What if she didn't turn up? She had sounded a little distracted on the phone. 'I'm Nina,' she had announced. 'I dropped the Baby. Haven't been Baby for years. Will I do?' Was stumped at first by the name Hilda Blessman. But when he amended it to Hilda Pendergast she was effusive, flustered.

'You're Hilda's boy? Well, hardly a boy I suppose . . . Dear me. Dear me.' She had repeated this several times. Yes, she knew poor Hilda had died. 'Tragic. At such a young age. Such a lovely girl.' Of course, they hadn't met since her return to America the first time. Such a long time ago.

The first time? What had she meant by 'the first time'? Had his mother made more than one trip? Tom looked again at his watch. Baby – no, he must remember, it was Nina – had agreed to meet him at three thirty. 'They do a very nice tea in the Shelbourne,' she had said.

An enormous tea-tray, laden with old-style genteel silverware and china, was placed in front of him. She was late. But that didn't have to mean she wasn't coming. She'd sounded like the unpunctual kind. Around him the tea-drinkers at other tables chattered on, enviably careless, urbane.

A small, slight woman in a powder-pink suit entered the Tea Lounge. Behind her a girl, tawny-headed, slender in a clingy T-shirt, stood at a slight distance. The woman looked as if she would like to be steered to a table by someone. But the girl was clearly oblivious of this wish. The woman was girlish still, her face faded-pretty. But anxiety had taken hold of it. Her hair, escaping wispily from a clasp, was a frizzy cloud, the drained colour of soft fruit, a peach or a melon. She stood there by the door, searching the munificent room with a myopic gaze.

Hesitantly, Tom half-rose. Her expression changed swiftly to one of recognition. She came to him with her arms outstretched.

'Tom!' she cried.

'Baby!'

'Nina,' she said firmly. She stood at arm's length to inspect him. 'I'd know you anywhere. You're the image of Hilda.'

'You think? I've always been told I'm a Blessman.'

'No way. It's the eyes, Tom. The eyes are all Hilda.'

He realised that Nina in no way resembled his mother. He was feeling slightly calmer.

'My daughter, Eileen,' she said then, bringing the girl forward.

When Tom took Nina's arm and led her to the couch he was aware of a slight tremor in his fingers. Nina gave a sigh as she sat and arranged her bags and umbrella around her. Perhaps this seat or this spot were not to her liking? 'Is this all right?', Tom blustered. 'We could move to a different sofa if you like.'

'It's fine,' Eileen said with a sympathetic smile. Her tawny, spiky hair gave her an urchin look. Large feline eyes, greenish. Her expression half provocative, half demure. Half urchin, half goddess. The T-shirt stretched across her small shapely breasts read 'I Shagged The Drummer'. That surely must mean she hadn't . . . God, she was more beautiful than a girl had a right . . . She refused tea.

With an automatic movement that was largely defensive, Tom raised his cup to his mouth and scalded his tongue. He had forgotten to add the milk. Red-faced, watery-eyed, he broke into a strangled cough. Nina patted him on the back and at the same time bit into one of the tiny damp sandwiches.

'We have so much to talk about,' Tom said shakily.

She patted his knee. 'First I want to hear all about your father.'

While Tom described Hank Blessman as best he could she listened consideringly, her head to one side in an old-fashioned pose, and sipped her tea. 'And to think he too is gone from us,' she sympathised. 'Still, I'm so glad poor Hilda found happiness in the end.'

'Was she not happy before?' demanded Tom.

'Can any girl be truly happy until she's married, Tom?'

Nina looked with meaning at her daughter. The girl, biting into a large fruit tart, was sprawled on the sofa, one foot under her shapely thigh, the spindle heel of her golden strappy sandal making what looked like a potentially grievous depression in the soft upholstery. The sandal looked familiar. It resembled the strappy footwear the girl in the street had on. He remembered the girl's small mottled feet that had made him want to rescue her. At least Eileen fitted hers.

'But she was no more than normally unhappy?' pressed Tom.

'No more,' Nina agreed.

The girl was a distraction, gorging on a tart, attacking it whole like a waif or a rude child. Despite himself he couldn't stop looking at her. Tom knew that sensation; he distrusted it. The wish to feast on a face . . .

Nina's brow wrinkled thoughtfully. 'You have an uncle, haven't you, Tom? Hilda used to talk about an uncle.'

'That would be Uncle Pender. My great-uncle. What did she say about him?'

'He was difficult, wasn't he? Demanding?'

Tom laughed. 'Still is.'

'Going strong?'

'You bet.'

'Poor Hilda,' Nina repeated sadly. She selected a cake from the tiered stand. The girl stood up and stretched with the languorous reach of someone just out of bed.

'I'm going outside for a smoke,' she announced.

'Can't you wait until Doll comes?' Nina appealed in a low murmur, as if she expected a refusal but would prefer it not to be broadcast aloud in the gentle atmosphere of the Tea Lounge.

'Doll? She mightn't even show.'

'Of course Doll will come.' Nina spoke with the voice of conviction. Doll is reliable. Unlike this daughter who has already left her, moving towards the pillared lobby with the eagerness of desire or escape.

Nina threw Tom a wan smile. 'She should not be smoking,' she remarked.

'She shouldn't,' agreed Tom.

'Your mother was a demon for the cigarettes. Of course we all were in those days.' Girlishly Nina laughed.

A demon? Tom started. Must be a figure of speech.

'My mother smoked?' He digested this scarcely surprising but intriguing piece of information.

They fell into the well-rehearsed conversation of former smokers. Date of commencement, number consumed per day, the undeniable pleasure of, date and circumstance of, moment of conversion . . . The relative ease – in Tom's case – of giving up, in hers the hardship.

'I'm sure if Willie gave up, the children might,' Nina mused.

'But I suppose the poor man has to have something to keep him going.'

'Willie – he's your husband?'

'My husband.'

Kinane Kitchens. 'He's in business, right?' asked Tom.

Yes, but in a small way these days. Used to be very busy, indeed too busy, in the past. Specialised in handmade kitchens. Always good with his hands, Willie was, though of course he had a team to do the carpentry work. His real forte was design, the hand-carvings. Known for his original touch. But he lost interest somehow, along the line. What they want now is the streamlined look. Standardisation he calls it, steel, high-tech. And then you see, there's his heart condition. Nothing too serious, but all the same, he should be careful. His daily consumption of Marlboro Lights, rarely more than ten. However. No, not bad, considering . . . Used to be Majors. Forty a day!

'Majors, Tom. Did you ever smoke Majors?'

'Can't say I did,' said Tom. 'They're heavy-duty?'

'Heavy-duty? I'm not joking.' She gave her girlish laugh.

'Has Eileen bunked off?' somebody asked. A dark-haired young woman had appeared, to loom flamboyantly over Nina and give her a theatrical kiss.

'Oh, she went off for a smoke. Tom, this is my daughter Doll. Spelled D-o-l – short for Dolores.'

'Not dolorous however,' interjected Dol. 'No way.'

'And this, Dol, is Mr Tom Blessman,' Nina continued.

'I know,' Dol breathed. 'You're Mum's American friend.'

Her handclasp was strong, formidable. Greenish eyes like her sister's, but fiercer. Beaming, she sank back into the cushions. Attractive, but a little on the rounded side, a little too strong a character perhaps to be truly a doll. The older sister obviously, competent, effective. Bossy, the younger would complain. But Tom wanted to return to the subject of his mother. It was hard to keep Nina on track.

Dol sat up again, restless, active. Picked up her mother's pot of tea, put it down. 'I think I'll have a drink,' she announced.

'Do, Dol,' said Nina indulgently.

Tom summoned the waitress. 'How about some champagne?' he said. 'I think the occasion merits champagne.'

'Lovely,' Nina murmured.

'I adore champagne,' sparkled Dol. She rearranged her various wispy garments lushly printed in the hues of summer berries, and in a friendly but businesslike manner, as if she were interviewing him for some hard-to-get position, commanded, 'Now, Tom. Tell me about yourself.'

Tom described himself as an investment consultant. He was sure, he said, that Ireland presented interesting possibilities. He had a backer, naturally. Elided the fact that this backer was his great-uncle and represented him as a man with an eye to profits and returns but who was also at the more benign end of the corporate spectrum. A man who had made his money, a great deal of money . . . his hunger abated . . . No, nobody they would have heard of, there were many such guys in the States. But he still liked to dabble, to keep a hand in, to have morning calls to take, decisions to make, the old muscles to flex.

To tell the Kinanes that he had been sent on some kind of a bizarre rescue mission, not to make money but to give it away – that he was deployed by his born-again sentimentalist great-uncle to save people like themselves – well, he could look naive; he could lose respect . . .

Neither did he tell them he was a novelist, though he wasn't sure why. For some reason he wanted to let them gaze for the present at least into the transparent waters of an all-American clean-cut if fictional life.

'Property, Tom,' advised Nina sagely. 'You won't go wrong if you invest in property.'

'Spectacular returns in property,' Dol agreed. 'But why don't you think about art? There's quite a boom in Irish art right now.'

She eyed him speculatively over the rim of her glass. Tom

suspected that there was a good brain at work in there behind the cool pussy-cat gaze.

'You bet,' he said. 'It's something I'll be looking into for sure.'

The Kinanes nodded approvingly. Tom felt he had impressed them. He paused as he poured more champagne. 'Shouldn't we get a glass for Eileen?' he asked.

'Eileen?' said Dol sardonically. 'I don't think Eileen will be back. She'll be hitting Temple Bar by now. Eileen can't stay in the one spot longer than five minutes.'

'Once Eileen goes, she goes,' sighed Nina.

'Temple Bar?' Tom repeated. 'What you call the Latin quarter?' For a moment he was downcast. Eileen appeared to have judged him not worth staying around for. 'There must be some good Irish pubs down there, I guess.' Low-lit, dusty and melancholy, sparsely populated by gaunt men supping the dark draught . . .

Dol gave a sardonic laugh. 'We don't do Irish pubs any more. We export them. Like the emigrants before them they've gone out into the world and multiplied. There's a very nice one in Murcia,' she mused.

'Murcia?'

'Murcia, Spain. The Murcians drink whiskey there in little black dresses surrounded by portraits of Joyce. Here, we crowd into tapas bars and drink Coronas.'

'Citizens of the world,' suggested Tom consolingly.

Without undue modesty Dol informed him that she was a key figure in the art world. Programme director of the Irish Gallery of European Art, or IGEA – 'just down the road'. She gestured towards the Georgian streets running east of the hotel. 'We're preparing a retrospective of the Seventies movement, Neue Merz. It's going to be big. Gibbon Fitzgibbon is sponsoring it.'

She uttered the words 'Gibbon Fitzgibbon' with an off-handedness that seemed to lend them a contradictory significance. Leaning towards Tom with the air of imparting a secret, she murmured, 'tax shelter'.

'Ah,' said Tom in a tone of understanding. In fact his knowledge of finance was rudimentary.

'Money may be our king,' declared Nina. Her mind was clearly drifting in other if ancillary directions. 'But it can't be our god. Can it, Tom?'

'What other god do we have?' demanded Dol. 'Golf, I suppose?'

Nina made melancholy eyes at Tom.

'Art?' he suggested.

Dol flashed him a buddy smile. He found he was liking Dol. But all the same the conversation was wandering far from what he really wanted to discuss.

'I'm kind of confused about her movements,' he remarked to Nina. 'Did she come back to Dublin after she was married? Like, you mentioned you hadn't seen her since she went back the first time. But my great-uncle mentioned only one trip. Could she have made two trips? Or maybe more? She called you, I guess? But you didn't see her?'

Nina was gazing at him with an absent expression. 'Who?' she asked vaguely.

'My mother. Hilda.'

'Poor Hilda.' Nina's face crumpled. Her eyes moistened.

'Well, back to the fray for me.' Dol was briskly gathering up her stuff. Wraps, bags, shiny phone. 'I'll see you to a taxi, Mom.'

'Mom. Spelled M-o-m,' said Nina automatically.

'She likes to be called Mom,' put in Dol, apparently by way of explanation. 'As opposed to Mam, or Mammy, or anything old-style. Though Eimear refuses to go along with it.'

'Ah,' Tom said, though he was quite mystified. He sprang to his feet. 'I can get you a taxi. Do you have to go? There's so much more I need to ask you.'

Dol gave him a complicit wink. 'You can talk again,' she said firmly. 'Plenty of time to talk. You're staying for a while, aren't you?'

'Sure,' Tom heard himself say.

'Tom must come to lunch, mustn't he, Mom?'

'Lovely,' Nina murmured.

'When?' he demanded.

'Give me your poca,' instructed Dol.

'My poca?'

She giggled. 'Your mobile. It means pocket in Irish. So your pocket phone, right? It's what Gibbon calls it. Give me your poca number.'

'Ah. My cellphone.'

'Okay, cellphone,' she laughed. 'I'll call you on your cellphone.'

14

About midday Tom asked for more coffee to be sent up and bent with renewed determination over his novel. But it proved no less intractable than it had all morning. Sentences refused to form. The very words seemed as foreign and remote as the fictional world he was wrestling with. His thoughts so hard to pin down . . . What a meeting that had been! To think he had talked with Baby – no, Nina – Kinane. But how was she to be pinned down? She was nice but so weirdly . . . fey? Absent-minded? Emotional? Keeping his great-uncle happy was one thing but it looked as if Nina could be another.

She would have to be approached with delicacy, circum-spection. Very upset plainly about his mother – more than he, her own son, was – on a conscious level at least. Her friend after all. She had more to remember, her memories real, accessible, her grief likewise. His memories were non-existent, his grief, if it could be said to exist in any actual sense, deeply buried, unreachable. And probably it was best to keep it that way. For sure Pender would say it was best.

He switched on the radio, just in time to miss a further broadcast from the honey-tongued philosopher. 'The task we are facing is not easy, but it's a task I believe we will not shirk,' Maconor was saying as he was faded out. But Tom was excited to then hear the presenter say, 'I'm sure we'll be hearing more from Etching Maconor on that topic.'

He had the fellow's full name now. But who was he? How

would he find him? Tom leaped up, found his poca and called Dol Kinane.

'Tom. How are you today?' She sounded gratifyingly pleased to hear from him.

'I was wondering whether you know who this Etching Maconor guy is,' he told her.

'Etching Maconor?' She repeated the name, considered. 'Oh,' she said at least. 'You mean Etching Maconor. But it's not Etching. It's Etching.'

'Can you spell it?' he asked.

'E-t-c-h-e-n M-a-c-A-n-a-r. He used to be a politician. Got into some kind of trouble, I forget what.'

'Too radical?' prompted Tom.

'Politicians are bad news,' Dol said. 'I'd keep away from them if I were you. Why do you want to know, anyway?'

'He's a pretty good speaker.'

'Yeah?' She sounded doubtful.

'Do you know where I could find him?'

'No idea. But you'll run into him. MacAnar gets around.'

'How's your mom?' asked Tom.

'Mom? She's fine. Tom, I'm glad you called. There's an art show I know you'd like. A big group exhibition. It'd be a great introduction to the art scene for you.'

'Sounds good.'

'It's an annual ritual, the Academy show. One of those things that kick off the season. Goes with lilac blossom and tanning sprays.'

'Love to,' Tom said.

The evening sky was swelling and billowing with blackish clouds, the hard dark light stripping the delusive beauties of nostalgia and romance from the streets. In high spindly shoes Dol hobbled along under the lowering chestnut flowers of the Green with the awkward sacrificial gait of a horse bred for racing and gambling.

'My sister got selected,' she was telling Tom. 'She has a picture in the exhibition. Can you believe it?'

'Sure I can. I'm not surprised to know Eileen is an artist.'

Dol snorted. 'Eileen an artist? Well, sure – if painting bits of your anatomy makes you an artist. Like your toenails. No, the artist is Frog. My kid sister.'

Dol's legs looked startlingly golden. In the grim light, her flimsy finery appropriate to a balmier clime, projected both optimism and an incipient pathos.

'Spelled?' prompted Tom.

She looked at him wide-eyed. 'What?'

'Frog. How do you spell it?'

'Don't you have frogs in America? F-R-O-G. She's actually Frances but we've always called her Frog.' Dol cackled indulgently. 'She had this lovely froggy look when she was a baby. She used to hate it; now she thinks it could be a good name career-wise but she can't decide. For the present she's showing as F. Kinane.'

Relieving Tom of the black umbrella that Cerise had supplied him with she used it as a walking aid.

'You'd only lose it,' she assured him. 'I'll mind it for you.'

'Is Frog a talented painter?' asked Tom.

'Talented? She got selected, Tom.'

The various rooms of the Academy were thronged with sleek, well nourished and happy people. Any perceptible gauntness, any trace of pallor, was clearly due not to hunger but to the low-fat regimes and gymwork of the western urban dweller. Tom saw no sign of the kind of artist that he had naively half anticipated: ragged, and pale from intensity and disdain, eking out their impassioned days with potato meals. The busy cacophony of talk and laughter had the same timbre that you would find at such an event in Manhattan – the stamp of correct thinking and correct action leading, as night follows day, to achievement justly accompanied by prosperity . . . As Pender would say.

In her role as a player on the art scene, or perhaps as a sister of a selectee, Dol stood propped on Tom's umbrella in the attitude of a hostess receiving her guests, at the centre of the mill. She had grimaced when she first tasted the wine and described it as 'vile', but all the same she was supping now from a glass of white with a degree of voracity. They stood beside a maze of partitions put up to provide more hanging space, and as faces emerged into view from behind them wearing the glazed expressions of the ecstatic or merely lost, Dol waved to one or other as she felt inclined. When she talked, loosened strands tumbling from her artfully arranged hair dipped into her glass. The regrettably conventional nature of contemporary art in comparison with the brutalism of Neue Merz was her first topic and Frog's selection her second.

'It's rather good,' she was saying. 'You should have a look. It's hanging on the south stairs. About halfway up.' Dol preferred to say 'south stairs' which she had coined herself, to the universally used 'back stairs'.

'It's gruesome, actually,' she murmured to Tom. 'Well, as a likeness it's gruesome. Doesn't look like my mother at all. It's called 'Ada' so Mom won't know it's her. She thinks it's some elderly Italian professor out at UCD.'

'Must be nice to have a mother to paint,' said Tom a little wistfully.

'Oh, she only did her because she was handy for doodling at the breakfast table. Frog is convinced that if it sells, it'll kick off her brilliant career. I can't imagine anyone wanting to buy it. But she'll be wild if it doesn't sell.'

'Oh, Dol! I've just seen an incredible landscape,' a young woman exclaimed. 'It reminds me of Killeigh. It's uncanny.'

'You'd better buy it then,' said Dol with a note of impatience. 'Killeigh is where our mother was born,' she told Tom as an aside. 'Tom, my sister Eimear. Eimear, Tom Blessman. You know, Tom. I was telling you about him.'

'She certainly was.' Eimear gave Tom an enigmatic smile.

'Another sister?' exclaimed Tom.

'Another sister,' Dol echoed.

'I don't know. They're asking nearly four grand for it,' frowned Eimear.

Her blue tweedy two-piece was of a flattering but peculiarly dated cut – and was totally appropriate to the temperate conditions in the streets this evening. Eimear gave the impression that she would always wear what was appropriate. Though obviously physically comfortable she seemed somewhat psychically stressed however. That remote expression of hers as if an inward eye was bent elsewhere . . .

'Spelled E-I-M-E-A-R,' Dol muttered as Eimear drifted off in her easy low-heeled courts. 'She used to be Amor: A-M-O-R – I don't know what my mother was thinking of. She changed it when she got converted to a Gael. Can't say I blame her. She's trying to bring back old style. Did you see what she's wearing? That suit was my grandmother's. She wears ancestral clothes.'

'It looks good on her,' remarked Tom.

'If Eimear had her way,' said Dol grimly, 'we'd be living on spuds and hairy bacon and dancing at the crossroads.'

'Sounds like it could be fun.'

'Huh.' Dol rolled her eyes. She was greeted now by a round-shouldered artistic-looking man who appeared to have something confidential he wanted to impart. He took her aside and spoke in a low voice into her ear. Perhaps a devotee of Neue Merz. Even a practitioner?

Tom moved away to inspect a large triptych, listed, he saw from the catalogue, as 'How Life Could Be' by T.J. Forde. Painted in heavy reds and browns and deep blues it had an unexpected airy and buoyant quality. In the rich swirling cloudiness he thought he could make out a cow – or was it an antelope? A tram – or possibly a train? A smaller cow, possibly the cow's calf. A wispily naked figure, an ethereal table . . . Each object and others not so easily identifiable floated above sketchy tracks that seemed to randomly begin and end in umber space. The figure and the train or tram were spliced in half by the separated canvases which gave the scene a sense of movement and change, even progression.

The meaning was opaque. The artist's eccentric idea of how life could be . . . Sure, Tom got that. But it remained provocatively unreadable. Of course, everyone had their own idea on that question.

It was oddly appealing. For some reason it made him think of Katya. The sombre but illuminated colours . . . The figure stepping busily, hopefully, from one frail path to another . . . A present for her? Might she unwrap it in the blue clarity of Colorado and be appeased? Appeasement – is that what I want for Katya? Too late, anyway. A man stepped in front of Tom and officiously slapped a small red dot beside the painting.

'I was falling for the triptych.' Tom turned around to Dol who was standing briefly on her own between greeters. 'But it's sold.'

She gave 'How Life Could Be' a cursory glance. 'A bit Chagall for my taste. Was it going to be a present?'

Tom nodded. 'For my wife.'

Dol made a face. 'Typical. You meet a nice guy and he turns out to have a wife.'

'She's a former wife, I guess.' It was the first time he'd used that phrase.

'Oh. Poor Tom. Is she—' Stopping in mid-sentence she gripped Tom's arm. 'Christ. There's Gibbon,' she muttered tersely.

In creamy glazed linen garb that evoked the sparkle and glint of tended lawns and a summer sea and crystalware in a commercial for some chic continental aperitif, Gibbon Fitzgibbon was moving in on exhibit after exhibit. A little more portly than he should be, he looked closer to middle age than he was. He moved briskly however, with the intent of a man loosing a firearm on fowl that rose in squawky profusion from their cover at the behest of minions and dogs. Once or twice he halted to thumb his catalogue and write in it with a stout and gleaming pen. Dol's grip on Tom's arm tightened. Whether for support or to suggest possession, he couldn't say.

'You buying, Gibbon?' she called out. Her manner was flirtatious but combative.

'Hi there, Dol.' His smile was simple and hearty. 'I'm in the market for a few pieces to furnish a new building. I found a couple of Lawless's that'll do the job.' He gave a knowing laugh. 'Size matters when you're talking offices. And this fellow here, I believe. I bought that on spec.'

He stood back and critically surveyed 'How Life Could Be'. 'Not bad. What would you say?'

'Not bad,' agreed Tom.

'He's a good prospect, young Forde. In fact there's more than a good prospect or two in the younger lot. I'm keeping my weather eye out.'

'Have you seen Frog's portrait?' asked Dol.

'Frog?'

'My sister. She was selected.'

Gibbon's brow cleared. 'Frog is an infant. Time enough for Frog.'

The introductions were made. Gibbon had a large and impressively firm handshake.

'You stole a march on Tom,' chided Dol. 'He wanted to get the Forde.'

'Sorry, Tom,' beamed Gibbon. 'But you have to be quick on your feet when you're buying.' He was a man who took pleasure in stealing marches. 'What's your line, Tom, when you're at home, as they say?'

'Oh, I'm looking around. Something to put a few bucks into. At home . . . here . . . Wherever.'

'Wherever there's a buck to be made,' smiled Gibbon.

'Tom has a big backer, Gibbon,' cut in Dol. 'You'd want to be looking out.'

'I never mind a bit of competition.' Gibbon's beam widened. 'Hi there, Yasmin,' he suddenly called out. 'How's it working out with Steve? I hear Yasmin is talking to Spielberg,' he murmured as Yasmin came up. 'The word is he wants to option.'

Yasmin O'Brien's latest cross-genre novel, intriguingly described by one reviewer as Kafka crossed with Binchy, was said to be the read of the season. Like Dol, she was gauzily dressed. But on her the effect was elegant. Statuesque, Tom thought.

'Steve? Who's Steve? Do I know a Steve?' Yasmin's smile was not warm.

'Spielberg. I hear you're talking to Steve Spielberg.'

'Oh, did you now?'

'Your agent is talking to Spielberg, right?' pursued Gibbon.

The novelist smiled enigmatically.

Gibbon was thrown. He decided that perhaps contrary to rumour, Spielberg wasn't in talks after all. 'You should talk to Tom here,' he ploughed on. 'Tom is in the money business.'

Yasmin gave a polite murmur and inclined graciously in Tom's direction.

'I'm in investments. Investment management,' he agreed.

Yasmin's smile grew spectacularly brilliant. 'But I have nothing in the world to sell.' Leaning with a gracious enquiry towards a chalky still life of Greek urns she was soon absorbed in the melée.

'I admire that woman, truly I do,' Dol declared. 'I can never tell what she's up to.'

'That's the artistic nature for you.' Gibbon seemed to have a genuine reverence for artistic natures.

'Artistic is as artistic does.'

'What does that mean?' Standing very close to Dol Gibbon was looking down at her with a mix of annoyance and fondness.

'Come on. It's a silly book.'

'Seoda was gobsmacked by it.'

Seoda, Gibbon's wife, had strong opinions on many subjects. 'I see. Seoda likes it.' She said *Seoda* with a knowing archness. 'There's a recommendation for you.'

There was going to be a tiff. A lover's tiff, Tom saw. It required space and privacy. With some difficulty he made his way to a desk through the clusters of parading art gazers and socialites.

'I am interested,' he informed an efficient-looking man in a sharp dark suit, 'in purchasing the work of a deserving artist. Could you recommend somebody who is both needy and gifted?'

'All our artists are deserving, sir.'

'Sure. But I'm interested in somebody who's especially deserving.'

'I'm not supposed to recommend any particular artist,' sniffed the assistant. 'Anyway, nearly everything of note is sold already.'

He examined his lists on which an array of red dots crowded and jostled. 'Let me see . . . I do have an excellent piece by J. McMurrough. Titled "Hercules". Diptych, mixed media on board. Priced at twelve thousand.'

'Is it big?'

'Very big. Enormous, in fact.'

Tom hesitated. His great-uncle would object to a classical subject like Hercules. Not Irish enough – 'What's Hercules got to do with anything over there?' – And where would he put it? He'd have to deal with shipping . . . It could be a liability.

'Is Mr McMurrough very needy?'

'Ms McMurrough actually. As I said, I'm not in a position to discuss individual artists. But I doubt it. Ms McMurrough is an artist of some reputation.'

Concluding that price rather than neediness was the issue, the man perused his lists again. 'What about "Ada" by F. Kinane?' he offered with an air of condescension. 'A debuting artist. Asking only seven fifty.'

F. Kinane. Frog's portrait of Nina. Of course. He should have thought of it himself.

'Yes. I'll take it,' said Tom at once.

By the time he had made his way as far as the back stairwell where Ada was hung a red dot had made its appearance under his new acquisition. He inspected it with some astonishment. As a likeness it bore no resemblance to its subject, apart arguably from the hair, which was an exaggerated electro-shocked version of Nina's frizz and was painted in mauve. The mouth was a green gash, the eyes lupine yellow pools. The bones – and Nina's bones were by no means prominent – were aggressive slashes protruding at odd angles like a smashed skeleton's. It was uncompromisingly hideous. Was Frog simply a bad painter?

On further contemplation Tom came to the conclusion that the work was derivative – early twentieth-century expression-ism crossed with Warhol, he speculated. And yet it showed ambition. Both could be forgiven in one so young – Dol had referred to Frog as a kid, after all. The face filling the canvas, powerful, threatening to break free of its confinement . . . A remarkable depth of meaning really, the artist locked in an awesomely passionate conflict with her subject. And she had certainly succeeded in implicating the viewer in the conflict. As the proprietor of 'Ada' Tom felt doubly implicated. It was a heady feeling.

He padded forward and back in front of Ada, fired with enthusiasm, purpose. Frog was surely not alone. Out there behind the prim facades of red-brick there must be any number of neglected talents, needing only encouragement, patronage; embodiments of investment opportunities, opportunities for philanthropy. Tom seized a glass of wine from a passing tray. Couldn't Pender fund a gallery? The Gast Gallery – The Gast Foundation? The kind of thing the more enlightened among the rich turn to when the yacht is beached and the golf swing arthritic and the spectre of oblivion is looming up. The Gast Museum? A monument to Pender in his native land. Well-positioned in a prestigious address – maybe one of those old Georgian squares?

Suddenly deflated, Tom sighed. No, his great-uncle was not like his peers, enlightened or not. To him the word 'monument' would be tantamount to 'mausoleum'. A red rag to a bull. As for artists – artists, writers, idlers: to him they were all one.

When he rejoined Dol he found her wreathed in smiles. 'Gibbon,' she said, 'is hoping you'll come and have a bite with us.' She and Gibbon had obviously made up.

'Oh Tom,' she exclaimed, 'did you hear? Frog's painting has been bought. And by a mystery buyer. I've just called Dad. He thinks it could be McGallen. The fellow who's buying up some of the best young talents.'

Tom wasn't sure why he didn't tell her that the mystery buyer was himself. Anyway, the Kinanes seemed to enjoy speculating about who it could be.

They crossed a couple of streets to a grubby old-style bar where Frog Kinane was waiting in tipsy vigil with Aaron, her artistic collaborator, for confirmation of her success. 'Animal,' she squawked. 'Deadly.' Not that she ever had any doubts about the outcome. 'Well, it is a fantastic portrait,' she remarked complacently. Frog enjoyed the confidence of the youngest child.

She had her mother's receding chin, a feature that did not figure in 'Ada', to Tom's recollection. But then it was a portrait in which features of any kind were hardly recognisable. Frog's work soared beyond mere verisimilitude, as she said herself. Her face was blurry, the not fully formed face of the just post-adolescent. Her light-coloured eyes were fierce with pride, though right now they were directed much of the time at her mobile as she texted her friends with her news.

To toast Frog's debut as a selling artist Gibbon graciously ordered champagne. A dusty bottle was produced and was quickly followed by a second and a third, possibly a fourth. Nobody was keeping count. In this company Gibbon was indulgent, patient, slightly apart. He placed an avuncular arm around Tom's shoulder.

'You need any advice, you come to me, okay? Here, give me your poca.' Taking Tom's mobile he punched in his details. 'My personal number. You'll always get me.'

Tom took Gibbon's and put his own number in.

'You're a fan of Neue Merz,' Tom remarked.

Gibbon shrugged. 'It's really Seoda's thing to be honest. Keeps her busy.' He laughed. 'You have to keep the wife busy, don't you, Tom. No, I like the really contemporary stuff. Apart from Sheil of course. Our only artist in the last century who's worth a toss.' He leaned forward. 'I had lunch with Ryan Boylan the other day. He heads up IGMA, the Irish Gallery of Modern Art. A good fellow. He has a superb show coming in. The Infanta. An installation by Demis Schwartz. Now, there we're talking contemporary.'

'Demis Schwartz,' exclaimed Tom. 'Wow.'

'Absolutely. Ryan Boylan was in a bit of a fix; one of his sponsors fell out. I told him I'd fill the gap.' Gibbon drained his glass. 'Should be fun.'

Tom took over the tab now, just as Eimear Kinane and Yasmin O'Brien arrived with an intense fellow with large, morose eyes. Introduced as Vasile, he sat at the edge of the company and said very little. More dusty bottles were downed. When the bar's reserves of fizz ran out they left in a mood of rampant hilarity and reeled down a few streets to a cool, low-rent restaurant called the Cosmo Prole on the fringes of Temple Bar. This, Dol explained to Tom, was an abbreviation of the Cosmopolitan Proletarian, which excused perhaps the rather dismaying choice of dishes.

Gibbon, who was sticking to champagne, looked with sympathy at the large and unappetising bowl of pork and beans that was placed in front of Tom. 'I'm a steak man myself,' he murmured.

'So am I, actually,' Tom told him.

Gibbon nodded. 'There's a good steak to be had here and there. I'll show you a few places.'

Yasmin was getting rather heated in a discussion about truth and the contempt for it in the present time. 'So you're all happy, are you, to live in a racket?' she challenged the table at large.

Gibbon looked mournful. 'You're quite right,' he said. 'But in our time none of us would get far if we had that attitude.'

Yasmin subsided into a sullen silence.

'The Shelbourne is fine, isn't it, as they go?' Gibbon mused. 'But I take it you could be here a while?'

He could, Tom agreed.

'A hotel is kind of temporary, I find,' Gibbon continued. 'Transient. To do anything halfway serious you need to be settled. I do, anyway. Can't do business out of a hotel.'

'I guess,' Tom agreed. He was thinking of his novel that was gathering dust on the little mahogany desk – or soon would be . . . His word count today was fifty-three.

'What would you say to moving into a little place of mine? It could suit you down to the ground. There's a Hungarian chap who'll be taking it but he's not coming into town until later on in the summer. Why don't you check it out? Ranelagh isn't a bad spot. Central. But outa town enough to keep you outa mischief.' Gibbon winked. 'If that's what you want . . . Of course,' he added, 'I want you to be my guest.'

'No need for that,' Tom protested. 'I'd be more than glad to—'

Gibbon silenced him with a gesture. 'I insist.'

15

In the comparatively clearer light of the following day Tom surprised himself by still thinking he'd check out this apartment. A breezy call from Gibbon renewing his generous offer had roused him from a stuporous slumber. Gibbon had put him onto an assistant called Marette and Tom had been only able to croak that he'd call her later. Ranelagh, she'd mentioned, he remembered later when he'd had his coffee – the apartment was in Ranelagh. A familiar name. Kinane Kitchens . . . Wasn't it where the Kinanes lived? He checked the phone book and there it was, confirmed. He called Marette and made an appointment to meet her there at five o'clock.

A mild afternoon sun was gleaming on the low mauvish roofs, the topmost foliage of the stand of trees lining the central promenade of Dame Street, the metallic lid of the over-sized Central Bank; glinted on the beer cans of a sprawling assembly of flush-faced winos, of alienated youths wandering about the concourse in search of soul mates and drugs. Little different from their New York counterparts down in the Village. Through a venerable stone arch a bridge spanning the river appeared. He was going northward, he realised, when he should be going south . . . Have to get that hair of the dog.

Turning into shady South Great George's Street he inhaled the cheesily pungent breath of pizzas baking. The prevailing downtown smell of a western city. In a neo – what? Fifties? Sixties? – café bar he watched a pensive Indo-Chinese girl draw him a pint and drank it in grateful gulps at the counter. Maybe she was thinking of the East, steamy and verdant rice fields, lowing oxen . . . Missing it? More likely to be love troubles, the universal tristesse of youth.

The russet solidity of the Victorian street, poignant somehow. A sense of lives lived, passed away . . . But this afternoon was his. And shared by the throng, the mill of individuals going busily along, preoccupied. Fellow feeling. A moment to be indulged, not seized. Possible here still behind all the hurry. In New York, he thought, you grabbed the moment greedily. Of course here he was acting like he was on vacation.

Tom quickened his pace. Slowed again as he passed the dark cavern of an indoor market. Grim sturdiness of its Victorian grilles, a whiff of spicy comestibles, exotic coloured garments hanging out on poles. Soukish. A big grocery store, fitted out retro New York style. The modern intent on looking like somewhere else or of some other time. This store Twenties style, those bell-shaped lightshades in ribbed glass . . . The days when they made frugal purchases, flour and coffee, sardines and potatoes, and went home to the walk-up and the single burner. Here, the walk-up would be two flights max. Or a low-slung cottage that you walked into off the street and went to poke the grate under the tea-kettle.

In a doorway a heap of blankets was heaving like a beached fish. As he came up it was resolved into a woman. Raddled, drink-abraded. She fixed Tom with a seawatery stare, and held out to him a ruddy hand, creases sketched out in grime. At once he brandished his wallet, bent down and presented her with a few of his blue euro bills. Sharp, strong features behind the ruin of her face. In a scatter around her lay a homely stew of empty bottles, frayed plastic bags, and the comatose body of a man making ardent stifled grunts like a dog dreaming of the chase. With an absent movement she tucked the notes into the pocket of her distressed leather jacket, raised her eyes to the sky and uttered a moan. It was a moan more of ecstasy than of pain.

'I love God – I love God – I love God –,' she chanted. The words were suffused with feeling.

Tom was at a loss as to how to respond. The connection, if any, of the words to the pocketing of the money was unclear. But she didn't appear to expect a response. Her eyes had blankly traversed his face, and were raised to the opaque sky. Tom followed the ecstatic gaze but could see nothing up there apart from a wheeling seagull and a mesh of construction cranes in the distance.

As he moved on, her chant was swallowed up by the din of the street. In the grip of one of the everyday delusions of the psychologically challenged? Or might he, on the strength of the gift of a few euros, appear to her as the God she loved looming down from above? Absurd but humbling. Or was it a statement of general love on more general grounds? Gratitude for the clemency of the afternoon, the mouth of her tartan sleeping bag ready to receive her, her man beside her safe in his.

Whatever the interpretation, these mystic down and outs could very easily appeal to Pender as representatives of his noble wretches – if only Pender would be reasonable. The distribution of largesse, the good feeling it bestowed on the giver . . . Was this what Pender was seeking at last? It was something he had always found easy to resist.

The mountains, a dilute of cobalt blue, rose into view. Not far off enough to induce restlessness, nor near enough to be oppressive. Why the southsiders were said to be complacent? The line of mountain a buttress to their backs like a plush, well-upholstered sofa . . . The emollient swish of traffic on sun-softened tarmac, a tarry smell mingling narcotically with exhalations from high-rise lumbering buses. Small trees here and there were dressed in pert new leaves.

Giggling, three babes went by. Sleek, skimpily clad, playful like lion cubs. A black-bearded man almost afloat in a white shalwar kameez . . . Two elderly Chinese sitting on a bench. A couple, lined faces, seated apart . . . Apart but together, together but apart . . . A sudden whiff of dried fish, the smell of Chinatown . . . Olfactory nostalgia? A second guy in a shalwar kameez . . .

He crossed an intersection and paused to appreciate a nice old shop-front. Slender gilted wood, Cigars-Tobacco-Provisions ribboned in gold italics. His mother could have bought her cigarettes there. In her kaftan, smoking as she drank her tea. Incongruous – wasn't his father attracted to a different kind of woman? Sensible, brisk, organised . . . Like Cerise?

Dad and Cerise . . . Nights when Tom was bought off with pizza and Häagen Dazs in front of the TV while they dined . . . Yeah, right! But the Cerise type could have been a reaction. He was stung. Why, wondered Tom, do I see Dad as having being stung – hurt even? So he went for the opposite. Suddenly the creamy air, the prosaic streets were filled with absences.

Before him the street climbed to meet the hump of a bridge. A canal bridge, the Grand Canal, he saw on the city map that Cerise had filed among his documents. Beyond the bridge rose the great half-moon of a church dome, chalky green, eclipsing the blue ridge of the mountains.

Tom halted to peer into the interior of a junk shop. Select Antiques. A collection of collapsed couches, lugubrious vases, brown-hued portraits of women in oleaginous gowns. Gloomy – but these places could hold hidden stories.

Groping his way through toppling stacks of shelving, crippled chairs, and precariously heaped chests, he came into a chamber hazy with dust motes and filled with what looked like theatrical jumble or the erstwhile train of a broken-down circus. But soon he saw that the artefacts had a religious character – the remains possibly of an ecclesiastical theme park? Here were marble columns, plaster figures swooning on chipped plinths, tall candlesticks and huge candelabras; there brassy altar rails, an altar cloth, its red and purple faded to hues of raspberry and lavender. Fractured objects, tarnished, peeling, mottled, most of them surmounted by a cross, or incorporating a cross somewhere.

Prayer benches he had seen heroines kneel at in old movies to plead for heavenly assistance in resisting earthly temptations . . . *Pries-dieux* – wasn't that what they were called?

'Twenty-five per cent off everything today,' he heard a man call. Slumped in a grimy armchair that was oozing its stuffing the man had the understandably melancholy expression of a dealer in unprofitable goods. Light seeping through the prism of a piece of stained glass washed him in stagey tints of green and yellow.

'You have some interesting stuff,' called back Tom.

The man stood up and came around to stand beside Tom and survey his stock.

'I have any amount of ciboriums,' he said hopefully. 'Or would you be into the saints by any chance? Anything you want to know about them just ask. They all have their specialities. As good as any consultant, the saints. Eyes, bones, ears, you name it.' He looked speculatively at Tom as if he might have come for a medical diagnosis.

'Dympna, she was for sore throats,' he continued as if Tom might be too shy to name his symptoms. 'Saint Theresa over there, better known of course as the little flower – the TB was her thing.' He patted the fissured head of a once gaily painted plaster bust. 'Christopher here, for travellers. Jude, hopeless cases. It was Jude got me my Leaving Cert, the mother always said. I got no credit for it at all myself. Oh no, would never have made it on my ownio.' The dealer sighed. 'That was all fado, fado.'

From a heap of textiles he pulled out a cloak-like garment, the gold and saffron colours dulled with age. 'Vestments. Some men the clerics were all the same, to be able to carry the weight of that on their backs. The gold gives it the weight. Should be worth something? What'd you say?'

'I'd say,' Tom agreed.

Recognising his lack of interest, the dealer threw the vestment back on the pile.

'You look like you might be in the bar trade,' he speculated with his hopeful look.

Tom laughed. 'No, I'm not in the bar trade.'

'And if you were, what interest would you have? Minimalism, that's what they're into now. But we had a while there when pubs were mad for the ecclesiastical stuff. Pulpits, pews, candlesticks . . . I could have sold any amount of them.' He sighed. 'I was into them too late.'

Tom looked at the despondent face of a plaster figure who appeared to gaze with longing at the Chinese carryout across the street. Why were saints so despondent? Could be why they'd fallen out of favour; didn't suit the zeitgeist. He looked at the inscription on a wooden panel: Jesus Falls A Third Time. The thorny-crowned figure bent under his crucifix . . . How post, how decadent was that? Would you take it for an ironically salutary comment as you ordered your third mojito?

'These style-setters. They're a curse. They never stay still long enough to let a chap settle into a line,' said the dealer sadly.

'Baroque is the next big thing,' Tom asserted. 'If I were you I'd go with baroque.'

He stepped over a heap of rolled-up banners to inspect the figure of an angel. He could tell it was an angel because of its gold-tipped outspread wings. Her expression was both grave and pouting, demure and provocative. The eyes were languorous, the gilted hair shingled in the style of a silent-movie-era starlet. Chipped slightly here and there but the small nose intact. She was rather a gorgeous angel. Tom had an intoxicating sensation of revelation. She reminded him of someone, though who it was he couldn't place.

'I quite like this,' he said with a hint of bashfulness.

The dealer approved his taste. 'You could do worse than invest in an angel or two. The angels are very popular. In fact, I have an archangel over here if you're making up a collection. The top man, the Archangel Gabriel himself. Pricey of course. But he could be worth going the bit extra.'

Tenderly, Tom brushed dust from a wing. 'This will do me fine.'

'I have to tell you now,' the man put in quickly, 'this style of angel is very rare. I wouldn't put an exact date on her. But you can see for yourself, she didn't come off a production line.'

'I guess,' said Tom dubiously.

'You have an eye, I can see that. Look, I'll let you have her for eight hundred.'

'I'll give you six.' Tom heard the man's crafty tone and knew he was expected to hustle.

'Six? Are you joking? She's in good condition. There's no way I could do her for six. Seven fifty?'

'Seven.'

'Will we say seven twenty-five?'

'Okay. Seven twenty-five it is.'

Triumphantly the dealer bore the angel aloft as in a ceremonial procession to his gored and listing chipboard desk. With great care he swaddled it in a tattered but lustrously satin cloth worked with elaborate crosses and the letters IHS in a gothic script. The cloth, he said, implying an unusual and uncalled-for generosity, was lovingly embroidered by long-gone nuns and he was throwing it in 'for luck'. Then he stuffed the lumpy and shiny package into a large black garbage sack.

Gibbon's apartment was on the fourth floor of an impassive modern development that looked out on a public garden. Marette was waiting to meet Tom at the lift as the doors opened and he emerged bowed under his burden. The outspread wings provided good leverage but the angel was a great deal heavier and bulkier than the ethereal creature she had seemed languishing among the pillars of marble and stone. Marette obligingly took hold of one wing in its black camouflage and with the bowed gait of conscientious adults taking a small child by the hand, they bore it between them into the apartment and placed it on a blondwood console.

Marette was the kind of competent and maternal woman rich men like to gather around them. She had placed an arrangement of flowers in a chinoise urn, made up the bed, brewed coffee. Now she threw open the floor-length window. The toll of a tram's bell drifted ceremoniously across the treeage of the garden. Lower than the regular warbling of town birds, the urban traffic was but a distant hum.

'It's quiet,' said Marette encouragingly. 'Homey.'

She pursed her mouth when Tom took the angel from its wrappings.

'What do you want it for? I grew up with all that stuff. Bad associations.'

Throwing open the wardrobe doors she displayed the capaciousness of the storage facilities. Running a plump manicured finger along the countertop, she assured him it was real marble from Tuscany. Then she busied herself with the coffee and instructed him to take a walk around. 'Get the feel of the place. See if it suits you.'

He wasn't sure about the drifting, vacuous look of the rooms. But as Marette had said, the apartment was quiet, the block in which it nestled in its allotted space pretty well silent right now. Homes for people who went out early to progress their busy careers and came back late. He was reminded not too happily of days spent in that silent apartment they took one summer on Long Island . . . When I was up to the deadline and hardly went out all day – the longing then for Katya to come home. And at last she would arrive, to peel radishes, or do something else that to most other people life was too short for . . . So competent, orderly, too much . . . Made me feel incompetent. At the kitchen table, peeling radishes . . . Wearing the blue kimono I got at the airport in LA on the way back from that Artists And Asia conference. Let her think I had got it custom-made for her by a tailor in Singapore . . . But she wouldn't have been happy with it if she'd known . . .

He wandered back into the living room. The open balcony door showed a panorama of sky and trees. And on the shiny wood floor by the door Marette had posed the angel, to gaze out on the view and the invisible hills. She looked like a captive nymph confined to the town.

'What do you think?' asked Marette.

'Well, she sure looks at home there,' Tom said.

Marette laughed. 'I mean, what do you think of the apartment?'

'It's cool. I like it.'

'She could do for a hat-stand, I suppose,' Marette conceded as she gave him his coffee.

16

'Oh Tom, what beautiful flowers,' Nina cooed. 'I don't know when I last got flowers.'

'I suppose Mothers' Day doesn't count?' grumbled Dol. 'I seem to remember you complaining only a few weeks ago that you couldn't move around here for flowers.'

'But that was family, pet.'

The Kinanes' Sunday dinner could be a fractious affair. The very terms in which it was referred to had divisive potential, an indication of the tensions of aspiration, culture and generation within the family. To Nina and her husband Willie, 'dinner' was any meal in which cooked protein, vegetables and preferably potatoes was the central dish. But to Dol any dish eaten in the afternoon was strictly 'lunch'. And forget meat and potatoes – some ethnic combination from far-off lands consumed in a bleached-out café with plenteous white wine was Dol's idea of a good lunch. Eimear on the other hand was stern in her use of 'dinner'; not however as a gesture of solidarity with her parents as individuals but in homage to the traditions they unconsciously if haphazardly embodied.

Another source of acrimony at Sandalwood Avenue on Sunday afternoons was the race for a parking place. The forecourt, which had recently replaced an old-style daisied lawn, could, with a degree of parking expertise, accommodate three cars. There was always at least one car too many for the space available and this would have to be parked on the public road, inciting in its owner a bitter sense of exclusion. Being forced to park on the street had clearly been engineered by those in prior possession of parking on the forecourt to symbolise exclusion from the family fold, a fate any Kinane was only too ready to suspect at any time.

The presence of an outsider such as Tom had a soothing effect on these fractious breasts and guests were eagerly sought by the Kinanes for their Sunday assemblies. For the sake of courtesy feuds would have to be put aside and battles suspended, the family obliged to contrive a front of cheer and harmony to the visitor. Foreign and personable, Tom Blessman was fine for this purpose, if not quite perfect. An actor fresh from a recent success, an artist ditto, or a writer with a new preferably contro- versial book, would perhaps be more exciting – the Kinanes liked to participate in artistic life. Today, as well as Tom, they had hoped for the presence of Yasmin O'Brien. But she had called to say something had come up and she couldn't make it.

'Yes, that Moldovan poet has come up,' murmured Dol. There was a general laugh.

Really, they would all prefer in principle at least to be any- where else on Sunday afternoons. They did have other options. They had friends to meet, as each regularly pointed out. They could walk around as the foreigners did in a kind of paseo after attending a religious service, wearing their best and eating ice- cream. They could go shopping. But the ritualistic lunch/dinner at home was traditional; there was a tacit recognition that the obligation to attend strengthened the fragile family bonds. It was virtuous, like doing a fast.

Tom was sitting on a rather lumpy sofa in the somewhat gloomy drawing room – another disputed term as some Kinanes favoured 'sitting room' – with a glass in his hand and feeling both happy – he had been eagerly anticipating this lunch – and nervous. He was nervous because he was finding it difficult to keep Nina focused and because there was so far no sign of Eileen. Nina sat opposite him now in the window embrasure, her mascaraed lashes heavy on her cheeks as if she could be dozing off. He had seen the lunch as an opportunity to engage with her in a heart to heart. He was eager to pursue the mystery of his mother's movements to and from Ireland.

'I understood from something you said before that she made two trips – possibly even more?'

'Did I say that?' Nina seemed bemused, even a little confused. 'But we were girls, mere girls.' Her voice was wistful, full of sentiment for a vanished youth.

And all the time Dol was bouncing back and forth from the kitchen to offer wine, daintily arranged bouchées and remarks he was finding inconsequential. 'So, Tom, you took the apartment,' she said. 'What's it like? Standard issue?'

'I guess. But I like it.'

'Gibbon does standard very well.' Dol appeared to be a bit disenchanted with Gibbon at present.

Nina got up to check the joint.

'Tom likes his beef rare, Mud,' Dol said in a warning tone.

'I like it any way at all,' protested Tom.

'He likes it any way at all,' called Nina triumphantly. 'Well, it's roasting very nicely, I must say. Have a pretzel, Tom,' she offered brightly as she came back. She had got them especially for him; she believed all Americans adored pretzels. Outside the tall curtained windows a placid sea of foliage foamed down the arboreal vista of Sandalwood Road, white and yellow and lilac, the frilly frothy flim-flam of early summer. The companionable mountains were pale like distant ethereal sails. Big bossy cars glinted in the sunlight.

In the near distance Carey's glittering navy-blue Augusta dominated the forecourt between a chipped ornamental urn and a large blue van with Kinane Kitchens written along its side in faded red italics. Dol's little banger occupied the third position, a car that signified she was saving up, notionally at least, and almost definitely in vain, to buy an apartment.

'Carey? Will you have a pretzel?'

Carey absently took a handful and returned to his perusal of the Sunday newspapers, uttering an occasional disbelievingly sardonic exclamation. His mother looked on him with tenderness. He was the eldest of the Kinanes. And just as his Augusta was alpha transport Carey was a fine specimen of an alpha male, with his success and his carelessness and that man-about-town aura as if he had just come from all kinds of manly pursuits. She had always believed in him but his success was a surprise to everyone else. Carey had been regarded as the least clever member of the family, boisterous and hardly educable, when the younger ones were doing well at their exams. But it was Carey who turned out to have the head for money.

Eimear too was doing rather well. But her business, concerned with nothing less than the preservation, and when necessary the re-invention, of Old Ireland, was philanthropic and visionary, threatening always, as she boasted, to bring her to the brink of bankruptcy. Generally, the Kinanes were happier with concepts like 'philanthropic', 'visionary' and 'bankruptcy'.

'Willie is greatly looking forward to meeting you, Tom,' said Nina, turning her attention to him once more and with a certain reluctance, Tom feared.

'I guess Willie never knew my mother?' Tom suggested. 'You were girls, as you said. You met your husband later?'

'I believe Willie and Hilda did meet,' said Nina slowly. Obviously, it was not too easy to recall those remote times. 'We weren't yet married. But I do believe we may have been going out.'

'It looks like Grogan is to be called up,' interjected Carey. 'Marguerite won't be pleased.'

'Called up where, Carey?' asked Nina.

'The tribunal. The McCarthy. The Hangman McCarthy as we call him.'

'Are you talking about Denis Grogan?' asked Tom.

'Denis it is. You know Denis?' asked Carey.

'Oh, slightly. But just enough to let me think I'm an insider already. I had a drink with him in the Shelbourne. Nice guy.'

'Doesn't take long to feel like an insider in this town,' grinned Carey.

'Why would they want to be badgering a nice man like Denis Grogan?' asked Nina. 'I can't make any sense of these tribunals. Can you, Tom?'

'No,' said Tom. 'But one of these days I mean to have a go.'

'Don't bother,' Carey said. 'A waste of time. They're a waste of everybody's time.'

'And everybody's money,' called Dol from the kitchen.

'Grogan's accountancy firm is major,' said Carey thoughtfully. 'He has all the big hitters. A lot of his dosh must come from the Augusta concession. But I don't think they'd have anything on him to do with Augusta.'

Tom turned eagerly again to Nina. 'I've been wanting to ask you – how did you get to know my mother?'

'Would you believe it? We met in New York.' She laughed. 'You'll be wanting to know now what I was doing over in New York, I suppose? Well, you see, there I was on a weekend break in Killarney . . .'

Nina embarked on a fulsome story about her love for dancing, especially to the sound of Foxy Bracken and the Cubs, her favourite showband of all time. In Killarney she had discovered that Foxy and the Cubs were playing at the Buttercup, a large dancehall in a small village nearby, so of course off she hopped . . . And as luck would have it, wasn't the Miss Buttercup Contest on.

'And, Tom, wasn't I picked,' she wound up delightedly.

'Wow,' Tom said. 'That must have been something.'

'And what was the prize?' She leaned towards him confidingly. 'A trip to New York!'

'Wow,' said Tom. 'And where in New York did—'

'Willie! There you are. I was just telling Tom how I won the Miss Buttercup back in – oh, we won't go into when it was.'

'And you'd nearly win it again tomorrow,' declared Willie

gallantly. Then two large hands clutched Tom's and two large moist greenish eyes looked into his. 'You're the spit of her,' he murmured.

'You think I look like my mother?' exclaimed Tom. 'So you knew her pretty well?'

'Ah, I didn't know her that well,' said Willie quickly.

He went and stood by the dusty black mantelpiece, lit a cigarette and appraised the sky through the window.

'A few weeks ago there I was afraid we were losing our prevailing wind,' he remarked. 'You wouldn't know what this global warming will be up to next.'

Willie had a more pronounced accent than his family, his Dublinois tinged with a harshness that Tom thought must have been swaggering and sexy in his youth.

'You and your prevailing wind. As if we didn't have enough problems,' called Dol from the kitchen.

'But I'm glad to say I appear to have been wrong,' continued Willie.

'Did you know her in New York?' pursued Tom.

'Oh, Nina's trip to New York was before my time. No, I met her here, when she came over. But sure as far as I remember, we only met a couple of times. Anything you want to know, you should ask Nina. Nina was her pal.'

'We were great pals,' murmured Nina.

Willie sported a beige moustache, sparse greying hair, and a florid complexion that had the perhaps ominous hue of rude good health. He looked like an entirely docile family man. But his flamboyantly cut check suit suggested a touch of individualism too in his nature. Padding across the floral carpet in his easywear canvas house-shoes he peered out at his son's Augusta.

'No problems with her so far, Carey?' he asked. Willie had always had problems with his cars and he had spent a good part of his time discussing them.

Carey winked across at Tom. 'Problems, Dad? With an

89

Augusta?' He gave his breezy hooting laugh, tossing back his reddish fringe.

'You're sure you won't have a drink, Willie?' suggested his wife graciously. This was for the sake of form; Willie had been on the dry for some time past.

'No thanks. Don't feel like a drink just now,' he replied laconically. 'Maybe later on . . . Ah, there's herself now.'

Footsteps came crunching lightly along the gravel. Tom sat up, his pulse running a little faster. The hall door, under the fanlight with its arc in relief of white shamrocks and the words 'St Eithne's' in faded lettering, banged. But it wasn't Eileen after all.

'Eimear love. Did you get a park?' asked her mother solicitously.

Wanly, Eimear nodded. 'I'm outside Murphy's.'

Dol whistled. 'You had to go as far as Murphy's?'

With an air of martyrdom Eimear sat on the sofa next to Tom. Again, she had on a tweed suit, similar to the one she had worn at the Academy. Murmuring about the warmth of the day she took the jacket off to reveal a chaste but rather alluring little top, crossed her legs demurely and, with a forgiving air, remarked on Frog's success in selling 'Ada'. As if on cue, Frog came clattering in from the upstairs regions, a distracted streak of yellow paint in her hair. Nobody could be in danger of underestimating Frog's genius and dedication.

'So who bought it, Frog?' asked Eimear.

'Oh, someone nobody's heard of,' said Frog. 'Some fellow called Pendergast. Must be a bogger.'

'I've asked around,' Dol said. 'No one has heard of anyone who's buying called Pendergast.'

'It's a Westmeath name, I believe,' put in Nina.

For some reason, Carey winked at Tom. Tom shifted uncomfortably.

'Is dinner ready?' Eimear asked. 'I'm starving after all that driving around. I must have driven up and down Sli Chualain ten times.'

Dol handed her a consoling glass of wine.

'Sli Chualain,' chortled Carey. 'That's Ranelagh Road to you, Tom. To Eimear here, it's still a grassy old chariot track.'

'Ranelagh Road, as you insist on calling it,' said Eimear stiffly, 'is merely the modern name for the ancient road from Tara in the days of the kings. I think it merits an occasional reference.'

'Did you tell Mammy – I mean Mom – that you bought a picture of Killeigh?' asked Dol.

'So she said. And I'm sure it's very nice,' said Nina. 'But my opinion is that when the past is over, it's over. What would you say, Tom?'

'I guess,' Tom agreed, a little lamely.

'Shall we proceed to the table?' suggested Willie.

'Isn't Eileen coming?' asked Tom diffidently.

His question hung in the air, unanswered. No one appeared to have heard it.

'Bring your glasses now,' instructed Nina.

The kitchen was a cavernous expanse of golden pine, the height of kitchen fashion a couple of decades before and a fine example of Kinane Kitchens' products in its heyday. Filing in, the Kinanes drifted to their accustomed places to sit under an enormous painting by Frog that hung with a lurid menace over the pine dining table.

'What a lovely old table,' Tom remarked.

'One of our big sellers,' Willie said.

But while at first glance the table seemed to be the kind that stressed-out New Yorkers wistfully stroke in furniture stores, like that swish place on Lexington Avenue, as they dream of living somewhere picturesquely rural upstate with kids and dogs and a stable of SUVs, on closer acquaintance it did not quite live up to the fantasy. He found, seated next to Nina at its head, that there was an extension which was liable to sag and bow if a diner's elbows rested on it too weightily. A Kinane however knew, without thinking about it, not to do that.

Along the table's length stood bottles of red wine, an essential accompaniment to any gathering of Kinanes, to assuage and soften tongues, to smooth animosities, to get them through. Glasses rested unsteadily on the lumpily fashioned flowers of the white tablecloth which had been embroidered by a great-aunt. Despite the dangers it presented, Eimear insisted on the use of this tablecloth because of what she claimed was its cultural significance.

A starter of bresaola, prepared by Dol, was consumed in relative silence.

Seated all together like this Tom noticed how, though they were not alike, there was a similarity in the Kinanes. They shared a tendency to unruliness of hair, a mobility of expression, unrestrained laughter. And their slight Dublin twang was often overlaid with modish notes of tortured vowels and that end-of-sentence upswing taken from American soaps.

The wine wasn't bad, Carey remarked. Not bad at all. After a little exhortatory pressure from Dol, Nina conceded that she did quite like the bresaola; adding however that she would have preferred pâté.

As knives and forks were put down again there was a movement that emanated from Frog and spread like a wave through the others, towards trouser pockets or into bags slung over the backs of chairs; furtive and implicitly apologetic to start with, then blatant. The Kinanes were getting out their mobile phones. The phones were placed on the table in front of each diner, a sign, Tom saw, that all felt the urgent need of a lifeline to the outside world or at least the comfort of this reminder of its existence. Like treats at a children's supper to be seized once the boringly wholesome stuff has been eaten, they lay, bright and tinselly as wrapped sweets alongside the dessert spoons at the head of each place.

Nina regarded them with a certain maternal indulgence. The mobiles of her children represented the continuance of her maternal duty. Morning and night, depending on their schedules, she would collect their phones from whoever happened to be around and would tether them to their chargers that she had assembled, like a small *baterie de cuisine*, in what had become a dedicated charger section on the counter-top. Fussing over them with the diligence of someone raising a brood of chicks, she could be proudly confident that no one left the house incommunicado.

'Any sign of this downturn affecting you, Carey?' Willie asked.

Carey guffawed. 'What downturn?' Then he decided to indulge his father. 'The fundamentals are sound. I can't see property not holding up.'

'I can't wait for this whole fucking property racket to collapse,' said Dol bitterly.

'Now, now, Dol. That wouldn't be nice for Carey,' protested her mother.

'Oh, saving his presence then.'

'Art. There's a real goer for you,' continued Carey. He looked across at Tom. 'If it's a low-risk placement you're after, you couldn't go wrong with a few Shiels.'

'Shiel . . . Thanks. I'll remember,' Tom said.

Nina beamed on her clever son, possessor of arcane and insider knowledge that he could generously bestow on greener fellows.

'Fitzgibbon could be a bit exposed, I hear,' suggested Willie.

'Who's putting that out?' demanded Dol.

'Ah, Gibbon is well placed to ride anything out, I'd say. He'd always see it coming,' Carey said.

'He would, he would,' Willie hastened to say.

Carey looked over at Tom again with meaning. 'Quality. That's the secret. There has to be quality. Whether it's property or art or anything else you're talking.'

'Dead right,' said Tom.

The younger Kinanes fidgeted with impatience. Carey, they suspected, was trying to impress Tom; it was how he carried on

in his own peer group when he wasn't talking about cars or golf.
Or he was doing a practice run for his next meeting with the
moneymen. Only Willie and Nina gazed at him admiringly,
expectantly.

He did in fact have an important announcement to make.
'Actually, I've put in a bid myself on an Aodhgan Shiel. It's
going up at Sotheby's next week.'

'An Aodhgan Shiel,' breathed Dol. In spite of herself she was
deeply impressed.

'Will you get it, do you think?' asked Willie. He was trying,
rather poignantly, to sound like a connoisseur of the art market.
Willie felt keenly his relative eclipse as a player on the
contemporary business scene.

'I've put in an honest bid. Shiel's prices are going up but it
should do the trick. Anyway I'll have my man on the phone to
raise it if necessary.'

The silence around the table was respectful. In fact it verged
on awe.

'A Shiel,' exclaimed Frog at last. 'What do you want a fucking
Shiel for? He's, like, totally old.' But she was blustering. She too
was deeply impressed.

'Aodhgan Shiel is somewhat overrated in my opinion,' said
Eimear, consideringly. Eimear's opinion mattered to the
Kinanes. 'That aside, he's a sound investment, no question,' she
concluded. 'Well done, Carey.' She raised her glass.

Another bottle of wine went down the table.

The joint was served. As a symbol of his position as head of
the household, Willie carved it, though badly. There was a
dutiful clatter of knives and forks. The meat was dun-coloured,
overdone. Frog, as she ate, often put her knife insouciantly in
her mouth. Where Frog was concerned you could not be
confident that she had absorbed the traditional manners and
courtesies.

'I'm in heritage management,' Eimear, who was sitting opposite him, informed Tom. 'I produce spectacles to illustrate and

celebrate the glories and the sorrows of our heritage. I call them shows.'

'Spelled S-e-o-s,' Dol interjected.

'As in the Irish. What the French call *etalages*,' Eimear continued helpfully. 'I do battles. The Battle of Clontarf, for example. You know, where Brian Boru vanquished the Danes? And then was tragically murdered in his tent? And I've put on several evictions. The evictions are very popular.'

She was an enabler, she explained, a conduit for the rich culture that lay buried in the psyches of the people and that only had to be given the opportunity for expression. Another exciting project was the transmission to adults and often to their children of the idiom of the country regions from whence they had come – often only a generation ago. But in some cases the heritage had been in abeyance through several generations. Right now she was sourcing people still in possession of the patois of their native place who were prepared to pass it on to the urbanised.

There were so many people out there, she said passionately, who were nostalgic for what they had lost in the standardisation of speech and of values brought about by urbanisation, globalisation and especially by the media. Women who had come to feel marooned in their comfortable but empty lifestyles and who longed to recreate the simple pasts of their forebears were her keenest clients.

Eimear's eyes gleamed with a fiery ardour as she spoke of the individuality and the uniqueness of the different county dialectic heritages; the tongues of Limerick, Monaghan and Roscommon, South Tipp and North Tipp, East Kerry and West Kerry . . .

'In fact any county you could name. They're all marvellous, all unique.'

The differences were subtle. But to the sensitive ear, accent, phraseology, nuances of stress and idiosyncrasies of attitude . . .

'She's teaching them to say horrrse,' put in Frog derisively.

'The subtleties and nuances can be extraordinary,' Eimear went on, ignoring her. 'Absolutely extraordinary. And right now I'm planning on closing right in. Getting down to the town, the village, even the townland . . . And of course there's the American market. America's going to be mega. You have such respect for your forebears over there.' She assumed an interrogative intonation. 'I'm hoping to open up in America shortly?' She looked speculatively at Tom. 'You could be a help with that maybe?'

'Maybe I could,' Tom agreed.

However, the phrase 'respect for forebears' in combination with his great-uncle did not strike him as promising.

'It's all horrrse to me,' guffawed Frog.

Eimear smiled forgivingly. 'Watch out, Frog. You'll be coming to me any day now. Shouldn't you be giving some attention to your image? Do you want to sound as if you came off the assembly line of artist girls straight out of NCAD?'

'There's no way you're ever going to get me to talk like I came out of the bog,' said Frog stoutly.

Frog's rotic rendition of 'horse' was familiar to Tom. He knew he had heard it somewhere before, but where? Then it came to him. It was reminiscent of the enchanting burr of Etchen MacAnar.

'You know, I think you're working on something of huge value,' he told Eimear fervently. 'Can I ask you a question? Have you ever heard of a guy called Etchen MacAnar?'

'Heard of him? I would nearly go so far as to say that Etchen MacAnar is a hero of mine.'

'MacAnar can definitely talk the talk,' put in Carey.

'The man has vision, anyway,' said Willie.

'If you ask me he has all the froth of a glass of warm beer,' Dol stated with what sounded like an unnecessary degree of contempt.

'I must say I do like his voice,' mused Nina.

'I find it something quite special,' Tom declared.

'He's a bogger,' pronounced Frog. 'We have our faults,' she

mimicked. 'But we arrre a good people. Though we may not be any longerrr a grrreat people.'

'And thank God for that,' smiled Carey. 'The only trouble with MacAnar is he doesn't quite believe it. He'd like us to be fighting noble battles and milking flocks of cattle like in the grand old days.'

'What's wrong with having ideals?' demanded Eimear.

Nina was becoming anxious at this sign of imminent inter-sibling acrimony.

'How did your jam come out, Eimear?' she asked brightly.

'Oh, it came out well.' Eimear's tone expressed some lack of conviction.

In homage to her grandmother, who every summer would assiduously and expertly preserve the fruits of her orchard at Killeigh, Eimear was buying up at huge expense slim punnets of raspberries imported from the southern hemisphere and was potting her own jam. However, she hadn't quite got the hang of it yet, it wouldn't set or it set too much. She claimed to be allaying the heavy expenditure by wearing her mother's cast-offs and sourcing her household articles in Guiney's. This was the old-style bargain shop that the grandmother patronised on her twice-yearly trips to Dublin.

'Guiney's is incredibly good value,' she mused. 'Really incredible.'

'You can't beat Guiney's,' Nina agreed with a note of dutifulness.

There was the peal of a mobile phone. Everyone looked hungrily at their phones for signs of life. It was Frog's. Languidly she reached out and picked it up. 'Yeah?' Her tone was low-key, an I'm-getting-calls-every-minute kind of tone.

Suddenly galvanised however, she leaped from her seat and paced up and down the floor, the phone clasped to her ear. At intervals she uttered delirious shrieks and expletives. 'Ohfuck, I don't believe it, ohmygod, you're kidding, fuckman, ohfuckAaron . . .'

Dol raised her eyes to heaven in big-sister mode. Nina made clicking noises to express her displeasure at her daughter's over-use of expletives. 'Language, language,' murmured Willie. Carey fingered his mobile and his spoon, rearranging them so they lay in ever more precise parallel lines.

Finishing the call, Frog went to the counter and calmly, gravely served herself a large plate of the rhubarb fool put out in readiness − for 'pudding' according to Dol, 'dessert' to her parents, 'sweet' to Eimear − and returned solemnly to her seat. Her workmanlike manner as she spooned it up implied a necessity to refuel as if some great and arduous task lay ahead. The Kinanes sat in expectant silence. Finally there was a pause in the action of Frog's spoon. She held it poised in the air.

'We're going into IGMA,' she announced. 'Myself and Aaron. They want our installation.'

'IGMA? You can't be,' squealed Dol. 'IGMA schedules years in advance.'

'Yeah, I know. But there's a hole in the schedule. That German performance artist was coming in. Margareta Boss or something? She was scheduled for IGMA after her gig in the Reina Sofia. But she's not coming. She can't, Aaron doesn't know why. And they think ours is hot, they really want it. In fact they say now is the very best time for it. They're offering us the slot.'

Frog's incrementally breathless news was received with mews of pleasure and congratulation. 'Attagirl,' from Carey. 'Go maith thu, a chailin,' from Eimear. 'Lovely, Frog, lovely,' said Willie and Nina in unison.

But almost at once there were hints of insinuation and criticism.

'Shouldn't you stick to painting, Frog?' frowned Dol. 'At this stage in your career it may not be a good idea to cross genres.'

'Particularly when you're making such a spectacular success of your painting,' Carey drawled.

'Yeah, I know.' Frog glowed happily. 'But an artist has to move on. You have to take risks, experiment. Do the unexpected. If the public doesn't like it, that's their problem. Once an artist stops experimenting, she's stuck, she's dead. You should know that, Dol.' She got up and helped herself to more rhubarb fool.

'Gibbon's "Infanta" is scheduled for the same time,' mused Dol. 'You'll be showing alongside Demis Schwartz.'

'Wow,' exclaimed Frog. 'Well, I bet ours will be way bigger.'

'What is your installation?' asked Eimear.

'It's titled "Dream Home".'

'I see. An exploration of the housing problem.' Frog did not contradict this quite acute interpretation from Carey.

'Cool,' said Willie a little self-consciously.

'It's cool in this house, anyway,' agreed Dol.

'Why don't you call it Teaghlach? Make it culturally germane.' Eimear couldn't help being prescriptive.

'Teaghlach? What does that mean?' Frog was dismissive.

'For God's sake. What do they teach you? It means family.'

'Well, whatever it means it has no vernacular resonance. Anyway Aaron wouldn't have an Irish name. He says they don't travel.'

'Fair dues anyway, Frog,' said Carey, raising his glass.

'Fair dues,' echoed Willie.

Frog pushed her plate aside. She had to be off now, she announced. She had a meeting with Aaron in his studio at the Abattoir. They didn't have a minute to lose if they were to get the installation up in time.

Already she had left the family gathering, so obtuse and domestic, far behind. Blowing a perfunctory and patronising kiss in the general direction of the table she vanished. The others turned to the ruins of the rhubarb fool.

'Mel is doing very well,' remarked Eimear. 'AIB has commissioned a Virgin.' Her air was challenging.

'Who's Mel?' asked Carey.

99

'He's the artist she commissioned to do her Sacred Heart,' Nina explained.

'An artistic interpretation of course,' said Eimear.

'Eimear started him off,' said Dol. 'Now he's planning a pantheon of the saints. Should keep him going for years.'

'Well, as long as he keeps on the right side of kitsch, he should be all right,' pronounced Carey.

'Will we repair to the deck for our coffee?' Willie spoke with diffidence. The deck was his own design and construction and he did not wish to presume on its popularity.

'Sounds good to me,' smiled Tom.

Nina stood up and put on the kettle.

Carey's phone rang. 'Yes? Two . . .? Sounds steep. But sure, I could be interested . . .' Tossing his fringe, he was making for the door as he talked. Carey's business was always secretive and always important.

Suddenly there was a cacophony of ringing mobiles and a more general exodus as Dol and Eimear also left in search of privacy.

'Well, I'm off for my nap,' Nina announced to Tom's disappointment. He had been waiting for the right opportunity to reopen their discussion about his mother. She had given him the impression earlier, though probably he was being over-sensitive, that he was being intrusive, even tiresome . . . She withdrew, carrying the small china teapot for one that communicated her wish to be alone.

The deck was surprisingly chic, furnished with Grecian-style urns and artfully shaped pots containing well-trimmed heads of box and bay and a huge striped parasol above a wrought iron garden table. Willie poured the coffee and reclined, legs crossed, thoughtfully, even sadly, surveying his domain.

'The roses could do with a bit of dead-heading,' he remarked.

'Willie, do you happen to know how Nina met my mother in New York?' Tom heard himself asking.

'Oh, some Irish function, I believe.' Willie frowned. 'Was it a Ceili?'

Tom looked bemused.

'An Irish dance. Or maybe a session? One of those Irish-American things anyway. Very big on native culture, the Irish-Americans.'

Tom leaned forward. 'My mother was big into Irish culture?'

'Oh, massive. Well, you all are, aren't you?'

'I guess,' Tom said lamely. 'Was she happy in Ireland?' he ventured. 'Like, what did she do over here?'

'Oh, the usual things, I suppose.'

'Did she stay in Dublin?'

Willie frowned. 'She may have gone touring. Yes, I believe she went touring.'

'In the country?'

'To the west I'd say. They like to go to the west, don't they?'

Tom had a vision of the west. Wild Atlantic waves, great sea-smooth grey boulders by the shore, a vast, pale sky . . . And a kaftan'ed dark-haired girl walking barefoot on the sands, the wind playing with her hair.

'How much are you paying for a litre of petrol over there these days?' enquired Willie.

'A litre of gas?' Tom couldn't say. He didn't drive in New York. But he did his best to answer further questions about life in what Willie called the US of A. He was interested in facts. The populations of different states, the cost of houses, speed limits on and off the expressways. Tom was able to explain what a condominium was.

Sun-warmed blossoms were fragrancing the deck. To left and right the old red-brick terraced houses of Sandalwood Road gave off a rosy warmth, a somnolent and timeless air.

'Great to see these old places surviving,' Tom remarked.

Willie sighed. 'Keeping them up. Maintenance. They're a big responsibility, Tom.'

Carey appeared on the deck and stuck out his hand. 'I'm off. But we'll talk, Tom. Okay?'

'Sure. Let's do that. Anytime.'

'I'm surprised, I have to say, to hear my mother was interested in Irish culture,' said Tom, breaking the silence when Carey was gone. 'We're not exactly the usual kind of Irish–American family.'

'Looking for something, I suppose,' suggested Willie. 'Or the streak of rebellion.'

'She was rebellious?'

'I couldn't tell you that, Tom. When it comes down to it, what does any of us really know about anyone else?'

They heard the low throb of the Augusta's engine as Carey backed out onto the road.

'Did she drive?' enquired Tom.

'Now, Tom, Nina would be able to answer all your questions much better than I can. Tis Nina was Hilda's friend.' Willie's voice carried a suggestion of exasperation, even unwillingness.

'Sure,' Tom said. 'Sorry.'

He went to the bathroom. Coming back he heard Willie, definitely querulous now, as he spoke to someone. As he stepped onto the boards Tom saw in the hammock, striped to match the parasol, a tousled tawny head, long legs idly swinging. Suddenly at a loss, he paused. The decking creaked. Eileen sat up.

'We've met,' she announced. 'I'm Eileen.'

'I know we've met,' Tom stammered. 'I remember.'

She looked astonishing. Gaunt, a little pale perhaps, but beautiful. A goddess who has spent hours hunting in the damp glades eating only an occasional wild berry.

'Tell me now, have you eaten anything at all today?' demanded Willie.

'Please, Dad.' Defensively, she pushed a strand of hair behind her ear. 'Just because I missed lunch doesn't have to mean I haven't eaten. I told you before. I don't do family lunches.'

'Your mother kept you some dinner.'

'I'll have it later.'

'I've heard that one before. You'll have it now.'

Eileen got up from the hammock. 'I'll eat when I like.'

Tom was alarmed. It looked as if she was about to flounce off and disappear again.

'If you don't mind me saying, Willie,' he said hastily, 'I know you have Eileen's interests at heart, naturally. But to my way of thinking a person can't be made to eat. Doesn't do any good.'

Willie sighed. 'You could be right.'

'Would you say I look as if I'm starving myself?' Eileen asked Tom.

'Well, let's say on Park Avenue you'd look quite well nourished.'

'Now, Dad. There you are.' Eileen subsided again onto the hammock and smiled across at Tom.

'Maybe you'd take a bite of dessert?' suggested Willie.

'What is it?'

'Rhubarb fool,' put in Tom. 'It's very good.'

'Okay.'

Willie hurried away to the kitchen.

I could ask her out to dinner, Tom thought. But in the circumstances it seemed a little inappropriate. He hesitated. Not far away a tram rocketed along the embankment, its brief thunder exciting, festive, like a vacation train racing to a beach resort, flags flying. Somewhere like Coney Island . . .

'You know, Tom,' Eileen remarked languidly, 'don't mind Dad if he's acting weird. It's just that he's been dying to meet you.'

'Has he? Why?'

'Well, your mother and all that.'

'What do you mean?'

'Don't you know? They nearly got it together.'

Tom gasped. 'What makes you say that?'

'Oh, I know my Dad. The way he acts when her name comes up. Hilda . . . Oh yes, I've seen him get quite red. And things he's said, without meaning to . . .' Eileen looked at Tom, eyes narrowed. 'I think they were in love.'

'This is news to me,' exclaimed Tom.

'I'd say,' she mused, 'it would have been Dad who'd have gone off to New York . . . Why would she have wanted to stick around?'

There was a familiar shrill. Eileen scrabbled under the hammock for her bag and pulled out a mobile.

Her gaze was abstracted, her voice brisk. 'Yeah? Right now? Okay, I'm out of here . . . Have to go,' she informed Tom. She gave him a bright courtesy smile. 'Nice to see you again.'

Her footsteps clacked on the kitchen tiles and faded into the distance.

Willie appeared, carrying a large bowl. The spoon protruding from it had an air of pathos. 'She's off again,' he said dolefully.

17

The prevailing wind that Willie had spoken of seemed to have shifted again. Between blackish sails of cloud and downpours the sun would come out and flash itself around with a naked brilliance only to hide itself again a minute later. Sometimes the mountains appeared like grim sentinels, startlingly near. Sometimes they retreated into a blue forgiving mist. Often they disappeared as if they had never been. Tom's angel, as she looked out on the dripping trees, seemed to wear a sulky, even faintly malign expression.

Tom's spirits too as he gazed on the unsettled skies, deserting his novel, rose and fell by turns. 'Tell me everything you know about my mother's movements in Ireland,' he emailed Cerise. 'I've discovered that she seems to have made more than one trip over here. Probably even a few.'

'Tom,' responded Cerise. 'I'm sorry but I'm totally in the dark here. All that was before my time. And your father didn't talk about it, as you know. Do you want me to ask Pender? Though I wouldn't be too hopeful; I guess he's told you as much as he's ever going to. You know what he's like . . .'

Tom did know. In any case what would his great-uncle be able to tell him about the Kinanes? He had never met them. Although could he even be sure about that? There seemed to be a lot, if not quite of evasion, of shilly-shallying going on. At the least, they had short and cloudy memories . . .

Something to do with the weather? In this capricious clime, he wrote to Pender, the inhabitants are bound to be unsettled.

Cast down and euphoric by turns, embroiled in a volatile state of raised and thwarted hopes, disappointments, reformulated plans . . . If the sun could be made to shine uninterrupted in its due season, their discontents might be burnt out, their issues melted away. No amount of money of course could tame the skies but he shared this thought with his great-uncle anyway. Pender was not sympathetic.

'He says half the world is crying out for water,' wrote back Cerise. 'And you want him to be sorry for these guys because they get too much? We're not talking paradise, we're talking goddam reality. He'd like you to get realistic, Tom. And to be honest I'm inclined to agree with him. Now, honey, look on the bright side. Isn't it good novel weather?'

It was, in principle. But he was at an impasse in his novel. He had the idea of bringing his protagonist, whose wife had just walked out on him, to Dublin. More research would be required.

Wandering from bar to bar, losing a succession of umbrellas – Cerise's had been only the first to go – and drinking a great deal of black coffee and whiskey, he brooded on the Kinanes. It was plain that Willie did not wish to talk at any length about his mother. Hilda, as he called her. It was strange hearing her referred to as Hilda. It made her less abstract but also more strange.

'What in God's name made Eileen tell you that?' This was more or less all Willie had had to say on the matter. He seemed indignant. Or was he embarrassed about being found out? But what was there to find out? That he'd been a bit of a Romeo in his youth? 'I'm flattered to hear it,' he said then, with a little laugh. 'Your mother was a lovely girl. But Eileen can be a bit fanciful. Young girls. They see love all over the place, don't they?'

'How many trips did she make over here, Willie?' demanded Tom.

'I couldn't say. Three? Four maybe? It's all a long time ago,

Tom.' Pleadingly he spread his hands. 'It's over thirty years ago now, for God's sake.'

Just then Dol had come onto the deck and after a perfunctory remark or two Willie excused himself. He did not come back.

'In love with Dad?' Dol gave a sceptical laugh. 'A nice thought. But Tom – really? No, I'm sure my mother could have been the only one. Eileen must have made it up. She's always making things up.'

Could Willie's statement be taken as a complete and outright denial, however? Hadn't there been a hint of prevarication? But why should he want to conceal an old affection? He was not a man to boast or talk about his feelings, but all the same . . . Could an old love survive so long? And if it did survive, had it been so painful – and still was in retrospect – that he couldn't talk about it? She was Nina's friend, but before she was married. Nina had confirmed that.

Since Sunday the Kinanes seemed to have gone to ground. On the Tuesday he went around on impulse – Cerise often teased him about his impulsiveness – to Sandalwood Road. But his repeated ringing of the bell wasn't answered, though Willie's blue van stood in the forecourt. On reflection Tom was relieved they weren't in. What would he have done? Accost Nina with the news? My mother was in love with your husband. Discuss.

The silence was such that he might have suspected a summary exclusion from the Kinane family if Eimear hadn't called to ask him to lunch at the Braised Shamrock. Eimear chose for Tom a truly Irish dish, according to her, of Clonakilty black pudding and colcannon. Today she was wearing glasses for her long-sightedness. They made her gaze very large, earnest and trusting.

The spartan ambience of the Braised Shamrock, she informed him as they ate, was the comparatively authentic representation of the house of a cottier eking out a frugal living somewhere on the western seaboard in the early years of the last century. It was an era to which she herself was deeply drawn, a time when Irish culture was at its most vibrant and its most authentic. She gave an ardent description of the meaning the Braised Shamrock had for her, and the meaning that the Irish nation in general should invest in places like it if it wished to be restored to itself.

'But does it?' asked Tom.

'What do you mean?'

'Does the Irish nation wish to be restored to itself?'

She gave him a reproachful look. 'Of course it does. Even if it doesn't know it.'

With food, she went on, one has the same relationship as one has with one's mother. To adopt foreign cuisines, as the Irish had done en masse, symbolised the rejection of the mother.

'And what is the mother, symbolically speaking?' she demanded. She held up a professorial forefinger. 'All that is of value to us, our culture, our history, our traditions.'

'Do you know anything about my mother?' he asked.

'Only that she and mine were pals. Right?'

'Right.'

Eimear gazed at him with her large, trusting eyes.

'What do you have if you don't have a mother?' he asked. 'Do you get none of those things?'

Eimear was stricken. 'Oh, Tom . . . I didn't mean . . . But of course I'm speaking symbolically. What I only mean is, it's essential that we bring the realities of our past to life. That's basically what I'm trying to do.' She looked at him consideringly. 'In your case it might be the culture of the native Americans.'

'I did write a piece for the *New Yorker*,' Tom told her, 'about native American poetry. But that's quite a while ago.'

'You see? I knew you weren't merely commercial.' Now she sounded professional. 'I'm not talking returns or profit. But there's a project of mine I'm hoping you might like to have an input into. It's really important, and I'm talking nationwide. Really significant. It's about the famine.'

'Famine?' cried Tom. He felt a rising excitement. 'Is there a famine? Where? How long has this been going on?'

'I mean the real famine. You know, the potato famine. Back in the nineteenth century?' Her laugh was slightly nervous.

'Of course,' said Tom. 'Sorry. The famine way back.'

'Well, my Famine Seo is going to be a re-enactment. Maybe you don't remember? I was telling you about the battles, the dramatic events in history – how we do re-enactments?'

'Sure, I remember. It sounded really interesting.'

They ate a pretty good apple tart. Eimear was disappointed however, when she tasted the custard. 'The eggs are real. It's not authentic. Should be Bird's Instant.'

Over a pot of tea, Tom wrote out a cheque to Heritage Unlimited for twenty grand. He was delighted to be able to do it. It was the first sizeable donation he had made to Ireland. He felt relieved of a burden.

These days he was seeing quite a bit of Gibbon Fitzgibbon. They would meet for 'a few scoops' either in the Shelbourne or the neo-art-nouveau place nearby where Gibbon threw around in terms of familiarity the names of personalities, politicians and business moguls that Tom recognised from the newspapers. He took Tom to Kirwans – 'the best steak in town' – and it didn't disappoint. A few times they ended up in the Horizontale – 'the only decent night-spot in town' – to 'quaff a bottle or two of shampoo' – though it would turn out to be considerably more – and bask in the attentions of a bevy of beauties, though unfortunately Tom could remember none of their names the following day.

There was no sign of Dol at the Horizontale. Tom got the impression that Gibbon and Dol could be cooling off.

Then Tom was summoned to dine at the Caravanserai. 'We'll be a bit of a gang. Seoda, the wife, will be there. She'd love to meet you. Mind you now, I'll have to be on my best behaviour with Seoda around. No Horizontale for us tonight, Tom.'

18

When Tom arrived in the Caravanserai, Seoda was already there. She beckoned to him with an imperious enthusiasm and patted the place next to her halfway down the long table. This table at the centre of the vaulted room was for larger parties, not for those who wanted a discreet or quiet dinner. Gibbon took the host's place at the top, his cheerful countenance a contrast to the lugubrious figure who was fastidiously buttering a bread roll at its end. This was Norbert Leddy, the noted lawyer.

Friends and associates jovially filed in to fill the table. Tom was pleased to see Carey Kinane take a seat next to Norbert. Carey winked across at Tom. A comely junior minister, in possession of an imposing cleavage, sat down across from him.

Denis Grogan, the first of Tom's Shelbourne acquaintances, came up to heartily shake his hand and went to sit on Seoda's other side. Some of the Kinanes seemed chary of Denis, displaying little sympathy during the family lunch at Carey's remark that he was to be tribunal fodder. But Tom was well-disposed towards him, and not only because he had led him to the Kinanes. There was something likeably shy, even vulnerable, about Denis.

'Deirdre. For fuck sake will you stop acting like a ghost at the feast and sit down there beside Tom Blessman,' called Gibbon in a jocular manner.

The graduate student type whom Tom had met in the Shelbourne in the early days – it seemed so long ago – pulled out the chair beside Tom and sat down with the reluctant air of obeying a faintly disagreeable instruction. She was not wearing the capacious coat this evening however. Tom took this as a sign of a willingness to be sociable. And yes, her name was Deirdre, he remembered.

'I hope, Deirdre, I didn't do anything too wild that night,' he murmured.

Nicely, she smiled. 'I don't think you did. Not that I'd remember. I'm inclined to amnesia I'm afraid.'

'Where did we go, anyway?' Tom asked. 'I recall being some place by the water but that's about it.'

'Was it Skerries? I often wind up in Skerries.'

'Must have been Skerries.'

He had been thinking that Seoda looked familiar and now he remembered where he'd seen her before. She was happy and relaxed this evening but she was definitely the blonde super-chic but bad-tempered woman he'd seen shake off the porter as she hurried into the Shelbourne from the chauffeured Augusta. Must have been having a bad morning.

Fresh drinks were poured. Seoda raised her glass. 'To Gibbon.' There was an enthusiastic chorus. 'To Gibbon.'

'You know, Tom, Gibbon is very fond of you,' breathed Seoda. 'And I have the feeling that I'm going to be just as fond.'

'Gibbon is a good guy,' Tom said.

Seoda sighed. 'He is, actually he is. Do you know what he told me last night? He said he has the sense he's known you all his life.'

Up close, the healthy gleam of her eye had an unexpected fierceness. Dol, Tom considered, should enter her territory, if she entered it at all, only with extreme care.

'Now, Tom, tell me, what are you doing in this funny little country of ours?' Seoda gave a husky little laugh.

So far, Tom told her, he hadn't jumped into anything major investment-wise. He was assessing potentials, he was trying to get a handle on the place, culturally, politically, historically, all that stuff. It was important to get to grips with a place before you could identify its needs, its operational readiness—

'Tom,' broke in Seoda, 'can I say something here? You know, as an American, you may be inclined to be a little bit sentimental. I take it you're looking for some kind of native character or native soul. Am I right? Well, you can stop looking right now. There's no such thing. The Ireland you came here probably hoping to find is obsolete. It's a fantasy. Well, a construct at least.'

'A nice little bit of basil mash for you also, sir?'

The waiter stood at his elbow. He was bent, elderly, his bow-tie slightly askew.

'Certainly not, Jimmy,' said Seoda crossly. 'Mr Blessman will be having the peppered chicory.'

Tom had a hankering for the basil mash but he let it go.

'The old mashed potato. Jimmy thinks it has to be served up with everything,' sighed Seoda. She resumed her discourse. 'You can forget the last century. And you can definitely forget the century before. Ireland as we know it – and let's thank whoever or whatever – was born some time around nineteen ninety-four. Or ninety-six?' She smiled. 'Let the historians fight about the year. Historians like to have something to fight about.' Consolingly, she patted his arm. 'Of course it must be a bit disappointing to come all this way and find we're exactly the same as everyone else. But there's always the theme park aspect. That's an area that's really thriving.' She laughed. 'No horrible muck to wade through. And usually to be experienced under cover from the elements.'

'I think it may have been Greystones, not Skerries,' whispered Deirdre in his right ear. 'Tom . . . Did I go back to your place?'

'Definitely not,' murmured Tom. 'I'd remember.'

'I'm not sure.' Deirdre frowned.

'Seoda, do you know Etchen MacAnar?' ventured Tom.

'I do not. And I don't wish to know him.' Seoda pronged a

piece of grilled meat and seemed to swallow it entire. 'I really don't know what you all see in that fellow. I believe he could be a real danger.'

'A danger?'

'He has the demagogic instinct, Tom. He's a fraud but he has a surprising number of followers. Simple people are easily taken in by a fellow like MacAnar.'

'Who is MacAnar exactly?' enquired Tom.

Seoda gave a disdainful sniff. 'He used to be some kind of a politician.'

'Don't you think he has charisma?' ventured Tom.

'Apparently he's thinking of running for president,' replied Seoda darkly.

'Have you ever thought of running for election, Seoda?' The topic of Etchen MacAnar was threatening to be contentious.

Clearly pleased, Seoda tossed her head and laughed. 'Why do you ask?'

Seoda had been languishing as an unusually glamorous teacher of economics in a rural secondary school in her – and his – native Mayo when she met Gibbon. She was very glad to 'move on' as she would say and devote herself to a calling more appropriate to her talents. She was still mulling over what the nature of this calling would be.

'You strike me as someone with the potential to make a fine politician.'

'Do I?' Seoda's smile was glowing.

'Well, you have ideas, you have convictions – that's rare, I guess.'

'I do believe in progress,' Seoda agreed thoughtfully. 'Passionately. As any politician should. I believe, Tom, that to move on the first thing you do is, you jettison the past. Bin it. Don't you think?' She sipped thoughtfully at her Château Margaux. 'You have to be convinced that progress is not only inevitable but also desirable. It's something people often don't understand.'

'We can't accommodate the past and the future, is that what you're saying?'

Seoda made a dismissive gesture with a taloned hand. 'Absolutely. No way. You have to be ruthless.'

'That's kind of radical,' Tom said a little doubtfully.

'Tom believes I'd make a good politician,' she flirtatiously told Denis Grogan. 'A radical politician, in fact.'

'My dear Seoda, Tom is absolutely correct,' Tom heard Denis reply.

'Would you like to have my basil mash by any chance?' murmured Deirdre in Tom's ear.

'I certainly would,' said Tom eagerly. At once, Jimmy, the waiter appeared, seized the dish from Deirdre's grasp and spooned the herby buttery potato onto Tom's plate, directing a reproachful look at Seoda as he did.

'I'll bring you some more in a minute,' he confided to Tom in a whisper.

Deirdre told him that yes, she was writing a PhD in semiotics – something to do with integrity and social exchange – but also she was the social diarist on a national newspaper.

'Are you going to write this up?' he asked.

She nodded. 'Possibly. Gibbon would like a mensh.'

'A nice mensh?'

'What else? Glowing.'

'Gibbon likes publicity?'

'He always makes good copy.' Thoughtfully she sipped some water.

From a faraway crisis somewhere in the city came, like bloated cicadas, the buzz of an emergency siren. A fitful late sun was dappling the tables of the Caravanserai, swelling its opaque mellow blinds. Along the pavements outside went the busy clickety clack of high heels. An optimistic sound, girls released into the evening, going to meet their dates. Katya stepping out . . . No, it would still be afternoon where Katya was, or only morning even . . .

Was Dol sulking in the Cosmo Prole over a rude bowl of fagioli and sausages? Eileen might be there. Tom had a sudden wistfulness for the old Cosmo Prole.

'No, Tom, I won't be standing for election,' announced Seoda, 'Not in the short term anyway. Not when Gibbon needs my support.' She looked over at the junior minister to check that she was safely engaged in conversation and wouldn't over-hear what she might consider heretical. 'In any case a woman has more power,' she continued with a conspiratorial air, 'when she stands behind the man with the power. And she gets none of the hassle.'

'That's an intriguing attitude. But kind of anachronistic, no?'

'Not at all,' retorted Seoda. 'Look, do you know what I believe about women – well, history and women? You see, I believe history is actually the story of the female project – and a very successful project it has proved to be – to control men. Rein them in.'

'That's certainly an original view. History is usually seen as a male project to rein in the women,' said Tom.

Seoda was placated. 'Exactly. Now, women are the keepers of civilisation, right?'

'I guess.'

'And what is civilisation about?'

Tom found himself at a loss.

'Let me tell you what it's about. It's about men wanting to keep the respect and loyalty of their women. You see? We can make them do exactly what we like. It's simply a question of demanding the ultimate from them while allowing them to believe that they're the ones bestowing the favours.'

When Gibbon was not answering the call of his poca, a surprisingly moody Chopinesque dirge, he was laughing uproariously as he lolled at the head of the long table. Seoda gazed at him now admiringly as if he represented a challenge at which she had not yet fully succeeded, as if he still contained elements of the elusive and the untamed. 'How brazen he is,' she murmured.

And how alarming she is, Tom thought.

'Did you know that he's been summoned to the tribunal?' she murmured. 'I have to be there for him. I couldn't stand for any election until it's all died down. These tribunals can take years, you know.'

'All the guys seem to be going before some tribunal or other,' smiled Tom.

Seoda also smiled. For some time past she had been disillusioned with Gibbon, had been confronting him behind closed doors with her trenchant perceptions of his mis-behaviours and inadequacies. But she was much happier with him now. She looked on him with a newly appreciative eye. It was just so hunky somehow to be summoned before the tribunal. All his flaws, his secretiveness, his relentless bonhomie and his periods of moodiness she was able to see in the different and totally agreeable light of archetypal masculinity. He was revealed to her as a player, a member of a formidable club from which she was only rightfully excluded. Where before she had seen mere deviousness she now saw depths, mystery, and masterly intrigue.

And she saw that he needed her as never before. He needed her by his side with her generous unquestioning womanly sympathy. The whole thing presented her with a reprise of the first exhilarating days of their relationship that nearly a decade of marriage had blurred. It was time for the Fitzgibbons to close ranks.

Above the splash of the urinals and the rinsing noises in the men's rest-room rose some piped music of a surpassing beauty. It was a choir of male voices, grave, soulful, deeply spiritual – though wasn't it a bit unsuitable for a public bathroom? Anyway, Tom liked it so much he washed his hands twice and rearranged the parting in his hair several times to prolong the experience.

Gibbon returned from the gloomy little smoking-yard behind the Caravanserai where he had been puffing rather amateurishly on a cigar.

'There you are,' he exclaimed to Tom's face in the mirror. 'Getting on well with the boss-woman I see. Seoda's a great girl when you get to know her. Now don't forget, Tom – you're coming out to my place in the country, right? Big party. Midsummer's night. Should be fun.'

'Love to, Gibbon.'

'Bring a guest. Anyone you like.'

'Thanks. I'll have a look in my little black book.'

'I won't bother giving you directions. It's hard enough to find. Let me send a car.'

'Great.'

As he left Gibbon turned and came back to murmur, 'Did Seoda tell you about this tribunal rubbish? Hangman McCarthy's circus?'

Tom nodded.

'I'll get out of it. I'll get out with colours flying.'

'Sure you will, Gibbon.'

'Fantastic music in the rest-room,' Tom remarked to Deirdre as he sat down again.

'Rest-room,' Deirdre repeated. 'I like it . . . Yeh, it's Gregorian chant. Actually, we get the same stuff in the ladies' rest-room.' She leaned back to murmur in his ear. 'Some bad apples in there.'

Tom was baffled.

'Monks.' She looked at him significantly. 'Monks . . . Boys . . . Right?'

Tom shook his head. 'Hard to believe.'

Slowly Deirdre spooned up the last of her beetroot and ginger sorbet.

'Tom, have some more Margaux,' ordered Seoda.

But Gibbon was already on his coffee. Now he rose. 'I shall bid you good evening, my friends,' he announced. 'I have promises to keep. There's a little person at home impatiently awaiting my return.' He managed to sound both proud and bashful. 'Has to be read her bedtime story. Can't keep the little lady waiting.'

'That's Saibhir. Our daughter,' Seoda whispered to Tom. 'She'll be six next week. Gibbon is besotted with Saibhir. Absolutely besotted.' She too got to her feet.

Gibbon's words of farewell were not followed by applause as such. But there was definitely the echo, or the aura of it, as if a bright wave of unheard acclamation eddied around the table and engulfed him in its warmth. With a graceful exhortation to 'have another on me' he swept from the Caravanserai, with Seoda, after a regal wave to the gathering, hanging from his arm.

When Seoda was around, Gibbon eschewed the pleasures of the Horizontale and went straight home to Gortbeg Hall, the commanding buttermilk-coloured late-Victorian mansion – which he'd renamed Gortbeg after his native townland in Mayo – on a scenic curve of the south littoral. But devotion to family life was also an aspect of the new regime recently instituted at Gortbeg Hall in the interests of confidence-maintenance, domestic and public.

The waiter seemed much happier now that Seoda had departed.

'You enjoyed your mash, sir. You ate it up, anyway.' He gave Tom an indulgent and comprehending look.

The taciturn Norbert Leddy, who had moved up the table to sit beside the junior minister, arched his thumb and forefinger in Jimmy's direction as a sign to make his whiskey a double. Denis Grogan stood, made a theatrical bow and bade the company good evening. Carey too got to his feet and winked significantly at Tom, inclining his head. As they left, Norbert, who seemed considerably more relaxed now, was breaking into song, an old-style rustic ballad, low and meditative as yet but promising volume and passion before very long.

19

Tom and Carey walked up the street together. The air was humid. Carey mopped his brow with a snowy handkerchief that he took from his trouser pocket.

'Grogan stayed on to the bitter end,' he remarked.

'Yeah?' questioned Tom.

'Well, they're no great buddies, himself and Gibbon. Used to be one time. But that's fado, fado . . .' Carey lowered his voice. 'The word is he has a few beans to spill on poor old Gibbon when he goes up.'

'Up before the tribunal?'

'Yep. Before the tribunal. Tom, do you want to chill? Why don't you come back to my place? Have a drink at home. I do a mean mojito.'

Carey's place was on a superb Georgian street off an even more superb Georgian square. The glow of the weirdly long Irish twilight warmed their brick facades to a powder pink, diffused their grim stature, deepened the colours of their brightly painted doors. Pushing open the door of his house, an electric yellow under a pale limestone lintel, he gestured at the vast spaces inside.

'What do you think? Smashing, isn't it? The planning was a bitch to get but I managed to swing it. I was lucky.'

In tune with the fashionable trend Carey had had his hall floor taken out. The forward-looking were taking out ceilings wholesale. Was this because, Tom speculated, it expressed a subconscious desire to breathe a bigger, more bracing air, a desire for openness and untrammelled freedom? So many lids had been taken off, culturally speaking, there was nothing left to uncover. So they were taking the lids off their rooms.

Over a chic rail of brushed steel he looked down into a cavernous space extending from front to back. On the black marbled floor far below, steel-trimmed columns stood like dreamworld tree trunks, giant steely kitchen appliances oddly forlorn at one end. It was achingly cool. Tom could imagine Carey sitting here in one of the pools of futuristic light, his silk tie loosened and askew, surveying his lofty domain and contemplating the exhilarating bleakness he had created.

'Come on,' ordered Carey, 'I'll mix you that mojito.'

In the chilling cabinet of the vast refrigerator he was able to find a luxuriant bunch of fresh mint. 'Lola knows to make sure I always have the mint in,' he said. 'Lola's my housekeeper. Fantastic. Can't beat the Slovenians.'

It was slightly chilly down there. 'These old houses,' muttered Carey. 'Can still be the devil to heat.' He lit something like a brazier, a gleaming oval object resembling a Roman bowl. It seemed to burn some mysterious fuel that resembled ancient winter leaves.

Drinks in hand, they moved towards the upper regions of the house, via a circuitous route. Carey showed Tom his cinema, decorated in a playful interpretation of Art Deco. In the bad old days this was a dark and freezing warren of pantries and cheerless quarters for cook and skivvies, as Carey said. He showed him his lavishly equipped gym. He led him outdoors to show him his garden, a long vista of orange trees and box, bathed in the moonlike — a soft southern moon — beams of an invisible lighting system. It was like a very grand and original version of Willie's deck.

As they climbed the broad and graceful stairs Carey brushed with his fingers the banister so gleamingly polished by Lola and gave a happy sigh of proprietorship. 'There's something up here I want you to see,' he said.

They crossed a beautifully proportioned mezzanine, fleur de lys plasterwork whitely ethereal overhead in the strengthening dusk. Carey, going ahead, threw open double doors with a commanding flourish and ushered Tom into a large and elegant room. To Tom's bemusement the room was empty, unfurnished except for a rather fine blue-upholstered gilded chair in the French style positioned just slightly off centre on the polished wood floor. Like ghostly faces the white waxen flowers of a chestnut tree crowded eagerly against two tall windows as if clamouring to be admitted to the mysteries within.

'It's a fine room,' commented Tom dutifully. 'And that's a pretty fine piece. Louis . . . something or other, is it?'

The far wall suddenly sprang into brightness. Carey had flicked on invisible lighting.

'There you are now.' His voice was low and husky. 'Take a look at that.'

An invisibly controlled blue velvet curtain moved smoothly aside to reveal a vacancy. There was nothing on the wall it had draped. However, impeccably centred in its solitude, an empty square was perfectly illuminated, top, bottom, every which way.

'It's for the Shiel,' Carey murmured.

'You got it,' Tom exclaimed. 'The picture you were after?'

'Not quite in the bag yet. But it will be.'

As trophy pictures go, Carey's would not be large. The white wall, receding into shadow, was huge around the space. For now at least, the blue curtain, gathered into folds at one side had, to Tom's eye, a slightly ominous look as if the space might conceal the entrance to some kind of a ceremonial funeral pyre.

'Sit down,' Carey ordered.

Tom lowered himself onto the French chair.

'Can't you just see it? Won't it be fantastic?'

Behind him Tom heard the floorboards creak as Carey shifted his stance. He was expecting a meaningful response.

'It sure will,' he declared.

With a pleased expression Carey emerged into the light to stand beside him.

'Shiel's middle period,' he explained happily. 'And his best, the experts say. I'm inclined to agree. His early stuff is easier to get into, of course. But I wanted to get in at the top end. You don't want the latent genius, you want the real thing, don't you? If you're going to get in at all.'

'Sure you do.'

'A fellow could do worse than get into Aodhgan Shiel.' Carey spoke with his complacent air of a man of experience giving a younger chap the benefit of his advice. 'You know, this chair is positioned at the optimum distance for observation.'

'He's big in the States, of course,' Tom ventured.

'They go mad for him over there,' agreed Carey. 'But we like to keep him at home, now we have the bucks to beat 'em at the game.' He grinned. 'There's a kick up the backside for the lads now.'

Who were the lads? His would-be peer group, Tom assumed, the guys who were a few rungs up the ladder of success. Bigger guys than Carey but guys he intended to catch up.

'Dead right.'

'You know, it's going to mean a lot to me. Can you understand that?'

'Sure I can.'

'I thought you would.'

Carey lapsed into silence, the serene silence of contemplation or reverie. Tom went over to one of the tall windows and looked down. The street below was veiled in a lattice of foliage, green leaves spot-lit a violent lemon from a hooped and curlicued old street lamp. In the tree the room's reflection was suspended, a room filled with luminous floating leaves. It looked, Tom reflected, as if some aesthetically awesome but catastrophic event had occurred in the room . . . Probably an act of nature.

Carey sat in the French chair, his legs comfortably splayed, took a sup from his glass and gazed at the illuminated wall as if his Shiel was already hanging there in all its glory.

'Carey?' began Tom diffidently. He was afraid he might be getting to be a bore on the subject. 'What do you make of this story about my mother and your father?'

The chair's gilded paws screeched on the boards as Carey wheeled around. 'What story?'

'Eileen says they were linked up at some point.'

'Did she?' Carey whistled. 'Fuck . . . Though I can't say I'm surprised. There's bound to have been more than my mother in the frame. He was a good-looking fellow in his day.'

'So you believe it?'

'See no reason not to.' Carey frowned. 'Willie lacks confidence, always did. That's his Achilles heel. But she could have been smitten.'

'Tell me about Willie,' Tom said.

'Poor old Dad.' Carey's tone was morose. 'There's one story he tells about when he was a kid. He's never forgotten it and he never will. It made him what he is, I suppose, for better or worse. Don't tell him I told you now. He can be sensitive on the subject.'

'Sure I won't.'

Carey considered his glass. 'He must have been about seven or eight. Dead poor. We're talking the Fifties here. Poor children often went barefoot. My father did. His father over in England, trying to put a few bob together. I don't think he was doing too well. The family mightn't see him from one end of the year to the other. They were living in a little cottage in Ranelagh . . .'

Carey gave a dry laugh. 'The place must be worth the best part of a mill now, of course. And there was one morning when there wasn't a thing to eat in the house. Not a crumb. And of course not a cent either – well, a halfpenny in old money. So Willie was kept back from school. His mother wrote out a note and told him to take it over to her sister in Donnybrook. The sister was in the same boat but' – Carey grimaced – 'hers hadn't sprung quite as many leaks. His auntie read the note, put on her coat, took Willie by the hand and led him up to the school where Johnny, his cousin, went. Down the long corridor they walked, hand in hand, and into a classroom and up to the teacher. His auntie whispered to the teacher while Willie squirmed – it was a big thing to walk into a strange classroom with your auntie, really embarrassing. Especially when you didn't know what she was up to. And he couldn't look for embarrassment at his cousin sitting in his desk but he could tell he was feeling the same.

' "Take off your boots Johnny, and bring them up here to your mother," ordered the teacher then in his big voice . . .

'And little Johnny bent over and unlaced his boots and padded up to his mother, a boot swinging from each hand. Willie talks about how white and soft his cousin's feet were compared to his own little grubby pair. In the front row a boy started to snigger but the teacher put a stop to that with one look. His auntie put the boots in her shopping bag and took Willie's hand and they turned and walked out of the classroom and hand in hand they walked in silence as far as Portobello to the pawn.

' "I'll be getting them out on Saturday," his auntie told the pawnbroker. Whether she did or not . . .' Carey made an unknowing gesture. 'Anyway with the few coins he gave her they walked to the grocer's and got bread, milk . . . The basics I suppose. And Willie took them home to his mother in the shopping bag.'

Carey heaved a sigh. 'And that's how they got fed, for that day anyway.'

'Such a sad story,' murmured Tom. 'But kind of heroic. How they stuck together.'

'Yeah,' Carey agreed.

'Is there still poverty as bad?' Tom asked after a while.

'God no,' said Carey. He rubbed his eyes as if he were sleepy. Tom suspected he was hiding incipient tears.

'Why don't I fix us a drink?' he suggested awkwardly.

'You do that.'

When Tom came back with the drinks Carey took the glass and thirstily knocked most of it back in one go.

'Do you know what, Tom?' he said. 'We could have been brothers.'

'Only we wouldn't be us.'

'Better how it stands so . . .' Carey slumped tiredly back in the gilted chair. 'Tom?' He opened one eye. 'Don't say anything to Dad. He can still get tearful about it if you bring it up. We try and keep him off the topic.'

In a little while more there was a sharp tinkle of breaking glass. Carey's crystal tumbler had fallen to the boards from his slackened grasp. And from the French chair came a slow tide of increasingly ungentle but contented snores as Carey slept.

20

The muted chorus of morning in the apartment carried Tom in and out of a dreamy half-slumber. Bird trills mingling with the jingle of distant car or house alarms so it was difficult to tell them apart, the faint abstract music of church bells, the distant churning of traffic on the motorways that ringed the city . . . A deep monotonous seething, like a great pot on the simmer. Converging on the city to consume, to be consumed . . .

Carey's story about his father, Tom realised, had a familiar ring. The old Ireland. His great-uncle and Willie Kinane, they were a generation apart but their memories were similar. Yes, to go around, like the Yank in the yellow car, randomly distributing largesse . . . Was this what on some level Pender basically wanted Tom to do for him? Pender had once told him a story of the Ireland he had left, though he had presented it as a story about America. To his great-uncle it was a mythical experience of Irish misery versus American munificence. For all his wealth, for all the overflowing bowl America had given him to sup, America had never looked to Pender so wealthy, so extraordinarily munificent as it did on that afternoon in his childhood . . .

He is hardly more than an infant. He is playing – to him 'playing' means a lesson in holding his own among the bigger boys – in the mud at a river bank. There are other children all around down there by the river, bigger boys, tough, hoarse, freckled. He can still recall with dislike the faces of a couple of them. He is wary of these boys. Like them he's barefoot. The mud is cold and oozy; it swells between his toes. His feet are white; they have a bluish tinge. He fears the mud and what might be lurking in it. But the big boys seem to have little objection to it and that's why he's here.

Suddenly a boy is shouting. The shout is both hoarse and high-pitched. 'He's coming. The Yank is coming.'

Wildly, roughly, the boys at once start to scramble up the bank towards the bridge. 'Get out of the way, Pendergast,' shouts one of them, not much bigger than himself. He's pushed aside, he falls face down in the mud, he has to wipe mud from his eyes with his muddy fist.

Thunderous in his ears he can hear the deep throb of the engine of a car. A car engine is rare music in those days, longed-for, marvellous. Sliding, falling down again in his hurry, desperate but no less determined than the biggest, the roughest boy, he scrabbles up to the bridge, to where the pale ribbon of road crosses the river.

He makes it in time to watch a big yellow car slowly approach the bridge from the direction of the town. Never has he seen a yellow car or such a glittering array of headlamps as this one carries. The car is hooded in black. Gracefully it sways as it comes as if the hood is playing with an impalpable wind blowing above his head from some other marvellous world far away.

The driver is wearing a peaked cap at an impressive angle. His passenger seated behind is a large dark man shape, a hulking solidity both slack and powerful. The boys press forward into the path of the car, jostling and pushing. Savagely the big boys push the small lads to the back. Their breathing is heavy with excitement. But Pendergast flails out with his fists. He kicks, he curses. He fights his way back to a position at the front again.

The car comes to a halt. He is close enough to it to see the plaited gold braid on the driver's cap and that the passenger is a large silver-haired man wearing a fawn overcoat. The man's expression, shadowed by the black hood, is unreadable, but its effect is one of impassivity. The protective weight and texture of his fawn coat suggests, for this is a summer afternoon, clouded but mild, that the man is accustomed to a warmer clime. Suggests the place he has come from, and will return to, is rich, kind, warm and infinitely generous, and he has taken the appropriate precautions to keep the cold of this poorer alien world at bay.

A boy jumps onto the wide yellow-striped running board of the car and peers in at the man through the rolled-down window. 'Are you the Yank?' he demands.

The driver's reply is quiet and measured. At once the boy gets down off the board and skulks shamefaced back into the crowd.

From his seat the passenger-man observes the boys. The boys observe the man. The driver looks straight ahead. Pender is pressed close to the car at the front of the crush of silent boys. The silence is expectant. The boys seem hardly to draw breath. The spoked wheels look enormous, the man high above him huge as the statue carved in stone in the village square. It is not a searching look. The man's look is detached. And yet he seems to absorb their presence, to be taking them into himself. He is consuming some essential thing in them.

'Okay, Harry, let's go.'

Little Pendergast hears the man's deep voice. His foreign accent has a painful music.

Slowly the car starts to move. Breathless, still, the boys wait. Pendergast knows they're waiting. But what they're waiting for he doesn't know. Now the rear of the car has passed. He notes the two brown leather valises lashed above the splendid spoked wheel. 'That's the spare,' he tells himself. The formerly abstract word 'spare' now made actual is infinitely pleasing to him.

As the bulbous yellow rear with its cargo of luggage and the wheel that is the spare passes the last boy in the line, a fawn-sleeved arm emerges through the window. The man is waving, bestowing the languorous wave of one who has received due homage. But the gesture is more than a wave. Falling from his hand to float briefly in the air before they flutter to the ground are small sheets of greenish paper.

'Dollars,' the boys shout. 'Dollars.'

They leap into action. They run after the paper sheets, scrabbling in the ditches, clambering over springing thorns. The yellow car is picking up speed and still the dollars float from the extended arm. The boys follow in its wake, becoming small distant running figures, shrieking, kicking, plucking dollars as they go.

Little Pendergast doesn't go chasing after the dollars. Standing alone in the middle of the road he watches the yellow car until he can't see it any more. In his memory now the whooping barefoot boys have vanished; he sees only the car. He is only the smallest of the boys, his understanding of what dollars can mean is limited. But he knows that to the others, older than him, they are precious treasure. He knows that if he did get his hands on one, it would only be taken off him. And he's beyond fighting; he's washed clean of mud, of rivalry, of wanting. He is contented. He knows now what he will be.

Later, a boy holds out a dollar to show to Pendergast. He's not allowed to take it in his hands but he is allowed to feast his eyes on it. There's a red smear of the boy's blood on it from where he stabbed his finger with a thorn. Pendergast is sorry about the blood, but his regret is not for the boy's bleeding finger. The dollar has for him the beauty of mystery and rarity. He doesn't like to see it smeared.

The trouble was, Tom thought, Pender wanted to be the Yank, but he didn't want the barefoot boys. He would have nothing but contempt for the boys. So, to whom should Tom be distributing dollar bills, in a manner of speaking? In any case, there were no barefoot boys. Only the youths slumped by ATM machines and pub doorways wrapped in sleeping bags who thrust a cup in front of you as they made a request for change . . . Just the same kind of panhandler you got in New York. Generally Tom obliged while he played out the arguments in his head.

'You're feeding his habit . . .', 'It'll sap her motivation . . .', 'He makes more begging on the street than I get in my job . . .'

The same arguments you got in New York. You got them anywhere. His great-uncle's arguments, except he would be more vociferous, more blunt.

'He's happy,' Cerise assured Tom. 'He says you're to carry on just as you are. You're doing fine.'

'He likes to see results,' protested Tom. 'And I'd like to see results. I was thinking about something maybe infrastructural?'

'Like what?' She sounded not ill-disposed exactly, but maybe uninterested. He sensed her yawn.

'Like the health system. The health system over here isn't great, to say the least. But that'd be huge. Would you say—'

'Health? No way.' Cerise was very firm on this point. 'Pender has a horror of sickness and disease. You know how he hates hospitals.'

This had always been the case. It was one of his superstitions. His great-uncle avoided the antiseptic milieus of the maimed and the sick as if they harboured the plague.

'But since his own brush with ill-health maybe he's changed? Doesn't he see it's normal?'

'No way. He's in denial. He's convincing himself it never happened. Look, Tom,' she went on. 'Believe me. He's happy. He's not getting the dream since you went to Ireland. And he just wants to keep it that way. Okay?'

Pender was happy because, as Cerise said, he wasn't having the dream, he was restored to himself. And why wasn't he having the dream? Because he was keeping it at bay. How? By keeping Tom in Ireland, on location, as it were. Like an animal tamer, Tom's role was to keep the rampant beast supine and subdued in its corner; in actual terms, dormant in the unexplored regions of Gast's subconscious. The beast would not emerge from its cave while Tom guarded the gate. The fact was, his great-uncle didn't give a damn what he did or didn't do over here, just so long as he stayed.

'Keep him over there,' he would have instructed Cerise. 'Keep him sweet.' An unscientific ploy, but effective.

Yes, the reality was he was marooned over here, exiled, captive you could say, until – until the beast was overcome? And when would Gast be persuaded of the beast's final domestication or demise? And how? Of course he could always take his life back, tell his great-uncle he was calling it a day, dream or no dream. But the truth was, Tom ruefully recognised, that he had his own beasts to keep him here.

Here there were presences, elusive but alluring. And maybe the most alluring was Eileen Kinane . . . A beautiful vulnerable creature, adrift in the forests of the night, rarely sighted, so difficult to hunt down . . .

The other day he had been on the tram and as it halted outside the bar called the Odeon he had caught a glimpse of her, or thought he had, at an outside table. When the tram had wound its way with a tortuous slowness as far as the next station he had jumped out and sprinted back to the Odeon. But by then she, or her phantom, had gone.

He sat down at the table where he thought he had seen her sit and drank a coffee. He hardly knew her; he had exchanged no more than a few words with her. And yet, the little she uttered seemed to contain the promise of mysteries unfolding. Like an oracle. The possessor of confidences. He would have to talk to Willie again, penetrate the caginess, break open the guarded bank of memory.

Printed on the paper wrap the sugar cubes for the coffee came in there was a proverb. A folksy Irish proverb obviously as there was also a version in the inscrutable language that Gibbon liked to throw words around in.

'What fills the eye fills the heart,' he read.

Well, Eileen certainly filled his eye.

A call from Dol broke into his speculations. Her greeting was cursory. She had something on her mind.

'Tom, I take it Gibbon has invited you to his midsummer party?'

'He has. He's sending a car, in fact.'

'So you're going?' She sounded both bossy and defensive.

'I guess.'

'Did he say you could bring a guest?'

'I'm sure he did. Are you going?'

'I'll go as your guest. If you don't mind.'

'Of course I don't mind.'

Dol's tone relaxed. 'Love to be your guest, Tom. That's really sweet of you. Thanks.'

'I'd like to have another word with your folks,' he said.

'Oh, Mom and Dad are in Spain. They have a little place over there.'

'When are they back?'

'Who knows? When it gets too hot, I suppose.'

21

'Your car is waiting outside, Mr Blessman,' a punctilious voice said on the intercom.

Gibbon's driver was a young man of extreme discretion and rectitude. He was disinclined to conversation, indeed he did not converse at all. His silence however did not appear to be an expression of either deference or respect.

He looked like a slightly shady banker. His navy-blue suit was elegantly draped. His face was bloodless and ascetic as if he disdained to dine on anything but unsauced white meats and thinly nourishing soups. The car he drove was the sleekest of Augustas, also navy-blue. He drove it as if it had been chosen to accessorise his suit and the superiority of his manner. When he asked it for thrust the car answered with a low courteous hum and was hushed again.

He hushed even Dol into silence. Tom had seen the driver's eyes narrow and his mouth pucker when he saw Dol emerge in her party gear, one of her most experimental-design dresses. But he walked smartly around and held the door open for her with a politeness that couldn't be faulted.

In a whoosh of silence they glided up O'Connell Street. Past the public monuments, the velvety texture of some hero's stone frock coat, the pencil stroke in the sky of the gangling Spire . . . what Dubliners called the Spike . . . Cruising through the north-side suburbs of more struggling greenery and grimier brick, baking gently under a lightsome sun.

You could think special privileges had been granted to the

driver by higher authorities. For him the lights were always green, the evening traffic a turgid metallic river they floated effortlessly by, insulated, inviolable, as if under some invisible escort. Before long they had left the city behind and were in the countryside. A venerable smell from the car's impeccably cream leather upholstery mingled with a scent of meadow flowers and grass – and also a very faint and only occasional waft of sick. Somebody had been sick in the Augusta, not perhaps last night, but recently.

A female, Tom decided, for no good reason other than prejudice. Some girl of Gibbon's who, after being entertained all too well in the Horizontale, was being conveyed home in the early hours. Could have been Dol; she was the most likely candidate, with her habit of knocking back the Chablis like water though she had neither the head nor the stomach for it. Easy to see her throwing up, even wilfully doing it just to provoke the driver . . . In the absence of having Gibbon to provoke.

Tom observed the subtly blonded hair, the inscrutable gaze in the mirror fixed on the subjugated road. The guy would not have been at all pleased – surely even Dol would falter at having to face up to him from a vomitous slump. A possible explanation for her subdued demeanour now?

The day was still, the green fields peaceful, replete. A small town cruised by, tall new apartment blocks on one side shutting out the sun from the old low houses huddled on the other. A man was being tugged along by a small dog. Pulling a twin baby-buggy a woman backed into a Centra. Then a long ribbon of road, lined with cottages of a frugal and utilitarian style, clothes hung outside to dry. Modern piles, American style, brash in their newness . . . An occasional bucolic villa in the old style lost among trees.

Cows recumbent in springing pastures were chewing on yellow flowers. Gast's dream of the famished land had not contained cows, the copious supplies they gave of milk and yellow butter . . . Yes, Jacques had been right about the butter.

'Cool scenery,' Tom remarked. His voice sounded a jarring note in the rarefied world of the car. The Augusta seemed to slow momentarily in surprise. The driver raised his gaze to meet Tom's briefly in the mirror. Tom thought he could discern the sardonic lift of an eyebrow. But the remark seemed to have restored Dol to mundane reality or at least to speech.

'I had a dream,' she announced ruminatively. 'I dreamt about this party we're going to.'

She described the dream at some length. The midsummer party was in full swing. Faces with the customary pallor of faces in dreams weaved brightly around her. The atmosphere was festive, even joyous; there was dancing. She described the bottles on the tables – there were many small tables in rows as in a restaurant – their jewel-like hues, the particularly iridescent quality of their coating of ancient dust. But the bottles contained only water.

'Weird,' she concluded. 'What do you think it means?'

'I have no idea,' Tom said.

'But I do.' She leaned close to his ear. There was no way her stagey hiss could not have been heard by the driver. 'It means that around Seoda there is no sustenance. There is no nourishment.' She lapsed into silence again and lay back and gazed calmly out of the window.

For a short while the road became a cool dark cavern of over-arching trees. When they came out into the sunlight again it ran alongside what seemed like an endless vista of gunmetal barrelled railings, a proud and intimidating defence lining the little country road.

'Ah. The noble demesne of Iveragh,' Dol loudly announced. 'She had the old stone demesne wall taken down, you know.' Her tone was indignant.

'The railings show a fine view of the park,' suggested Tom. Dol gave him a look of disdain, searched in her bag for a compact and inspected her face in the mirror.

They passed through high granite columns on which stone

figures of some species of a noble and solitary bird were posed. A retainer stood by a picturesque little lodge and tipped his cap. At a more ceremonial pace now the Augusta bowled along a generously curved avenue, a coiffed park on either side furnished with lofty spreading trees, broad-boled and vernal. The silence in the car seemed to have assumed a reverential quality. They rounded a corner and in the distance at the end of the straight the Fitzgibbons' country bolthole hove into view winged, festively glittering in the evening sun. The car slowed to quite a stately pace of homage.

'Iveragh, sir,' announced the driver. His tone was perfectly balanced between urbanity and controlled emotion.

'It's beautiful,' murmured Tom.

'It's not a grand house, you know,' Dol bossily pronounced. 'Not technically. It's only what we call a house of the middle size.'

'Well, it's sure grand enough for me,' said Tom with a determined levity. Certainly, in the light of his preconceptions before he came, it was grand for Ireland. He felt a faint stirring of anxiety. Was Dol going to be difficult?

'You should've seen the dump it was before he got the kangos in.' The driver spoke with unexpected force. 'You wouldn't give two cents for it.'

'Must be pretty ancient. He gave it a makeover, I guess?' Tom was aware of a rather craven sense of gratitude for this man-to-man overture.

'Makeover? He gutted it.' This was delivered with relish, the force of a man who loves a gutting.

There was perhaps more meat to the chap than met the eye, but there was no time to find out. As they made their stately approach, Gibbon came sauntering out of the shade of the portico, planting his legs squarely on the low-rise granite steps, cigar in one hand and glass in the other. A snowy-clothed drinks table was set under the stone canopy and a comely and smiling servitor stood behind it, an assurance from the start to thirsty and travel-weary arrivals of the free-flowing hospitality to come.

'Tom. My old pal. Great to see you, a chara . . .' Putting down his glass, Gibbon gave Tom's hand a lengthy and really first-class shake. His was slightly moist. Well, inevitable in a host, a touch of nervousness.

'And hey, look who's here. Dol . . .' Deftly his lips brushed Dol's proffered cheek. 'Love the guna, baby.'

Dol's appearance was welcomed by Gibbon with admirable aplomb, though she had not been invited as such, as she had admitted to Tom, to the party. In fact Tom had gathered that she had been more or less discouraged from coming. But then Dol was not a girl to take discouragement, and especially not from Gibbon.

'Enjoy the drive, did you? A first-class driver, that Luke.' Gibbon gave a meaning wink. 'Went to a good school. Served his apprenticeship early at the joy-riding. Best driving school to be had.'

Dol sniffed. 'Pity he didn't go to good-manners school.'

Gibbon ignored that. 'A Bolly, Tom? And you, Dol?' He led the way to the drinks table. Yulia, the Lithuanian bartender, poured them each a glass of frothy champagne into which she inserted a trio of small and perfect wild strawberries with a pair of tiny silver tongs.

'Beautiful evening,' said Tom appreciatively. He looked across the panorama of luscious parkland bathed in the limpid light of midsummer.

'Glorious,' Gibbon agreed. 'I bet our weather over here is a bit of a surprise to you, Tom. Thought you'd get nothing but rain, right?'

His inflection was American again. Gibbon was boisterous with a genuine American-style confidence this evening, which had a lot to do with its gloriousness. It persuaded him that fortune would continue to smile on him with the effulgence that it always had.

'You're in good time. Well positioned. Get a few scoops into you now before you face the throng, right?'

'Will there be dancing?' Dol's reference to dancing when she was talking about her dream had reminded Tom of its pleasures.

'Dancing? Sure. If you want.' But Gibbon didn't seem very enthused by the prospect of dancing.

Dol had obviously been at Iveragh before. With a chilly smile she drifted away through the great grey-painted door. Confidentially Gibbon inclined his head towards Tom. 'There'll be a few lads here I'm sure you could find of interest, Tom, that you haven't met. Nothing like a party to grease the wheels, eh? But no business now, d'ya hear? You're here to play. Have a good time.'

In a vast drawing room about a dozen guests were already gathered. They stood about in small clusters on opulent rugs, making noisy talk and laughter with the slight edginess of first-comers. Among them were two rather stunning model types, tall, blonde and polished to a sheen. But Tom was led over by Gibbon to a bunch of guys, their large shoulders phalanxed against the room as if fencing off some possibility of attack. These were obviously a cohort of the 'lads' of whom Gibbon had spoken.

'Here's the boys for you,' he confirmed in a whisper. Waving his cigar expansively in the air he made the introductions.

The cigar was unlit, a prop only. This was because Seoda had forbidden smoking in the house. It was yet another test in compliance for Gibbon. And Gibbon was being submissive and not smoking in the house. She had considered extending the ban to the park but realising this could give him an excuse to stray beyond her sight and control, at the least to withdraw behind some tree or clump of verdure, she had thought better of it. Permission to smoke on the portico kept him domestic.

Seoda had not yet made her appearance at the party. Just now, she was reclining, smoking successive Marlboro Lights, in a state of undress on the couch in her dressing room, ignoring the arriving cars and her husband's hearty shouts that wafted up at intervals from the portico below. She was watching a bumper edition of a Brazilian soap called *Underwear* – although apparently it had a raunchier title in Brazilian – centred around a lingerie factory in Rio.

She had felt quite virtuous about following *Underwear* since that brilliant fellow in *Brutus*, the formidably hip journal, had treated it to a serious critique. To engage with it was obviously to participate in a cultural experience. He had referenced it with *Carmen*.

'Make yourself at home now, Tom,' beamed Gibbon before he returned to his post. 'We're all free and easy here.'

Tom recognised a couple of the lads. They had often been in Gibbon's train or at his table in the Caravanserai. Barry and Ber they were called, one dark, one fair, both at the top of their game. 'Listen here to me now, lads. No deals tonight, okay? You're here to have fun,' Gibbon chided facetiously.

'Deal?' cried Ber. 'Sure I'm only from Cavan. We wouldn't know the meaning of the word up in Cavan. Not like the Leitrim boys.'

This elicited chortles all round. They resumed their discussion about golf, or at least the potential for golf courses in Azerbaijan – Jan as they called it. Jan, they were of the opinion, was the place to get stuck in. And fast, before that other lot did. Tom had the disconcerting sense that if the Irish hadn't yet bought up the whole world, they were soon going to.

'Isn't that a kind of unstable part of the world?' he enquired.

'Could be, I suppose,' Barry agreed. 'It's the Caucasus after all. But no bother. Uncle Sam will sort them if they get out of line.'

'Won't ye?' demanded Ber. They all looked expectantly at Tom.

'Sure we will,' he answered with a laugh. 'All you guys have to do is ask.'

'Ask? Sure all we have to do is flash a cupful of Mazola oil under their noses and they'll be in on top of us, guns blazing.'

Tom's laugh was slightly cagey. Ber gave him a friendly no-harm-meant type puck. 'No one to look to these days but Uncle Sam. You wouldn't want to be depending on little Granny Europe when push comes to shove.'

The conversation split amicably into two sectors: one concerned with the failure of Granny Europe to come to the aid of small nations in their hour of need, the other with the optimum number of hectares required for a first-class second-division golf course, both with and without a shopping outlet attached. Every minute or two one of them stepped aside to respond to the call of his mobile and the others would josh him indulgently. 'Ah come on now. Would you ever turn that thing off? Give yourself a break.'

Tom wondered whether he might approach the model-type girls who were perched now on either arm of a lengthy and handsome chesterfield upholstered in a lustrous golden satin, their corn-coloured manes reflected in the gilted antique glass behind them, itself freckled with a sun-kissed tarnish, as they tossed their heads flirtatiously to and fro. But they were already surrounded by admirers. To gain a jockeying position he would have to elbow his way to the fore with a determination he was not sure he was up to right now.

The room's golden and gilded decor bestowed a sunshiny sheeny look on everyone. It could have been designed to show off a blonde – such as Seoda – to her best advantage; and it probably was. In heavily ornate frames paintings from bygone ages hung on the saffron-clothed walls. There were portraits of sleek high-achieving horses, short of tail and small of head, portraits of grim-faced gentlemen in high collars or soldier's crimson, likenesses of women with sad expressions and complicated coiffures who seemed to turn aside with affected hauteur from the sight of the happy gathering below.

Through the tall elegant windows draped in lemon-coloured silks you could see the file of Augustas proceeding up the drive with the predictability of a military convoy and drawing up at the portico. As their cargoes were disgorged, more and more guests were advancing steadily in twos and threes into the room, armed with smiling mouths and watchful eyes.

These arrivals by public road however, glossy and haughty though they might appear, were, in the hierarchy of guests, the party's raggle taggle. The top rankers were those who buzzed down onto Iveragh's sward in their own 'copters, a little late. Later on in the evening they would leave a little too soon. Below them on the ladder were those who came in a hired 'copter. Tom, ferried by a chauffeur-on-call, figured in the lower ranks – but of course above those who were obliged to drive themselves, even if in an Augusta. There were a few also who came shambling up the avenue in a family saloon or a Japanese jeep and they were received with no overt sign of condescension whatsoever. But the fact was noted; it was absorbed.

Whatever their status, there was an undeniable tendency to ambivalence or even a faint furtiveness among the guests at Iveragh on this midsummer. It was a regrettable reality that Gibbon Fitzgibbon's pending appearance at the tribunal, technically guiltless though he might be, meant there was the possibility that he could shortly become a person with whom you would prefer to be no more than casually associated. This was a condition of course emphatically not yet his. And his party, an annual mainstay of the social calendar, had this year the significance, the added frisson, of asserting that it never would.

But the danger, remote though it was, nevertheless did exist. And it was eliciting from Gibbon an especially hearty and swashbuckling performance and was the cause of an undefined unease in his guests. It was not at all palpable, but there was a hint, a tricklet of an undercurrent of discomfort at what choices might lie ahead and an unusually keen computation of who had not yet shown up at the party and therefore might even, God forbid, be suspected of having already jumped ship. Most of the Fitzgibbons' acquaintance empathised with Gibbon's position.

They were in revolt against the grinding machinations of the tribunals. They wouldn't wish to be the first to jump. But neither would they wish to be on the loser's side. They were watching their backs, they were observing each other with something of the suspicion of conspirators kept unaccountably in the dark about the plot. To banish these unspoken intimations of treachery and danger they drank more and more Bolly and a somewhat premature buzz of merriment was soon filling the golden drawing rooms of Iveragh.

Yasmin O'Brien made a rather grand entrance in an important-looking robe-type dress. Tom recognised her look as Celtic themed. Relieved at being released from 'the lads', he made his way over to her. Yasmin introduced him again to Vasile, her poet friend who came from some ancient land in the foothills of the Urals. They had met, she explained, some months before at a literary conference in Rome. Vasile was the fellow who had sat mutely through all the drinking on the night of the Academy Exhibition. He was looking no less gloomy now than he did on that occasion.

Yasmin's presence soothed the socially anxious in a way the wealthy men of affairs and the bunch of politicos, full of apparent candour though they were, could not. She had intellectual cachet and enough celebrity to placate any fears afflicting the timid that one might be in the wrong place just now. All the same she did not come gilt-edged. Could artistic people really be counted on? Weren't they often lax and unpredictable in their moral judgements? Liable to make gestures of support that could be considered rebellious merely for rebellion's sake? They could be perverse . . .

This evening Yasmin was eager to speak of her distress, though in her admirably controlled way, at the tragic destiny of the Irish salmon. Her snake bangles clinked emphatically as she waved her hands around in a generous display of indignation.

'. . . Noble and courageous creatures . . . Their natural habitat the waters of the wild ocean and the rushing rivers . . . Gifted

with instincts we can't even begin to fathom . . . Deprived . . .
Depraved! Yes, depraved . . . Confined from birth in tanks. In
tanks! In ponds grey and filthy with murk and disease.'

'Poor fishes,' murmured Vasile. 'But of course, pigs as well,
they live the same.'

'Pigs? But pigs aren't salmon, Vasile. Salmon are noble
creatures, courageous . . . Still,' she conceded, 'it's not a bad
comparison. Actually, those ponds are exactly like pig-sties.
Filthy and smelly and disease-ridden.'

'A pig may be happy in his smelly little house,' objected
Vasile. 'To him it may be a palace.'

'I don't see what the perceptions of a pig have to do with it.'
To show her displeasure Yasmin turned aside, raising her eyes to
the lofty ceiling where moulded bows and trailing ribbons were
delicately picked out in gold.

'How beautiful,' she breathed, distracted from her cause.
'Would you say it's Italian?'

Vasile refused to share in her enthusiasm. He kept his eyes
morosely bent on the burnished parquet.

'Executed of course by Irish craftspeople,' Yasmin continued.
'We mustn't forget how gifted were our craftspeople.' Her long
heavy robe had vaguely druidic motifs painted down the front
and was held together with an array of metallic pins in the shapes
of swords, snakes and fishes. With an affronted air, Vasile
wandered off towards the French doors thrown open invitingly
to the exterior. Out there he could nurse his wounds and have
a smoke.

'These artificial habitats – can't they be cleaned up?' asked
Tom.

'I want those farms shut down, I want them banned,' Yasmin
told him firmly. 'The salmon must be free to roam in the
independence of their natures. They must be liberated.'

'Have you talked about this to Etchen MacAnar? Sounds to
me like it could be an issue he'd be happy to go with. I'd say he's
a man to get something going.'

Yasmin gave an ironic laugh. 'Etchen MacAnar? I'm sorry, but you must be fucking joking. MacAnar's in the thick of the fish farm interests.'

'Really?' Tom eyed her doubtfully.

'Yasmin! You're looking absolutely splendid.' A guy with a little goatee beard and round spectacles, obviously a Joyce admirer, came mooching over. 'Where's your wolfhound?'

Yasmin beamed. 'Would you bring that hairy beast into polite company, Finn? What would Seoda say?'

The room was filling up. Tom saw quite a few familiar faces, among them Denis Grogan. He seemed to have beaten back the competition and was seated in monopolistic position beside one of the blonde stunners. She listened to him with a rapt expression as he talked, but Tom was sure he saw her cast covert and wistful glances around the room.

Dol, who had disappeared for a while, was now back in circulation, calmly and decorously, he was relieved to see. And at last Seoda had made her long-awaited entry. In gracious hostess mode she was moving from group to group, the glittering folds of her diaphanous sea-coloured garment providing an occasional flash of comely limbs.

Any remaining trace of discomfort felt by the guests at accepting hospitality from a possibly soon-to-be-outed malefactor had evaporated clean away by now with the arrival of several noteworthy faces equipped with impeccable credentials. There was that up-and-coming actor whose name hardly anyone could remember – but what did that matter? And Voxy, the fiercely politically conscious and famous rock star, sitting cross-legged on the floor in front of a chair occupied by an important-looking woman in a feathered headdress, was a great coup. There were at least two wholly respectable film directors. And an emissary from the American embassy, of lesser rank than the ambassador, but considered to be far more formidable. It was also gratifying to spy Lord Nenagh, who, though admittedly not all that choosy about the milieux he patronised, was definitely a catch for any host. A token lord had to be better than none.

Lord Nenagh had at once made tracks, albeit in a slouching and circumambulatory manner, towards the end of the long sofa opposite Denis Grogan's where the other stunner was reclining, and had seen off her suitors with a penetrating glance from his blue eyes. He was now dropping references into his conversation that caused her sheeny skin to tingle with the most delicious sensations and her eyes to sparkle. She was looking more and more beautiful.

Indeed everyone and everything was. The perfect evening too was growing more and more beautiful as the sun fixed the room in its sultry rays on its infinitely slow trajectory towards a balmy twilight and the dancing. It was a perfect setting, and a perfect party. Above the lyrical din Gibbon's boisterous laugh could be heard as he entertained the ambassador's emissary with tales of old Ireland. He looked both boyish and masterful, the inheritor come into his estate. He looked like a man that nothing could hurt or damage or hinder. He turned now and gripped Tom's shoulder.

'Meet a compatriot, Tom. Mr Sontag. But maybe you're acquainted already? Mr Sontag is from your part of the world.'

Tom and Mr Sontag were not acquainted but they both agreed that they were more than glad now to be. Tom described himself as a vice president of the Gast Corporation – among other things of course – and his business agenda as having an exploratory nature, valiantly depicting his great-uncle's absurd delusions in conventional and acceptable guise. The First something-or-other nodded sagely and adverted to Ireland's tax breaks for business which – here he dropped his voice significantly – the Gast Corporation would be finding more than favourable.

'Couldn't do better than that kind of accommodation, in the short-term certainly . . . But I have no doubt, Tom,' he added as a grace-note, 'that you know a lot more than I do about all this.'

Tom managed to both demur and assent to this proposition which seemed to please Mr Sontag.

Here they were interrupted by Seoda to demand of Tom whether somebody called Johnny had approached him about his Platonique concept. Platonique, she assured him, was totally wonderful. And then to Tom's relief she carried off Mr Sontag to meet Lord Nenagh – and also, perforce, the stunner, to Mr Sontag's obvious pleasure.

Tom wanted space to recoup, especially after his encounter with his compatriot. He thought he had been pretty successful in his handling of him but felt a bit of an impostor. Evasiveness and vagueness disguised as urbanity weren't easy to pull off. If only he could find something his great-uncle was willing to invest in. Something normal, corporate, approbatory, some-thing he could present like a badge or an office to people like Mr Sontag. Pender was impossible. He should never have got himself into this situation. Well, a breath of fresh country air would be good. With a purposeful manner he shouldered his way through the mirthful throng towards the gardens.

Beyond the French doors a walled court, what Seoda called the 'piazza', lay between him and the open spaces of the park. In a former life this had been the kitchen garden, an area given over by the previous inhabitants of Iveragh to the cultivation of the humble vegetable and a gnarled forest of cooking-apple trees. Seoda regarded the production of kitchen fodder to be lacking in the sublime. There were enough organic smallholders scattered across the county for that. 'Let us cultivate beauty,' she instructed Gibbon.

The mundane and the utilitarian had been banished from her estate. The piazza's sun-baked walls now contained exotic and rare trees, their foliage fascinating and unseasonal shades of hot pink and lemon and subtle water features poetically murmuring. There were other intriguing artefacts such as a huge modernistic sundial inspired by the Incas.

And wrapped in the still shadows of the trees were disposed

this evening, like life-size and remarkably novel garden statuary, persons with mobiles pressed to their ears. Smoke wafted from many cigarettes. Along the paths that looked in their bright glister as if they had been gravelled with precious stones from the mines of Arabia, around the serried complexes of recherché shrubs and plants, numbers of others wandered in single file like seekers of solitude, talking into their phones and dragging on their cigarettes. Often, a woman would have to stop to shake a pebble from her flimsy footwear and she would stand expertly on one stilettoed foot as she talked, her buttocks pertly outlined in her thin dress. Sometimes one of them – he had run into her in a bar perhaps? – would throw Tom a preoccupied 'Hi Tom' as he passed. But mostly they gave him only a bright and abstracted smile.

It was an impressive sight, these people who seemed never to sleep, behaving here on a festive evening in the deeps of the countryside like city dealers in a trading room, the intent words they spoke to their pocas lost in the chattering evensong of birds. But they were more likely, Tom knew, to be listening to the game in Cordoba or setting up the golf for the weekend . . . Setting up a girl, a score for later . . . Or they could even, however humdrum Seoda might find it, be checking up on the babysitter. Of course, the sitters Seoda found for Saibhir were the kind one didn't ever need to check and she was irritated by those who couldn't do the same.

Passing through a small powdered-steel door Tom found himself in the park. In front of him, grassy acres of an astonishing green rolled away towards the flat horizon, on which flocks of small, very white and winsome sheep were grazing, picturesque and playful as the sheep of Marie Antoinette. At stately intervals, trees spread out their spacious boughs. He strolled along a broad and mossy track, like a way for drovers and carts in some long gone and more pastoral century. He had walked some distance when he came upon Yasmin's poet. Vasile was hunched under one of the chestnut trees in the very attitude of one of those drovers taking a rest from his trek to the eastern port.

'Beautiful place,' called out Vasile in greeting. 'Very beautiful.'

Languidly he gestured towards the surrounding landscape. Tendrils of bluish smoke floated from his nostrils into the motionless sunlit foliage above his head.

'I am seeking the consolations of nature,' he informed Tom.

'I can't imagine a finer spot for it.'

'But I am sad. I do not find what I am looking for.' Vasile looked very mournful. 'Maybe I am homesick. Maybe a poet is always a little bit homesick? Even when he does not know where is his home.'

'Even more, perhaps, then,' Tom agreed. 'You don't like it here?'

'Like, dislike . . . these are questions of preference. They are questions for children. They are not important, Tom.'

'I'd have said they're fundamental,' Tom protested.

'Okay. You are right. They are primitive so they are fundamental.' Vasile's ennui was too great for argument. 'And yes, to answer your question, I do not like it here. What's to like?' he demanded. 'If you are a poet like me, what's to like? Tell me that. All I see around me is that the soul of this people has flied away.' With his long poetic fingers he made weary undulations towards the blue vault above. 'And you see? They have lost the land.' He gestured towards the lush parkland of Iveragh. 'Oh, I am foolish, I have the Irish imagination. No, I must correct myself, I used to have it. Since I was a boy I know all about them. Do you know their little people, Tom? And their banshees? I loved them to death. I was inspired . . . Listen, only to think about this wild crazy people and I would cry. The poet Yeats . . . I loved that guy. And what do I find when I come at last to his homeland? He is some old guy nobody cares about, fading on the wall in an old pub. Have you seen him hanging there in those places? He gets no respect. I come here and I find people who think only about money. Greedy people. The soul is lost. They would be happy to have a dictator to boss them and then they would not have to think. Not to think at all. Never.'

Stubbing out his cigarette, Vasile gave a weary sigh. He had something else too on his mind. 'Yasmin is a difficult woman,' he remarked heavily.

'She's a strong woman, I'd say,' said Tom helpfully. He was moved to encourage Vasile, put forward a positive view of Yasmin.

'She would like me to be different. She wants to change me. But it is not possible. I tell her, I do not change myself for any woman and she will not be the first to make me do it.'

'She's on a no-hoper there for sure,' Tom agreed. 'No woman can change a man. Or vice versa.'

This was a truism nobody could argue with, and Tom should know. He had produced it often enough for Katya.

Vasile gave a sardonic laugh. 'Maybe I would like to change Yasmin a little. But I would not try. I would have no chance, I know it.'

The echoing tones of a gong came faint but clear from the house.

'Supper, I guess,' suggested Tom.

'You are hungry?' Vasile sounded surprised, as if mere hunger was something he had long left behind. 'Okay,' he conceded. 'Maybe I could eat something.'

Slowly and languidly he stood up. Together they began to retrace their steps towards the house.

'These sheeps,' Vasile complained. 'Their fur so white. It's terrible. I think they are washed in expensive shampoo.'

Tom laughed. 'Could be the rain, I guess. They get showers on a regular basis . . .' He came to a stop and looked at Vasile. 'You were talking about the soul,' he said. 'Do you think the soul of a people, if it's been lost, can be found? Can it be . . . you know . . . put back somehow?'

'You mean, like in a house? Can you replace an old thing . . .'
Vasile frowned. 'An old bath . . . Restoration?'

'Something like,' Tom conceded.

'No. I don't think it's possible,' said Vasile firmly. 'No way.'
Mirthlessly he laughed. 'Oh, they will try of course. Crazy
foolish people with crazy ideas. Some crazy religion . . . Many
religions, the health of the body, the soul, it is all the same to
them . . . they will give themselves to anything.'

'Yeah, I know. Just like back home,' said Tom ruefully.

'Like everywhere.'

Back in the piazza Yulia and her colleagues were going
around proffering trays of tempting tit-bits. The poca users
munched abstractedly on morsels of fruits of the sea and other
delicacies as they talked. The trees were making long filigreed
shadows that reached far across the paths, evoking faintly
melancholic intimations of the passing of beauty and of time.
Rather a pleasing melancholy, Tom thought, when time and
beauty are still on your side. Vasile picked a single quail's egg
from a passing tray and ate it slowly and wincingly as if it were
some kind of medication.

'You know, life can be simple,' he ruminated. 'That is a nice
life. A little bit eat, a little bit drink, a bit love . . . What more
can they want? Okay . . .' He qualified his statement. 'A bit
truth. But not too much . . . Of course a little bit melancholy
also, for the soul.'

In the drawing rooms the crowd was thinning out. People
were drifting downstairs to graze on the more substantial fare
now being served in the dining hall. Gibbon ambled purposefully
by, a straggle of guests in his wake. He caught sight of Tom.

'Hey, Tom. Do you want to come up to the gallery to have
a look at my Shiels?' Graciously, he seized Vasile's arm. 'I'd be
glad too to have a poet's opinion. The poets are said to have the
best eye, you know.'

Vasile gave a charmed smile. 'Let me tell you already, Mr
Fitzgibbon. I believe Mr Aodhgan Shiel is first class.'

Gibbon beamed. In convivial and ragged file, the guests trooped behind him up the grand staircase and into the Shiel Room. This was a low ivory-painted salon with ivory-satined couches disposed down the middle and lined ivory-coloured blinds drawn down to protect the works of the renowned artist from the rude light of day. At least a dozen of Shiel's works were hanging there and each one of them was displayed, bright with the panache of established genius, under its own superbly positioned arc of artificial light. All of them, Tom saw at once, were larger by far than the space awaiting Carey Kinane's single beloved Shiel. Making loud murmurs of appreciation, the guests moved slowly from one to another, pointing out their favourites.

After a little interval had been allowed for individual appraisal, Gibbon planted himself in front of the largest of his Shiels and embarked on his Shiel lecture for the benefit, as he explained, of newcomers among his guests – and here he gestured at Tom – 'such as Tom, my American friend here'. Gibbon liked nothing better than an excuse to give his Shiel lecture.

Aodhgan Shiel, he began, could be regarded as the holder of the position of national painter. The position might not be officially recognised but it was implicitly his in the way James Joyce was implicitly the national author. Gibbon hadn't yet got around to reading Joyce but he knew that his man could only gain from a presumption of association with the great modernist.

However, while Joyce had presented urban man – Gibbon knew enough about him to confidently make this assertion – Shiel presented the vibrant world of the countryside. He painted a world, now sadly lost – 'the world of my own people, my antecedents', said Gibbon – in the middle part of the last century, itself a period also lost but now repositioned in the past patinated with nostalgia, romance and innocence that were not so evident when it flourished.

Untainted by the power-hunger and the corruption and the repression that were undeniably a part of those years, Shiel had gone about his solitary art. He painted the people, the small people of the small fields and the small towns. The people who were the real stuff of the nation.

In eulogistic terms Gibbon spoke of the seminal figure of Jack Devine. This was Jack Devine of Devine Plastics, one of the founding fathers of Irish industry and arguably the greatest of them all. Jack always had a superb eye for a business opportunity. When he turned that eye on art, it fell at once on Aodhgan Shiel. The boys coming up behind him, seeing that Jack's eye for a picture was, as for all things, good, followed his lead. Soon there was a brisk and dizzy trade among them in Aodhgan Shiels. In the auction rooms they bid against each other for a Shiel in the same friendly spirit of competitiveness with which they met on the golf course.

'That's Fitzgibbon's take on it, anyway,' someone muttered enigmatically into Tom's ear. It was Denis Grogan, standing with something of a skulking demeanour behind Tom's shoulder.

'Is it not true?' Tom whispered.

'Whisht, whisht,' Denis murmured stagily in reply.

'They're certainly worth a few bob,' Gibbon was telling his listeners. He was jocular now, cutting to the chase, pleasing the crowd. After all, you couldn't give wall space, the implication was, let alone an entire salon at Iveragh – not if you were Gibbon Fitzgibbon – to pictures that weren't worth a few bob. This would suggest a serious failure of taste. 'But I don't give two cents for that. To me they're priceless.'

There were murmurs of approbation at this forthright statement which seemed to cloak everyone in goodness, followed by a rising tide of applause.

'The FitUp Comes to Ballintubber,' read out Tom, peering at a title. The painting was of one of Shiel's most characteristic subjects, vintage conveyances or farm machinery emitting clouds that could be steam or exhaust fumes, the picturesquely attired crowd around it, also characteristic, indistinct in the miasma.

'A fine piece of work,' Denis assured Tom. 'A classic. Worth every penny Gibbon paid for it. There were three of them after it on the day, all ready to go the distance. I remember it well. Here he was holed up at Iveragh, putting the calls in to Sotheby's. But he beat them all.'

Denis described Gibbon's devil-may-care attitude as the bidding went through the roof. 'Once he's at the races Gibbon will always go the distance. And I must say it's a fine thing to see one of our own rated with the likes of Picasso.'

'Sure is,' Tom agreed. What was it Carey had said about Grogan? He had beans to spill on Gibbon. Just now he seemed to be see-sawing between muted antagonism and muted affection.

'A bit of a genius, Gibbon, for all his faults,' mused Denis. 'Always was hard to tell what he'd be into next.'

'Oh, you have to keep a weather eye out with Gibbon, I'd say,' smiled Tom.

'You keep an eye on him, Tom.' Denis gazed thoughtfully at Gibbon's buoyant stance not far off as he explained the finer points of a picture to the intent faces surrounding him.

He lowered his voice. 'He could be getting into a bit of stormy weather. He's not used to storms. He'll try to ride it out. But will he? That's the question.'

'Well, even the best of men has his enemies, I guess,' remarked Tom.

Denis's expression was brooding. 'We all have our enemies.'

A fresh horde of Shiel enthusiasts had made an appearance in the gallery. As Tom began to descend the stairs Gibbon was embarking on his lecture once more. Denis had taken Tom's arm in a firm grip and every couple of steps he would come to a halt the better to emphasise a point in his discourse. Now he was talking about money and how it was misunderstood. When Tom attempted to move on, he would extend an arm in front of him, ably barring his progress.

'It's innate, it's an instinct. Was there ever a man who made a few honest pence and didn't want to turn it into a quid? I'm talking old money, Tom, cents and dollars to you. What about the talent for money? How are they going to talk that away? They won't breed that out. Money is like a rabbit, Tom. Money has to make money like a rabbit has to make rabbits . . .' Denis halted again. 'The small men with their small minds – all they want is to harass and hinder fellows like ourselves. But they have the power, Tom. And so they are dangerous men. The power and the danger, there's a bad combination . . .'

Tom had managed to steer Denis as far as the second bend of the gracefully curving staircase. Absently his gaze took in a pink head bobbing swiftly upwards through the melee on the stairs. She had done something to her hair, she had done quite a deal. It was a bright acid-pink, a tufted mop of pink. But he would have known that face under any guise.

Denis Grogan's clasp tightened. 'We have dangerous people among us. Very dangerous.'

'Don't worry, Tom, it may never happen,' Eileen called out with a whimsical laugh as she passed. He wheeled about but she had already rounded the bend and vanished. And Denis was moving on down, his grip on Tom no less determined. His face had reddened. Was he drunk? Paranoid? He was using words like 'sabotage' and 'conspiracy' . . . but Tom had lost any capacity to listen.

The bottom of the stairs was in view. Denis stopped again and fixed Tom with a challenging look.

'Well? What do you say? Is that a rosy outlook?'

'You're absolutely right,' Tom answered distractedly.

Grogan's expression relaxed. 'Good man,' he said. He released Tom from his grip and ushered him onward down the remaining steps. He had the air of someone who had concluded a deal. Zestfully he rubbed his hands together. He seemed in much better form now. 'Well, I'm ready for a bit of nosh,' he declared.

She must have been making for the Shiel Room. But would

she be so interested in the Shiels? Looking for a bathroom, maybe? But there must be several bathrooms disposed around the ground floor. She could be anywhere; the house was vast . . . Tom turned to go back up.

A lanky young man in a bow-tie was standing in the hall calling out brisk instructions and directing with arm extended like a traffic policeman wandering guests towards the dining hall below. Firmly, Denis steered him in their wake.

'This way, Tom.'

A flight of narrow candle-lit stairs, formerly the service stairs and still atmospherically chaste in contrast to the grandeur above, led to the lower regions of the house. One of the golden girls swayed sexily towards them. They stood at the bottom of the stairs to let her pass.

'Go on, you knackers,' she smiled in her husky voice. 'If you don't hurry up they'll be out of caviare.'

'You're making me hungry now,' called Denis gamely back. She swung her glittering little shoulder bag playfully in response.

'Knackers?' asked Tom. 'What was that about?'

'Oh, she was just being friendly.'

Denis turned to watch her retreating back. 'She's off to the jakes now to do a line, I'd say.' He gave Tom a buddy-like slap. 'Come on. Let's see what our host is cooking up.'

The big old gloomy kitchen of Iveragh, at one time the smoky den of mutinous and ill-trained menials, was a spacious and well-lit hall where a staff of handsome young people were carrying around platters bearing appetising arrangements of high-protein, high-vitamin-content comestibles. The eggs of small fowl and large fishes were replaced now by the choicer parts of exotic baby animals cut with ingenious artistry to be dipped in thin densely flavoured liquids or seasoned with highly coloured and concentrated powders. Others were proffering wine bottles swathed in snowy napkins which they unravelled with a ceremonial flourish to display the label as they poured.

'Château Fitzgibbon,' they would gravely announce.

Denis promptly accepted a glass. 'Go on, it's not bad at all,' he said.

Cautiously, Tom tasted some of the red Château Fitzgibbon and made a grateful murmur. It was quite drinkable.

'Hails from his vineyard,' Denis explained. 'Not exactly what you'd call a grand cru classe. But a fair enough sup as they go.'

'Gibbon grows vines here? At Iveragh?' demanded Tom.

Denis chortled. 'Irish vines? What do you want? Château Bally-in-the-rain? What kind of respect would that get you? Oh no, like all the boys, Gibbon bought into France.' He looked meaningfully at Tom. 'Let me tell you, we can count ourselves lucky that mein host tonight bought where he did. And more to the point, that he has a fellow down there who knows his oenology. We can safely knock back the Château Fitz.'

An increasing peril of these house parties, he confided, was often such a 'wine of the house', proudly presented. It might be the only wine on offer. From the perspective of the guest, there was a natural but potentially unfortunate tendency in a viticulturist host to look rather too fondly on his own production, shipped in from his outpost in France.

'Although I do have an eye on a place myself,' Denis confided. 'In fact, I'm going down next week to check it out.'

And you were entitled to the bit of pride, he pointed out. After all you were following in an old tradition; you could regard yourself in a way as a descendant of the Wild Geese, at one with nobler men and nobler times.

Denis suddenly looked morose again. 'The exiled. The betrayed. Do you know what I'm saying, Tom?'

Tom didn't know. He was particularly ignorant about the reference to wild geese. But he didn't feel up to to a history lesson just now. He was looking restlessly around for a sighting of a pink head.

'Sure I do,' he assured Denis.

Gibbon came bounding over. 'Hey guys. What do you think of our château bottled?' He had a boyish bashfulness.

'Excellent,' Tom said. 'Very drinkable.'

'Top class,' said Denis. 'Though maybe not quite as good as you gave us last year.'

Gibbon smiled as if he hadn't heard. He placed a friendly arm around Denis's shoulders. 'Could have been an appellation of course only I got into the Grenache. I fell for the old Grenache.'

Tom nodded. He was impressed by Gibbon's oenological erudition.

'That's the rebel in me, I suppose. The Wild Goose, you could say?'

Denis shook himself free. 'That might be going a bit far now.'

Gibbon stepped back and looked keenly at Tom. 'If you're thinking of doing business with Grogan here, let me tell you now you couldn't do better.'

'I'll bet,' said Tom lamely.

Gibbon turned and surveyed with satisfaction the festive mill he had gathered about him. 'Good party. You know, it's great to know the old crowd won't let you down.'

'We're all with you,' said Denis. 'You know that, Gibbon.'

'Course I do,' said Gibbon softly. But the expression in his large eyes was not soft.

Denis took a sip of his Château Fitz. 'A good vintage. It'd be a few years back, I'd say. Two thousand?'

'Ninety-nine,' said Gibbon shortly. He looked at Tom. 'Where's Dol? I've hardly seen sight or sound of her all evening. What's she up to?'

'Oh, Dol is around,' said Tom. 'I caught a glimpse of her upstairs a while ago.'

'Happy?'

'She seemed happy.'

'Good. Hope she stays that way.'

'Dol,' meditated Denis as Gibbon bounded away. 'One of the Kinanes. A bit of a handful. Have you run into the Kinanes, Tom?'

'I have,' said Tom stoutly. 'Great family.'

'Ah,' was all Denis Grogan said. He bit into a small but luscious thigh. 'God knows, Fitzgibbon would get up on a back rasher . . .'

Gibbon came hurrying back, at his heels a smiling floppy-haired man in a pinstripe suit of a debonair cut.

'Tom . . .' He ushered the man forward as if he were a bearer of gifts. 'You wanted to get acquainted with Etchen MacAnar. Well, here he is. The man himself.'

'Etchen MacAnar,' exclaimed Tom. He put out his hand. 'I'm honoured indeed, Mr MacAnar. May I say I've been looking out for the chance to meet you.' He found that in his fervour he was stammering a little.

'Certainly you may, Mr Blessman. Are you telling me my fame has spread as far as that great city to the west?'

'I've heard you speak. On the radio. I'm a big fan. One of many, I guess.'

'On the radio, was it? Marvellous medium, the radio.'

Appraisingly, Etchen MacAnar looked at Tom. It was a look, Tom saw, that conveyed keenness, candour, a deep intelligence. Perhaps also a hint of defensiveness as if he expected attack from some quarter. But with it there was a forceful conviction of his own strength of character, the knowledge that he would be more than equal to dealing with the attack when it came. It was a look, Tom felt sure, of one hundred per cent proof integrity.

'Etchen is very impressed with my Shiels,' put in Gibbon. 'He says I have the best collection in the country.'

'And I'll say it again,' said Etchen.

As Etchen MacAnar spoke of Shiel's painterly qualities and his seminal importance, Tom listened to the rich and wholesome voice that had so impressed him in its broadcast guise. He found it, now that he was face to face with the great man, even richer, more wholesome and more true. He took in the distinguished presence of Etchen MacAnar in the flesh: the arched imperial nose, the silky greying locks, the timeworn honesty of his expression. An expression suggestive also, Tom thought, of a vulnerability that must inspire anyone to give him a hand, to assist him in his work. Etchen was not a big man, but his presence was big. He had not been mistaken about this man.

Denis Grogan, shifting from one foot to the other, was clearly bored by the subject of Aodhgan Shiel. Murmuring something about 'going to find Marguerite', he excused himself with a nod and moved off. Giving Tom a self-satisfied pat, Gibbon too moved off though in the opposite direction.

'I've heard you refer to certain problems here in Ireland, Mr MacAnar,' prompted Tom. 'You're very concerned with them, I know.'

'Indeed we have great problems, Mr Blessman, in this little land of ours. Sadly my role at present is confined largely to the contemplative. But we can only try to do what we can.'

'What are the problems you consider to be the most pressing?' asked Tom humbly.

Etchen sighed. 'A difficult question, Mr Blessman. Many are not amenable to easy resolution.' He paused, contemplated. Decisively then he spoke. 'Top of the list, I'd love to be able to do something for our travelling people. Our lucht siul. Yes, our lucht siul are dear to my heart. Always have been.'

'Your travelling people?' queried Tom.

'They are our nomadic tribe. Our native nomads. Their origins are obscure and much debated. But I'm not alone in believing them to be an ancient and a noble race. Their lot is a hard one, Mr Blessman. Marginalised, despised, like all nomadic tribes in settled communities. Oh yes, they've had a great deal to endure. A great deal to put up with.'

Etchen accepted a top-up for his glass from a passing waiter.

'Where are these people? Are there many of them? Can I meet them?' Tom's excitement was mounting.

'Oh, you'll hardly find them here.' Etchen gestured at the flushed and baying company around them. 'No, Mr Blessman, they are to be found on the edge, the fringes. The forlorn edges of our towns and cities, the fringes of society, wandering about from place to place. And there's a fair number of them, if you count in the diaspora . . . It might be merely a question of costumery of course,' he mused intriguingly. 'Tell me, Mr Blessman, do you know the history of the red squirrel and the grey squirrel?'

'I can't say I do. Maybe you'd tell me, Mr MacAnar?'

But just at that moment, a plump young woman in a red dress splashed with green hieroglyphic motifs thrust herself on Etchen and whispered confidingly in his ear. He laughed and, to Tom's dismay, allowed himself, like a patient and beloved guru in the hands of a breathless disciple, to be led away.

'Can I call you?' Tom yelled.

Etchen turned and waved in gracious assent.

22

The noise level had heightened considerably. It was that moment in a party's life cycle when it has reached its prime. The many and various inebriants on offer have well and truly kicked in, the happiness and the self-confidence of the guests know no bounds and they're at their most assertive and, it has to be said, raucous. A fragile moment but great while it lasts.

With benign favour, Tom looked about him. He himself was filled with a sense of optimism and power, although of course in a higher key. He felt his sense of purpose renewed. Travelling people. Nomads. People of no property, descended, if he had understood Etchen MacAnar correctly, from noble Irish clans, wandering the small country roads and by-ways . . . It was nothing less than Pender's dream actualised. His dream people had come to life. And Etchen MacAnar would know what was to be done for them; he would direct him to the solution. What was that about the red squirrel and the grey? An enigmatic reference, in the context of the discussion.

There was a dogged aspect to Tom's personality that he shared with his great-uncle. He did not take on a task lightly, and this one he had taken on with extreme reluctance. But once he did he generally saw it through. Right now his great-uncle's conviction seemed to be uncharacteristically weak but Tom's was strengthening. He had found a focus, and in Etchen MacAnar a man who promised to be an inspiring guide and helpmeet. Through the waves of rosy jolly faces and brandished egos he made his way upstairs. In the more or less deserted salon, the long optimistic twilight glowed in the windows, dusky and velvety, the long twilight of midsummer in these parts that would never quite give way to night.

He drifted out onto the piazza. Tapers had been applied to the outdoor candles. Steady and unflickering they burned in the motionless air. As he meandered along the shining pebbled paths Dol's familiar voice hailed him. As he came up to her he was struck by the impression she gave of loneliness and despondency. She had lapsed onto a kind of throne, carved from the limestone native to Iveragh to look playfully regal. She called out to him and patted the wide scrolled arm-rest for him to sit.

'It's a Callaghan, you know. Big name in parkland sculpture.'

'Comfortable, is it?'

'Comfortable? It's fucking torture.'

She looked rooted in her chosen solitude. She had kicked off her party shoes and was chafing her long knobbed toes with one hand and dragging on a cigarette with the other. Tom placed himself on the arm-rest. It was warm to the touch – from the heat of the day probably. Though the seats on the piazza might very well be fitted with their own ingenious heating apparatus . . . The lengths to which Gibbon and Seoda might go in the name of innovation and luxury could not be overestimated.

The air was fragrant with something strong and opiate. Tall upright flowers stood in clusters a little way off, their colours washed pale by the dusky light. Dol tossed her fag-end in their direction and rooted in her pearlescent evening bag. Moodily she extracted a fresh smoke.

'Light up that for me, will you?'

'Sorry, I don't have a lighter.'

She pointed to a candle nearby. 'You can take a light off that.'

'But you don't smoke, Dol,' Tom chided.

'I'm a smoker tonight.' Her voice was drowsy.

'Did you take something? What are you on?'

'What are you on!' She laughed as if the question was hilarious.

'I've been talking with Etchen MacAnar,' he told her. 'He seems like a really good guy, I must say. A fantastic guy.'

'A fantastic guy!' Dol found this hilarious also. 'I saw you talking to Gibbon,' she stated then. She had an accusing note as if some rule or agreement between them had been broken.

'You did? He was looking for you.'

'Keeping a watch, I suppose . . . What were you talking about?'

'I don't recall. Small talk, I guess.'

'Naturally. Does Gibbon do any other kind?'

'He does good enough talk,' Tom protested.

Dol affected an ingratiating voice. 'Oh, excuse me. Gibbon can be very deep. Oh yes, you'd be surprised at how deep darling Gibbon can be. Oh, Gibbon's okay,' she conceded then. 'But he has terrible taste.'

'I don't see all that much wrong with his taste.' Tom looked agreeably around him.

'Oh, the place is fine. He has his people to do that for him. But he has bad taste in his friends. Don't you think? I really don't like his friends.'

'Your sister is here,' remarked Tom.

'I know.' She blew smoke into the air. 'Seoda must have invited her.'

'Seoda?'

'Seoda wouldn't do a party without her sweetie supplier to hand.'

'What do you mean?'

'What do you think I mean?' She gave a sardonic laugh.

Tom considered the proposition. With a grinding noise the dark mass of a helicopter climbed into the sky above the piazza walls and lurched away towards the east.

'Let's get out of here,' said Dol with decision. 'Let's get back to the capital for God's sake.'

'Back to Dublin? Now?' Tom did not sound eager.

'We can find the driver. He's waiting backstage to take us.'

Dol gestured towards the graceful group of reconstructed coach-houses and granaries beyond the wall. 'He has his riding orders to take us whenever we want, whether he likes it or not.'

'I'm not sure I'm ready to leave,' Tom said.

'Don't, Tom,' said Dol after a little. 'Don't do it.'

How heavy and drowsy her voice was.

'What are you talking about?'

'Don't go falling for her.'

'Who said I'm falling?' hedged Tom.

'You guys are always falling for her. And it's never any good. Look, I'm telling you. It won't work.'

'Why won't it work?'

'She's a mess. She's dysfunctional.'

'Who the fuck's functional?' His laugh was forced.

'Yeah, okay. You're dead right, Tom. To be human is to dysfunction.' Gloomily she fished for her sandals. 'Even my fucking feet are dysfunctional.'

She trailed ahead of him along the glistering paths. The laughter that wafted now onto the piazza from the salon sounded unrestrained, histrionic. It seemed to carry possible undertones of belligerence. Behind them, another 'copter thundered into the stubborn glow of the sky.

'Forget it,' advised Dol tiredly. 'Forget anything I said. You're not going to listen to me anyway. Look, I completely agree with you. In fact, I give you my blessing. All my sister's in need of is the love of a good man.'

'Get yourself some coffee or something,' Tom advised. 'You're not seeing straight.'

The party was drifting back into the salon. The women's hairdos were unravelling now, the men's laughs were slightly awry. There was still no sign of Eileen. He thought maybe he should make sure Dol got something to clear her head. He was about to follow as she set off a little unsteadily across the room but was held up, rather forcibly, by a young man. In a moment she was lost to sight. The young man introduced himself as

Johnny – spelled J-o-n-n-y. Jonny had been looking out for Tom all evening. He wanted to tell him about this fantastic thing he was working on. For the time of night Jonny was very determined and very focused.

It was his own idea, Jonny told him, totally original. He had sourced several experts who were eager to come on board once the finances were in place. Chemists, two top cosmetic surgeons, a fellow in elastics . . . The idea was some kind of a face-lift product.

'No cutting. No stitches. No blood. Nothing invasive. Just the mask. A second skin, perfect, tight, fine as silk . . . Oh, finer than that, supersuperfine. But you grasp the idea? She gets the exact face she wants, bespoke. The face she's dreamed of. Platonique – that's how we're branding it. The platonic face. Get it? Oh yes, platonism is alive and well and living in the suburbs. Platonism is a fantastic opportunity for business. The best we've had for a long time. Pure genius. And it has association power. Sounds a bit like plastics, right? Only fresh, new, the next level . . . The face wouldn't have to be original, mind you. Wouldn't sell if it was. Originality, that's absolutely the last thing she wants. She's had original all her life, it's what she wants out of. No, what she's after is the Hollywood face. A composite of, mind you. No one's face in particular. I've looked into it, the cost would be prohibitive. We'd be heavy into copyright. For the market we're targeting, the product has to be affordable.'

Jonny pulled a face. 'Think of what we'd have to pay some-body like Kidman. Or what's her name . . . Could be Dietrich of course. Or Monroe. Somebody who isn't around to argue. We could talk about it but I don't think so. That kind of face is dated, wouldn't appeal. No, my feeling is we'll go for the babyface look. Regular features, blue-eyed, blonde. That's the kind of look they want. They all want to be the same, basically. Just imagine it, Tom. Put yourself in a woman's place. No more lines, no more blotches, bumps, bad colouring . . . Ever again. The instant lift. Who wouldn't go for it?'

'Sounds great,' said Tom. 'But what about the eyes? The eyes can be a giveaway.'

Experienced eyes. Wise, or pained, or original eyes, looking out from a babyface mask . . . Mightn't be a good look.

'That's no problem. We've thought of that. We'll work on the eyes with contacts. I have a big eye-man coming on board. She'll get any colour she wants. A bit of colour, a bit of shine . . . Brilliant colours, fantastic shine. It's all sorted.'

'I love it,' said Tom. Shameful maybe, but if your enthusiasm was feeble, the easiest way out generally was to fake it.

'Who wouldn't love it? Right, Tom?' Jonny lowered his voice. 'You want in?'

'Good of you to offer, Jonny. But you know, I'm not sure it's my kind of thing.'

'This is a moral product, Tom, if that's your worry,' protested Jonny. 'It'll save lives. They can die under the knife, for God's sake. I have the figures. With us, there's no risk whatsoever and no pain. No abrasion, no stripping down, nothing to come off . . .'

'No pain, all gain?' offered Tom.

'Hey, that's good. I like that.' Jonny knitted his brows. 'No pain, all gain . . . We could nearly run with that. You sure, Tom? I don't think you'll want to pass. This is a product made for you. You're in tune with it already.'

'I'm sure,' Tom said firmly. He could see Jonny was the persistent type. 'Much as I love it I'm afraid my guys back home wouldn't be too keen. They're kinda conservative. Traditional? More into bricks and mortar, that kind of thing.'

'I only asked because Seoda said you'd be interested.' Jonny looked doleful. 'Seoda is going to be in bigtime.'

They both looked over at Seoda who stood leaning sinuously against the back of the saffron sofa. Her fingers were playing seductively with tendrils of her glossy hair as she attended to a voluble discourse from the ambassador of Roumania.

'Maybe you should talk to Seoda,' Jonny suggested. 'I think you should talk to Seoda.'

'Let me do that,' said Tom absently. He was watching Dol, who had come back into the room and seemed to be advancing towards Seoda and the ambassador. There was an impression of intent in her advance as if she had something important to say or do. She looked, he thought, like the character in a play at whose entrance the audience sits up, expecting action. She was staring fixedly ahead, Seoda in her line of sight. But on the other hand she could have been looking at anything or anyone on that side of the room. Tom waved to her but she took no notice. Probably she hadn't seen him.

'You should, Tom,' Jonny was saying. 'It's an opportunity you'd be sorry to miss. Why don't you think it over, get back to me. But don't leave it too long, there's a lot of people who'll be wanting in . . . Anyways, here's to good old Gibbon. He sure throws a good party.'

Jonny clinked Tom's raised glass. Dol had crossed the room now, was almost upon Seoda. She seemed more alert, must have got the coffee or something restorative. Arriving at the sofa however, she veered off, ignoring Seoda, who was still deeply absorbed in the ambassador, Tom was glad to see, and sank into its plump depths. Slowly she crossed her legs and took out a cigarette. Dammit, she was going to smoke; that could cause a situation . . . Or might Seoda be able to resist the opportunity to make a scene? From her bag Dol slowly took out a lighter, a cute little silver lighter . . . Where did she pick that up? She didn't have it out on the piazza . . . With uncharacteristic deliberation she flipped it open and brought it up to the cigarette.

Tom gave a low groan. Dol's behaviour really was too provocative.

He saw her turn sharply to the right. She appeared to be gesturing to somebody behind her. Any minute now Seoda would notice the cigarette, or sniff the smoking nicotine . . .

The slender flame of the lighter caught, fattened, flared. For a moment Tom watched it blaze. Like some terrific lambent hat, flame framed Seoda's head. It took him several seconds to realise that Seoda was alight. Her hair was on fire.

The gaze of the ambassador, concentrating on his discourse, was raised to the high and gorgeous ceiling. And while Seoda's eyes may have glazed over, they were still only for him. Oblivious apparently of what she had done, Dol got up from her seat and sauntered towards the fireplace.

Tearing off his jacket, Tom hurled himself forward towards the sofa. Flinging the jacket over Seoda's flaming head he bundled her up in it, clutching her to his chest. She screamed. The scream was muffled but it was shrill with outrage and fear. Unimpeded, the ambassador screamed much louder in his own language. Out of nowhere two large men in matching dark suits materialised at his side and flung him to the ground.

'What's going on?' Dol cried. Her cry had something artificial in it or theatrical. But it was a theatrical moment in fairness. She continued to stand at a distance by the fireplace taking urgent drags on her cigarette, a foot resting on the fender. The previously subtly scented air was acrid with the smell of burning.

'It's okay, everybody. Stay where you are,' shouted Tom with impressive authority. He had once taken a class in crisis management. The assembly stood quite still, their petrified glasses poised in front of them. Somebody uttered a deep and dramatic moan.

The ambassador stood up, shook himself like a dog and straightened his tie. 'Is she fine?' he asked. Legs splayed, his security stood by, challenging all comers. Gingerly, Tom freed Seoda from the restraints of the jacket.

Her hair came into view. In front and around her temples all was glossy and fair and lovely as before. But behind, there was a charred mess. A ragged and gaping nest made by a drunken sparrow, a tangle of shrunken and reeking frizz. She raised an arm and felt the back of her head. Black fragments of frizz floated wispily in the air like giant dust motes and settled on the golden cushions.

Seoda's horrified gaze found Dol Kinane. She was keeping her place by the fireplace, calmly smoking the fag-end of the cigarette. Seoda screamed all over again, even more lustily. At a run, Gibbon appeared, Saibhir's paediatrician at his heels.

'It was that woman.' Seoda's scream was angry now. 'She did it. Get her out of here.'

'I'm sorry,' Dol murmured. With remarkable composure she threw the fag-end in the cave-sized grate and walked away from the outraged faces and the baying that would follow and out onto the piazza. She walked with an air of sorrow and dignity. Or with as much dignity at least as a person can muster when she is wearing difficult footwear.

Weeping, Seoda left the room via another door, Gibbon's arm protectively wrapped, like a good well-trained bear's, around her heaving shoulders. They were followed closely by the paediatrician who, in an initial examination, had confirmed that the injury was cosmetic only. Behind him went Tom. An appalled and vociferously supportive cohort brought up the rear. She was guided upstairs to her quarters.

Luckily – Seoda was always lucky somehow in these ways – Felix was a guest at the party. Felix was the most celebrated of celebrity hairdressers, and of course Seoda's own coiffeur. And by some miracle he was still more or less compos mentis. But then Felix was famed for not losing the head no matter who else was losing theirs. He went straight to Seoda's side, shooed the hapless wringers of hands away and took full control of the emergency. Seoda's suite was closed even to Gibbon.

'Thanks, Tom. You're a hero,' murmured Gibbon.

In a subdued manner they descended the stairs together. Mutely Gibbon ushered Tom into his sunken library. The library was calm, cool, blessedly redolent of the rational sphere of time-hallowed paper and ink and intellectual enquiry. There was a smell of leather mixed with an agreeable smell of must.

Designer-library aroma. Tom was familiar with it from a few private libraries he was acquainted with back home.

Nothing for it but to attempt to restore a sense of calm and normality, Tom decided. He appraised the book-lined walls with a show of interest.

'Well, you appear to have a fine collection here, Gibbon,' he said heartily.

Gibbon emitted a kind of groan in reply. Lowering himself onto an opulent leather divan he broodingly buried his face in his hands.

Upstairs in the shaded dressing room, Felix was closeted with Seoda and was embarking on designing her new look. But she would not engage. Mopping her ravaged eyes and taking great gulps of Cristal she was refusing to look in the mirror.

'We wanted it off anyway – didn't we, darling? Too heavy, wasn't it? Dated, my darling Seo, if I'm honest. Really, pet, it was. And you're made for the gamine look, simply and utterly made for it. That bone structure, darling. Maybe I shouldn't tell you this, but I've been wanting to give you gamine for so long. I've been itching to do it, darling. Only you have such gorgeous hair . . .'

At this, Seoda emitted an anguished sob. Felix took a quick fortifying sip of champagne. He cupped her chin, tilted it upwards and gave her his most sparkling, his most flattering smile.

'I see it exactly. You'll look wonderful, Seo. Sleek on top. Feathery sides, shaped at the back, kind of wispy . . .' At the word wispy Seoda widened her eyes in renewed horror. 'What we want is a shape to display that fantastic skull.'

Gently he turned her head towards the mirror. Violently she twisted away from it. But in her eyes he read a furtive faint glimmering of hope, the tiniest dawning of a willingness to be consoled. Felix could tell, he always could tell, when victory was near, when a woman was close to submission.

'Are you going to do it now?' she whimpered.

'Oh, Seo, I wish I could. But I don't have my magic scissors, do I, darling?'

Accusingly she turned away from him.

'Now, Seo, I'm hardly going to carry the tools of my trade to the do of the year, am I? But first thing tomorrow – snip snip snip . . . We can do it here, if you like. We can have the magic scissors sent down the minute the salon opens. I'll close off all my appointments. Those Ballsbridge biddies will just have to wait. Seo, do you know something? You're going to be glad this happened. You'll be grateful to that stupid girl, flailing around with her lighted cigarette. Honest you will. And of course you'll have to get a new wardrobe. Think of what you'll be able to wear, darling. Lovely gamine kind of things . . .'

In the library Tom was examining, on the wall behind the divan on which Gibbon was slumped, an appealing and familiar image. He had recognised it almost at once as 'How Life Could Be', the painting he'd fallen for at the Academy. Gibbon had beaten him to it, unwittingly of course.

'Works well here,' Tom remarked. 'Good colours.' He felt a slight but quite unjustified resentment. It was certainly more appealing than his 'Ada' of which he had recently taken delivery.

'Yeah,' grunted Gibbon.

Tom set to leafing with a determined display of keenness through the tomes that he plucked at random from the shelves. Predictably they were first editions one and all, and more often than not signed by the long-dead author. Collectors' books, beautiful with the handsome bindings of other eras. In some of them he was surprised to see passages that were marked, albeit with delicate pencil strokes, and evidently by the same light hand. Was it a good idea, he suggested to Gibbon by way of distraction, to annotate these obviously valuable artefacts?

'Valuable? Who fucking cares?' Gibbon waved a slack hand around. 'They're my books.'

'Dead right,' Tom said.

'I go for the melancholy bits,' Gibbon explained tiredly. He was slumped in a supine attitude now on the divan. He looked exhausted. 'If you're basically a cheerful chap, you like the bit of melancholy. Do you know what I mean? Keeps you balanced.' He cocked an eye at Tom. 'Or do you think that's weird?'

'Not at all.' Tom laughed. 'Though I can't say it's a side of you I've seen a lot of.'

'Nobody sees it,' said Gibbon with a hint of petulance.

From what Tom could muster the concentration to read, Gibbon liked passages of philosophical dejection, the moments in a protagonist's story when his yearnings crystallise and he arrives at a perception about the world and his place in it; generally a view of the world as a place of grimness and fatalism. He was fond of asides about the passage of time and its irrevocability. He was very partial to descriptions of bad weather.

'Where do you get the time to read them all?' asked Tom.

'I don't. Jesus, man, where would I get the time? No, Sheila reads them for me. She's an assistant of mine. Sheila knows what I like. Fantastic understanding. She marks out what I like.'

Gibbon gave a hugely despondent sigh. He looked over at Tom.

'Anyhow. Talk to me.'

'I'm talking.'

'You're not talking about it.'

'What's "it"?'

'The event.'

'What event?'

'Come on, Tom. You saw it from beginning to end. Did she do it deliberately?'

This was a question Tom was anticipating. He had been hoping to turn it away. He played for time.

'Deliberately?'

He repeated the word as if it was neutral, and the question merely curious. He took down another volume, sumptuously bound, turned it over in his hands.

'Fine binding. Is it original?'

'Tom – tell me. Did she do it with malice aforethought?'

'No. No way she did.'

He hoped to speak with force, but not too much. He hoped to speak with indignation, just enough to shame Gibbon for having the effrontery to ask. And to speak with enough conviction to convince him he was wrong.

Again he saw Dol's weaving motions with the lighter and how they might have been not wild but studied. He remembered how he had glanced over at the fireplace to see who in its vicinity she could be waving to and there had been no one there . . . How she had not run to Seoda as her hair flamed, or alternatively away from her. Either response more natural surely than staying where she was, a foot resting indolently on the fender, smoking her unwonted cigarette . . . And then her cry . . . 'What's going on?' . . . A line you might give to a chorus in a play to say when it already knows the story and the outcome that is now to follow.

'Are you sure?' Gibbon was suddenly alert, hopeful. Then he slumped backwards again. 'Dol can be very volatile,' he sighed. 'You never know where you are with her.'

'Is she?' Tom's tone seemed to suggest that the volatility or otherwise of Dol was neither here nor there in this context. 'I guess she needs a short rein all right,' he conceded.

Gibbon looked at him with meaning. 'She needs a husband. Somebody to keep her in order.'

Was he saying he'd like to get her off his hands? In that case no wonder she was volatile . . .

'A charming idea. But it doesn't happen in real life, does it?'

'You mean marriage only makes them worse?' Gibbon gave a low laugh.

Tom grimaced. 'Well, that's been my experience.'

Gibbon sat up. 'You're married? I had you down for a "no ties" kind of chap.'

Tom told him a little about Katya. He described how they'd

met, guests at a dinner party given by his ophthalmologist. 'I had myopia,' he explained. 'Got it lasered.'

Anyway, Katya was the ophthalmologist's date. Tom's date was a girl he was seeing at the time. 'Nice, but . . .' Tom gave a rueful smile. He and Katya took one look at each other – well, several looks – and that was it. But that dazzling thing had dimmed, dispersed . . . The bewilderment of finding little left behind.

'It happens,' Gibbon said.

'She'd have been better off with the ophthalmologist. Practical. She likes practical. She wanted to change me, I guess,' he wound up. 'She wanted me to be different.'

'They can't leave a man alone,' said Gibbon mournfully. 'They can't let a man be.'

'But Dol's a good kid,' offered Tom.

'Good? Man, we're talking about Dol here.' Gibbon lay back and closed his eyes. 'Read me something, will you?' he said.

'What do you want me to read?'

'Anything. Anything at all that Sheila's marked.'

Tom plucked a slender leather-bound volume from a shelf. 'The Letters and Journals of George Gordon, Lord Byron . . . Let's see.' Flipping it open at random he found a passage at once.

'The lapse of ages changes all things – time – language – the earth . . .' he read.

'Slower,' instructed Gibbon from the divan. 'And start again.'

'The lapse of ages changes all things,' Tom enunciated gravely, 'time – language – the earth – the bounds of the sea – the stars of the sky, and everything about, around and underneath man, except man itself, who has always been, and always will be, an unlucky rascal. The infinite variety of lives conduct but to death, and the infinity of wishes lead but to disappointment. All the discoveries which have yet been made have multiplied little but existence.'

Gibbon sighed with pleasure. 'Give it to me again,' he ordered. Tom read it again. When he had finished there was silence.

'Dol is some woman all the same,' mused Gibbon then. He stood up and stretched luxuriantly. 'I could do with a bit of cheering up. Let's go see how the party's doing.' He sounded cheerful already.

The festivities were winding down. In the gilded salons two large brindle-coloured dogs, let out by somebody from the boot room they had been confined in for the duration of the party, were leaping wildly from sofa to sofa, molesting the guests and carrying off in their mouths the evening bags they found lying about on the occasional tables. Nobody cared. They were past caring. They lay about in attitudes of satiation, not bothering to push the dogs off. The servitors still went around with loaded trays but the guests were neglecting even to drink.

They were replete. There had been an incident of note at the party, indeed a near tragedy. It had rarefied the air and fed the soul. They could ask for nothing more. Only the hired entertainment, the tarot readers and conjurors brought in to mingle among the guests and delight them with their skills, were drinking steadily, having put away their props. A couple of them were sprawling on the ominous sofa.

The Roumanian ambassador came hurrying up. 'How is she? I am unable to take my leave without reassuring myself about dear Seoda. But she is fine? It was only the hair? Not to worry, that is a replaceable commodity. Of course in the case of Seoda, the hair so beautiful . . . A great pity . . .'

Tom moved on, to a chorus of smiles and empathic murmurs. People reached for his hand and shook it tenderly. He was a great fellow, they assured him.

Vasile told him he was as good as Superman – 'Your coat that you have used like his red cape.' Denis Grogan proudly introduced him to his wife, Marguerite, a tiny woman with attractively simian dark eyes, who breathed fulsome words of admiration. Carey gave him a heartfelt shoulder-clasp and murmured, 'Good man, Tom.'

But some of the gestures and the words were tinged with guilt and even a modicum of resentment. He had been there for Seoda, he had leaped to her side in her hour of need, when they had not . . .

Caught up in his admirers, he nearly collided with Eileen Kinane. Just in time he was aware of the pink head blocking his path. She was crouched on the floor, extracting from the jaws of a dog a small glassy vial. Looking up at him she smiled. 'Don't worry. It's only lip gloss. Made to be eaten.'

With a practised movement she dabbed at her mouth and returned the vial to her pocket.

'All gone, the narcotics, unfortunately. They always run out, eventually . . .' Her head flopped sideways as if she was admiring the marquetry of the floor. Then her body followed. Tom caught her and set her upright. She was very white, made whiter by the freshly reddened mouth.

'Would you like me to read your Angel cards?' she asked. She sounded a bit drunk, but not incompetent. 'I've been reading them for all the guests.'

'Why not?' said Tom.

'Where did I put them?' She gazed with surprising alertness around the room. 'Fuck, I'd love to get out of here,' she said then. 'Have you seen Carey?' She seemed to have forgotten about the Angel cards. 'Carey has a driver. Or what do you think? Will we get another drink?'

'I have a driver,' said Tom.

'You have a driver? Cool. Let's go.' She reached out a hand to him and he pulled her to her feet.

But first he should find Dol. Dol, he felt, had to be got safely out of Iveragh.

'Where's Dol, I wonder?'

'You mean my sister the pyromaniac? Hiding in the shrubbery, I'd say.'

'Let me go find her.'

Eileen sat down with unexpected primness on a tub chair. 'Okay.'

'Don't move,' he instructed.

She smiled up at him. He trusted it was not too whimsical a smile. 'I'll wait,' she said. Her head dropped sideways; her eyelids drooped.

It took a while but at last he tracked Dol down. In a small room shelved with boxes of magazines and journals beside the cloakroom he came upon her coiled uncomfortably in an office chair. She was flicking through an art review, frowning over an illustration of some intricately contorted clay objects. She showed him the page.

'Interesting, yeah?'

'Not bad,' he agreed. 'What do you say to getting out of here?'

'You know,' she said thoughtfully, 'he takes that Sheila twice a week to lunch in Guillaume's.'

'Course he does. Any guy is going to have to take his assistant out to lunch once in a while.'

'Not to Guillaume's. And not twice a week.'

Tom shrugged. 'I wouldn't read too much into it.'

'I wouldn't mind hitting the road. If you wouldn't,' she said then. Her manner was neutral, amenable.

'Let's go,' he said.

Miraculously, Eileen was where he had left her. She appeared to be fast asleep but was co-operative once she was woken. The sisters exchanged no word of greeting nor fell into conversation. But united all the same, palpably intimate, they made their way ahead of Tom through the depleted salons. With sundry guests they exchanged words of farewell. The farewells Dol received were hearty, carrying no discernible trace of animosity. But the crowd parted before her like waves of the sea, an example of the deference and appearance of solicitude that polite society grants to the pitiful and the guilty.

They stood on the granite steps, waiting for the car. Tom looked around briefly for Gibbon so he could bid him good-night. But he wasn't anywhere to be seen. The night air was grateful, filled with the fragrance of flowers, old style flowers, roses, peonies, lilies . . . In an orderly file along the gravel, the Augustas came nosing their way out of the shadows like superbly trained dark beasts, as if directed by an invisible ring-master, and up to the forecourt. Their dimmed but powerful headlights cut the massed darkness of the shrubberies, illuminat-ing to phosphorescence the spray-rinsed greenery. Among the drivers there was a jealous hierarchy of rank and importance and they engaged in jocular but deadly battles for position and one-upmanship. Jokey shouts came from those stationary in the line.

'Be more professional, will you?'

'Tis gone very common since last year.'

'Get those civilian cars to the back of the line.'

Luke must have been watching out for them because very soon he came purring up to the steps. As he was Gibbon's man the other drivers at once gave way to him.

'Both the ladies to go, Mr Blessman?' he murmured as Tom came up. There seemed to be the implication in his question that the sisters were regrettably disreputable cargo. Luke would have heard of course all about the incident, the charred tresses. Drivers were always in the know about everything that went on inside or out.

With a bravura show of defiance Dol got unbidden into the front seat.

'No harm done to your jacket, I hope,' Luke murmured as he held the door open for Tom to get in the back. Eileen took unassisted the place next to him. The driver's door closed with an elegaiac clunk and the car moved slowly off. They had gone only a short distance when a man, stepping smartly out of the shrubbery, materialised in the glow of the lights. He stood spreadeagled on the gravel in the car's path. The car came smoothly to a stop. He jumped in beside Tom.

'Right. Let's get back to the capital,' Gibbon instructed.

For a while there was silence in the car. But soon it was broken by Gibbon's nasal snores as he slept. Dol's head lolled contentedly on her headrest in front. Comatose as a sleep-hungry child Eileen was curled up beside Tom. When the car rounded a corner they were brought swaying gently together. How, he wondered, was he to prevent her from returning to the obscure fastnesses of the city from which she had miraculously reappeared? Could he ask her back to his place? He should at the very least be able to get her mobile number. Though if the Kinanes were to be believed, she never answered her phone or responded to her messages.

Like a docile panther the car was loping through the dawn, eating up the miles far too fast and efficiently for his liking. He became aware of fumbling movements in the region of his crotch. Glancing down in surprise he saw by the blue light from the dash the glimmer of Eileen's fingers attempting to undo his fly. They were finding it difficult to manipulate the buttons. But she was one down . . . Dammit, a zip would be simpler . . . Her head was lying slackly now against his chest. But her fingers had definite intent. His first impulse was to take over the job.

'Eileen. Stop it,' came Dol's commanding voice from the front. 'For chrissake. Tom isn't one of your D-list wannabees.'

'Sorry,' muttered Eileen drowsily.

The fingers withdrew. She curled up again, her back turned.

Stealthily Tom re-did his fly. The panorama of foliage and sky was giving way to brick and painted doors lurid in the tangerine glow of the city street lamps. I can't ask her back to the apartment now . . . It would look opportunistic. Hell, it would be opportunistic. Taking unfair advantage. Can't do it; she's blitzed.

They were cruising past Christchurch. Gibbon gave a series of snorts. He was waking up.

'Stop please, will you?' Eileen ordered, suddenly clear-voiced, peremptory. She sat up. 'I want to get out here.'

Luke brought the car to a halt.

'Let me come with you,' urged Tom.

'Thanks. But I'll be fine.'

'It's not safe.' He appealed to her sister. 'Dol, it's not safe, is it?'

Eileen laughed. 'Of course it's safe.'

'Oh, she'll be fine,' said Dol. 'She's been fine so far.'

Before she slammed the door, Eileen turned. 'See you,' she said.

'Night, a cailín,' said Gibbon. Dol said nothing.

'Sure,' shouted Tom with fervour.

Through the back window as the car moved off he watched her drop into a side street leading down towards the river.

'You're staying in town, Mr Fitzgibbon?' enquired Luke.

'Town it is,' agreed Gibbon.

The car drew up at a Victorian neo-gothic style building. Another example of Fitz Inc's apartment conversions. Gibbon jumped out and opened the door on Dol's side. She murmured something Tom didn't catch and giggled. Gibbon laughed, a low, amused laugh.

'And home for you, Mr Blessman?' suggested Luke.

'I guess,' Tom said reluctantly. 'Where else?'

23

'The question is, Tom,' Etchen MacAnar was saying, 'should Ireland take her place among the nations of the world as one of them merely? Or as herself?'

'As herself, I guess?' suggested Tom.

'Yes. That seems obvious. But what is herself? What is her identity? This is the question we must answer. We have moved on, Tom. The church is lost to us. The land is lost. But is there more to us than faith and field? What is to take their place?'

Lunch with Etchen MacAnar was, unsurprisingly, turning out to be a stimulating experience. They were in Grille, a small and select establishment on a lane behind the old houses around Baggot Street. Etchen had selected Grille.

'I suppose I'm a bit of an old gourmand,' he said with a charming bashfulness, pronouncing the word with an unpretentious hard 'd'. 'But I can't eat under-par. I'd be no use to anybody. The other day for example, I had what they were calling a tarte tatin' – he waved in the direction of the town and its various inferior eating-places – 'and they served it to me on choux pastry. Tarte tatin on choux pastry!' He shook his head at the chicanery of the world.

Between them sat Etchen's disciple and assistant, Bernard. Bernard was working for Etchen on a voluntary basis. He was a gangly young fellow who spoke rarely but when he did, pointedly. Listening with rapt attention and undisguised appreciation to everything Etchen said, he was taking plenteous notes with the diligence of a professional secretary. His dark-grey suit was pressed but dated in cut, and even impressively threadbare in places. It lent him an air of having an unusual commitment to some noble cause. However, between his note-taking Bernard took care to eat plentifully. He was a country lad, as he explained, both accustomed, and committed for health reasons, to taking his dinner at noon. He could not, as he said, get into the panini culture at all – 'No way could I work on a panini.'

Grille provided an excellent French-inspired cuisine with all the traditional components – foie gras, truffle-infused sauces, rather delicious *amuse gueules* . . . But it also offered some native dishes, exquisitely prepared and with their own native accompaniments – bacon-and-cabbage, steak-and-onions, rhubarb tart . . . The presence of these dishes on the menu was for Etchen and Bernard the principal reason for Etchen's eschewal of the more brash and fashionable spots such as Caravanserai or Dosh or Guillaume's where this kind of artlessness and simplicity had no place on the menu. It was a tenet of Etchen's that simplicity equalled sophistication. The truly sophisticated favoured Grille.

Another reason for his patronage was that in those other places the hectic pace of the conviviality induced a stress that was bad both for the digestion and for the orderly progress of the business in hand. The patrons of Grille kept their heads down, eating wholesomely, conversing constructively and doing good work. They valued anonymity and privacy as they lunched. They were the hardened veterans of the lunching circuit, chairmen and chairwomen of commissions and boards, most of them devoted to virtuous endeavours.

The social columnists did colour, they did glamour. They did not circulate at Grille. A *cordon sanitaire* of discretion surrounded its calm and muted rooms. Grille, as Etchen put it, was for the real players.

As far as Tom was concerned – and as he had hoped – this was turning out to be no mere business lunch. It was inspirational, an educational opportunity. It was practically a seminar.

Casually, generously, Etchen dropped his words of wisdom, the fruits of his ruminations and his learning, as freely as the patrons of Dosh or Guillaume's dropped the names of celebrities. Much of it was over Tom's head, for the moment at least. The references to recondite aspects of Irish history, to political movements and figures past and present, to the vanished culture and habits of the old Ireland . . .

But they furnished his imagination like stray pieces of a jigsaw. If he listened with sufficient attention the kaleidoscopic chaos would surely before long make a coherent picture. He was learning all sorts of apparently disconnected but important things. Jewels of erudition spilled from Etchen's lips with the mellifluous sparkle of the recherché blend of whiskey he was splashing with a pleasing show of largesse from the decanter into his glass. And his thoughts were not confined to the parochial. Etchen's was a world view.

'What we must strive for is the healing of our culture. We must liberate ourselves from our restless and ceaseless wanting. We suffer from wanting. The tragedy is that so much of the rest of our world suffers from want.'

'That's a really interesting perception,' Tom said.

'But at the same time – the perennial longing for purity and order. This is what we have to resist,' Etchen warned.

'Can you explain?'

'I mean the lure of ideology,' explained Etchen. 'Ideology may be seductive but it's a fraud. The struggle against the natural disorder and chaos of life, attractive though it may be, is always misguided and ultimately hopeless. And it's dangerous, Tom. A rupture will always occur, the evil will leak and seep out unregulated. Do you understand me?'

'I do,' Tom assured him.

Etchen's expression was mournful. Tom reached for the decanter and refilled his glass.

'We have lost something,' Etchen pronounced, 'somewhere along the way.'

'Could that something be the soul?' suggested Tom. 'Whatever that may be.'

Bernard's pen was poised expectantly above his notebook.

Etchen sat back in his club chair and regarded Tom. 'I'll be honest with you. I don't know what it is that we've lost. But I'm searching for it, Tom. I'm searching.'

'To search may be the best any of us can do,' offered Tom to encourage him.

Etchen ate a forkful of the buttered 'boiled new potatoes' which he had declared himself very happy to see on the menu.

'You're Irish, Tom, I presume?' he asked.

'Partly. A couple of generations back.'

'And this is why you're here? You're looking for your roots?'

'Yes and no, I guess.' Suddenly Tom found himself confiding in Etchen. And it was a huge relief to come clean at last, to candidly relate the story of his great-uncle's dream, to describe a little of Pender's idiosyncrasies and his obduracies and the resulting difficulty of his own position.

Etchen found Pender deeply interesting and not particularly absurd.

'A fellow who dreams can't be all bad,' he pondered. 'What is the dream but a conduit for change and transformation?'

'Do you remember,' Tom demanded, 'when we talked at Gibbon's? You spoke about the native nomads? The travellers?'

'The travellers?' queried Etchen. 'Ah yes. Our lucht siul.'

'Yes, yes. The travellers.' Impatiently, Tom waited.

Slowly Etchen wiped his mouth with his napkin. He was deep in thought. He looked piercingly at Tom.

'The travellers could suit your great-uncle down to the ground,' he said.

'Exactly. That's my feeling too,' Tom replied happily.

He had long been concerned by the plight of the travellers, Etchen assured Tom. A noble, proud, but indigent race, obstinate in their allegiance to the old culture, the old ways. Had he not in his youth witnessed the last vestiges of that culture?

The characteristic apparel of shawl and earring worn by the women as they tramped the roads – here Tom's heart leaped with a sense of recognition . . . The hooped caravan, the tarpaulin camp, the droves of horseflesh that travelled with them. He had even learned some words, a few phrases indeed, of their ancient and private language.

But they had moved with the times. They adopted the motor, the engine, contemporary business practices . . . It showed adaptability. And yet a great richness had been lost. But Etchen had accepted this must be their destiny as yet another strand of the native spirit and tradition vanished into the maw of history.

Until one day, as he was walking along Dame Street, a pretty woman in gipsy dress approached him. In an enchanting sing-song voice she asked him for alms. It was gladly he gave it. She appeared to him a revenant from his youth, an insouciant bearer of all the romance and all the poignancy of that distant time. However, she was not an Irish traveller. She was a gipsy, from some country to the east where the traveller still had the ancient pride and the confidence of their tribe.

And as he watched her sway down the street in her colourful flounced skirts, her babe at her breast, an illumination had come to him. What chance had the native tribe in the face of such colour and such romance? Everything was against them. Society of course – but they themselves must take some of the blame as well. Their pride was eroded. They had abandoned their tradi-tional costume, they had given up on their traditional trades. They were on the road, yes. But they were not heading for the horse fair of Ballybay – 'or wherever' – here Etchen gestured expansively. No, they were on the road to extinction.

Suddenly, in mid-flow, he halted. Somebody at another table had claimed his attention. Leaning across the table he lowered his voice. 'There's Norbert Leddy now,' he said. 'I wouldn't have expected to see him here. It's Gibbon's first appearance at the tribunal today of course. Norbert will be wanting to lie low. Wouldn't want to be showing his cards.'

'Gibbon is up today?' asked Tom.

'He is. And I hope he's keeping the head.' Etchen looked at his watch. 'You know, I think we'll make a good team, Tom,' he said as he stood up. 'Ourselves and Mr Pender Gast.'

24

Gibbon had hoped to sail through the summer without receiving his summons to appear before the McCarthy tribunal. But in the last week before it went into its holiday recess the tribunal chose, in what seemed to him its typically arbitrary and discourteous manner, to examine him. The hottest topic now in the bars around town, and picked over with the keenest appetite in the bars and halls of the Shelbourne, was the exact nature of Gibbon's 'activities' or 'misdemeanours'. Whichever phrase was employed depended on the level of warmth towards him felt by the speaker.

His activities were nothing more than normal business dealings involving friends and acquaintances, explained friends such as Carey Kinane. Of course Gibbon was friendly with a few politicians. Some of them found it hard to live on their ridiculously meagre salaries. It was only natural that a fellow of generous instincts like Gibbon should lend an occasional helping hand.

But from a lower level of acquaintance, the kind of person with a lesser affection for Gibbon, Tom heard whispered allegations of illicit and hugely bloated overseas bank accounts. There were mutters of dealings – almost certainly at a remove, this person would hasten to add, undertaken even in all innocence – with the underworlds of gangsters, native and foreign . . . International Mafiosi-style outfits trading in drugs, diamonds, or dry-cleaned South American currencies. 'Dodgy?' somebody would guffaw. 'We're talking more than dodgy here.'

As the night wore on, rumours would sweep across the tables, spoken loudly and with relish, and gaining by the minute in luridness and exoticism to encompass enterprises such as the louchest aspects of the sex industry or dealings in arms of the most lethal type. Like hot-air balloons the rumours heated and expanded and were sent floating into far-out and incredibly fanciful realms.

All this was fuelled by the fact that there was more than one tribunal on the go. And they had all been sitting for so long and had extended their enquiries into so many areas of corruption, bribery and scandalous activity that it was quite forgotten what the original remits of their enquiries had been.

Soon no member of Gibbon's circle was safe. Indeed it was surprising that he himself had escaped until now. The fate of many of these men was not a happy one. It might be compared to the situation of lepers in the last century who, despite the assurances given to the citizenry that they were no longer contagious, still bore the scars of their dreadful disease. These modern-day outcasts avoided media attention, disappeared from the places they had once frequented. They sold their racehorses, their companies no longer sponsored highly publicised events. An example of this pitiable tribe – the survivors of the tribunals – was once or twice pointed out to Tom, lurking like a shade in a dark corner of his favourite watering-hole out of which a tribunal had rudely plucked him a year or two ago, and from which consequent disgrace had to all intents and purposes banished him.

This melancholy example was, for some still unexplained reason, always male – a fact that could incite in female players both a righteous smugness and a paradoxical bitterness. Women were still being excluded clearly from the big boys' club, and from the share they too deserved surely in the spoils, even if they were ill-got.

Such a man was not actively shunned however. No policy or decision was taken in club or committee that he should be shunned. No, the new reality of his fallen state was transmitted to him through other means. There was as ever the fervently civil, even solicitous deportment of his old buddies who accepted a drink from him and bought him one in return. But this return drink seemed to be called for and placed in front of him with an undue and disturbing alacrity. And the buddy somehow always had a pressing engagement at home or elsewhere when a move to a table in a well-loved restaurant nearby was diffidently mooted. The offer even of 'one for the road' would be, though with fulsome regret, declined.

The old buddies were always in a hurry somewhere these days. Oh, it was all so changed from the salad days, so recent and yet so distant, when he could swagger forth in his armour of arrogance and intrigue. True, he still had his wealth. But how long more would they leave him that? He walked on shifting sands.

Another topic that whiled away the drinking hours was whether some survivor of a tribunal, keeping to his luxuriously appointed mansion on the south littoral, was pining away for the pleasures of society and the envied name he had formerly enjoyed. Opinion was generally inclined, with the pietistic relish of schadenfreude, towards wretchedness and decline – the poor fellow was sinking rapidly. Since the state seemed unable to punish him – for the tribunals were confining their activities to naming and shaming – the righteous must.

In these days of his travails, Gibbon Fitzgibbon made it plain that he did not intend their sorry fate to be his. Standing in the glare of the ever-eager cameras on the steps of the tribunal, photographed in domestic mode in his local shopping centre, grocery sacks in either hand from which garden-fresh greenery tumbled, he took every opportunity to appeal to the public. He was innocent, he assured the country. The tribunal could have nothing on him, for the simple reason that he had done nothing wrong.

And if by some perversity they did succeed in turning up

something on him that might, viewed in the wrong light, be considered transgressive, this would be from a merely technical point of view. Any broad-minded non-judgemental person would see that. It would be revealed as a little oversight on the part of a busy man which was patently not dishonourable in intent. In the future he would face all their sermonising and condemnations with a brave and truthful indignation. He would not be defeated by their small and legalistic minds.

Gibbon's approach was novel. Pundits were using the word 'attaque' to describe it. 'Fitzgibbon's attaque is first class,' Tom heard again and again. Other celebrity defendants had adopted a tactic of dignified silence. However, their approach was now negatively interpreted as indicative of cunning and shiftiness. Gibbon's accessibility, his freshness, his candid appeals to decency, the endearing impression he gave of a certain naivety were, by comparison, deeply impressive. He might have been wholly convincing had public confidence in everyone and everything not been badly shaken by all the scandals and all the lies that had gone before.

On the days of his appearance before the McCarthy tribunal, Gibbon could be seen on television entering the courts alone. He held his head high, his handsome boyish face wearing an uncharacteristic and, to Tom's eyes at least, totally convincing expression of unjust injury. He had a wounded look; his face crumpled easily as if he was not at all inured to the hard and mean ways of this world. And all questions and accusations he met firmly and courageously with staunch and unyielding negatives.

Norbert Leddy, the best lawyer in town, was guiding Gibbon through his daily interrogation. Norbert was the best a man could get. And at the same time, to have called on Norbert was possibly a confession that Gibbon was more worried than he admitted. It signalled to the sceptical that he was in need of the best for his defence, the wile and the guile that only big money can buy. But what was he to do? protested his friends. When all was said and done a mere rumour of guilt had to be better than innocence mismanaged by some mediocrity.

When the day's machinations were over, Gibbon would arrive in the bars. Moving from one table to another he accepted hearty words of encouragement and jocular words of praise on his comportment and forbearance throughout the long hours of confrontation with the blustering lawyers. Indeed there were many lawyers who themselves joined in the chorus. It has to be said that tribunal lawyers were rather happy with men like Gibbon and even happier with themselves. Their fees were enormous and were assured long into the future.

Long-suffering still but somewhat cheered now, and mollified, Gibbon would sweep off with a strong entourage to the Caravanserai to be greeted by a gratifying show of welcome, especially from the likes of Jimmy, and given the long table in the centre of its vaulted rooms. He had achieved his first aim. Until the tribunal should produce unanswerable evidence against him – and with Norbert's formidable legal brain in his arsenal that was highly unlikely – any criticism, any hint of doubt, of the cold shoulder or the boycott, was unthinkable.

Another unusual aspect of Gibbon's diurnal appearances was Seoda's absence from his side. She did not accompany him to the court, nor to the venues where he conducted his walkabouts in the media glare. And unexpectedly, the absence of a wifely figure hanging on his arm in the time-hallowed gesture of wifely support added to the impression he gave of embattlement, a kind of solitary heroism. It gave him the poignancy of a noble but slightly clumsy beast at bay in a corral of smaller and fiercer breeds; a beast who would fight valiantly to the end whatever the enemies ranged against him.

In the bars the names of his PR people were bandied about with admiration. 'I wouldn't use anyone else myself,' they declared. Only a PR genius could go against the grain so audaciously and dispense with the prop of the supportive wife. There were a few people – women mostly – who proposed that

Seoda's absence was due to her unhappiness with her new gamine look and her reluctance to be seen on television not looking what she considered her best. But this was not taken at all seriously.

In the evenings however Seoda could come up trumps. Any suggestions that she was bored by her husband's friends or even by her husband himself were nipped in the bud. She was often in his company, or mingling with a brave conviviality close by. From a distance she could look, assisted by her new image, delicate and tender, the very picture of a woman standing by her man.

Tom, too, was there for him. As Seoda said, it was a solace to Gibbon to have Tom around, an open-faced, open-minded American unperturbed by over-the-top allegations of shady practices.

'The tribunals should set up in Texas,' was Tom's quite sincere comment on the situation, 'if they're looking for some real shady practices.'

The cohorts would nod wisely and knowingly.

'If we're talking anything at all here, we're only talking peanuts, right?' Tom remarked. 'Like, you guys, you're not into murder, are you? No stiffs, right?'

'Not yet,' murmured Carey.

There was laughter all round, comfortable and complacent.

25

Over several lunches at Grille Etchen outlined his plans by which, with the assistance of funds from Mr Gast, the journey to extinction of the traveller might be reversed. First off, they would set up an organisation. An organisation was vital – an office, committed workers, a public profile. And the organisation would have to have a title, a catchy but meaningful title.

Bernard duly came up with a list of imaginative names and Etchen and Tom thrashed them out around the table. Finally they settled on The Association for the Preservation of the Irish Traveller. Its acronym would be PAIT. This was not a real acronym, it was true, but Etchen assured Tom that the little stretch was permissible. PAIT was so warm to the ear. And after all, it was how Pat, the most friendly and typical of Irish names, was spelled in Irish – 'the sweet and kingly tongue of the Gael', as Etchen described it.

Champagne did not seem appropriate in the ambience of Grille. It was too frothy somehow, just a little bit out of place, even ever so slightly vulgar. When they were celebrating one of their worthy achievements Grille's patrons preferred to discreetly choose obscure vintages from its unpretentious but distinguished wine cellars. Nonetheless the inauguration of PAIT was toasted with an excellent champagne selected by Etchen. 'When you think about it, isn't PAIT all about celebration?' he declared.

Etchen's long-term plan for PAIT was slowly formulated but obviously all the better thought-out for that. Together he and

Tom would nurture it to the level where it would be umbrella'ed as an independent NGO, a publicly funded non-governmental organisation. To get to this level there would be intermediate stages. Expertly Etchen counted them off on his fingers; start-up, public recognition, leading to its establishment in the public consciousness as the essential body – standing head and shoulders above those already in place – for traveller support.

Finally the imperative for public funding would be clear to all. When this came through he and Tom would become redundant, freed up to move on to further endeavours. Of such endeavours there would be a ready and urgent supply. Here, Etchen sighed deeply, weighed down by the Sisyphean self-appointed and thankless task that awaited him of turning Ireland around.

In the short term meanwhile, there were PAIT's immediate needs – and in the short term Tom would be on call for the provision of the necessary cheques. The lease of an office and its fit-out, the hiring of an administrator . . . Bernard happened to be absent that day and it was discussed at length whether he would be willing to take on the task and whether Etchen could spare him.

A PR would be retained. The right PR was vital. There would be enormous opposition to PAIT at first, warned Etchen. They would have to be prepared for that; they would have to stand firm, display strength and commitment. Etchen's voice trembled and broke with a particular sweetness as he described the misguidedness of current policies on the nomadic people. It was integrationist, anti-conservation. Basically it came down to one word, and that word was dissolution.

But it was the medium-term plan that excited Tom the most. There would be the purchase of the materials for the re-creation of the artefacts of traveller heritage. Great rolls of canvas and tarpaulin for the construction of the traditional wagons. The horses to draw them. The sourcing of extensive tracts of land at appropriate sites around the country from whence they could come and go as they pleased as in the old days, in the great annual cycle of their circumambulation of the island. The building of structures at these places – Etchen envisaged them as state-of-the-art barns or silos – where they could carry on their traditional trades of metalwork and horse dealing. For the unhindered practice of the age-old profession of begging, pitches would be purchased or leased in the cities and towns. Once officialdom saw the light, these pitches would be guaranteed by statute unto the future generations.

The mendicant pitches, as he called them, were very dear to Etchen's heart. He saw the giving of alms as vital to the re-creation of the nation's heart. But they could be controversial, he conceded. PAIT might be obliged to answer legal action, to take its case to the highest courts, even as far as the International Court of Human Rights. Sadly he remarked that you could certainly expect little in the way of justice or rights in these parts. Etchen appeared to relish the prospect of litigation.

Education and training were a lynchpin of his plan. Basic education for the young in their lost culture and language, their threatened way of life, refresher courses for the older generations . . . All this would be very costly, Etchen warned. However, Tom need not fear that all this would or could be rolled out at the expense of the Gast Corporation alone. Once the right PR and the right fundraiser was in place, the benefactors would follow.

Temple Bar had assumed something of a poetic quality for Tom now that he associated it with Eileen. Wandering around the cobbled streets he came upon the lush who loved God. She was propped against the graffitied wall of a pub in the same attitude as before. The same purple jacket, the same male companion – presumably – slumbering in a variety of coverings by her side. She had acquired a tan since he last saw her. It didn't suit her. It gave her skin a yellowy rather than a golden tinge. It made her

look unhealthy. Her eyes were clouded and filmy. Their sleeping arrangements couldn't be too good . . .

Discreetly he dropped her a large note; very large by anyone's
reckoning. She examined it with suspicion. May not have seen,
let alone possessed, a note of such a denomination before.

'Is that a fake?' She squinted up at him.

'It's not a fake.'

She looked sceptical but pocketed it anyway.

'Maybe you should try and stay out of the sun,' he suggested.
'Too much sun can be bad.'

'Fuck off, you,' she retorted with remarkable vigour. 'I'll do
what I fucking like.'

She betrayed no gratitude or surprise at the size of his
offering. And on this occasion she made no reference either to
love or to God.

26

An incongruous smell, a homely compound of frying sausage and tobacco, was wafting with an insolent pungency through the white and airy halls of IGMA. Interrogatively Dol sniffed the air. 'Definitely coming from Home,' she pronounced. 'Frog adores sausages.'

Tom had been pressed into service as an audience for Frog. 'She's feeling a bit sidelined by Gibbon's "Infanta",' Dol coaxed. 'She could do with a show of support.'

The cloying odours strengthened as they passed through the crowded Great Hall where the Infanta was on display, adding an unintended homeliness to the exhibit. This excitingly nihilistic and sentimental work by Demis Schwartz, the big international heavyweight, was proving hugely popular. And certainly it was doing Gibbon, as the principal sponsor, no harm at all as a counter-balance to his present notoriety. However, to Frog's chagrin, the Infanta was stealing what she considered to be 'Home''s rightful acclaim.

And this state of affairs looked set to continue. The Infanta was going to be on show for the entire summer and beyond, while in a few short days Home would be history. As it was, after viewing the Infanta very few visitors were willing to dilute the experience by continuing on to the small gallery called the Annex where Home had languished for just ten days, garnering, for all the commitment and determination that Frog and Aaron had brought to it, no more than a couple of small polite notices. A modest controversy about Aaron's smoking had not even outlived the afternoon's news bulletins.

In his Infanta, the artist had constructed, as in his other works, an ingenious mix of the chemical and the mechanical, with, most radically, a soupçon of the natural. Schwartz had made his name with robotic fantastical creatures of a surpassing cutesyness. With the Infanta, his model of a human baby, he was taking the idea a step further. It was admiringly critiqued as a provocative and devastating statement on parenthood. By the public who were flocking to see it, it was regarded as simply adorable.

The Schwartz baby was supremely lifelike and supremely idealised. Its skin for instance was made of the fused ineffably soft skins of hundreds – some said thousands – of a breed of Antipodean lizard. Of course these were lizards, the artist was at pains to explain in interviews, that had been especially bred, allowed to live their natural life span and to die in their due time before offering themselves up for the creation of art. The resulting artwork was designed as a comment on, and to afford, the pleasures of parenthood – the feeding of baby, the cuddling, the sweet rewards of coos and smiles. The more tedious aspects of the role, the nappy changing, the responsibilities of night feeds and making sitting arrangements were discretionary.

And perhaps best of all the Infanta would not grow older or change or mutate in any way. What you saw was what you got. And you could have it for ever and ever, or at least until you tired of it or wanted to recoup – several times over undoubtedly – your investment. For its most provocative aspect – though this the public was finding the most attractive – was that its copy in a strictly limited edition was for sale. Moreover the copy could be tailored in the matters of gender, colour of eyes, hair, musicality of coos etc. to suit personal tastes. Naturally, the price of such a piece was extremely high. High even for a work by Demis Schwartz, prohibitive even for the richest and most serious of collectors. But the possibility of owning an Infanta, remote though it was, was gripping the imagination of the public. Musing on the prospect of a huge lottery win, they stood around it in silent communion. And the prospect of such a win seemed more and more likely as one gazed on the Infanta. It produced a feeling of optimism and wellbeing in all who gazed on it.

Seoda Fitzgibbon was negotiating a purchase with Demis Schwartz, it was generally believed. Seoda had certainly entertained Schwartz on his fleeting visit to Dublin for what he called the Incarnation of the Infanta. Pictures of the two walking together on an empty stretch of beach, she sporting a fetching hat to protect her from the light breeze, he burly and bear-like in a striped matelot vest, had appeared in the latest edition of *Hello* magazine for all to see. There had been a select supper for him in Guillaume's where even Gibbon listened in reverent silence as Mr Schwartz discoursed on the various football teams of the German provinces. Tom had found himself leaving unusually early to work on his novel, passing on the Incarnation ceremony.

But now, as he stood in front of its cradle that was placed on a dais in the centre of the long oak-panelled hall, he surprised himself by being very taken with the 'Infanta'. Around it also was a crush of spectators, some in silent contemplation, others uttering low cries of delight. The tall Georgian windows of the Great Hall – Schwartz with his characteristic audacity insisted on natural illumination – cast on the cradle a kind and pure light from the exterior of rinsed green lawns and clear sky.

The very cradle was gorgeous, quaintly bunched in flurries of white lace that formed a canopy, dotted with delicately embroidered satin flowers and suspended in intricate loops by means of blue bows and green-tipped pastel-pink rosebuds. But the Infanta itself was charming. In truth, it was completely enchanting; the fine silky hair of a novel tint, a kind of mauvish gold, the chubby but androgynous features . . . Its rather inane expression was particularly adorable. This inanity of expression had been described by more than one critic as a devastatingly sophisticated comment on humanity, on life itself. By the public however it was deemed to be simply and gorgeously babyish.

Right now the Infanta was in wake-mode, clapping its little hands at artfully irregular intervals and seeming to look with a half-smiling pleasure at the faces that peered at it over the restraining cordon. The mood prevailing around the cradle was one of a gentle repletion of spirit that can be lent only by feelings of tenderness and love. This at least was what Tom felt as he gazed at the Infanta.

'Don't they know it's not real?' muttered Dol loudly.

Owing to the demands of the tribunal on Gibbon's time and image-presentation, Dol was seeing little of him at present. Understandable as this was in the circumstances, her antagonism towards him, which was no less understandable, was directed towards his protegée, the Infanta.

Perhaps the atmosphere was always thus in the classically proportioned spaces of the Great Hall, whatever happened to be on show, but anyway the mood this afternoon was joyous and serene, reverie and speculation blending harmoniously. Drifting towards the fine windows, surfeited Infanta-gazers were looking out with new-found contentment on the peaceful springing gardens while others came to take their place around the cradle. Odd snatches of talk could be overheard.

'I think I'd go for a female . . .'

'But I thought it was gender free?'

'Two? Who could afford two?'

'Red hair, darling. Like yours . . . I'd take nothing else.'

With but a small sigh to denote that it was tired, the Infanta had fallen imperceptibly into graceful sleep-mode. The eye-lashes lay long and moist and delicate on the soft cheeks.

'Poor old Frog must be feeling really neglected,' Dol urged. Stealthily, as if not to disturb the exhibit, she pulled Tom away.

As they neared the Annex, the domestic smells were rather more unpleasant and a tinny sound of broadcast voices grew louder. Around the 'Home' exhibit a small group of children were gathered in a mute and trancelike state, their eyes fixed on the widescreen television set in the corner of the dingy room.

'Can we please go now?' pleaded their minder, an aunt or au pair perhaps. The children paid her no heed.

On a small shabby pea-green sofa Frog was lounging in front of daytime TV. She was watching what looked like some kind of a gardening show crossed with striptease. Hunched over the small kitchen table, Aaron was maniacally punching buttons on his mobile phone. Absorbed in these individual forms of entertainment, they appeared to be as oblivious of each other as of their audience. Also they were neglecting their domestic tasks. Home was looking profoundly homely, the kind of homely that some might consider plain old dirty.

Frog was steadily munching through a family pack of Mikado biscuits. Aaron was chain-smoking a pack of John Player Blues. They gave the impression of being morosely mired in pervasive crumbs and tobacco fug. But of course that was the whole point, if anyone took the time to think about it properly.

By smoking within the walls of 'Home' Aaron had attempted to spark a controversy about the status of 'Home'. Was the installation an art-piece merely? Or was it to be regarded as the personal home of the artists for the duration of their stay? Basically, was 'Home' a public or a private space? If it was judged to be the former, smoking should bring the wrath of the law and public opinion on his head. However, meeting with disappointingly little opposition, he had won his argument that it was the latter. The debate had prematurely collapsed after a respected pundit opined that 'Home' was indeed a reality show. Somehow after that nobody could get exercised about it.

As an aside, the pundit also asserted that reality shows were dead in the water. And the public appeared to agree. But Aaron saw his smoking as a great victory that in the course of time would be recognised as seminal, a victory for the sovereign rights of art over the laws of the land and societal conformism. And his commitment to art could not be doubted – in real life he didn't smoke and had taken up the habit purely as an instrument of battle. His greyish and sickly complexion now was testament to that.

The children's minder was very indignant.

'When kids are placed in front of a screen they're going to watch it, aren't they?' she whispered loudly in Tom's ear. 'I brought them here to get them away from their screens at home. It shouldn't be allowed. Would you call that art?'

'I would,' Tom said stoutly.

She looked unconvinced but was cowed into silence all the same.

Switching off the television, Frog pushed her feet into a pair of stained moccasins and shuffled over to the fridge. She was wearing leisurewear-type costume and looked plump and sluttish. She seemed to be playing a domestic-slattern-type person. As if in response to a Pavlovian signal the children turned away from the newly blank screen and tramped off.

'The only way to get rid of that shower,' Frog remarked. She sighed. 'Shoot. I'm getting to kind of like daytime TV.'

'So you're being authentic. You're not, like, just doing a performance?' said Dol excitedly.

'Is it a performance?' Frog considered the question. 'You know, we've been discussing that. And we're not sure any more.'

Aaron looked up from his game. 'Would you guys like a beer?'

'Ah, that's interesting. You're engaging with your audience,' commented Tom.

'If we feel like engaging, we engage,' Frog explained. 'If we don't, we don't. Like life really. Also, another question we're asking ourselves: is the audience actually an audience? Maybe you're, like, callers? Visitors?'

'My offer of a beer is symbolic,' announced Aaron. 'Art is hospitable, art is welcoming. My idea there is, art gives beer to the people.'

'Thanks, I'll take a beer,' Dol said.

Tom said he would like a beer also. Pushing aside some food cartons Aaron cracked open four cans. Dol stepped towards the sofa with the intention of sitting down.

'Hey, stop right there. You don't come in,' said Frog sharply. 'This is art. There's an invisible wall, you know. Respect, please.'

'The boundary between art and life is sacred,' rebuked Aaron.

Dol rolled her eyes. 'Still a work in progress, obviously.'

But she consented to move back into the public space. Frog returned to her place on the sofa and switched the TV back on, though with the sound lowered to mark her generous willingness to engage. She unscrewed a bottle of orange nail polish and started to carefully paint her toe-nails.

'Big crowd around the Infanta?' she enquired casually.

'Not very big,' answered Tom and Dol in unison.

'No?' Frog looked pleased. 'Well, that thing isn't art, is it? It's fantasy. Fantasy is the opium of the people.'

Tom and Dol contemplated the exhibit. The artists swigging real beers, real cigarette smoke rising into the air, the hyper-realist detritus of daily life filling the cramped hard-edged spotlit room . . . A room of our times?

'Do you not get bored?' asked Dol.

'No way. We like it here,' said Aaron.

'We love it here,' corrected Frog.

'Well, you'll be out soon. Freedom at last, yeh?'

Frog placed her can on the litter-strewn floor. 'Can I tell them, Aaron?' She had an air of suppressed excitement.

'No,' said Aaron.

'She's family,' begged Frog. 'I want to tell her.'

'No. In here, I'm family. Remember?'

'Have you got engaged or something?' Dol was excited now.

'Engaged? Are you crazy?' Frog was derisive.

'Engaged . . .?' pondered Aaron. 'That's something we could consider . . .'

Staring thoughtfully at Frog he blew incompetent but significant puffs of smoke in her direction. Steadily Frog returned the look. It was the conspiratorial comprehending look of the artist.

'Are you planning a wrap party?' asked Dol brightly.

'Why don't we give you a call? Once we know what we're doing. Okay?'

Frog turned the TV sound back on, nestled into the shallow depths of the sofa and closed her eyes. Aaron put his stockinged feet up on the table in the manner of a man-of-the-house and began to flick through the pages of the *Evening Herald*. To the spectator the exhibit was now a vivid portrayal of exclusion, dismissal. Home as the cave, the refuge from the outside world.

'Please yourselves,' said Dol stiffly. She hesitated. 'Well. See you later.'

Frog, training her eyes on the lofty decorative ceiling of the Annex, made no response. Aaron gave a grudging grunt.

27

Tom's image of himself these days was that of a pioneer, of somebody solitary and questing, moving into uncharted territory. The virgin landscape ahead appeared to be benign but undoubtedly it could hold hidden dangers. His only guide was Etchen.

Etchen had, as he put it, several projects moving along on the conveyor belts in his head but of them all PAIT was the cause dearest to him. He was chafing to get PAIT's belt going. He wanted to fast-track it.

Tom was no less keen. All the same, exciting though the project was, he would have liked to run it past Gibbon, who was moreover an admirer, even an associate of Etchen's. But Gibbon was proving inaccessible. He had a great deal on his mind. He had retreated, only temporarily, of course, into the world of lawyers and image-management and also, Tom saw with sympathy, worry-management.

Sometimes he thought he would also have liked to run it past his great-uncle for approval. He knew that Pender had a deep-seated objection to what he called 'bogged-down goddam bureaucracy', which was anything to do with offices, computers, paper and more than one female secretarial help. Pender often boasted that he was able to run an empire with only Cerise and her little laptop as back-up. But the truth was his empire had long existed only in the abstract world of numbers. It had nothing to do with people. Well, now people had reared their heads, even if they were dream-people. Was he ready to accept that helping them out entailed some engagement with bureaucracy?

By now, however, he would have relocated to the Hamptons for the summer as he always did. Each year, Tom briefly wondered what the point was of this seasonal move. Out in the Hamptons Pender's daily lifestyle differed little from his lifestyle in Manhattan and he seemed to enjoy it even less. But then the concept of enjoyment was one of those things he had long discarded.

Sure, out there on Long Island the air was fresher. But since he firmly kept the fresh air in its place out of doors and the conditioning on inside, this counted for little. He did have the ocean to look at instead of the city traffic, circulating endlessly on the Avenue below on one side of the penthouse, and the moody river on the other. And look out he did, but only with his habitual air of gloom and disillusion. Year by year he complained that the ever-increasing numbers of vacationers thrashing in the waves interrupted his view. But he had never liked the view of the ocean in any case. He liked nothing that was unstable or shifting.

Nor did his move to the Hamptons bring any change in his eating habits. There was an Italian restaurant nearby that brought to his Boston-ivied door exactly the same dishes as were delivered to him in the city. At lunchtime a person he called 'the boy' – actually a mature and grizzled man with a moustache – came with pizza triple-pepperoni. In the evenings osso bucco and roast potatoes alternated with spaghetti bolognese, again brought by 'the boy'. His Manhattan vintner supplied him with the same cases of wine that he always drank. On the weekends, the 'lady' – she favoured lumberjack-style shirts and a cropped haircut – who took care of the housekeeping in the apartment rode out on the Long Island railroad and cleaned the vacation house. Same face, same level of clean.

The one significant difference Tom could see in this summer-life of Pender's was that he saw less of Cerise. During the annual migration, she worked only half-time, commuting out there as it suited her and when she did, spending a good portion of her time on the beach. July and August she took several weeks away with her husband in their time-share in Hawaii. This present husband was a shadowy presence of whom Tom knew little, except that more than once his great-uncle had referred to him – out of Cerise's hearing luckily – as 'that zero'. Maybe one reason he took a summer break from the city was to get a break from Cerise. Pender had always found propinquity a burden. An alternative and intriguing possibility was that, on the contrary, he took it because he found life in the Manhattan apartment without her familiar presence intolerable.

Still, as far as Tom could recall, his great-uncle had given him carte blanche. By the time Cerise was back at her desk and he was talking to Pender again he would have PAIT up and running. Tom liked the idea of presenting it as a fait accompli. A fully organised, fully functioning operation. Not merely a plan of action, but action itself. In fact not just action, but proaction. Tom was like his great-uncle in that he liked to cut to the fundamentals. He liked results.

The first step clearly was to locate a locus operandi, a headquarters for PAIT. Etchen had too much on his plate, naturally, to do the necessary footslog. And, selfless and willing as Bernard was, he was already burning the candle at both ends, hunched over laptop and telephone as he multi-tasked Etchen's multifarious affairs.

'Why shouldn't I do it?' Tom offered without hesitation. He would be happy, he assured Etchen, to take on the task of talking to a few estate agents around town and inspecting the office accommodation on their books.

Etchen let him know that his preferred option was an HQ in a central location, for the sake of convenience of course more than prestige. But he did point out that the importance of a prestigious address could not be overestimated when the advancement of their clients from disadvantaged to advantaged status was a primary aim. Tom advised the estate agency people of this requirement. Nodding sagely at the words 'convenient' and 'prestigious' they added another zero to the rent.

Tom approached his task of finding the right HQ with some tenderness of feeling. He could not help seeing it in the light of 'finding a home for Pat'. 'Pat' he visualised vaguely as a long-suffering and noble individual who had been thrust out of his ancestral residence by the avaricious and the heartless. With patience and dignity Pat was waiting for his home to be restored to him.

Daily Tom had meetings with one property agent or another. This new role as a man of affairs pleased him. At last he could regard himself as bona fide.

Sometimes the property agent would be a pressured young man who shot his box-fresh cuffs, loosened his college tie and, complaining about the heat, went out to smoke on the steps while Tom looked over the putative HQ. Other times it would be a maternal woman who made tut-tutting noises about the brown estuarial marks on the ceiling of the property and shook her head over the ever-repeating waterfall in the bog. Then, pulling the door of the offending property behind her as they left, she would give him her considered advice, which was to snap up the place while he could. There was a big run on this kind of property at present.

He examined bright new suites in Docklands where the steely river loomed on the other side of the sound-proofed plate-glass and seabirds swooped past, their mouths open in noiseless squawks. In Georgian squares he examined dim-lit and cosy suites. In old northside neighbourhoods he inspected buildings with peeling stonework or soft brick crumbling like nibbled sponge. Beyond narrow flights of stairs smelling of damp and ancient disinfecting fluids he would wander through high rooms where even the sun looked mellower and older, as through short squared windows it fell in warped angles of light on a patch of carpet or a painted floorboard.

He was touched by some of these rooms. They could remind him of those sour-sweet afternoons he had passed with Katya in a hotel on the Fotanka in St Petersburg. Pat, he felt, might have been happy in such rooms. He could be again . . .

Etchen said that certainly he understood Tom's hankering after these places. But he dismissed them. Lovely of course, but rackety, he chided, archaic. Anything that could be construed as rackety or archaic they must avoid like the plague. Etchen's vision of Pat and Pat's requirements was different altogether from Tom's. His Pat was a muscular, androgynous sort of fellow. He was modern, ambitious, upbeat. He had youthful blood surging in his veins.

PAIT belonged to the future, not to the past, Etchen said. It didn't carry a sell-by date. HQ had to reflect that. Tom heard the appealing rotic sounds as Etchen enunciated 'surging' and 'androgynous' and 'future'. He declared himself to be in total agreement. He returned to Docklands.

A morning appointment had been arranged. 'A fantastic property, Tom, in a wonderful new development,' Maureen from LOK Commercial told him. 'I have a feeling this is the one for you.' But she cancelled at the last minute. An hour later she called to reschedule it for a 6 p.m. viewing.

Coming into the new plaza by the river that Maureen had directed him to he could make out, through the glare of the late sun fiercely reflected in the bright glass and steel structures, a girl perched on marble steps. She waved to him. 'Hi Tom,' the girl called out as he came nearer, 'surprised to see me? I thought it had to be you when Maureen said I'd be meeting a Mr Blessman.' With a start of pleasure he recognised Eileen Kinane.

'I didn't know you were showing properties,' he exclaimed.

'I don't. But Nicky does. He couldn't make it and told Maureen I'd go along.' She shrugged. 'I'll get a few bob for it.'

'Who's Nicky?'

'Oh, just a friend.'

Her hair was tawny again but darker than he remembered, and heavier. More carnal somehow.

'You washed out the pink.'

'A bit cheerful for me.'

'Yeah? You always seem cheerful to me.'

She pulled a face.

As they strolled around the enormous open-plan office Eileen admired the views – the sky, the water, the sporty figures tacking around out there with sails and boards – while Tom admired her. She was wearing an uncharacteristically demure costume of linen skirt and cotton shirt.

'Oh, I can do business dress when I want. Well, do you think it'll suit?' she asked.

'I don't know. I'm going to have to think about it.'

He didn't give a damn just then what kind of a place the HQ might end up in. Later he could visualise nothing about the property except Eileen standing there on an acre of green carpet looking both autonomous and magnetic.

'Should I snap it up, do you think?' he asked as she pulled the door behind them and they came out into the plaza.

'If they take half the rent they're asking, maybe. But don't tell them I said that.'

'Would you be free for dinner?' he asked.

28

Grille was for serious business. Guillaume's was froth and glamour. He took her to Guillaume's.

She settled herself on a white sofa in the glamorously minimalist ante-room, kicked off her prim high-heeled shoes and frowned in concentration over the menu. Her skirt slid up her bare thighs. Rather mottled thighs, Tom noted with a degree of tenderness.

'Could the cappuccino de légumes be counted as a vegetable experience?' she asked the waiter.

'Mais bien sur, mademoiselle,' he assured her.

Apart from this clarification she knew exactly what she wanted. Briskly she gave her order, then leaned forward and gazed into Tom's eyes.

'So what do you want a fancy office for?'

Etchen MacAnar had impressed on Tom how important it was to keep PAIT under wraps until it was established on a firm footing. 'Hold your fire,' he had advised. 'We want to come out guns blazing.'

'Absolutely,' Tom had agreed. But he found himself embarking now on an impassioned account of the project. Eagerly he described the ancient lifestyle of the native nomadic tribes and his plans for its restoration.

'Yeah,' Eileen would murmur at intervals, 'yeah, that's really interesting . . .' She had seized her bag and was rooting in it for something, fruitlessly so far.

'The mendicant pitches, you see, are crucial . . .'

She took out a small tattered notebook covered in red leather, a lipstick tube . . . Tom paused.

'Go on,' she insisted. 'I'm listening.'

'It's a question of recreating an ancient culture,' he explained, 'as Etchen MacAnar puts it, of privileging the . . .'

Eileen had found her mobile at last and was nimbly pressing its buttons.

'Fascinating,' she remarked without looking up.

'Tom, a chara . . .' A friendly hand patted his shoulder.

'Gibbon!' Tom stood up to return the greeting.

Behind Gibbon at a little distance the guy called Jonny who was selling the Platonique concept waited with a restless smile. Turning to usher forward a clever-looking young woman – though the impression of cleverness could be down to her wearing spectacles – Gibbon introduced her as Sheila.

He declined the offer of a drink. 'We're on the eight thirty to Zurich. Late already.'

Tom felt that the recent events, which were obviously trying though he had weathered them well, had altered Gibbon. He seemed steelier, remote somehow. But he would be back to himself before long for sure. He wasn't figuring in the news bulletins any more; indeed you could think he had melted away in the night like the snowy blossoms. The tribunal had gone into recess until the autumn. No judgement had been arrived at – the deliberations of the judges tended to be lengthy. It was predicted that they would require further sessions with him to arrive at a judgement. For the time being however he was off the hook, though his new air of disillusion, of a man who had come through but had learned from the sullying experience a grave lesson or two about the perfidy of the world, implied he believed he was off it for good.

'How's Seoda?' enquired Tom. He felt a certain quasi-fraternal responsibility for Seoda since her accident at Iveragh.

'Seoda's grand. Headed off to Quindong the other day.

There's some hot architect that she's keen to get over here for her Wired to the Moon thing.'

'Ah yes. Her charity event,' said Tom. 'That should be fun.'

Eileen looked up from her mobile. 'Where's Quindong?' she asked brightly.

'Quindong's in China,' said Gibbon shortly.

'China's hot all right,' she observed.

'Tom?' murmured Gibbon with his newly businesslike air, 'could I have a word?'

'Sure.'

Gibbon drew him aside. 'Tell me, has Leddy been in touch?' he asked.

'Norbert Leddy? No. Should he?'

'The thing is, he's planning a little dinner. Himself and Noreen. They'd like to pair you up with Ciara . . . Oh, not to worry. No romantics required,' he smiled, seeing Tom's slight frown. 'It's only that Ciara broke up lately with Mark Donovan. And she's kind of old-fashioned, you see, won't go anywhere without an escort. She's a grand girl, nothing wrong with Ciara . . . It's just that . . .' He inclined his head in Eileen's direction . . . 'It would be better if you didn't bring herself along.'

'We have to go, Gibbon,' called Sheila.

Gibbon looked at his watch. 'Yep. Gotta go.' He patted Tom's arm. 'Thanks, Tom. You should try the mousseline,' he advised as he walked off.

Tom and Eileen watched them go, Gibbon moving purposefully ahead, Jonny and Sheila a pace or two behind. Jonny's right arm was extended ever so slightly, giving him the look of security, a professional minder; an air that can appear sinister even when it's no more than solicitous. Gibbon's long strides, his brisk handshake with the maître d'hôtel . . . Outside Luke would be waiting by the Augusta at the bottom of the steps to whisk them to the airport. And if they were late and missed their slot another would open for them at once. Gibbon's jet seemed to enjoy a mysterious right of way.

'What a sleazeball,' Eileen remarked for no reason Tom could see.

Of course there was the Sheila factor. Eileen would, on Dol's behalf, naturally resent Sheila's presence in Guillaume's with Gibbon.

'Gibbon is very fond of Dol,' he said reassuringly.

'Is he?' She smiled. 'Okay. Maybe he's not a total sleazeball.'

The waiter led them to their table.

'Maybe there could be a role for you in PAIT,' Tom suggested diffidently when they were seated.

She shook her head. 'Don't think it would suit me.'

'Are you not enthusiastic about PAIT?'

'Oh, there's nothing wrong with it, I'm sure.'

Already the contents of her bag were dispersed about the table: several sets of keys, lipsticks, contact lens accessories, the notebook, a pair of diamante hair clips, her enigmatically blinking mobile . . .

'You don't think it's a runner?' he persisted.

'Why not? It's a runner for you and Etchen MacAnar.'

'What do you mean?'

'It's what any organisation is for, isn't it? The people who run it?' She looked at him wide-eyed. 'Hey, Tom, you're a businessman.'

'You're saying it'll be good for us? But not for the travellers?'

'Oh, I'm not saying it'll do them any harm.'

Tom was baffled. Did she not see that PAIT was radical, altruistic? She must be repeating something she'd heard from some resentful type . . . Half the country seemed to be multi-millionaires and the other half would naturally resent them. She was repeating a scrap from the street, a soundbite that allowed her to appear knowing – all the Kinanes liked to appear to be in the know.

'Forget it,' she insisted. 'I wouldn't have a clue. I know zilch about business.'

'PAIT isn't business,' he explained. 'Not in the way you think.'

She opened her eyes wide in that wannabe dumb and sexy way of hers. 'Tom, you're really clever. You know that?'

What was she playing at? Some dumb advice-manual stuff about flattering your date? All the same he couldn't help feeling flattered. Her phone rang then and she got up and went off to the privacy of the salon.

All through dinner it rang. Half of the time she was in the salon conversing with it. Half of the time he ate alone. But when she was there, in the seat opposite, disposing of occasional forkfuls of prawn and mousseline of veal she made lively and practised conversation. She spoke of movies she'd seen, the actors who starred in them, their personal lives, the personal lives of celebrities in general. She prattled. She appeared to be a girl with a great number of things on her mind, all of them superficial. Somehow he wasn't convinced by this gloss of superficiality. But he was at a loss as to how to break through it.

'When are your folks back from Spain?' he asked.

She was constructing little hills with the crumbs from a chunk of walnut bread. 'Don't know. Could be back by now.'

'You haven't been home?'

'I come and go.'

'You don't get along too well with your mother, do you?' he ventured.

Her brow puckered. 'My mother is in a state of confusion. Tom, should you be allowed to be confused when you're nearly sixty? Like, I'm entitled to be confused but she's, like, totally . . . Eimear says she should be going off to Medgugorje on pilgrimages and praying for us, like the country mothers . . .'

No topic was enough to keep Eileen in her seat for long. When she was not on her phone she was padding about, boldly charming in her bare feet, greeting acquaintances at different tables. Her laughter travelled across to him as she prowled the room.

From his seat he studied her mercurial features. Her face resembled Nina's: filled out, smoothed down, washed in milk and roses. From the back she could seem a fairly everyday type, a rangy blonde . . . But the face when she turned – an original. Flawed, probably, as they say in novels . . . but he liked her too much, he thought ruefully, to care. She seemed young for her age – she was what? Twenty-two, twenty-three? But there was something older in her too, world-weary.

From other tables, diners he was acquainted with smiled to him and waved.

'Come and join us,' pressed Denis Grogan, when he came over to say hello. Denis was dining with Marguerite and a couple Tom didn't remember meeting. Marguerite raised her glass to him in greeting. She was drinking Campari, the same scarlet as her nails.

'Sorry,' Eileen called over at once from a nearby table, 'Tom's with me.' She came back to him as if staking possession. 'I want to get the chocolate fondue,' she instructed. And almost immediately she was off again.

The waiters hovered attentively. They seemed particularly deferential and kind as if they were in tacit sympathy with Tom. The chocolate fondues were set down with quiet ceremony. Eileen came promptly back. After a few spoonfuls she pushed the plate away.

'Do you want to see my shrine purse?' she asked with the air of a concession. Her manner was confiding, artless.

Tom knew about shrine purses. Katya's was a receptacle for small reminders of Russia, playful and pathetic, religious and profane. It also contained – or at one time it did – a lock of his hair. A shrine purse was private. Katya at least rarely let anyone see hers.

'I'd be honoured,' he smiled.

She handed him a small brown leather pouch. Face cupped in her hands she gave a running commentary as he took out one scrap after another. A small white feather represented her guardian angel. 'We all have one, you know,' she said gravely. The faded rag was cut from a dress she had when she was a child – 'My only dress. I didn't do dresses after I was six.'

'You do cool dresses now.'

She threw him a smile. 'Do I?'

The green pebble was from a beach in the West of Ireland – 'washed by the ocean'. The bleached lock of hair was 'Benny's'.

'Benny?'

'A friend.'

Wordlessly she placed a hand over her mouth to denote tragedy. 'He overdosed. Bad stuff.'

'A bad drug?'

She gave a theatrical shiver. 'Bad stuff.'

A ring made of a base metal with a stone of a cloudy indeterminate colour was a present from Una. One-time best friend, now in India studying the arts of acquiring wisdom. Una had a new name now, a gift from her guru.

'I should be there. I should be in India,' brooded Eileen.

'Why don't you go?'

She shook her head. 'I can't. I'm afraid.'

Her open gaze slid away. She looked down at the dazzling pattern of the rug . . . Suddenly she seemed moody, unsure. Her fingers were crumbling and shredding the wrappers from the petit fours. The russet paper fragments lay on the white tablecloth like crumbs of withered leaves. Tom leaned forward and caught her fingers in his.

'What are you afraid of?'

Her forehead puckered again. 'Nothing. Only this fucking carpet is making me feel weird.'

Seizing the shrine purse she rapidly re-packed it, stuffing the fetish-objects back in as if they were no more than rubbish coins.

He nodded to a waiter. Eileen was toying with a coffee spoon. She looked up. 'What are you doing now?'

'Nothing in particular.' He felt his pulse quicken. 'What about you?'

'Come on,' she said. 'We're out of here.'

29

He had a sudden vivid image of Katya. A way she had sometimes of unexpectedly pulling away from him just when things were getting warm . . . And then slowly, with a kind of ritualistic care, she would undress, undoing fastenings, unpeeling her stockings down her short smooth creamy legs. Absorbed, reverent, like a woman undressing for him, perhaps for a stranger even, for the first time. Katya liked underclothing, soft, thin, old-fashioned colours, rose or eau de nil. Though he liked black, so occasionally, kindly, she would wear black. Was it some kind of a game, a fantasy? He never quite knew.

'Let it alone,' she would say. 'Don't audit.'

Stagily putting a finger to her lips. She could be so foreign sometimes, provocative . . . At last, naked, she would turn to him, unbutton, unzip . . . Lie back then, grave, pale, expectant. Something ceremonial, sacrificial even in her pose. Her eyes never left his face.

Wanton in her only half nakedness, Eileen coiled, uncoiled. Kissed him feverishly, feverishly stroked his back. No, not exactly feverish. But with enthusiasm. The detached enthusiasm, well tried, with which she despatched a few forkfuls of some dish she'd said she liked, before pushing it aside. She insisted on leaving her shirt on; she wouldn't allow Tom to take it off. She slithered in the disordered sheets, claimed his mouth, chewed it greedily but expertly with soft lips, her tongue, her teeth caressed him, nibbling his neck . . . But she did not look in his eyes. A fleeting glance, maybe, possibly not intended, that would veer off at once.

Shouldn't think of Katya. His confidence could be shot . . . Eileen pulled him close and he forgot.

When they lay sated and companionable, Eileen's attempts at smoke rings rising raggedly above their reclining heads, he realised he felt oddly fearful. Not for himself; for her.

He lay propped on an elbow, watching her face. With an unlikely chasteness she had slipped on her skirt again. There were hollows under her eyes that, too soon, would age her. A case obviously of burning the candle at both ends. They made her look troubled, as if she had endured a good deal in her life. She would probably be the kind of woman who'd want to get them fixed. He thought he'd like to be around to tell her she didn't have to.

'I'm glad,' she was saying whimsically, 'that you don't call yourself Thomas.'

'Why can't I be Thomas?'

'I don't like names with two syllables.'

'Can I take it that means you like me?'

'The absence of a negative doesn't have to mean a positive.' She looked at him and smiled.

'Well, I think you're gorgeous.'

'Do you? Do you think I'm crazy as well?'

'I've known worse. Sorry to disappoint you.'

'But I'm the real thing.'

She got up to wander around the room. He wished she hadn't dressed. It made her like a character on family viewing.

'You don't have much, you know . . . stuff,' she commented.

'Should I?'

'How else can I know you? I need to see your clothes, your car, your . . . stuff.'

'I do have some clothes. You could pick out a night-shirt to wear if you want.'

From the rail she smiled. 'I like your clothes.'

She went and hunkered down in front of 'Ada'.

'So it was you who bought it! What did you do that for?'

'Shouldn't I have?'

She considered the painting. 'It's hideous. But a good invest-ment, probably. Frog is determined to be famous. An early work in oils,' she intoned in a pompous voice, 'by Frances Kinane. Hideous. But of exceptional rarity value . . .'

'Stop snooping round and come back here.' He patted the bed.

'What are you doing with this?' She was inspecting the angel.

'She looks like you,' he said. 'No, actually I'm wrong. You look like her. I acquired her first.'

She turned. 'Hadn't you met me in the Shelbourne? With my mother?'

'Correct,' he smiled.

'Bad,' she said sadly. 'Only bad to be got from looking like an angel.'

'You don't want to look like an angel?'

She shook her head. 'Nowhere to go but down. Mind if I smoke?' she asked, lighting a cigarette.

'Not on my own behalf.'

'The great sin of our time,' she mused. 'You can do anything as long as you don't smoke.'

'Tom?' she asked then. 'Do you think something can be wrong in one year and not the next? Do you think God or somebody might come down one morning and pick you up out of hell because they'd decided your big sins weren't such big ones any more?'

'Wasn't hell abolished?'

She didn't answer. She looked away into the darkness beyond the terrace.

'Why did you tell me that story about my mother?' he asked.

She grimaced. 'I shouldn't have. Dad gave me hell over it.'

'For being fanciful?'

'Is that what he said?' A look of mischief crossed her face.

'He's used to that. No, it was because he doesn't want you to know.'

'Know what exactly?' Tom sat up.

'The truth.'

'What truth?'

'That they were hooked up, of course. They were having a relationship.' She said 'relationship' with an exaggerated note of irony. 'He being married, she being married . . . And there was Carey. Dol maybe . . . I don't know.' She twisted to look at him. 'Even you, I suppose.'

'I don't believe it.' Tom was surprised by his sudden sense of indignation.

'But wasn't it romantic?' Eileen protested. 'Don't you think?'

Tom was silent.

She lay back and closed her eyes. 'They ran away to Connemara,' she recited dreamily. 'He drove. He had the old Jag then. They walked on the beaches. In the nights they swam naked in the waves. They were in love . . .' She glanced up at him. 'And then when they came back, for her to die – can you imagine, Tom?'

'But that was later,' he protested.

'No, it was after that weekend, I'd say.'

'That's crazy. What makes you say that?'

'Okay, maybe I'm guessing. But I know Dad. I conjecture . . . And he does tell me things. We're alike, I suppose.' She pulled a face. 'We can't keep a secret.'

'He seems to be pretty good at keeping them from me.' Tom was pacing up and down. 'It can't be true. But if it is – does Nina know?'

'My mother? I can never tell what she knows and what she doesn't . . .' She bit her lip. 'Look, really, I don't know anything. Not for sure. Are you annoyed, Tom?'

'No. Not with you, anyway.'

'You should talk to Dad.'

'I tried. He's not talking.'

'Maybe he needs time.' She stifled a yawn.

'You're tired,' he said.

'Nicely tired,' she agreed.

He sat up for a long time smoking his way through her cigarettes until the pack was finished. He was thinking of the file Cerise kept, so neat and tidy, so oddly meagre . . . Why was her death certificate not among the few papers it contained? He should take the first flight back to New York and confront Pender. No, whatever about Pender, who was always cagey anyway, what about Willie? He was more than cagey; he was being deceitful. First he should fly out to Spain and confront Willie. He doubted everybody. Pender, Cerise, the Kinanes one and all.

Did he doubt Eileen? Looking at her sleeping form he saw that he had thought her, at least, capable of telling the truth. He doubted the unknown creature who was his mother, and especially he doubted the creature he himself had created. He doubted himself. When the sky was paling to white over the trees he got in beside Eileen and fell into a deep sleep.

Blearily he awoke to the shrill of the phone. It was Norbert Leddy.

'Just checking, Tom. You're coming to dinner tomorrow, right? I believe Gibbon told you you're expected.'

'But Gibbon is in Zurich.'

'Oh, he'll be back.'

'Let me take down the details,' Tom said with a degree of reluctance.

'By the way,' Norbert ended, less apologetically than he might, 'Ciara will be your date. In a manner of speaking . . . I hope you don't mind.'

'That's all right,' Tom agreed, even more reluctantly. 'Gibbon told me.'

He pulled on some clothes and went down to the Spar. There were cloudlets high up in the bright sky, the kind likely to fatten later and merge. But for now it was an effervescent blue.

'You look happy today,' remarked the Asian assistant.

'Happy? It's not the word I'd use.'

As he moved off he turned. 'You know though, you could be right.'

She smiled. He hadn't noticed that smile of hers before.

When he came back he found Eileen sprawled on the couch watching TV. She looked contented and settled in that striped shirt of his. She reached out to accept the carton of coffee from Spar, her eyes on the screen.

'Another gangland murder in the suburbs,' she said. 'Gruesome.'

'So what's new? ... . Eileen?' he asked. 'What would you say to a weekend in Connemara? Someplace west? I should see a bit of the country.'

Looking at him she considered. 'I think I might say yes.'

'Great. I got you cigarettes. And some brioches.' He went to the bathroom.

'Hey, Tom,' he heard her call.

He came out. She was sitting upright, staring at the TV. 'Incredible,' she breathed. 'Frog's made the news.'

Over a newsflash alert a reporter was standing in a familiar courtyard, in front of the rather beautiful bulk of the Irish Gallery of Modern Art. Here at IGMA, she was saying, 'Home', an art-installation exploring the concept of homelessness, had been due to be dismantled at the weekend. But the exhibiting artists, Frances Kinane and Aaron Greene, had not taken down their installation. They were refusing to leave the gallery. These young artists, she announced with a rising note of excitement, seemed to be following in the tradition of artists' protests of former times. They had even decided it would be a betrayal of their artistic purposes to talk to the media. However, the director of IGMA, Dr Ryan Boylan, anxious for public good will, had agreed to be interviewed.

The director looked harassed. Speaking with a slight stammer that was not habitual with him, he objected to the reporter's use of the words 'sit-in' and 'protest'. He failed to understand, he said, how the 'Home' exhibit could be considered to have anything to do with protest. The artists had certainly not been engaged to install it on the basis of protest. Blatantly he hinted that the whole thing was no more than a publicity stunt.

'To give these people the oxygen of publicity may be to play into their hands,' he warned.

'How do you interpret the artwork, Dr Ryan Boylan, if it is not about homelessness?' demanded the reporter.

The director's stammer became more pronounced. 'Any piece of art is open-ended in its meaning or interpretation. The meaning is for the individual consumer to formulate. It is not my role to interpret any work of art.'

His voice broke slightly as he appealed to the reporter. She must bear in mind IGMA's complexity as an operation and its statutory obligations. Not only to artists but to society, indeed all the people of the city . . .

'And who, might I remind you, pay your salary, Dr Ryan Boylan,' interrupted the presenter in her most professionally acerbic manner, for which she was renowned.

With suddenly mounting anger the director responded that he failed to comprehend the relevance his salary, or who it was that paid it, had to the protest. Plainly he was not a man who functioned well under stress.

'You do accept then that this action taking place in your gallery is indeed a protest?'

The reporter was triumphant. No more was heard from the director. Before moving on to a water-charges story she stated firmly her conviction that the IGMA story was not going to go away. Her message was clear. If the protestors held their ground, a plentiful supply of the oxygen of publicity would be available to them.

Tom's phone rang. 'Did you hear?' demanded Dol. 'Frog has

taken over IGMA. Crowds are massing in support. Isn't it amazing? I'm going up there right away. We should all be there.'

'I'll make it later,' Tom hedged.

But Eileen was already hitching up her skirt. 'Let's go,' she said.

30

Even your regular fed-up-with-the-whole-damn-lot-of-them taxi driver was showing signs of revolutionary fervour as they sped along the quays.

'There's going to be a right hullabaloo. They'll get a fantastic crowd. This is one in the eye for house prices and the whole cabal, I'll tell you. There must be hundreds of homeless officially in this city. Officially! The real figure must be in the thousands. Tens of thousands. Sooner or later someone had to make a stand.'

House prices? . . . Home . . . Homeless . . . Parents with adult kids on their backs into the foreseeable . . .

'You're saying this could be big?' Tom asked.

'Big? It's going to be massive.'

Nearing IGMA they got the latest bulletin. All other news was backing up now behind 'Home'. A crew sent in to dismantle the installation had been halted by demonstrators. The first skirmish in what could be a lengthy battle, declared the excited reporter, had resulted in victory for the artists.

'They won't get away with evicting them anyway, that's for sure,' said the driver. 'We won't put up with evictions.' He did not add 'over my dead body' but it was implicit. He dropped them at the gates of IGMA. 'I'd be joining you,' he said, 'only I have a fare to pick up in Newbridge. But I'm supporting these lads.'

He gave the V for victory sign as he drove off.

In the Italianate-style courtyard demonstrators were striding around smoking and conversing with their mobiles. They gave off an air of urgency as if something really major was about to happen. Inside the gallery, the Great Hall was deserted. The Infanta was smiling away and gurgling and clenching its little fists as adorably as ever. But today no crowd was gathered around the dais to gaze on it or to coo. There were only the attendants who stood around, evidently at a loss. And today the adorably musical sounds the Infanta produced were inaudible because the hall was humming with a low and vibrant roar, the familiar sound of a great and convivial gathering in progress not far off.

The roar was coming from 'Home'. The small gallery was crammed with people, seated cross-legged on the floor in the traditional posture of the demonstrator. They were facing the installation as if 'Home' was a stage onto which a leader would shortly leap to incite them to action.

'Home' looked smaller than Tom remembered, frail as a tent on a cliff top when a storm is brewing. And yet it also seemed more important.

The demonstrators looked happy, expectant, like a theatre audience that has taken their places again for the second act when the first has been a winner. They came in all shapes and sizes. There were students, pensioners, middle-agers – this was clearly a cross-generational issue. Many of them were people who had not had the chance of a good demo for years. Now they were having one, indoors to boot, and in a cultural atmosphere, surrounded by masterpieces of world art, and therefore safe from the possibility of alarming baton charges.

It was lunchtime. There was a matey share-out of sandwiches and panini and bagels and the crackling note of paper wrappers was added to the symphony of chatter and shouts from one end of the gallery to the other and the gales of companionable laughter. Frog accepted a sandwich presented to her and with slow hypnotic movements began to eat.

But mostly the artists were ignoring their laudatory public and were carrying on just as before. From her pose of lassitude on the sofa Frog gazed with the blank expression of the daytime TV viewer at an apparently soundless quiz show. Aaron was seated at the table in exactly the same position as when Tom had last seen him.

A cheer went up as an early edition of the *Evening Herald* was passed up to them. 'Home' had made the front page. With an admirable show of indifference Aaron threw it aside and returned to the dance of his fingers. The demonstrators, loving this show of artistic disdain for the corporate media and their lure of fame, loudly applauded.

Through the dense maquis of demonstrators Tom and Eileen managed to make their way over to Dol. Yasmin O'Brien was there. So too was Eimear. Yasmin gave an absent hello and bent her head again to write in her reporter's notebook.

'She's filing for the *New York Times*,' Eimear murmured respectfully.

'What's going to happen?' asked Tom.

'Who knows?' said Dol excitedly. 'They're saying it could be the new May sixty-eight.'

Truly, Eimear exclaimed, it was like the bygone days. She was finding it deeply inspiring to see that the Irish still had the spark of revolution left in them after all. She began to tell the story of her great-uncle's role, on the Kinane side, in the revolutionary period circa 1919-1923, to which no one listened. However she found an interested audience nearby in a group of Polish students of history.

Complaining of the discomfort of the pose of the demonstrator, Dol was fretting that she had not kept up her yoga classes. It was only now that she was able to fully understand the importance of the padmasana position.

'Did you know that some parish halls aren't allowing yoga classes to be held in them?' Yasmin looked up briefly from her reporting. 'Terrified of competition from eastern wisdoms.'

The others shook their heads in disbelief and made pious murmurs.

By now, Eimear was tremulous with feeling. 'Oh, it's beautiful. It's so, so beautiful,' she cried. She closed her eyes and swayed back and forth. When she opened them again they were brimming with tears. She rose to her feet and called forth in a high and ringing voice. 'We are worthy at last. At last we are worthy of our forebears.'

A cheer went up. Even Dol seemed for once to approve of Eimear's historical ardour.

A commotion could be heard coming from the back of the gallery. And soon the news rippled in a low hiss through the assembly. 'The shades are here, the shades are here . . .' Three officers of the Garda Siochana in their summer uniform of short-sleeved blue shirts had arrived. They stood at the back, severe and impassive above the massed ranks.

The demonstrators seemed to hug the ground now in a manner symbolic of the cowed and the oppressed. Silence passed across the gallery like a cooling breeze. In this first moment of their awareness of transgression, everyone looked expectantly at the artists, awaiting guidance.

The artists continued placid. Frog scratched her nose with the tip of the remote control and idly flicked to another channel where a woman was complacently displaying the dimensions of her enhanced breasts. Aaron, rocking to and fro on his chair, was watching the woman with a mildly lascivious expression. And in the silence you could hear that he was humming. The melody that could gradually be discerned in his hum was familiar and oddly ceremonial. It had resonances of another time and another world; a headier time, a headier world. Somewhere in a row near the front, close to 'Home', someone picked it up.

Rising, gaining strength like the chant of a choir in a lofty cathedral, the song spread through the gallery. 'We shall over-come . . .we shall overcome . . . I do believe we shall overcome some day . . .'

It was the old anthem of protest and hope. Sadly, few knew all the words, but most knew the refrain at least. It did not, as it might have done in the old days, swell and soar; rather it ebbed and eddied, the general hesitancy and one-string note keeping it earthbound. 'We shall overcome, we shall overco-o-o-me I do believe we shall overcome' rang out over and over with the predictability of a dirge.

But it was enough to persuade, even alarm the gardai. Powerful and fervent enough to make them withdraw into the Great Hall where they tightly regrouped around the consolingly domestic cradle of the Infanta and muttered about the necessity for reinforcements.

'Three days is apparently the optimum length of time for a successful sit-in,' mused Dol. 'After that the media lose interest.'

Three days? It was going to be a long haul.

'Dol, when do your folks get back from Spain?' asked Tom. 'I need to talk to your father.'

'Do you?' she said absently. 'Oh, they're back. But my father is in Mullingar or somewhere on a job these days.'

'All Frog wants is notice,' murmured Eileen. 'Frog always gets what she wants.'

Frog had had the bright idea of switching over to the national station – the bog-station as she called it – and was delighted to find an ongoing running commentary on her event. A hand-held camera was roving over the concourse in front of IGMA and the shadowy countenances massing there – well, news was thin on the ground just now with the tribunals in recess and anyone newsworthy on holiday . . . The not quite steady move-ments of the camera were giving the event an impressively subversive air.

The art pundits were out in force, asserting their pride in the fact that the first political revolt in what seemed like generations had emanated from the art world. They loved the passion of it, the riskiness, the absence of irony. They were eager to claim acquaintance with Frog Kinane and Aaron Greene, to confirm that their potential had been clear from their first days at

NCAD, the art college. Arguments raged as to whether the protest was primarily artistic or political. Opinion was generally tending towards the political. The idea of it as a political action certainly made it more risky, seminal.

'It's a cross-issue issue,' they were saying. 'That's why it's so important . . . That's the genius.'

Poverty and wealth, power and impotence, the homeless and the housed, the fusion of art and reality – miraculously, 'Home' embodied them all.

Frog and Aaron seemed to have appointed Dol as their conduit to the outside world. She was going back and forth, consulting in grave whispers for long periods with the artists and then popping up on television to make cryptically incitatory comments. She declared her pride in her sister and in Aaron, her confrère. Their protest was 'a landmark in the conformist climate of our time.' It was 'a message to the rich and the careless that they can't have everything their way any more.' Then she gave the victory sign.

'But Dol adores the rich and the careless,' Eileen exclaimed.

All the members of the 'extraordinary' Kinane family were in demand.

A researcher arrived to escort the two other Kinane sisters through the throng to the courtyard. They were interviewed in turn.

Eimear, described as 'a really creative entrepreneur . . . original, committed . . . philanthropic . . . the kind of entrepreneur we could do with more of in this country . . .' spoke with emotion of the 'spirit of rebellion re-ignited here today.' Eileen, introduced as 'one of our most talented young actors' showed an unexpected judiciousness by echoing Dol's approval of her sister. Eileen had fantastic screen presence, Tom realised with a glow of pride.

Probably because it was ad hoc the commentary was free of the criticism or judgement of conventional news reporting. The people were speaking. There was almost the sense of a national event – the funeral perhaps of a great statesperson, or a tragedy for which all were deemed to be in some way at fault.

IGMA's director, Dr Ryan Boylan, seemed to have gone to ground. He was not to be seen or heard, nor were any of his staff. They were said to be awaiting developments. They were taking legal and political advice, consulting with the Garda Commissioner.

In excitement and chatter the day wore on.

At some point it was announced that the embargo on the artists had been lifted and they could speak if they wished. But they would not be speaking, it turned out. They would neither explain nor appeal. They would remain within the perimeters of their art. However, when the buildings of the courtyard were silhouetted in the angled sun of the late twilight, there was a further announcement concerning the artists' wishes. There was a matter of personal importance which Frances and Aaron wished to be communicated to the outside world.

What they wanted the world to know was that during their long incarceration in 'Home' they, who before had been no more than collaborators, had fallen in love. And today, in the midst of the drama gathering about them, they had become engaged. Considering the daily circumstances of their lives outside, they recognised that their future marriage must be a distant, perhaps unattainable hope. Notwithstanding they had pledged, however rashly, their troth.

The world found the news of the engagement better than moving. The couple's plight was now all the more powerful. A collective sentimental sigh could practically be sensed rising nationwide. The young couple wished to be together, to set up home. Everyone could sympathise with that. But it was not to be. When they were thrown out of 'Home' – and sooner or later this was inevitable – they would have only the single beds, the cots in a manner of speaking, of their childhood years in their respective family homes to return to. But meanwhile the hearts of the people would reach out to them.

The camera lingered on the helpful faces of the protestors as two sleeping bags emblazoned with the chic High Mountain logo, donated by the chic High Mountain chain, were passed from row to row and handed up to the affianced pair. As Frog ceremoniously received them, her alliance with those who had no choice but to sleep outdoors and whose most valued possession was probably a sleeping bag was strikingly clear.

Tom was looking anxiously around for Eileen. He hadn't seen her since her interview. She must have drifted off to receive the adulation that was her due now as a Kinane. But she had been gone a long time. Dammit, she had such a habit of disappearing.

'Have you seen Eileen?' he asked Eimear.

'Didn't she leave? I saw her leave after her interview.' Eimear lowered her voice. 'No staying power. Never had.'

By midnight, the crowd could be expected to have swelled enormously, the commentator was saying, conjuring up a thrilling picture of folk spontaneously leaving en masse their sofas and twilit patios to fill the streets and avenues of the city. The people had taken over the gallery. There were rumours that they could soon be taking over the city. Tom made his way through the serried bodies shaking down for the night and took a cab home. There at least, she would know where to find him.

In the Spar everyone was talking about 'Home'. 'We should be laying in provisions,' somebody said, inspecting the shelves of canned foods with an air of imminent panic.

'The whole city might close down.'

'This could get really heavy . . .'

'Are you saying it could get rough?' a girl demanded.

Rough . . . A heady intimation of danger yawning like a dark maw on the near horizon. But they were loving it.

Tom went straight to his laptop and, ignoring the messages from his publisher, his agent, and sundry others, composed an email to Cerise. He was insisting, he told her, on a complete account of his mother's movements in Ireland and, above all, of her death. He had been kept in the dark, obstacles had been placed in his way. But he would tolerate no further lies or prevarications. He would have left for New York by now to give his great-uncle hell if there were not some pressing issues still outstanding over here.

On a re-reading he changed 'lies' to 'mistruths' and then to 'evasions'. It took a while to get the tone right. He could depend on Cerise to empathise with his indignation but he didn't want to alienate his great-uncle. He would dig his heels in. Pender was not a responsive man but he was more likely to respond to coaxing.

Having sent it off at last, he sat with a beer waiting for the intercom to trill or the phone to ring. Some time in the early hours he fell, alone, into bed.

By morning the cameras had penetrated the inner sanctums of IGMA. Cursory glimpses of the abandoned Infanta were followed by long and tender takes across the huddled ranks of the steadfast who had withstood the siege through the night. Visible in the crowd were some familiar faces. Eimear yawning hugely, one of the models from Iveragh looking bright and bushy-tailed in a playful military-style outfit. Dol was highly visible as she moved to and fro.

Still apparently asleep, Frog lay huddled on the sofa in her sleeping bag. Aaron was slouched over a steaming carton with the word 'Home' printed on it. Some entrepreneurial printer had clearly been busy in the night. The camera followed Aaron's every movement as he raised the cup to his lips and took a sip. He was looking undeniably shaky. Slack-shouldered, bleary, and squinting with morning fatigue.

The famous artist Zube gave an interview in which he endorsed the radicalism of the happening and generously refrained from more than a modest mention in passing of his own show at IGMA's rival gallery, the City. A water-colourist – occasional – aunt of Aaron's who normally passed a quiet and retiring life in Greystones was there, ushered out of obscurity and delivered to 'Home'. Introduced as an important influence on Aaron, she herself was declared to be an artist more than worthy of note.

There was however no sign of Eileen. But as a kind of consolation a camera cut to the Italianate garden and found Etchen MacAnar there. Tom moved close to the screen to more keenly observe his friend and mentor. He thought Etchen looked taller, statesmanlike, as he stood between the low parterres of box hedges.

'There are moments in history, in time, when our true desires are revealed to us, when people take a leap forward into a consciousness of what it is they really want. There is a hidden destination in the human journey, hidden until some sudden revelation takes us by surprise . . .'

Etchen spoke in the same measured tones he always did, warm, engaged but free of unwonted excitement. The tone of a man who watches the chorus gather and begins to move towards the place he has prepared, a place pre-ordained . . .

'Such an event was the storming of the Bastille, the fall of the Berlin Wall. This could be another such moment. Could any of us have predicted that art would ignite the spark? This may well be a key moment in history. I hope and I trust . . .' Here he paused as if gathering breath. Summarily he was cut off.

'I believe we have with us now Mrs Nina Kinane, the mother of Frances,' said the reporter urgently.

Nina was found seated in a regal manner on a stone seat, as she perused a rather tattered photograph album. She had a new smooth hairdo and was wearing a pretty polka-dot mother-of-the-bride type outfit. Displaying a photograph of a sulky-looking child, she explained that this was Frog, aged nine.

Frances's talents were apparent from her earliest years, Nina said. A childish but competent drawing of a pony was lovingly traced by the camera.

'Were you surprised by the news of her engagement?' smiled the reporter.

'I certainly was surprised,' Nina agreed. 'Naturally I'm very happy for her. But it is a worry . . . Speaking as a mother, the way things are these days, how are Frances and Aaron to find a home?'

'Are you worried about the outcome?' The reporter's tone implied an imminent debacle. Water cannons, mass arrests . . .

'I hope and I believe,' said Nina with dignity, 'that the authorities will see the justice of my daughter's cause and that everybody concerned will behave reasonably.'

'Should they be allowed to stay?'

'I hope everybody will be reasonable,' said Nina firmly.

She had done well, Tom considered. The Kinanes were really good at this kind of thing. He checked his emails. Nothing as yet from Cerise. But then unlikely to be, when you took the time difference into account. He checked his phone: maybe the battery was out? But it was fine. He subsided onto the floor in front of the screen again, nibbling on yesterday's brioches.

Demis Schwartz was arriving now at IGMA, having come straight from the airport. He had flown into Dublin to show his solidarity with the artists. As a mark of his solidarity he intended to reclaim – symbolically – his Infanta from the reactionary guardianship of IGMA and present it – symbolically – to 'Home'. Schwartz was large and pugnacious and when he raised his clenched fist to denote his solidarity you were sure he meant it. The presentation of the Infanta was to take place in the afternoon and would be covered live.

A lull for advertisements seemed to go on for ever. The slots between reports from 'Home' were clearly in huge demand.

When was Eileen going to call? They would have dinner. Not Guillaume's, however . . . Tom remembered then that he couldn't do dinner. He had to go to Norbert Leddy's.

By lunchtime he was back at IGMA. Surely Eileen would show up there for the presentation. He found Dol in intricate

236

negotiations between the artists, Demis Schwartz and the TV people. The artists were refusing to leave 'Home' for what they described as a mere photo-call, while Demis was equally adamant that the Infanta could not be moved from its crib. The TV people were determined that they must be brought together.

Finally a compromise was reached. Demis would carry the Infanta's shawl, symbolically containing the Infanta, and present it to the artists as they remained within the confines of 'Home'. It all went very well in the end. Demis cradled the shawl very convincingly in his arms and Frog received it from him with evident feeling.

Afterwards Tom was able to have a word with Etchen. Etchen's round blue eyes were especially piercing and alert.

'The bottom line is there's a longing for expression. For a kind of salvation, Tom. The whole city is in a ferment. You know, you can clip its wings back to the bone but the spirit has to soar. And back to the bone it was clipped. But it will not be kept down. It has to be shown its direction, Tom. It has to be shown its direction.'

'Come to any decision on a lease?' asked Tom.

'I'm thinking maybe we should go for the Fitzwilliam Square property. A bit roomy maybe as you said. But sure, we'll fill it, no bother.'

Fitzwilliam Square. An elegant redbrick, several grandly proportioned floors. Wasn't there a dodgy lease? Minimum thirteen years. A prohibitive get-out clause . . .

'Sure, Etchen. We can go for it,' Tom said.

'Good,' said Etchen. 'Very good. Must head, Tom. I have a photo-call with Demis Schwartz.'

31

Norbert Leddy's house on Capri Road was one of a cluster of pastel-coloured period mansions set on a grassy lowland slung around an inlet of Dublin Bay. The houses looked close enough to each other to be neighbourly. But as Tom was driven up the tree-shaded avenue that led to the Leddys' he could see the seclusion they enjoyed, and the gratifying sense, even if it was illusory, of dominance and ownership of the bay it could give. No wonder Norbert expected people to jump to his summons, he thought with a tinge of resentment. Eileen's exclusion was rankling with him. He ignored the fact that he couldn't have got hold of Eileen, even if she had been invited.

A butler-type retainer provided Tom with a glass of champagne in which a blackberry, a portent of the turning season, was nestling lugubriously at the bottom. Then he led him through the house and onto the terrace looking out over the sea. Norbert's wife, Noreen, came to greet him. She was a plump, likeable woman with an accommodating manner.

'Who do you know here, Tom?' Noreen gestured towards the guests already assembled. Eight or nine of them, too few to properly populate the huge terrace, they looked lonely, insubstantial, like migrants on the deck of a large ship as it silently leaves the port. No one among them was immediately familiar to Tom, but then perhaps, one night or other in the Horizontale or the Shelbourne . . .

'What a lovely view,' remarked Tom to distract her from her social duties, making for the low balustraded parapet. He didn't want to chat with anyone, let alone the neurotic-sounding Ciara, just yet.

'Well, Gibbon should be here soon,' Noreen said understandingly. She looked up at him as if imparting a confidence. 'Have they told you what the plan is? How are you on the old vintages, Tom? We're going to give you a wine tasting. Fun, isn't it, a wine tasting? Something different?'

'Well, I guess it beats charades,' Tom said.

'It was Gibbon's idea. Though I'm sure Norbert had a hand in it. The two of them are as thick as thieves. It'll be fun, won't it?'

'Sounds like it,' said Tom unhappily.

Milky blue wavelets of the sea were lapping the stones below the emerald green tennis court, the buried roots of beech and evergreens at its edge. The trunks of the trees were dappled straw and greige by the evening sun. In a light breeze coming off the water, the leaves trembled and quivered. Tom thought he could hear the musical rustle of the leaves travel across the mossy grass. But on the terrace, deftly designed to be impervious to breezes, the air was still.

They watched Gibbon come striding towards them, bestowing a handshake here, a shoulder pat there.

'Gibbon! You're late, Gibbon,' Noreen chided flirtatiously. I was beginning to think you weren't going to turn up.'

'I'm like a bad pingin. I always turn up.'

'There's fourteen of us. Lucky number,' she said.

'Safety in numbers, yeh?' Gibbon gave a kind of lopsided smile.

'I didn't see you at the presentation at IGMA today,' Tom remarked.

'Would have been but I got in too late.' Gibbon smiled through eyes narrowed against the light. 'Mr Schwartz sure knows how to work the old publicity. Has Ciara turned up yet?'

'I don't really know,' said Tom. 'Look, Gibbon, I don't need a date,' he added with a note of irritation.

'Sure you don't, Tom.' Gibbon patted his arm. 'It's just a little matter of courtesy.'

Carey Kinane came up and they talked about 'Home'. 'They do seem to like the limelight,' he remarked of his family. 'But not me. No thanks, I'm lying low.'

Finally Ciara arrived. She had an earnest blinking manner that he might have found not uncharming in other circumstances. But tonight he had no eyes for charm.

They went inside and took their seats at the formidably long and wide dining table that took up most of the room. Like the guests islanded in their places, the individual table settings stood in solitary battalions of glass and silver. In the consciousness of the unusual distances set between them the banter of the guests faltered or sounded over-loud. On a sideboard a many-armed candelabra lit up a terrific number of darkly lustrous bottles.

Norbert took his place at the head of the table, Noreen at its foot. With a machine-gun delivery Norbert made rather perfunctory introductions. The guests seemed a rather motley collection. They were not well-acquainted with one another. There were a couple of family members – a brother-in-law of Noreen's, a sister of Norbert's . . . an airline executive who was obviously shaping up to be the principal butt of the banter, such as it was . . . An aspirant politician, a lawyer or two, a high-level civil servant . . .

A chilled soup was immediately served with remarkable efficiency by the retainer, introduced to the company as Michael.

Gibbon was seated a long way off, Carey equally far away at the other end of the table. Dilatory conversation travelled Tom's way from left and right, but by and large his attention was inclined to wander. Placed between the wife of the aspirant politician and Ciara, neither thankfully was proving voluble. To be heard you had to speak loudly and they were perhaps a little intimidated by this. Whatever the reason, Ciara was less eager to appropriate his attention than he had feared.

Risotto, a dish that a nervous – or merely unambitious? – hostess might settle on, was served. Could be relied on to be foolproof, fuss-free . . . Copious amounts of wine were offered and accepted. Soon, there was a discernible increase in the level of affability.

Briskly the dishes came and went. The cheese boards appeared in next to no time. The Leddys were obviously keen to get to the main business of the evening, the wine tasting, Tom moodily perceived. However there was an unexpected grace-note when Michael, standing at Noreen's side, recited the origins of the cheeses, naming euphonious-sounding townlands in the pastoral counties to the south and west. Describing their individual qualities of ripeness, sweetness, sharpness and nuttiness, he spoke with the expertise of an actor whose voice must carry to the farthest seats. Surreptitiously Tom looked at his watch.

'Eat up now,' ordered Noreen with laugh. 'You won't be able to see a thing once you have your foulards on.'

'Foulards?' There was a general murmur of enquiry.

'Blindfolds,' explained Ciara. 'We'll be wearing blindfolds for the wine tasting.'

'Fuck the wine tasting,' Tom heard himself exclaim.

'Sorry, what did you say?' asked Ciara.

'I'd forgotten about the wine tasting,' Tom told her apologetically.

Michael was moving smartly around the table with the coffee. When everyone had been served Norbert tinkled his spoon and called on a general thank you for the excellent service their waiter had provided. Michael bade the company a continuing good night and made a theatrical bow. An appreciative chorus of thanks and farewells accompanied his exit.

Any need for a visit to the heads should be indulged now, Norbert jocularly announced. He didn't want people to be leaving the table later on. They should remain in their places during the tasting experience as comings and goings would be distracting for everyone else. And of course they should remember that the best vintages would be bound to be quaffed in their absence. There was a small commotion as several guests pushed back their chairs, leaving the room to a series of jokey remarks about bladder capacities and the proximity of the pair of decorative urns that stood at either side of the fireplace.

Tom faced the prospect of the wine tasting with little zest or cheer. He had drunk a lot of wine already. He was feeling definitely woozy and also an uncharacteristic inclination to be truculent on the subject of vintages and terroirs – on any subject at all, in fact.

But already the foulards, voluminous strips of a soft black material, were being passed down the table and with a dispiriting display of vivacity his fellow guests were trying them on. They had a tremendous capacity for drink, these guys . . . He took some coffee and grimaced. It was weak and tasteless. Reaching for a cheese board, he proffered it to Ciara.

'Did he say one of them comes from Limerick?' he enquired. 'D'ye see, I might, ah, maybe I could summon up an appetite for a cheese if it hails from Etchen MacAnar's part of the country.' His words were coming out with a drunken slowness.

Ciara was donning her foulard. A fold slipped down over her mouth.

'Sorry,' she mumbled, 'I wasn't paying attention. I don't eat dairy.' At least he thought that was what she said.

As they masked their faces in black the erstwhile harmless company was taking on the sinister appearance of members of some secret society turning now, after a ritual supper, to casual pronouncements of execution by horrible and arcane methods. Tom had sudden lurid and grisly visions. The rat torture – death by hanging – by the garrotte – the breaking on the wheel . . . Really, he had drunk far too much already.

Come on, man, shape up . . . It wasn't as if he'd been drinking some poison or other like absinthe. Resigning himself to the game he reluctantly put on his blindfold.

Sounding more sober than he had a right to be, the now invisible Norbert explained the rules of procedure. After each tasting he or Noreen would record each taster's opinion of the wine in question and the decision he or she had come to on its provenance. Only considered opinions would be acceptable, he emphasised. He would prefer the participants to come clean and admit ignorance rather than take wild guesses. He was requesting from his guests a committed and conscientious approach to the tasting. Norbert spoke, as he generally did, like a man who does not expect a request to be refused.

'Isn't Norbert a stickler for the old protocol?' somebody said.

'But would he have got to where he is today without the old protocol?' called another.

'Will you chill, Leddy? It's only a game,' chaffed the airline executive.

'Is it?' An affectedly sepulchral note came from farther along. There was a faint intake of breath around the table, a delighted shiver of apprehension. This was cut by the same man adding, 'If you think he's serious about this game, you should see what he's like on the golf course.'

'Would you call this a game? When there's neither male nor female in the reach of a grope? Where I'm sitting, anyway.'

That would be the aspirant politician. Politicians were inclined to be bawdy when they had had a few drinks.

'Why can't we stick to strip poker?' Wasn't that Gibbon's voice?

A soft pad-pad could be heard on the thick Persian rug as the Leddys moved down the table distributing the first essay of the tasting. The plop of rich liquid being poured into glasses was followed by gurgles and swallowings and lip-smackings as the wine went down the hatches. Comments then were obediently delivered to order as Norbert or Noreen called out names at random.

'I'm going for the New World . . . Definitely Oz.'

'I'm with you there.'

'I'll stick with the New World but I'm going for New Zealand.'

'No way. Definitely Old World. It's a Burgundy. In fact good old Château Marman. Ninety-eight . . .'

'Napa Valley two thousand and two,' pronounced Tom sullenly. He hadn't a clue and he didn't care. His palate was furry, his ears singing. And the tasting was getting out of hand. For all Norbert's good intentions he was losing it, procedure wise. People were calling out of turn. They were passed over, returned to . . .

'Napa Valley? Surely not. Far too jammy.' Ciara spoke loudly, authoritatively. She was getting assertive.

'Ciara, please,' admonished Noreen. 'It'd be kinder if you didn't comment on someone else's opinion.'

'Well, when someone has clearly got it so wrong . . .' protested Ciara.

Despite himself, Tom felt offended. She was meant to be his date, after all.

And so it went on. Draughts – large draughts for a tasting surely – of Château this and Cuvée that, Bordeaux or Chile, Burgundy or Malbec, '95 or '99 or '03 . . . By the fourth or fifth experiment, dissension was rampant, voices raucous. And the tasters were finding that they were liking raucous. The orderly delivery and reception of judgements was completely breaking down.

'Red,' declared the politician's wife. 'That's all I'm saying. Definitely a red.' Her voice was slurred. 'On my husband's future seat of Dun Laoghaire Rathdown I swear it's a red.'

But whatever the level of disorder the blindfolds stayed gamely and obediently in place.

The cloying embrace of his blindfold was suddenly intolerable to Tom. The cool air of the terrace called to him, a respite from the cacophony of thickening voices and the force-feeding of rich wines. It was irresistible. Stealthily he raised his blindfold. With unfocused eyes he saw a blurred version of Noreen as she bore a bottle past the empty chair in which Gibbon had been sitting and advanced towards a woman whose rosy face was bisected in black. The bottle was swathed in a white napkin that hid the label. What were they wearing blindfolds for? A napkin would do just as well.

He made a would-be apologetic sign in Noreen's direction and with some difficulty got to the door. His head was floating, his feet heavy and a long way off. His legs didn't seem to be working as they should. And where was Norbert? He was meant to be pouring the wine. Neglecting his post after his display of seriousness. Leaving his wife to run the show.

Behind him, the din from the dining room fell away. The house was blessedly silent. No tinny voices from TVs or play-stations travelled from upper or basement rooms, the regions of family or the hired help. He remembered Noreen mentioning as they went in to dinner that the boy was away. He was in the Gaeltacht. 'A kind of holiday camp, Irish style,' she had explained.

'Learning the sweet and kingly tongue,' Gibbon had remarked, echoing Etchen's phrase. And Michael, the retainer – he had bid the company a good night and gone home.

Halfway along a passage he found a door left ajar. Hospitably a white washstand loomed out of the dusk inside. He groped for a light switch, couldn't locate it . . . The water he succeeded in drawing from the faucet spilled out fresh and copious into the basin. A marvellous, a miraculous achievement. In the lunar light his reflection in the mirror looked featureless, liqueous, clownishly pale. He was mouldy, as Dol would say. Definitely mouldy. He drank several mouthfuls of water from his cupped hands and gratefully rinsed his face.

Back in the passage he lurched on, blindly seeking the airy quiet of the terrace, the cool and lucent expanse of the sea. But he couldn't find the fine pair of doors that he yearningly remembered, flung open onto the kindly elements. However there up ahead was a small door with glass panes in it gleaming with the pale glow of moonlight. Surprisingly it was open. He stepped out and the terrace stretched before him, cool and empty and plain as far as the glistening water.

To his left a slope reared with the dark shape of a house beyond, ringed by trees. It was a smaller house perhaps than the Leddys', but no less fine. It featured turrets, lacy castellations, all light and evanescent under the moon. Neo something or other . . . Florentine? The air was delicious. He tried to steady himself as he drank it in but it seemed to make him even more dizzy. Quite near at hand, he heard a dull thud. It was followed by another similar thud. Then two more.

Tom knew what such thuds normally mean. He was raised in New York; he was not quite a stranger to the wilder sides of Manhattan, and of Queens and the Bronx for that matter. The thuds resembled gunshots.

He was too drunk to feel any alarm. And sober enough to remember that this wasn't New York, but the swishest, surely the safest road on Dublin's swish and safe south littoral . . .The next sound he heard was like a sigh or a moan. Who or what could that be? It definitely sounded like a person. Hey, was Gibbon around somewhere, could he have come out, like himself, for a breath of air? Had he fallen and hurt himself? Stumbling towards the direction of the noise, he swung himself over a low granite wall and set off clumsily up the slope. Like some large woodland beast, an elk on the rampage, a bear, he lurched wildly through the trees, the undergrowth . . . and very soon, crashed into some immoveable obstacle and landed on the ground. Well, Superbear had run into a damn tree.

He leant against the tree trunk for support. A warm trickle was running down his nose. He touched it, gingerly. Couldn't see what colour it was but it had to be blood. That had a steadying effect. And the fresh air was kicking in at last. What was he doing, running around on some stranger's property? And the noise he'd heard – must have imagined in fact – had nothing to do with Gibbon. If there was a noise, it was made by some animal, domestic or wild. They might have all kinds of exotic animals over here. Or a perennial sough, a wind blowing through the trees. And the thuds were no gunshots for God's sakes. Just a car backfiring up on the carriageway.

Below in the near distance the candles in Norbert's dining room were flickering with a cheerful light. He'd have to find that washstand again and fix up his cut.

There was the clatter of falling brooms. A rubbery hose was wrapping itself in coils around his neck. Out of the darkness of a corridor to his right Tom was glad to see Norbert appear. Norbert's stance as he approached suggested fierceness. He was breathing heavily. He looked battle-ready.

'Tom. It's only you.' Visibly he relaxed. 'Couldn't make out who it was there for a minute. What's going on? Looks like a fucking boa constrictor around your neck.' He was amused, cordial.

'I was looking for the bathroom,' Tom explained.

Norbert freed him from the embrace of the hose and pushed the vacuum-cleaner back in the cupboard.

'You've hurt yourself.' Solicitously he steered Tom into a bathroom, switched on the light and examined the cut.

'Only a scratch,' he diagnosed. 'Give it a rinse there.'

He ran the water in the basin and Tom splashed his forehead. Then he placed an arm around Tom's shoulders and amiably but firmly steered him back up the passage.

'Left the party, did you? You're a bold boy. That'll screw up your scores. Noreen won't be too happy.'

'I was screwing them up anyhow. Could never tell my côtes del Mar from my côtes d'Azur.'

'We're going to finish up with a few digestifs,' said Norbert encouragingly, as if he were offering a reward for obstacles overcome. 'I'd say you can tell your fine from your fino, yeh?'

'Doubtful. Where's Gibbon?' asked Tom.

'Gibbon? Gibbon is being a good boy, tasting his wine.'

'I don't think so.'

'Well, he's not with me. I only came out to take a leak.' Norbert sounded very firm and even a little bit unfriendly.

'Maybe he headed off to find Dol,' said Tom thickly.

'Dol Kinane?' Norbert laughed. 'Fine little piece, that Dol. Did you see her on the box?' he continued conversationally. 'Earlier today, wasn't it? She spoke well. That young sister of hers is some operator. She'll go far.'

Their slow advance had brought them to the dining room. Norbert propelled Tom towards the door. In their absence the hilarity inside had escalated to further heights. Tom came to a decisive halt.

'I'm sorry, Norbert, but you're going to have to count me out. Great fun, great party, but . . . My judgement's shot.'

Norbert pushed him onward. 'You'll be grand, Tom. It's only starting.'

'No. Had a great night. Don't want to spoil it. And there's this girl, you see . . . Eileen . . . She's my date. I kind of promised we'd hook up . . .'

The words gave him conviction. Tom turned the brass knob and the door swung open. He caught a glimpse of Ciara as she feebly attempted to climb onto the table. She was still wearing her foulard. Firmly he pressed Norbert towards the ferment of shouts, the intoxicating fumes of alcohol and smoke.

'Tell Noreen I said goodnight,' he remembered to urge. 'Don't you forget now.'

The impulse of escape lent him steadiness, speed, foresight. Swiftly he was in the empty echoing hall and had let himself out of the handsome hall door and was blundering along under the darkly ethereal roof of trees. Norbert might have offered to call a cab . . . But he did take the poor guy by surprise. I wanted out, couldn't hang around . . . Keep the head now, walk in a straight line, shoulders tall . . . There's the road straight ahead now. Easy. Flag something down . . .

32

'You wanted Temple Bar, didn't you? Are you getting out or not?'

He was roused from his stupor by the cabman's demand. Did the guy have to be so unfriendly? Fumbling with the door handle Tom attempted an exit. Briefly he took in a glimpse of the street scene outside: lurid, neo-Hogarthian. Roars and hilarity, the sidewalk surging with neonlit girls supping from small bottles, youths supine against a wall. Near at hand somebody vomited. The air was pungent with the exhalations of the night. He slumped back into his seat.

'Look, where do you live?' The cabman was frosty but resigned. 'I'll take you home, okay?'

Weakly, Tom registered his assent.

'You took in a fair bit, I'd say.' The cabman eyed him in the mirror.

'Wasn't my choice,' protested Tom thickly.

'Of course it wasn't. They held you down and poured it into you.'

'Yeh. Pretty much.'

She was hunched on the floor beside the lift, her head buried between her knees. He blundered towards her. 'Eileen. How did you get in?'

'One of your neighbours turned up. I told her I wanted to wait for you and she let me in.'

Once he had managed to find his keys and they were inside

he had to go straight to the sofa and lie down. Eileen sat on the rug, observing him.

'Your eyes look funny,' she told him.

'I can see you,' he slurred. 'Nice.'

When he tried to raise his head it hurt and he had to lie back again.

Reaching for her leopard-spot satchel she took out a small bottle of vodka and took several gulps. She wiped the neck with the hem of her dress and passed it to him. He waved it away.

'Do you want to get yourself a glass?' he offered.

Eileen shrugged. 'I don't need a glass.'

'Poor Tom. It's no fun coming down,' she said. 'No fun at all. I'm probably worse. Nothing heavy. I'm just a bit spaced out, yeah?'

'I sure drank a bit too much tonight.'

'Must be a while ago. Come on, take a hair of the dog.'

Reluctantly he took a meagre mouthful of vodka. It wasn't so bad.

'We all need a little something,' she said kindly, 'to turn away reality.'

Wriggling from side to side she shimmied out of her knickers and unhooked them over her ankles. Her head rested on his chest.

'Did you ever think,' she mused, 'how life could be if we were born with a steady drip of coke in our veins? It could have been arranged. Couldn't it, though? Really stupid that they didn't think of that.'

She was circumnavigating the rim of the bottle with a fore-finger. A low-life finger, green chipped nail polish painted onto short bitten nails. She was wearing a playful, pink, full-skirted dress. The dress disturbed him; it gave off a faint pathos. It seemed to him the costume of the desired from another system, a system that said, 'Do not touch. You may desire, but you cannot possess me . . .' A costume that had no power any more, nor meaning. It gave her the incongruousness of an actor who, after the performance, appears in the theatre bar dressed in his stage outfit. He would look the part but he couldn't be it. He'd changed systems.

He wasn't seeing straight. In the morning everything would look different.

'Where have you been all night?'

She shrugged. 'Does it matter? Here and there.'

'Why don't you take off your dress?'

'Are you saying you will if I don't?'

'Wouldn't be able right now.'

His fingers played tiredly with her hair. It was coarse, it needed attention. Her shoulders were bonier, slighter than he remembered or had imagined.

'I suppose you see me as the loser-type,' she brooded.

'What makes you say that?'

'Oh . . . I don't know.'

'Where do you go,' he asked, 'when you drop out of sight?'

'I told you. Here and there. Half the time I don't remember.'

'I had you down as someone who told the truth . . .' He groaned. 'Talking makes my head throb.'

She stroked his arm. 'Did you miss me?' she wheedled.

'Let's say I noted your absence.'

'I was thinking about you,' she said with the air of a concession. 'As in, giving you some thought.'

'Come to any conclusions?'

'Maybe . . .' Slowly she traced the bottle-neck. 'I think you're good, Tom. You're a good guy. You know that?'

'Like how good? A good guy? Or good in bed?'

She laughed. 'Show me.'

He groaned. 'I can't, honey. I'm beat.'

'That's okay.' She considered the empty vodka bottle.

'Why don't we get into bed?' he suggested. 'Tomorrow is another day.'

'Do you want to go to a bar for one?' she suggested instead.

'I have some whiskey somewhere. Must be in the kitchen.'

'Wouldn't mix. I'm on a vodka kick right now.'

'Eileen, you're drinking too much,' he told her.

'I know. I'm a dipso.' She looked up at him. 'Registered. Bona fide. Among other things. It softens things, doesn't it? Rooms, moods, people . . . People are more tender. It makes me more tender . . .'

'Let's get into bed,' he repeated.

She stood up. 'I have to go.'

'Where?'

'Home.'

'To Sandalwood?'

She laughed. 'That's so-o-o American. Yep, to Sandalwood.'

She pulled on her little black jacket. It had 'Life Is Great' emblazoned on it in pink letters.

'You didn't read my angel cards,' Tom said.

'No?' she said absently. 'Next time I'll read them. Okay?'

'Okay. Next time, right?' Momentarily he felt better.

She slung her satchel over her arm.

'Let me call you a cab.'

'It'll take too long. I'll find one in the street.'

He managed to make it down as far as the street with her. They stood in silence watching the traffic.

'You don't believe I'm going to go home, do you?' she remarked.

'No. Oh, what does it matter where you go?'

Why did he say that? He needn't have said that. Her face snapped shut.

'By the way,' she said, 'you'd want to sober up. Dad has agreed to talk to you. You should give him a call.'

A cab pulled up.

'Sandalwood Road,' she instructed the driver, very loud so Tom would hear.

The taxi pulled away. She would tell the driver she had changed her mind. She would instruct him to take her to some other address. He decided that was what she would do.

33

He awoke far too soon for recovery. Propped limply against the sofa he watched the footage from IGMA, scanning the crowd in the hope of catching a glimpse of Eileen. That could be where she'd gone. Returned to the haven of the family fame-fest. But the camera was on the move again, repositioned now on the scene outside the gallery and the arrival of a new body of supporters.

On foot, a small phalanx of young seminarians in grey clerical suits were approaching IGMA's entrance gates. But the gates had been closed by the hardening authorities against all newly arriving protestors. The morning faces of the clerics had the look of innocents, sprung into rude reality from a monastery or the fastness of some mountain retreat. They looked archaic, as if they could have stepped out of some old black and white Italian movie. Arriving at the gates, they symbolically rattled the ornate bars.

From its vantage within the walls the camera eyed them with dispassion. The reporter spoke of the 'pitifully small' number mustered from the seminaries. With more than a hint of condescension she allowed them to speak. The clerics wished, their spokesman said, to stand alongside the protestors within, to share in the hope they represented of a return to unselfish thoughts and unselfish actions.

'Are you talking about a return to Christian values?' The reporter sounded sceptical.

'We believe in spiritual values.'

'Do you believe this is what the artists believe in?'

'Certainly, though they may express it differently.'

'Fucking paedos.' A hoarse voice was heard off camera. 'Don't let the fuckers in.'

Tom, falling over the remote, inadvertently knocked off the broadcast. He collapsed again into sleep.

The clerics had come too late. By mid-morning when Tom surfaced again 'Home' had been wiped from the news. The media caravan had moved on to pastures new, to the plush location of a multi-millionaires' row somewhere on the south Dublin coast, and the murder in the night of the wealthy businessman, Denis Grogan. From the media perspective it was the juiciest of stories, the best of murders.

Already the story had advanced beyond statements of the facts of the case to fevered speculation and a wide-ranging eliciting of opinion. As yet the murder had no apparent motive, but plainly it was a murder that reeked of intrigue and conspiracy and the murky dealings of the rich. The commentators were agog, the rumours rife and increasingly imaginative.

Denis Grogan. Denis – dead. Murdered . . . Tom found it hard to take in. The shock would have been even greater were he not feeling almost on the point of expiry himself. His hangover was grievous. An incipient anxiety was also obviously due to the hangover.

For legal reasons the commentary was obliged to be vague, enigmatic. But the reporters were chafing at the bit. There were lustful shots of the Grogans' mansion taken from ingenious angles; a bird's eye view from the carriageway, its little turrets projecting above the roof . . . Close up from behind a screen of verdure – obviously a trespass situation on the part of some daring cameraman – the turrets rising gracefully skyward over a pretty oriel window . . .

Tom's anxiety increased exponentially. The turrets were unmistakeable. It was Denis's house he had blundered into last night. No, not the house, the grounds, he had only entered the grounds, hadn't he? The anxiety subsided somewhat. And sprang up again as he remembered the gunshots. But who said they were gunshots? Nobody was mentioning gunshots. Now a rockabye view taken from a boat in Dublin Bay. The sea was choppy today.

If Denis had been at the dinner, he might not have been shot, might have evaded his fate. Had Denis and Marguerite not been invited to Norbert's party? They must have had another engagement. Denis and Gibbon, and presumably Norbert, weren't great friends any more but they were making the best of it. At the very least they were civil.

The phone shrilled.

'This is going to be big,' Etchen announced. 'This could be Grogan-gate.'

'I'm not getting you.'

'The crows are coming home to roost, Tom.'

'What crows?'

'There could be a few of them for the high jump. Are you all right? You sound a bit beat up.'

'Oh, I'm okay. Just a bit hungover,' Tom said weakly.

'Take a hair of the dog. Look, Tom.' Now Etchen sounded evasive or at least hesitant. 'I'd like to ask you something.'

'Go right ahead,' Tom said.

'I'd like to know that whatever I do you'll stand behind me. I'd like to know you wouldn't let me down, Tom.'

'I'm with you. You can be confident of that. Are you in a difficulty, Etchen?'

'Any man likes to know he has a friend behind him. The friend a man can depend on is not easy found, any time, any place. But in this town . . .' Etchen paused significantly. 'We have to watch out, Tom. Watch to our left and to our right. To our fronts and our backs.'

He sounded weary now, weary from a long and lonely struggle, a struggle perhaps of the spirit.

'You can always be confident that I consider myself your friend,' Tom assured him.

'Thank you. That's all I'll say for the moment. Look after yourself. I'll be in touch anon, as the man said.'

With a groan Tom pitched onto the sofa. What was Etchen talking about? But the tragedy was rendering any such speculations irrelevant. Good thing he hadn't suggested lunch. Wouldn't be up to it.

The stern reporter from IGMA popped up in a far-flung suburb. With a tincture of smugness its residents spoke of their fervent hope that the kind of crime they were obliged to witness on a regular basis was not about to spread its tentacles into areas free of it until now. The reporter referred in passing to the fact that Gibbon Fitzgibbon, recently a subject of investigation at the McCarthy tribunal, also lived on the same exclusive strip of coastline as the late Denis Grogan.

Tom hurried down to the Spar to get an early edition of the evening newspaper and a supply of Ibuprofen. His girl at the checkout had been replaced by another, also Asian; lean, hand-some, a high receding forehead. A warrior look. He imagined her striding across the uplands of Nepal or Mongolia, breathing rarefied air, face raised to the high snows . . . And now fallen to earth here between the snack counter and the cache of smokes. She was haughty. Probably he'd never see her smiling pre-decessor again. She had moved on, another room, another Spar. Everybody kept moving, they moved on, moved out. They moved fast, it was what cities were for . . .

'Crime Comes To The Costa'. An enormous headline occupied the entire front page of the evening paper. Denis Grogan had been shot, the words inside screamed. His wife, Marguerite, had found his body, lying face down in the extensive gardens surrounding the house, in the early hours of the morning. Denis had gone out, she was reported to have said, to look out over the sea, as he always liked to do before retiring, and had not come back.

Again, Tom heard the bullets coming out of the blue, the dark blue of the night, as Denis stood gazing contentedly out on the water, phosphorescent under the moonlight. And thought with a pang of grief, of Denis, suddenly sightless. He wasn't a bad fellow, Denis. It was Denis who had led him to the Kinanes – Kinane Kitchens. Only incidentally of course but all the same . . . Denis's view fading, dimming . . . or turning to red, like a violent primeval sunset. Crimson and puce, fizzing and boiling in his large amiable eyeballs. There was no one probably who could say how it was. Anyway, quenched. Snuffed, like a candle . . .

'Died instantaneously,' the report said.

The killer, whose identity and purpose remained unknown, was believed to be a bad marksman. Not a professional. Several shots were fired and only one had hit home. A stroke of bad luck; perhaps the first bad stroke of Denis's life. A life that had smiled on him with all its munificence until that one terrible moment when it turned coat and blew him out. The same moment in which the murderer got lucky. Maybe the first stroke of luck in his life – a loser's life that beat him up, had rained down on him its blows of injustice or ignorance. Each of them, killer and victim, locked in the most significant of relations, each an instrument of destiny for the other.

The gunman had got away. On a waiting boat, the report speculated, a boat sliding out from its anchorage hidden under the low grassy headland. Or spirited away via the fast carriageway, to lie low in a safe house, perhaps in the anonymity of some new sprawl of a suburb where nobody knows anybody and if they do they don't talk.

'A taxi driver is believed to be helping the gardai with their enquiries.'

Did that mean that a taxi driver was the suspect? Or did it mean that the taxi driver had picked up a fare who was the suspect?

The phone went again.

'Hello?' Tom said cautiously, nervously.

'Tom? Carey here.'

'Carey!' The sense of relief was huge.

'You've been watching the news,' Carey stated.

'Bad stuff, Carey. What a tragedy.'

'You've said it, Tom . . . Listen, did you hear anything strange last night?'

'The weird thing is, I might have heard the shots. I was out on the terrace, getting a breath of air. Dismissed it at the time, but now . . .'

'We were all out of it, Tom.'

Tom groaned. 'I'm still out of it.'

'Was Gibbon with you?'

'No, actually I went looking for him because I thought . . .'

'Are you saying he left the table?' interrupted Carey.

'Well, he wasn't there when I took off that damn blindfold.'

'He must have gone out for a leak.' Carey paused. 'He could be in a spot of trouble if that got out. In the present circs . . .'

'Gibbon couldn't have anything to do with it,' protested Tom.

'Course he couldn't. But in the circs . . . I suppose, Tom, what I'm saying is, you know, if anyone should ask, maybe . . .'

'I shouldn't say?'

'That could be the best plan.'

Behind Tom, a shrill clamour went off.

'Who's going to ask?'

The clamour stopped, then started up again. He recognised the noise as his doorbell.

'Who's that at the door?' asked Carey sharply.

'Don't know. Might be your sister. I should get it.'

'That's all right. Which sister? Oh, never mind. You do that, Tom.'

'Right, Carey.'

Quickly putting the phone down, he leaped to the intercom.

'Eileen?'

34

'Would that be Mr Tom Blessman?' It was a man's voice, deep and countrified.

'It would,' said Tom.

'Garda here. Could we have a word?'

'Come on up.'

His fingers were trembling as he found the door-release button.

Like invited guests, the two detective garda officers courteously shook Tom's hand.

'I've been kind of expecting you,' he told them.

'Have you now?' The taller officer looked without any particular meaning at the shorter.

They introduced themselves as Frank and Larry. With a friendly officiousness they apprised him also of their surnames and their professional titles, but this information Tom was unable take in. 'Frank' and 'Larry' were more than enough to be going on with.

'Just making some routine enquiries, Mr Blessman,' said Frank mildly.

'Call me Tom,' urged Tom.

They declined his offer of a drink but agreed to take a cup of tea. Seated side by side on the sofa they surveyed the room with polite interest.

'Nice place you have here,' Frank called out. 'Renting, I believe?'

'Well, borrowing,' Tom called back from the kitchen.

'Makes sense. House prices are OTT.'

They all took deep draughts of tea and Frank made noises to denote his grateful sensation of recuperation and refreshment. Larry was lean and sharpish of feature, Frank large and open-faced. They both sported a navy-beige combo; Frank wore a navy blazer and beige trousers, Larry a beige blazer and navy trousers. Larry's open-necked shirt was blue and Frank's was mauve.

A picture of Denis flashed up again on screen. Larry picked up the remote and flicked it off.

'Lord rest him,' Frank pronounced.

Laying his cup on the floor at his feet, Tom leaned forward in his chair with a most helpful expression. 'I don't know if I can be of any help at all to you guys but, whatever . . . you know . . . Go right ahead.'

'No hurry, Tom. Whenever you're ready,' said Frank.

Tom bent to get his cup and took another gulp of tea. Ready? What did that mean?

'How did you know we were going to pay you a call, Tom?' asked Larry.

His manner was conversational. Serenely, ruminatively, Frank sipped from his cup with tea-moist lips.

'Because of the taxi driver,' Tom said eagerly. 'When it was reported you were talking to a taxi driver I guessed you might be calling around. Yeh, hands up. I'm the guy.'

'You're the guy?' Larry seemed a little put out.

'Hang on now,' said Frank. 'There's a fair few taxi drivers out there.'

'There is,' Larry agreed.

Tom flushed. 'We're talking about the guy who picked me up on the coast road, right?'

'There were a lot of fellows picked up on the coast road,' said Frank.

'Not to worry. You'd be on the computer all right,' said Larry reassuringly.

'Look, let's start at the beginning,' said Frank. 'On the night in question, Tom, you were at a dinner party, I believe.'

'I was indeed. I was at the Leddys'.'

Naturally they would know about the dinner party. There would have been house to house enquiries . . . Noreen would have obligingly furnished the list of guests.

'Tell us about it.'

Tom gave a full and detailed account of his movements around the dinner party. Approximate time of his arrival, the drinks on the terrace, the quality of the light . . . The time, rather more approximate understandably, of withdrawal to the dining room. The casual nature of his acquaintanceship with most of the guests, apart from one or two of them . . . His voice tailed off.

'Who did you know, Tom?'

'Well, Carey of course. Carey Kinane. And Ciara.' Dammit, he couldn't remember Ciara's surname.

'Gibbon Fitzgibbon, I believe,' prompted Frank with a slight impatience.

'Oh yes. Gibbon is a friend of mine.' Needn't have made that quite so plain.

'So I believe,' said Frank.

'Did anything unusual take place at the table?' Larry asked.

Tom frowned. A considering, co-operative frown. 'Not that I can recall.'

'Did anyone leave the table?'

'There were tos and fros. The usual.'

'Apart from the usual tos and fros?'

'Well, I did,' said Tom candidly. 'I left the table. To be frank,' he continued with a warm frankness, 'I don't remember a whole lot. The Leddys were more than hospitable. I had a good deal to drink. Could've held back I guess, considering how I feel today . . .' Painfully he laughed. 'But unfortunately I didn't. I think I must have been the first to leave. I left the table to go to the bathroom and I didn't go back. I'd over-indulged . . . You know yourselves.'

Tom gave a hopefully complicit smile. The officers nodded understandingly.

'I let myself out and I walked up to the road and I got the cab.'

He was keen to return to the subject of the cab. The cab was verifiable, the cab was an alibi . . . Put him on the spot for sure incrimination wise. But so transparently that it worked in reverse. An idiot would see he had to be telling the truth. But hey . . . Alibi? What was he thinking alibi for?

'Let's go back to the party, Tom,' suggested Larry.

'Sure. We can go back. Another cup?'

More tea was sipped.

'Very refreshing, the cup of tea,' said Frank.

With enthusiasm, Tom returned to the topic of the long Dublin twilights of which the evening before had been a glowing example. Lavishly he described the glorious ocean views that could be observed from his seat at the dining table.

'Actually, that is not the ocean, Tom,' frowned Frank. 'It's the sea. The Irish Sea.'

'Sure,' said Tom. 'Sorry. I'm not big on geography.'

'Call it whatever you want, Tom,' said Larry kindly. 'Let's go back. Was it a catered dinner?'

'I couldn't say. Noreen Leddy may have cooked, I guess. Norbert even? Michael may have assisted. I'd say Michael could be pretty good in the kitchen.'

He told them all about Michael. His impeccable deportment as greeter and server, his impressive knowledge of native cheeses, his expertise in general.

Larry shook his head. 'Michael Fitzgibbon can't cook.'

'Leddy wouldn't have had the time,' mused Frank. 'He was tied up all day.'

'Michael Fitzgibbon? Did you say Michael Fitzgibbon?' asked Tom.

'I did,' said Frank. 'He's a brother of Gibbon Fitzgibbon's.'

'That's weird,' exclaimed Tom. 'Why didn't he say?'

'Any thoughts on that, Tom?'

'Must have forgotten, I guess,' said Tom lamely.

'Anyway, you left the table,' prompted Harry.

'I went to the bog.'

That was a good thing to be able to say. It seemed to normalise the situation.

'See anything? Hear anything out of the usual?'

'Not that I can recall . . . Oh, the usual creaks – it's an old house. I guess I was making a bit of a noise myself.'

He told them about not being able to find the light switch in the bog. Painted for them a faithful, hopefully amusing image of himself blundering around in a strange house, colliding with broom cupboards, getting entwined with the coils of a vacuum cleaner. Blind with drink.

'What would you say, Tom, to the proposition that there was an intention to make everyone at the table blind with drink?' asked Frank.

'What do you mean?'

'There was an intention to make you drunk.' Frank spoke patiently, as to a child.

'Norbert wanted to make us drunk?'

Frank shrugged. 'Did Norbert want to make you drunk?'

'I'd say that would be going a bit far.'

The officers considered him. Their expressions were, as far as he could tell, impartial.

'Is that a scratch you have there, Tom?' asked Frank solicitously. 'Cut yourself shaving?'

'No,' said Tom promptly. He had seen this question coming up. It was like an examination. Be ready for the questions and you should get through. 'I got it in my encounter with the vacuum cleaner.'

'Of course, the vacuum cleaner,' said Frank understandingly.

They regarded him in silence. He offered to make a fresh pot of tea.

'No, thanks all the same.'

263

Larry stood up. 'Staying long, Tom?'

'No immediate plans. I'm waiting to see how a few business ideas develop.'

'Very good . . . Very good.'

'You also know a fellow called Mr Etchen MacAnar, Tom?' Frank was moving towards the door.

'Sure I do. He's a good friend of mine. In fact, we're business associates.' Tom met Larry's considering gaze. 'Why?' he asked after a pause.

'Oh . . . Just wondering.'

Now Larry had his hand on the door catch. But instead of flicking it he turned.

'What did you wear, Tom, to the Leddys'?'

'What did I wear? Let me see . . . I wore my navy blazer. Armani . . .' Tom laughed uncomfortably. 'Rather like Frank's here in fact. And a white button-down, I guess.'

'What footwear?' demanded Larry.

Tom hesitated. He hadn't cleaned his black loafers after his blundering trespass onto Denis's land. He'd kicked them off when he lay down. They would still be there right next to the sofa where the detectives had sat.

'I wore a pair of black loafers.' His voice was oddly hoarse.

'Can we have a look at them?'

'No problem.'

'Nice shoes,' said Frank, weighing the loafers appreciatively in his surprisingly small hands. 'Handmade?'

'Handmade,' Tom agreed. 'Vogel's.'

'Mind if we take them away with us, Tom?' asked Larry.

'You'll get them back safe and sound, Tom,' Frank assured him. 'No worries on that score, I'd say.'

Tom accompanied them to the lift. He punched the Call button twice, three times. The damn thing was not responding.

'Sorry I couldn't be of more help to you guys.'

What they all say, the liars and the murderers . . .

'You were a great help, Tom,' Frank assured him. He was

264

carrying the loafers under his arm wrapped in a plastic bag from Spar.

The lift began its sweet groan of ascent.

'If anything else should come to mind that you'd like to tell us . . .' Larry made a sweeping gesture of invitation. 'Anything at all.'

'Sure,' said Tom. 'I'll let you know.'

'Feel free now,' said Frank. 'Like, any time.'

'And vice versa. Goes without saying. Anything you want to check out . . .'

Returning to the apartment, Tom locked himself in and with the fugitive fumblings of the guilty poured himself a large shot.

35

What exactly had he told them? Or not told them? At least he had succeeded in steering them away from that question about who had left the table. Hadn't told any lies, couldn't be accused of lying . . . Of evasions certainly, prevarications perhaps, but not of deceptions – surely? The evasions seemed to be about looking out for Gibbon, he saw. But why was he looking out for Gibbon? He was fond of the guy, but he wouldn't look out for him if he had killed a man . . . Killed Denis. Only Gibbon hadn't killed Denis – sure he hadn't. Why then was he protecting Gibbon? For Carey's sake? Tom liked Carey, but more especially he liked the Kinanes, or the idea of the Kinanes. There was a bond somehow that felt almost like family. Or was it just the schoolyard contempt for the snitcher, the betrayer? But you didn't carry that very far into adult life . . . What would, say, Georgie Hertz do? Georgie would fess up rightaway. Great-uncle Pender would advise in no uncertain terms that he do the same . . .

Maybe he should call Gibbon? But what would he say? 'Just wondering, Gibbon. Did you shoot Denis?' Hell, they might be tapping Gibbon's phone. His poca . . . Tapping his own . . .

The sky was low, monotone. Through the windows the foliage in the park was a dull and clotted green. The mountains burdened the horizon, startlingly close. Tom had a sudden intimation of what it must be like up there . . . a stark brown wasteland of bog and windblown heather. All day he watched the news programmes, hoping for word of an arrest. 'A man is believed to be helping the gardai with their enquiries' – that was the kind of locution they used and he was waiting for. There was no such announcement.

However, the occupation at IGMA was over. The artists had quarrelled. There had been a shouting match in the early hours and Frog had walked off the set in tears. Their engagement too was over, though there was some ambiguity as to whether the break-up was artistic or actual. An exhausted and downcast Aaron had emerged into the courtyard to fatigued applause from the handful of remaining supporters. A cursory shot revealed Dol among them. Dol would always stay to the last, Tom reflected.

The big story now was the death on the costa. In fact, it was shaping up to be the story of the year. Tenderly, the camera pored over photographs of Denis in different phases of his happy and successful life, at work and at play. Wearing shorts, he posed on the deck of his gleaming yacht on a summer's day in the bay, under the plump eddies of a well-filled sail. On a paradise beach he sprawled in a steamer chair beside a younger, rounder and jubilant Marguerite in a bikini – this was taken on his honeymoon. The Grogans' marriage had been a happy one, Tom reflected.

Gazing out at the trees, Tom thought of the Fall at home, the turn of the year that was not so far off now, the dry crunch of leaves underfoot and the crisp blue skies . . . It was always Katya's favourite season. He was struck by a sudden longing for the Fall, for home, for Katya. Whenever he was in a situation before he talked to Katya. With one decisive remark Katya could straighten out his muddled thoughts. This situation was a tough one, but she'd know what to do. The practical and ordered was what you wanted sometimes. Right now it was all he wanted. She'd be exasperated, make him feel dumb and muddled, but she'd have a solution . . .

Hell, why not go back? Get on the plane, get back on the track, back to normality. Pass the Fall in Vermont, work, forget the craziness . . . No, not possible. He couldn't do that. It could look like flight, the guilty party fleeing the country. And there were issues outstanding; he had involvements here . . . He'd just have to face the muddle on his own.

He was better suited to marriage than to solitude, Tom thought wistfully. But next time around it would be more equal. Katya had wanted to take care of him and he had let her and then taken it for granted . . . Resented his dependent role. Next time he'd do more of the caring. It was time he grew up, dammit.

Between news programmes he went down and skulked around the Spar, bringing back junk food to consume while he watched more television. The angel's gaze, preoccupied with the distant view, was disengaged, ungiving. At some point, the top news story briefly became Etchen MacAnar.

There he was, lengthy footage of an Etchen of old speaking on various platforms in his varied career. In an ill-lit hall in Limerick, after an election defeat on a rainy afternoon in Norristown . . . And most recently in the bright sunshine of the gardens at IGMA.

A warrant had been issued for the arrest of Mr MacAnar, the newsreader was saying, on charges of misappropriation of funds. The funds belonged to a charity, based in Tullamore, devoted to the restoration of patriotic monuments. An image of a rumpled, haggard-looking Etchen was shown, taken on CCTV in the arrivals hall at Malaga airport. Interpol had been informed. The gardai were confident of an imminent arrest.

Tom began to laugh. It was slightly maniacal laughter, choked and painful. When the phone rang he looked at it fearfully before he answered. 'Yes? Tom Blessman here.' His voice had that odd hoarseness again.

It was only Eimear. 'Just checking that you're coming to the pageant tomorrow, Tom.'

'Pageant? What pageant?'

'Didn't you get the invitation? The Famine pageant. Your Famine pageant, Tom . . . You didn't? I really will have to find a capable assistant. Well, lucky I called then. It's at Duck Walk Square. They seem to be calling it Duck Walk Piazza.' Eimear sniffed. 'Should be Cearnog Duck Walk if they had any sense of . . . Anyway, it's at five o'clock. We're all expecting you.'

'Okay, I'll be there, I guess.'

'Great. By the way . . . Tom, have you seen Eileen today?'

'No. Why?'

'Oh, nothing . . . Well, we are a little worried about her. Something somebody said to Dol.' She sighed. 'Never mind, I'm sure she's fine.'

'Eimear . . . Eimear?'

But she had hung up.

In the darkness he lay cagily awake and listened to the howls of the emergency sirens criss-crossing the city. It was at dawn they came, he thought; they liked to take you by surprise. No show from Eileen. But it was too late to call anyone. Except maybe Cerise? What time was it back home? He had a sudden longing to hear Cerise's voice.

Cerise sounded reassuringly solicitous.

'Are you okay, honey?'

'I'm fine,' Tom quavered.

'You don't sound too good.'

'It's late. Well, early. Early in the morning.'

'Sure . . . Tom, I'm sorry. I was going to email but, you know. Summer's on here.'

'How is he?'

'Pender? He's good. We're getting a nice summer. Low humidity.'

Pender was obsessed with the humidity scales.

'Tom, he wants to talk to you. He wants you to come home. He's missing you. I'm missing you.'

'How could you miss me? You'd have seen no more of me if I was down in the Village all summer.'

'Sure. It's just knowing you're around, I guess. Listen, he had the dream again a couple of nights ago. And what do you know? The folks were all laughing and waving. They were happy. Mission accomplished. He says that whatever you've been doing over there, it's done. Time to move out. He wants to talk to you about your mother, Tom. He's very anxious to talk.'

'Wow, that's a concession.'

'You sound angry . . . He only wanted to protect you, honey. Look, you're to get back over here, now, before they get their hooks into you . . .'

'I'll do that. Maybe in a couple of weeks,' said Tom lamely.

'You must be having fun. Though you don't sound like it right now, I have to say.'

'It's early in the morning.'

'Tom?' Cerise's tone had descended a note. 'I should tell you . . . Katya called. Her lawyers want your address. She wants a divorce.'

'Why does she want a divorce?' Tom found he was more annoyed than pained.

'She's met somebody. Some screenwriter guy . . .'

'Where did she meet him?'

'Colorado. Tom, you knew it was coming.'

'I guess.'

'Lots more fish in the sea, honey . . . You okay?'

'I'm okay.'

'You get onto that airline now, you hear?'

Demanding as ever, his great-uncle, still expecting him to hop to his tune . . . By dawn, the encroaching traffic on the motorways was an urgent thrum of engines and rubber, a hostile force besieging the park, the room, the bed . . . But they didn't come. He fell into a deep sleep.

36

He would go and have a look at Eimear's pageant. After all, it looked like the pageant might be the only success story for the Gast Corporation. And Eileen might show up there. Once he'd showered, shaved, and eaten a late brunch of eggs and bacon he felt quite clear-headed. Almost buoyant. Braced by a sense of resolutions and departures, he set off for town on foot.

The air was close. In the almost lavender-shot light the smoky, plum-coloured buildings of Camden Street were wearing the bold yet sombre look of old downtown New York. It gave him a fleeting sense of stability, security. Going along the west side of St Stephen's Green he came upon his homeless-type lady. She was propped against the polished-stone wall of a bank, her head lolling at an awkward angle. Bending down he pushed a note into her flaccid outstretched hand.

'Can I ask you a question?' he said. 'Look, the thing is . . . why do you love God?'

She raised her eyes.

'Fucking bastard,' she said vehemently. 'Fuck off.'

She was looking bad. In the greyish penetrating light the yellow flush of her complexion could not be mistaken for a tan. Her blood-veined eyes were yellow. The very blood seemed yellow-tinged.

'I'd love a drop of tea,' she whimpered.

He pulled out another note and pressed it into her hand. Her fingers closed limply around it.

'You should go see a doctor,' he advised.

'Fucking doctors . . . Get me some tea,' she demanded with a surprising vigour. 'I want tea.'

He walked on a few paces. Then he turned and went back.

'Come on,' he said resignedly. 'We'll go get some tea.'

He helped her to her feet and led her along, down through the teeming concourse of Grafton Street as far as Bewley's café. She moved slowly and with difficulty but she was able to walk. Sitting her down on a corner banquette at a small marble table, he went to the counter to get the tea.

'Tom! My good friend!' A foreign accent, sweet to the ear somehow. Ahead of him in the queue a guy reached out and seized his arm. 'My good friend from New York.' It was Vasile. A beaming Vasile.

'I'm sorry, I'm not able to introduce you,' Tom whispered as Vasile came back with him to the table. 'She won't tell me her name.'

Vasile sat down opposite the woman. 'What is your name?' he demanded authoritatively.

'Joanie,' she replied at once. Thirstily she began to drink her tea.

'I have to say, she does not look well, your friend,' Vasile murmured. He bit with appetite into a cream cake.

'Well, you're looking good,' Tom told him.

'It is happiness, maybe . . . I am happy, Tom. I have my girl, my poems . . . Good poems . . . Very good. Yasmin is happy, I'm happy . . . We're going good.'

'Glad to hear it,' said Tom a little morosely.

'Fuck you,' Joanie exclaimed.

Tom leaned over to murmur in Vasile's ear. 'She talks to herself.'

'Ah yes. In the city, the sensitive ones . . .' Vasile nodded sagely. 'They talk to themselves. When you are a sensitive person the city is a hard place. But maybe the country is worse . . .'

'I hate I hate I hate I hate,' declaimed Joanie.

'I wonder if she'd like a cake,' Tom wondered aloud.

'Fuck your cakes.'

'She is not well,' Vasile murmured. 'She should see a doctor.'

He bit into another cake. 'Your friend, Dol Kinane,' he ruminated. 'Very sad. Very very sad. Very.'

Carefully Tom put down his cup. 'What about Dol?'

'Not Dol. No, her sister. The nice kid. Foolish kid, but a nice kid . . .'

'Which sister?'

'Dol has many sisters. There is the artist sister. Frog. Very smart kid.'

'Has something happened to Frog?'

'I love God, I love God,' Joanie intoned.

'Not Frog.' Vasile's tone betrayed a slight impatience. 'There is the businesswoman also . . . No, the other sister. She is blonde. Like a little lion, yes? But she likes too much to drink, she likes the drugs . . . Fragile girl. Sensitive.'

'Are you talking about Eileen?' Tom cried.

Fatalistically Vasile threw his hands in the air. 'What can you do? She goes and puts herself in the hospital. Myself, I would never do such a thing. Never, never, never. And I am a poet, I am entitled . . .'

'For God's sake, Vasile. Are you talking about Eileen? Eileen is in the hospital?'

Next to Tom there was a sudden thump, followed almost simultaneously by a loud crash as crockery smashed on the floor. In a spreading pool of spilled tea Joanie's head was lying inert on the table. She seemed to have keeled over. Tom gazed down at her. But his gaze was blind. He wasn't taking it in.

Vasile reached over, picked up a lifeless arm and felt for a pulse. He jumped to his feet. 'Oh my God,' he said slowly. 'I can find nothing.'

'Are you saying she's dead?' Tom yelled.

Vasile nodded. 'I think maybe she is dead.' He was paling visibly.

'Call an ambulance,' somebody at the next table shouted.

Tom clutched Vasile. 'Tell me. Is Eileen dead?'

Vasile stared at him wide-eyed.

'Which hospital?' Tom cried.

Vasile's look was blank. 'Are you able to give the kiss of life?' he enquired.

'Whatever you do, don't move her,' a waiter advised. 'She shouldn't be moved.'

'I have to try,' Tom shouted.

He rushed from the café. In the street he punched his mobile. 'Which hospital is running emergency?' he demanded of the operator. Then he was plunging wildly towards the Green, pushing aside pedestrians in his path. A taxi, to St James's . . . Try St James's, she'd said.

'Are you a relative?' the woman at reception wanted to know.

'No. I mean, I could be . . . Look, I have to see her.'

'Sorry. You'll have to speak to a relative.'

'I have to see her,' Tom shouted.

The receptionist's expression was alarmed but controlled. She was trained in handling this kind of occurrence. His arm was caught from behind. He tried to shake himself free but they weren't letting him go. Savagely he turned to glare at his captor – and felt a warm sensation of deliverance . . . It was Willie.

'Willie. Is she alive?'

'She's alive. She's doing fine.'

'Why didn't you let me know?'

'She didn't want you to know, Tom.'

'Overdose?'

'Overdose. And a wrist.' Willie heaved a sigh. 'The usual carry-on. It's not the first time.'

'Can I see her?'

Willie hesitated. 'She's still a bit under the weather . . . Not really up to talking . . . Okay,' he agreed at last. 'I'll take you up.'

★

She did look very ill, pale and small under the thin white hospital blanket. But her breathing was smooth. At the word 'Tom' from Willie, and the touch of his lips on her forehead, she opened her eyes and closed them almost at once, but not before the trace of a smile seemed to warm her pallor. Sitting on the bed, he held her unbandaged hand. Willie went off to gaze out of the window at the far end of the ward.

Suddenly Tom saw that all he wanted, could ever want, was to be around to take care of her for ever, for always . . .

'Eileen, I want to take care of you. If you'll let me,' he heard himself blurt out.

He was sure he felt the press of her fingers. And tenderly, he thought he saw the old mischievous expression cross her face. The soft hand was warm in his grasp. Her nails still showed endearing flecks of green polish. His love, he thought, would change her. She would learn to trust, to commit.

Willie came padding up. 'Let's go, Tom,' he murmured. 'We should let her rest.'

They walked down the corridor together.

'It feels like a punishment, you see,' Willie came to a stop and looked hard at Tom. 'A punishment to me.'

'A punishment?' questioned Tom.

'On account of your mother.' Willie's voice was shaky.

'My mother?' With a pang of shame Tom realised he hadn't given a thought to asking Willie about his mother.

Willie took his arm. 'We'll go and find a cup of tea.'

They sat facing one another in the fluorescent glare of the hospital cafeteria.

'From what I hear,' Willie said, 'you've been kept a bit in the dark.'

'You can say that again,' agreed Tom with more than a note of bitterness.

'You have a right to know. Though I'm not sure I'm the best man to enlighten you.'

'Looks like nobody else is going to.'

'But sure, which of us knows the whole story?'

'Eileen told me,' said Tom firmly, 'that she died here. In Dublin. My father and my grand-uncle, they never referred to Dublin.'

'On account of the circumstances, Tom,' chided Willie sadly. 'On account of the circumstances . . . Yes, she did die here. In the Shelbourne.'

Tom jumped up. 'In the Shelbourne? It can't be true.'

'It is true. That much I do know. Will you sit down, Tom, like a good man,' Willie pleaded.

Reluctantly, Tom sat. 'How?'

'Some kind of an overdose. But you see, the question is, was it an accident? or . . .?' Willie sighed deeply. 'I have to tell you Tom, it has preyed on my mind. Still does. The inquest came to no conclusion. Alcohol poisoning, they said. With complications. That was the decision they came to.'

'Alcohol poisoning?' demanded Tom disbelievingly.

Willie nodded.

'Who found her?' But already he knew the answer.

'We were going to go away together. Her bags were there, scattered around the room, half-packed . . .'

'You were going to like, elope?'

'We loved each other, Tom. She used to come over, stay in the Shelbourne . . .'

'Why didn't you just marry?'

Willie groaned. 'It was complicated. There was Nina to think of . . . Carey. And Dol on the way . . . And there was you, of course. She was torn up with worry about you.'

'She was?'

'Torn to pieces, I'd say.'

Tom found himself turning aside to hide his tears. Mutely, Willie handed him a paper napkin.

'Are you sure?' mumbled Tom.

'For God's sake. She was distracted over you.'

'Did Nina know?' Tom asked after a while.

'I don't think so. But then it's hard to tell with Nina. She's a smart girl. Nina knows when to keep her counsel.'

'Where were you going to go?' asked Tom. 'When you eloped?'

'Oh, the States. Out west somewhere. She used to talk about California. But she wasn't able to do it, Tom. She just couldn't. Maybe I'd have been able, but she wouldn't. She'd have had to leave you behind, you see. Your father was never going to give you up. And your grand-uncle was right there behind him. He was going to use all his money and all his strength. We'd never have got away with you. They never would have given us a clean break.'

'But would you really have walked out on Nina?' asked Tom.

Willie spread his hands. 'I just don't know. Hilda saved me from having to face up to that one.'

'It was an accident,' Tom said decisively.

'Would you say?' Willie demanded hopefully.

'I would.'

'I'm so sorry, Tom.'

Tom could see how sorry Willie was, how sorry he had always been. Even sorrier than he himself was, probably. Willie knew her, he loved her. He had lived with sorrow all these years. While he himself had known only an illusion, a creature constructed out of his imagination. In comparison to Willie's love, his was abstract.

'Willie?' he asked. 'Did you take her to Connemara?'

Willie looked bemused. 'Connemara? No, we never went to Connemara. Why?'

Tom shrugged. 'Oh, just asking . . .' Connemara would be his and Eileen's trip, a fresh new place to strike out for.

'I love Eileen, you know,' he announced. 'I want to try and make her happy.'

Willie reached out and patted his arm. 'I'm glad.' He gave a sad smile. 'Mightn't be that easy, Tom. But you could be the man to do it.' His smile widened. 'Funny thing though, isn't it?'

'I could do with a drink,' said Tom wrily.

Willie looked at his watch. 'Shouldn't we head up to this pageant? They're all at the pageant. There's a place kept for you in the VIPs, you know.'

'The pageant. I'd forgotten the pageant.'

'We can grab a taxi.' Willie's moustache quivered. 'The pageant and all that . . . You see, it keeps the mind off it for them. And she's safe now. She's out of danger.'

37

On Duck Walk Piazza, one of the recent developments of swish commercial and residential in the burgeoning new town downriver, a stand had been raised. The tiers of seating were reserved for the organisers and the dignitaries and their various invitees. Opposite the stand a small number of the city's populace was seated on long benches while others stood about munching on delicacies they bought from the food stalls.

Exotic odours of grilling and roasting spicy meats filled the air, Thai, Turkish, Mongolian fast food commingling with the more homely smell of the Irish burger. All around the piazza gleaming steel and glass structures reared, challengingly new. On its south side the piazza opened out onto the river, today a broad, still, watery road under the humid sky.

'Good,' remarked Willie heartily, getting out of the taxi. 'It hasn't started yet. We've time to get a kebab.'

A clash of cymbals seemed to announce that the pageant was about to begin. With an air of delivering a gift, Willie brought Tom to his place in the stand. All the Kinanes were there; Eimear was in the first rank, flanked by the mayor in his robes on one side and by Nina on the other, beaming graciously under an elaborate hat. Dol, Frog and Carey were seated behind them. Only Eileen was absent.

'We were afraid you weren't going to turn up,' hissed Dol.

All the Kinanes beamed hugely upon him. They waved happily, brandished thumbs and made signs to him to take the place they had ordained for him in the front row beside Nina.

Making apologetic signs in return Tom sat down next to Dol. The others subsided and turned their attention to the stage below.

'Not a great crowd, unfortunately,' Dol whispered. 'There's a big game on the box this evening.'

There were familiar faces, Yasmin and Deirdre among them. A couple of rows behind, Tom could see Gibbon Fitzgibbon, seated between Noreen Leddy and Norbert. Seoda was obviously still away in Quindong. He thought Gibbon was looking quite cheerful. And he thought too that Gibbon could take care of himself whatever befell him.

The cymbals faded. Shuffling along the quay from the east and rounding the corner into the piazza came a lengthy file of artistes. They were costumed in ancient dress . . . Of wood kerns perhaps? Some variety anyway of serf or peasant, steeped in ancient wretchedness, wearing a tattered motley of old-world moleskin and sacking and sheepskin. Their faces were daubed with a white wash that gave them a ghostly or spiritual aspect.

As they came onto the stage they divided into two halves. In the middle of the arena these came together, divided . . . Came together, divided . . . Swaying rhythmically, a section of them was making a wailing music and a great keen of a mourning nature. Another section performed a ritualistic mime, raising imaginary goblets and dishes to their mouths and flinging them aside again. Raised them, flung them aside . . . Writhing on the Tufcote grass, they stuffed what was perhaps imaginary grass in their mouths.

The actors were limber, athletic. They were obviously conveying anguish, possibly grief. Some extreme form of suffering in any case. Hunger seemed to be the most likely cause. Whatever it was they were doing they were doing it really well . . .

But Tom was distracted. His attention drifted. His mother's face and Eileen's were becoming one, super-imposed. He knew he would have loved his mother, whatever her flaws. And she had loved him. From what Willie had said, that was more than

280

apparent. He realised he had always doubted it before. He felt a sudden surge of exhilaration; the sense that anything would be possible now.

But Joanie . . . What had become of her? He had left her there in Bewley's, in distress, abandoned. Had Vasile been able to cope? Surely she had only fallen in a faint? Well, he would put her into rehab, the best rehab in the country . . .

'I must say, the choreography is fantastic,' whispered Dol.

Dutifully Tom bent his gaze again on the pageant. The artistes were shuffling along now in an elongated ellipse, their bodies distorted as if by pain or some terrible despair, their arms artistically clutching the empty air as if reaching out for sustenance. Gestures of hopelessness, yearning . . . They were beseeching the empty air . . .

Tom had a sudden sense of déjà vu. 'Funny,' he murmured. 'I'm sure I've seen this somewhere before.'

'You could have seen it,' Dol agreed. 'They played some festival in New York. The Festival of World Food maybe?'

Like a revelation it came to him. No, he hadn't seen it before. But it was well known to him all the same. He knew it only too well. The same yearning people, on the march . . . Well, more or less the same. The pageanteers were taking the dream a step further. They had arrived now at some destination or other. And they seemed to know what it was they wanted.

He became vaguely aware that someone had slipped into the vacant seat beside him. Glancing down he saw a pair of beige trousers. They were familiar and not in a nice way. And he knew those tan loafers. He saw there were two pairs of trousers. The other pair was navy-blue. His head jerked up. Beside him Frank and Larry were gazing with a benevolent and appreciative attention on the play below.

'No hurry at all, Tom,' murmured Larry. 'No hurry at all. Whenever you're ready.'

Tom stood up. 'I'm ready now,' he said.